I0670697

PRAISE FOR ALISON R. LOCKWOOD
AND *THE ARSONIST'S LAST WORDS*

"STARTLINGLY INNOVATIVE… An elegiac novel that deftly
combines elements of investigative journalism and crime fiction."
—Kirkus Reviews, Best Indie Books of 2013

"AN UNFORGETTABLE CHORUS OF LOST VOICES… The
author impresses with her bountiful embracing of humanity."
—IndieReader

"A POWERFUL, SUBTLE, DEEPLY-MOVING BOOK… Not only
is it beautifully written, with keen psychological insight and a
discerning eye for human character… it has really big heart. One
of the best fictional explorations I've read of the 'meaning' of 9/11."
—Paula de Fougerolles, author of *The Chronicles of Iona*

The Arsonist's Last Words

—a novel—

Alison R. Lockwood

Mansfield House Books

Published by
Mansfield House Books
P.O. Box 721266
Orlando, Florida 32872-1266
www.mansfieldhousebooks.com

Library of Congress Catalog Data:
Lockwood, Alison R.
The Arsonist's Last Words: A Novel/Alison R. Lockwood—First Edition
Library of Congress Control Number: 2012910202
ISBN-10: 0985535806
ISBN-13: 978-0-9855358-0-3

Printed in the United States of America

PUBLISHER'S NOTE
This book is a work of fiction. Names, characters, places and incidents either are products of the author's imagination or are used fictitiously. Any resemblance to actual events or locales or persons living or dead is entirely coincidental.

*For my parents, who must have
wondered what was taking so long,
and for Graeme, who always knew*

Though the mills of God grind slowly,
yet they grind exceeding small.

—LONGFELLOW

PART ONE

CBS News Transcript/Burrelle News Services
Show: 60 Minutes (7:00 PM EST)
Date: Sunday, Sept. 12, 1999
Segment 3: After the Fall

Program Intro:
LESLEY STAHL: In the months after the Parramore Plaza disaster, the "theme park capital of the world" began to forge a new identity for itself. The people of Orlando said—quietly, of course—that some good had come out of the tragedy.

[Video Clips]

DELPHI OWENS, Mayor: We're a real city now. We pulled together. The world saw us for who we truly are.

ROBERT F. TANNER, Exec. Director, Orange County Convention Center: Honestly? No more Mickey Mouse jokes.

GORDON LIMAN, Bishop, St. Barnabas Episcopal Church: Attendance went up by thirty percent. That day brought us closer to God.

[Video Clip/Juni Bruder talking to a firefighter at the Plaza site]

STAHL (voiceover): There were those who might have disagreed with the bishop, including the reporter who quoted him and won a Pulitzer Prize for her coverage of the Plaza fire and its aftermath. Her interviews with survivors, rescuers, victims' families—even the sister of the janitor who set the blaze— helped "make sense of a senseless act," as the *Orlando Herald* put it.

After her suicide, many wondered why such a gifted writer had failed to find solace herself.

Sadly, she left no note.

It's true Juni didn't leave a note. She left a 200-page manuscript. The writing took most of a year, though she wouldn't show me. Not until it was done, she said. At the time, her sudden fit of shyness struck me as funny—thousands of strangers read her stories every day—but mostly I was glad to know she was working. She almost sounded like herself again. My life was hectic, you understand, and I didn't have time to worry.

The last time Juni called, I was running late for a class and let her message go to voicemail.

A week after the funeral, I opened her laptop. Sacrilege, even for me. That computer was so much a part of her; she talked about her brain in terms of hard-drive space. Her password was easy: Excedrin2. Her desktop was clear, everything put away, like her room when we were kids. There were only three folders: Work, Financial and Personal. The first was a warren of stories and drafts for the *Herald*. The second held all the records of day-to-day life (expense reports, insurance forms, an old budget). The third was empty.

The little wastebasket at the bottom of the screen was not.

The document inside was dated May 31, the day Juni died. Forgetting to empty the trash just wasn't like her. The apartment was spotless when I arrived. She'd even cleaned out the refrigerator. Her transcripts and clippings were filed in plastic storage bins, indexed and watertight. No loose ends, except for one.

Did she mean for me to find it? Does it matter? She must have known what I would do. I'm a priest, after all. And her brother.

She left it to me to dispose of her personal effects.

Aria Interrupted

Dozens of witnesses later recounted Sunday night's phone call during the opening act of "Rigoletto." Due to the continental design of Bob Carr Auditorium (there was no center aisle, so patrons who bought the best seats had to cross a continent to reach them), some thirty people had to uncross their legs or stand to let Dante Costas sidestep his way to the exit. For most of the ticketholders in Orchestra Left, "Questa o Quella" was ruined.

Some remembered Costas apologizing profusely. Others said he was unforgivably rude. All agreed he was polite enough not to return until intermission, a span of forty-five minutes.

Three blocks away, no one saw a handsome man in a single-breasted tuxedo walk into the parking garage of the Parramore Plaza. The night guard was away from his post, making the eight o'clock rounds (in truth, sneaking a cigarette on the rooftop terrace, the building being smoke-free). The surveillance cameras would be destroyed in the fire the next day.

If Dante Costas's wife noticed the faint smell of linseed oil on his hands when he joined her in the courtyard at intermission, or if he seemed a bit distracted at the private fundraiser for the Orlando Opera Company after the performance, she never mentioned it.

Random Acts

On the last night of his life, Marko Abissi ate at his sister's house. He tried never to miss the traditional Sunday meal with Valerie and her kids, even though his wife, Rosanna, always refused to go along. After the separation, he'd been able to bring his two-year-old daughter on the occasional weekend when Rosanna needed a babysitter. Not tonight. Three days earlier, at the preliminary hearing in the divorce proceedings of Abissi vs. Abissi, the petitioning spouse was awarded sole custody of the couple's minor child. The Ninth Judicial Circuit Court had declared the respondent an unfit father.

By all accounts, Marko Abissi was suicidal.

His life had been in a downward spiral since the cold December night he'd fought with his wife and left the house. That in itself wasn't unusual. Valerie had given him a key for the times he needed a place to crash. Her boys were used to waking up and finding Uncle Marko on the couch. He cooked "private eyes" (grilled toast with an egg in the middle) for breakfast.

After those nights, Marko went to work in wrinkled clothes and waited for the storm to pass, as it usually did, with the requisite amount of groveling.

But this time was different. Instead of the silent treatment, he got a phone call. There was a hint of satisfaction in Rosanna's voice when she informed him that if he came home, she'd have him arrested. It was the first time he'd ever heard the term "restraining order" outside of a TV show.

Domestic battery—that was something out of a nightmare. He'd never struck a woman in his life. It didn't matter. Within a span of three months, he would lose his home, his job and his daughter.

He'd been in line for promotion at Cornerstone Homes, where he worked as a construction manager. Unfortunately, the company's zero-tolerance policy made no exceptions for a plea of *nolo contendere*.

With child support and legal bills to pay, Marko sold his truck and cashed in his 401k. When he applied for work with the cleaning service, he neglected to mention his conviction on a Class A misdemeanor. Another first, lying on a job application. He rented an efficiency apartment near the daycare center. He memorized bus routes. He tried to get on with his life.

But he couldn't live without his daughter.

He said so, breaking down at the dinner table, the night before he died.

Loss 'Catastrophic' in Plaza Collapse

Death toll climbs as rescuers search for the missing

Compiled by the Herald Staff/Tuesday, April 14, 1998

ORLANDO—Arson is suspected in the fire that raced through the Parramore Plaza on Monday morning, causing a series of explosions that brought about the collapse of the downtown office complex in less than sixty minutes. Scores of emergency personnel who responded to the first 911 call and entered the burning 12-story building are among those injured, missing and feared dead.

At a press conference Monday afternoon, Mayor Delphi Owens said the loss would be "catastrophic."

Firefighters struggled to bring the smoldering blaze under control, even as they mourned fallen comrades. Shifting debris and heavy smoke hampered the search for victims. A makeshift morgue was set up at the Orlando O-rena, where an ice-skating surface was ready for a Starz on Ice performance, now canceled.

Emergency rooms in Orange, Seminole and Volusia counties were inundated with the injured, many suffering burns, smoke inhalation and cuts from broken glass. Due to recent budget cuts that closed one local trauma center and left two others understaffed, many critical cases had to be airlifted to Tampa and Jacksonville. At least one victim died in transit.

Volunteers from across the country are arriving to aid in the recovery effort. Search and rescue units have been mobilized from as far away as Seattle. FEMA task force members were en route to Orlando within hours of the collapse, and FBI and ATF investigators have already begun collecting evidence.

'I'm in trouble here,' caller said

The first 911 call came at 9:03 a.m. The caller, identified as a janitor, reported a fire on the Plaza's second basement level. The building had an underground parking garage and maintenance wing, a rarity in Florida, where groundwater thwarts subterranean construction. "I'm in trouble here," the man said. "It's too far gone for fire extinguishers, and the sprinklers aren't coming on."

Within minutes, an explosion ripped through the atrium, opening a gash in the floor and destroying several businesses on the lobby level, including a cafe, a gift shop and a bank branch. A separate blaze was reported in the twelfth-floor restaurant, Douze. Witnesses saw a van speeding away from the scene, fueling a bomb scare. Based on the blast's proximity to the basement storage area, investigators believe industrial cleaning chemicals may have ignited.

Thick smoke had filled the atrium by the time fire and rescue units from OFD Station 2, a block away on Parramore Avenue, arrived at 9:06 a.m. According to reports, the basement floors were fully engulfed. Engine and ladder companies from two other stations reached the scene in minutes. Police and emergency personnel began organizing the evacuation and treatment of victims. A triage area was set up in the Central Avenue commons across from the building.

The Plaza had three main stairwells connecting upper floors to the ground. The central stairs were damaged in the first explosion. Survivors reported debris and smoke in the southeast stairwell; only the northwest side remained clear. Several groundskeepers were reportedly trapped on the roof.

Of the 350 people estimated to be inside the building when the fire started, at least 100 made their way to safety. The initial evacuation was orderly. According to fire department records, a building-wide fire drill had been conducted at the Plaza on April 7 as required by state regulation.

Countless lives were saved by an accident on the San Luis Bridge that snarled I-4 traffic, preventing at least two-thirds of the building's 1,000 employees from arriving at work on time.

A second, much larger explosion roared through the building at 9:23 a.m. Fire officials pinpointed a natural gas rupture as the likely cause. The Plaza, lauded for its fuel-efficient design, featured a prototype gas-fired air handling system, the first of its kind in the state. The tremor was felt across the downtown area, causing widespread panic. One radio station reported an earthquake.

Many people were feared trapped in the southeast stairwell after the second explosion. Radio calls between firefighters and the command post indicated that evacuees were "jammed up" on the second and third floors. Other victims may have tried to retrieve their cars from the parking garage.

Witnesses in the atrium saw both elevators stopped below the eighth floor. "People were banging on the glass," one man said. Engineers were conferring about the problem when the second blast severed the elevator cables. Several children on a field trip were among those trapped, but their identities have not been released.

At 10:04 a.m., a loud crash echoed from inside the building. "An ungodly sound," said one witness who watched from the I-4 overpass. "You could tell the whole thing was coming down." The northern side of the Plaza buckled, sending glass flying in all directions. "I held my breath, thinking, oh, my Lord, those poor people," the man said. Seconds later, the building collapsed, falling toward the commons.

Many victims and medical staff were killed in the triage area. All local fire units, including 65 firefighters and 19 vehicles from six stations, had responded to the scene. It is not known how many off-duty personnel also reported for duty. Countless fire trucks, ambulances and police cars were buried in the rubble.

Cause of the blaze unknown

Due to the intensity of the Plaza fire and the speed with which it spread, arson experts believe an accelerant was involved. Authorities focused their initial investigation on the janitor who reported the blaze, identified as Mauro Abissi.

Abissi, who had worked in the building for fewer than three months, was seen carrying a suspicious package into the atrium at 8:45 a.m. The security guard at the front desk told police he stopped Abissi and asked for his I.D.

badge. Abissi claimed to have left it in his basement locker and was allowed to pass. Abissi was later observed on closed-circuit camera in the maintenance area where the fire broke out.

Abissi is believed to have died in the collapse. The security guard, Harold Arnett, is being treated for third-degree burns at Orlando Regional Medical Center. Arnett remains under a suicide watch.

According to police, Mauro Abissi, 29, was charged with domestic battery last December. Records indicate an emergency restraining order was issued against Abissi by his wife, Rosanna.

The 911 operator who spoke to Abissi said his last words were, "Don't let TV forget me." His family could not be reached for comment.

Death toll expected to climb

Twelve people are confirmed dead in the Plaza collapse. At least 250 are still missing. The American Red Cross is compiling a list of survivors, hospitalized victims, confirmed deaths and those reported missing by family members.

The building's owner and architect, Dante Costas, is among the missing. He was last seen helping people exit the parking garage. Costas, an active supporter of philanthropic causes in Orlando, provided office space to many nonprofit organizations, including Habitat for Humanity, the Alzheimer's Research Trust, Planned Parenthood and the Central Florida Arts Council (CFAC).

A CFAC board meeting was scheduled for Monday morning. One attendee, Muriel Hutchins Montemayor, was reported missing by household staff. The heiress to the Hutchins Department Store fortune used a walker and may have been unable to descend the stairs from the CFAC boardroom on the fifth floor.

Several government agencies, including the Internal Revenue Service and the Department of Veteran Affairs, maintained satellite offices at the Plaza.

The building also served as headquarters for Gulf Breeze Savings & Loan, the recent target of federal investigators. Chairman Thomas Rhodes, acquitted on fraud and conspiracy charges in January, was reportedly in the building at the time of the explosion. His current whereabouts are unknown.

The offices of music mogul Stan Diamond, whose successful string of "boy bands" formed an Orlando entertainment empire, took up half the Plaza's eleventh floor. Two members of the singing group B4Me, Jason "Flossie" Cabanis and Joey Dixon, along with manager Rami Green, were among the victims. A third member, Zenas Witt, escaped without injury. Stan Diamond, scheduled to meet with the group on Monday, ran late for the appointment and survived.

In the days to come, investigators will focus on the many unanswered questions related to the structural collapse of the Plaza, the failure of the sprinkler system to control the fire, blocked exits that may have contributed to the death toll—and the motive for this heinous act.

Monday the 13th

Most people thought it was a shuttle landing. After more than a hundred flights from Cape Canaveral, the twin sonic booms of the orbiter's return were almost routine. Two problems: There hadn't been any launches that month—a fact pointed out by know-it-alls who read the paper—and there was only one boom.

Thousands of office workers who'd stood at their windows watching the double plumes of the *Challenger* would feel the same sick horror as black smoke obscured the downtown skyline.

Fifteen miles north, Juni Bruder was getting a root canal.

While news began to filter into the Lake Mary dental office, the *Herald* reporter drooled in her chair, lips numb, gums packed with cotton. The dental hygienist, a talkative girl named Marcy, had disappeared half an hour earlier to make a temporary crown. With the Novocain wearing off, Juni could feel the familiar tightening across her scalp, a deeper pressure, the onset of a migraine swelling against the bones of her skull. She'd taken the first appointment of the day, hoping to be back at her desk by noon. Now, she was afraid she'd end up with an ice pack in a darkened room. She'd forgotten to pick up her refill of Imitrex.

Someone at the front desk said, "Oh, my God."

What?

Something about an explosion.

Running footsteps, a slamming door.

Some kind of attack.

The "William Tell Overture" rang on somebody's phone.

Somewhere downtown.

Above the office's piped-in music, Juni could hear a radio being tuned. The receptionist and patients in the waiting room were grilling the mail carrier, as if every government employee had the scoop. In the absence of facts, the story was taking on a life of its own: a bomb, a terrorist missile, a towering inferno in the Sun Bank building, or the new city hall.

"I was there when they imploded the old one," a man said. "Remember they filmed it for a movie?"

"Lethal Weapon Two."

"I thought it was Three."

Juni wanted to scream.

Marcy peeked into the room, her eyes red and swollen. "Your crown's almost done," she sniffled, blowing her nose. "My husband works downtown. I couldn't get through to him on the phone."

What did that mean? Was he there? Was he hurt?

"He called from home. He's watching it on the news."

Goddamn drama queens.

Juni was thirty minutes away in good traffic. It was an urban myth, good traffic on I-4. At best, she was looking at an hour, maybe two—

"I-4's closed," the receptionist announced.

Marcy leaned into the hallway. "East or west?"

"Both. The expressway, too."

Jesus Christ, this was bad.

Juni tried to map different routes in her head, but the pulsing throb at her temple kept dissolving the lines. She could try Semoran, or 17-92, but so would every other driver who knew the roads. Traffic would be backed up for miles.

Bob Davidson was already on the scene, she assumed, along with Margaret Fuller and the other *Herald* reporters. Tomorrow morning's edition would be wall-to-wall coverage. Juni usually took the human-interest features—she'd burned out on the harder stuff—but with a story this big, the paper would need every able-bodied writer. Dear God, the obituaries.

No time to think about them now.

She needed to call her editor, Carl, as soon as she could feel her tongue. She needed to get back to the office. She'd make it by dark, if she was lucky. If she could drive with one eye shut. If Marcy could stop crying long enough to finish her tooth.

"Can I get you anything?" the hygienist asked.

Just tell me what's happening. I need to know.

It was a litany of sorts.

In the end, Juni barely made it to the bathroom to throw up.

Her Honor

The second Monday in April meant the monthly staff meeting for Mayor Delphinia "Delphi" Owens. By nine o'clock, the conference room would be stocked with fruit, coffee and muffins from the deli, and Delphi liked to be on hand to supervise. Not that she didn't trust the food—Eddie Pollard, the owner of Spoon River, handled the mayor's orders personally. Delphi believed in supporting young entrepreneurs, and Eddie never failed to express his gratitude.

He flirted with her shamelessly.

Delphi always wore a special hat on Mondays.

Her hats were her trademark. In fact, voters knew Delphi more for her millinery style than for her politics. Never mind. She used whatever advantage she could. At her swearing-in ceremony, the brim of her satin hat had been so wide, the judge was forced to stand three feet back.

Her first official act as mayor had been to hire Austin Dabney away from the biggest law firm in town. Fortunately, he valued public service over money, or she wouldn't have been able to afford him. Austin kept the locals in line without ruffling any feathers. It didn't hurt that he was a hero to every OPD officer on the beat. As a patrolman, he'd been wounded during a routine traffic stop and finished his law degree in a wheelchair. Last year, he'd finished the Boston Marathon in under two hours.

"Dibs on the blueberry," the hero was saying now as he wheeled into the conference room ahead of Hank Layton, Delphi's press secretary. Hank feinted left and ducked around the chair, making a dash for the food. He made it there first, but Austin rolled over his foot. As Hank yelped and hopped around the table, Austin held up his prize and took a bite.

"Children." Delphi shook her head and went back to her notes. Because of spring break, the agenda would be light this morning: a Green Space opening, a volunteer forum, a greeting at the Central Florida Home & Garden Show.

Lydia Humphrey, her executive assistant, drifted into the room and took a seat. The ex-English teacher rarely spoke. Delphi assumed she was busy in her head, taking notes and silently correcting people's grammar. Lydia's letters on the mayor's behalf were poetry; Delphi even relied on her to send condolence cards. She always knew the right words to say.

Hank, on the other hand, never knew when to shut up. He was a pro when it came to spreading the news—Delphi had seen him type a sober, thoughtful press release in minutes, never backspacing—but give him an audience, and he launched into stand-up comedy. He could be funny, Delphi had to give him that, and Lord knew he could liven up a dull party, but he wasn't always wise in his choice of targets. His joke about Commissioner Weirauch, whose hairpiece did in fact make him look like a cocker spaniel, was her first mayoral lesson in damage control. For that reason, she kept Hank on a short leash.

"What's burning?" he asked now, stirring his cup. Delphi smelled nothing but coffee, so she paid him no mind. Hank would go a long way for a punch line.

Austin, sitting next to him at the window, said, "Can't see." City Hall stood at the southern end of the downtown corridor, and the 36-floor Sun Bank Building blocked the view.

The door opened, and a receptionist leaned inside. "Mayor Owens, there's a call for you on line two."

Delphi's rule was simple. If your beeper or cell phone went off in her presence, you owed her five bucks. She didn't believe in wasting other people's time. In her former life as a real estate agent, she'd been a chronic offender. But now that Delphi attended meetings for a living, she didn't tolerate interruptions.

Everyone in the building knew the drill: Unless it was an emergency, take a message. Delphi had been in office for twenty-eight days, and her rule had yet to be tested, when the Parramore Plaza went up in flames.

For Immediate Release:

Mayor Owens Declares State of Emergency

ORLANDO, FL (April 13, 1998) — Mayor Delphi Owens has declared a state of emergency in response to the arson attack on the Parramore Plaza. Under the advice of Police Captain Reilly Killion and Fire Chief William Herndon, and in accordance with Section 13-25(a) of the Orlando City Municipal Code, the mayor issued an administrative order creating an emergency disaster area at 3:30 p.m. The order enables the city to apply for state and federal disaster assistance.

Access to a 30-block section in downtown Orlando, bordered by Robinson and South streets, Hughey Avenue and Westmoreland Drive, will be restricted to rescue and law enforcement personnel until the scene is secure.

Residents within the affected area are being evacuated. Dust, debris and unstable structures surrounding the Plaza continue to pose safety hazards. The American Red Cross has established an emergency shelter at the First United Methodist Church, 142 E. Jackson Street.

At the mayor's request, Governor Lawton Chiles has dispatched National Guard troops to maintain order and prevent looting. The Federal Emergency Management Agency (FEMA) will work with local officials to assess needs and damages.

The Mayor's Emergency Management Office (MEMO) will coordinate the work of various relief agencies participating in the recovery effort.

For details, contact Henry Layton, Public Information Officer.

A Family Way

Faith Browning braced her forehead on the toilet seat, praying for the flu. She'd been sick four mornings in a row, and it was becoming impossible to ignore the obvious.

She was pregnant again.

Web would have a cow.

They'd agreed to stop at three. Caitlin was in preschool now, and Faith finally had the house to herself again. The boys were barely old enough to tie their own shoes, let alone help with a baby.

At Christmas, Cait had asked Santa for a baby sister.

Another son, and Faith wouldn't have any good dishes left.

Ten fingers and ten toes—that's all she cared about. That and not gaining too much weight. It had taken her two years to get back into her skinny jeans.

It'd taken Web two minutes to get her out of them.

Last fall, the car seat and crib had fetched all of forty dollars in the garage sale. She'd donated the stroller to Goodwill. Perfect timing, as usual. Just last week, Web had mentioned taking a cruise for their anniversary, getting away, the two of them. Nude beaches, he'd said, crooking his eyebrows.

Guess what, honey? There'll be plenty of heavy breathing in your future, but not the kind you wanted.

If he so much as looked at her sideways, she'd kill him.

But what could he say? It was all his fault. He'd been too much of a baby to schedule the vasectomy. Big, strong cop, and he couldn't pull the trigger.

Bet he'd make a beeline for the urologist now.

She would need to schedule a doctor's appointment herself. Faith thought about calling Web in the car, but he hated talking to her in front of Ernie. His partner, who never cracked a smile on duty, thought Web goofed off too much as it was.

Ernie took his responsibilities seriously. Wouldn't he make the perfect god-father? Faith could see them at the christening: Ernie, the kids, her parents, Father Hubley. In her arms, she was holding a baby with the Mathenys' red hair—like every other boy in her family—and Web's blue eyes.

But Web wasn't there.

When the phone rang, she was already crying.

Famous Last Words

"Get something on the janitor." Her editor, Carl Hamblin, didn't bother with small talk. Juni had pulled off the highway, sick a second time, throwing up the coffee and Excedrin she'd swallowed at the dentist's office. The radio reports were enough to turn her stomach, even without the migraine.

The Plaza was gone.

She found a napkin in the glove compartment and wiped her mouth. A pair of sandhill cranes grazed in the field beside the road, heedless of traffic and the strange woman leaning out of her car. Watching the silent birds wade slowly through the grass, she began to feel better. For a few minutes now, she'd be able to think, almost function on a human level. The knifing pain behind her eyes had dulled to a throb. She could almost move her lips. While she'd been retching in the weeds, all southbound lanes on SR-417 had crawled to a full stop.

Juni tried her cell phone again, still marveling at the ability to dial from her car. Before today, she'd only used the new toy twice: once to activate her account, and once to call her brother in Chicago to say, "Peter, guess where I'm calling from!" Carl's number had been busy all morning, the network down. Radio announcers were begging people to stay off the lines, except for emergency calls. Like everyone else, Juni considered herself exempt.

It was a shock when she finally got through.

"Where are you?" Carl rasped.

"The Greeneway. Oviedo."

"Are you drunk?"

"Novocain."

"Hell of a time to be getting your teeth drilled."

Juni rubbed a pressure point along her brow and tried to concentrate. "What do you need?"

"Davidson's guy at the OPD says they're looking at a janitor," Carl said. "Got a pen?"

"Go."

"M-a-u-r-o A-b-i-s-s-i. He carried some kind of package into the building, and nobody stopped him. The Plaza security guard was talking in the ambulance, but he's out of it now. Third-degree burns or some such. Margaret's on her way to the hospital."

"Where's the janitor?"

"Under the building, with any luck."

"How bad is it, Carl?"

"Couldn't tell you," he said. "We can't get close. The whole area's cordoned off."

"No credentials?"

"State of emergency, babe. Do not pass Go."

Two lanes over, an idling semi released its brakes with a roaring hiss. The cranes took flight, wheeling away into the empty sky.

"What the hell was that?"

Up ahead, drivers were getting out of their cars to talk. Juni sighed into the phone. "I'll be home for Christmas."

"Remember that piece you wrote on the Plaza when it opened? We'll need that copy, fluffed and dried."

"When? Today? I don't think—"

"Do what you can. Get something on the janitor first," Carl said. "We pulled the records. Sounds like this guy beat his wife, among other things. He wanted his name on the nightly news, the fucking bastard. What's 'Abissi' anyway—Lebanese, Palestinian?"

"Fax the papers to my house, okay?"

"Will do. Tonight's print run is held up. Get something filed by ten."

"Carl?"

"Yeah?"

"How bad is it, really?"

"Honey, you don't want to know."

He was wrong, of course.

Juni turned off her engine, rolled down the window and changed the AM station to NPR. Hearing Cokie Roberts say the word "Parramore" made it real somehow. This wasn't just a local tragedy—it was national news.

Despite the sun's heat through the windshield, Juni shivered.

She wanted to go back. Back to this morning in the shower. Back when the worst that could happen was a root canal.

Jaysukh Chaudhary, Owner, The Clean Team, Monday, 4-13-98, 7:45 p.m.

Mr. Chaudhary, I'm sorry to bother you at home.
Who is this?
My name is Juni Bruder. I work for the Herald. *I'm trying to get some background on your employee, Mauro Abissi—*
How did you get this number?
You had the cleaning contract with the Plaza. You're one of few people who knew him—
My lawyer said not to talk.
I understand, and I'm not asking for confidential information. I'm just trying to find out what kind of person he was, anything you might—
He only worked for me three months. Call his family. They knew him better than I.
Frankly, they're not answering the phone.
Can you blame them?
No, and I wouldn't either. That's why, when something bad like this happens, we end up talking to people on the fringes, people like you who get thrust into the news through no fault of their own—
Thrust? What do you mean by this, thrust?
It's a matter of public record that Mr. Abissi worked for you. It'll be in the papers tomorrow.
He wasn't working for me! I fired him!
Mr. Chaudhary, do you mind if I record this? It's very important, what you're saying. When did you fire Mr. Abissi?
Five days ago. Write this down: I fired him on Thursday. He was not working for me when this terrible thing occurred. I have—I *had* his signature: Marko Abissi. Terminated as of Thursday, April 9. Five days ago.
He signed it "Marko"?
That is his name.
Not his real one.
My real name is Jaysukh. Nobody calls me that but my mother. It's Jay. Do you want to see my driver's license?
I'm sorry, Mr. Chaudhary. It's just that the details might…well, anyway. You fired Mr. Abissi—Marko—on Thursday. Why?
Let's just say they weren't too pleased with him, where he was. Three years I had that account. I could not afford any trouble.
How many of your people worked there?
Uh, fifteen, actually. Six on the day shift, nine at night.
All accounted for?
Yes. A miracle, truly. All of them, late for work. I should dock their pay.
Did you have any problems with Marko before, any other complaints?
No, only the one. He was a good worker, a hard worker.
So let me understand this. Someone at the Plaza complained about Marko on Thursday, and you had to let him go.

Correct.

Did he argue about it?

No. He left the building quietly. He came to my office to pick up his check. He asked me who complained, but I couldn't tell him.

Can you tell me?

No.

What was the complaint about?

When it's the owner of the building, you don't ask. You say, "Yes, sir. Anything you say, sir."

Mr. Costas? He called you himself?

No, I didn't mean—

Had you dealt with him before? I mean, I would have expected someone from his office to handle the day-to-day details.

Mr. Arnaud usually called, but I didn't—

Mr. Chaudhary, this is very important. You're saying Dante Costas called you on Thursday and told you to fire Marko Abissi?

I'm not saying anything of the kind. I need to go.

Did Mr. Abissi give you any indication that he meant to do someone harm?

Oh, yes, of course! He told me he was going down to that building this morning to blow it up! What do you think? Of course not! He shook my hand. He said he was sorry. He took his check and left. That's it!

What was he sorry for?

Losing his job? I don't know. It's what a person says in such a situation.

I'm just trying to understand—

You think I don't know? I keep asking myself, how could I not see? What did I miss? If you ask me, I'd say it's impossible! I looked him square in the eye. I saw nothing! Nothing like this! If I did, I would have strangled him with my bare hands!

Did you think he was capable of violence?

No! He was a nice young man, quiet, too good to be washing windows, but he worked hard, so what did I care? I didn't ask why he lost his other job. Now, I wonder if I should have—

Can you tell me where he worked before?

I don't know. Construction somewhere. It's on his application. One of our workers vouched for him, so I didn't care.

Do you mind if I swing by your office tomorrow for a copy?

Too late. The FBI took it.

The FBI? Already?

My files, my computer, gone. How am I supposed to work without a computer? They looked like accountants, these guys. No guns, no bullet-proof vests. Suits.

Did they ask for anything specific?

Do burglars give you a list before they ransack the house?

So any information you have on Marko is gone.

They left the phone book. I can look up his number for you.
It's unlisted.
Why didn't I think of that?
Mr. Chaudhary, I'm sorry to put you through this.
It's okay. You are only the messenger.
I hope your business doesn't suffer too much.
You mean, other than bankruptcy?
Why do you say that?
Miss—what was your name?
Bruder.
Miss Bruder, you cannot imagine this is what they call "good" publicity.
No, I suppose not.
And the lawsuits will bury me besides.
But as you said, Marko wasn't your employee anymore.
That won't stop the lawyers.
How long have you been in business, Mr. Chaudhary?
Eighteen years. My wife was nagging me to retire.
Well, you know what they say—
Please don't tell me "everything happens for a reason."
You don't think so?
I don't think these people died so I could join the AARP, no.
Did you know anything about Mr. Abissi's military record?
No. Only the cough.
What do you mean?
He had a cough. I asked. It came from the Gulf, he said. He took medicine.
That's it.
Did he talk about his divorce?
Miss Bruder, you seem to be under the misapprehension that we sat around
discussing life. I run a business. I saw Marko once a week on payday. We spoke
five minutes, maybe. He showed me pictures of his little girl. I bragged about
my grandson. We debated the merits of an arranged marriage.
You believe in that sort of thing?
No. The Unitarian Church frowns upon it. I am a U.S. citizen, Miss Bruder. I
met my wife at a drive-in theater. My daughters found husbands quite well on
their own.
I didn't mean—
No, this is good, Miss Bruder. Good practice. This is America. Innocent until
proven guilty. But when the people decide who is good or bad, there is no
argument. If they say Marko did this thing, he is a bad man. And he worked for
me, Jay Chaudhary, so I must be a bad man too.
Not if you didn't do anything wrong.
Tell that to the FBI.

Plaza Janitor Fired Five Days Before Attack

Suspect lost custody of daughter in Friday hearing

By Juni Bruder, Herald Staff Writer/Tuesday, April 14, 1998

ORLANDO—The suspect in the arson attack on the Parramore Plaza was fired from his job five days before the fire, according to the man who employed Mauro Abissi as a janitor. Jaysukh Chaudhary, owner of The Clean Team, says that a complaint about Abissi was filed on Thursday. Chaudhary would not comment on the nature of the complaint.

"He was a good worker," said Chaudhary, whose company supplied fifteen janitorial employees to the Plaza on contract. His records were seized by the FBI on Monday.

Little is known about the suspect, whose family remains in seclusion. On April 10, Abissi attended a hearing at the Orange County Courthouse in which his wife, Rosanna Roberts Abissi, filed for sole custody of the couple's 2-year-old daughter. The motion was granted.

The couple had been involved in divorce proceedings since January, when Abissi, 29, pleaded no contest to a misdemeanor charge of domestic battery. Police were called to the Abissi household on the night of Dec. 26, 1997, at which time an emergency restraining order was issued against Abissi.

According to military officials, the suspect was a Desert Storm veteran who received treatment for unspecified health issues after his deployment to the Persian Gulf in 1991. Abissi served with the 101st Airborne Division.

April 13 marks the seventh anniversary of his unit's return from Kuwait to the airfield at Fort Campbell, Kentucky. This week also marks the third anniversary of the bombing of the Alfred P. Murrah Federal Building in Oklahoma City.

To Sleep, Perchance

A church bell tolled for the dead.

As Juni marched in the funeral procession, she looked down and realized her shoes didn't match. One blue, one black. She turned to the man beside her and whispered, "Has anyone noticed?" He shook his head and kept sweeping.

No, not a bell. A phone—hers—ringing.

Wake up. She fumbled for the light and knocked a glass off the end table. The cordless phone was wedged between sofa cushions.

"Hello?"

"Were you sleeping?"

She recognized the cough. Carl had made good on his New Year's resolution to quit smoking, but she guessed this week would test his will.

"No," she said. "I'm up." Dark through the windows yet. What time was it? She glanced at her wrist—a little after six. Weird to be wearing her watch; she usually took it off before bed. Along with her clothes.

Oh, now I remember.

"You're going down to the site this morning," her editor said.

She'd taken an Excedrin PM around three a.m. after filing her stories and watching too many hours of CNN. But every time she closed her eyes—

"Excuse me, what?"

"The governor's on his way," Carl said, hacking again. "Oh, Jesus, hang on." She heard the crinkle of cellophane, a click.

"Those things will kill you."

A deep puff. "Only the good die young."

Even the old jokes weren't safe anymore. "The governor's coming," she repeated for him. Her socks were wet; she righted the empty glass and pressed her feet into the carpet, soaking up water.

"Governor Chiles is coming to tour the damage and talk to volunteers," Carl said. "The official word is no press, but the mayor made a special request for you to tag along."

"She did?"

"*She did?*" He mocked her in a high voice. "Like you didn't already know you're the teacher's pet. Shit. I went to school with girls like you."

Peeling off her socks, Juni wrung them into the glass. The water was gray. "When?"

"The mayor's chief of staff is meeting you at the South Street checkpoint at eight."

"Am I taking a photographer?"

"Negative. Not with what they're pulling out of there. Not yet." His voice caught on the last note, and Juni held her breath, waiting for him to regain his composure. Carl? Terrifying. "Hey," he said, clearing his throat. "Did you catch Dan Rather yesterday?"

"No. I stayed with NBC." She carried the glass to the kitchen and poured the dirty water down the drain. Her headache was back with a vengeance, not that it had ever left. A good night's sleep—

"You were probably still in your car. It was early yet," Carl said. "Without live feed, old Dan ran out of things to say, so they went to their local guy on the street, the Channel 5 affiliate—what's-his-name, the one who goes out in the hurricanes?"

"Phil Connors?" She downed two more Excedrins with the inch of cold coffee left in her mug.

"Yeah, Phil Connors at the hospital with his hand over his ear, doing his man-on-the-scene impression, and Dan says, 'Can you tell us, Phil, is Disneyland under threat?'"

It hurt to laugh.

"Now, you know Phil was dying to say, 'Uh, Dan, Disneyland is like twenty miles from here. That's a whole 'nother zip code.'"

"Actually, Disneyland is in California."

"Oh, man, wouldn't *that* have been funny?"

"What did Phil say?"

"He said, 'Dan, as far as we know, Walt Disney World is secure.'"

"'But the Goofy Police are on high alert.'"

Carl let out a hoot and went into a coughing fit. "The best part," he said, catching his breath, "was when they interviewed the tourists who were pissed off about the parks being closed. 'We bought a four-day park-hopper. What the bloody hell are we supposed to do?'" His British accent sounded vaguely Jamaican. "Un-freaking-believable."

Standing in front of her bedroom closet, Juni remembered the laundry she hadn't done. Fortunately, her wardrobe ran to black. "Is the airport open?"

"Governor Chiles ain't walkin'."

"Speaking of which," she said, "I need to jump in the shower."

"Comb your hair this week. You might get to meet Bill."

"Mr. President? Been there, done that, shook his hand. The tornadoes, remember?"

"Oh, right. No impressing you with the leader of the free world."

Juni stopped short in the bathroom. "I completely forgot. Dante Costas and his wife went to the Renaissance Weekend with the Clintons in December."

"The what?"

"Don't you read your own paper?"

"Not if I can help it."

"It's this annual think tank at Hilton Head," she said. "Invitation only. Mrs. Costas gave a talk on global trade. Al Franken was there."

"The guy who wrote *Rush Limbaugh is a Big Fat Idiot?*"

"Yeah. My hero."

"You pinko liberal feminazi."

"Aw, you say the sweetest things." Juggling the phone, she stripped out of her clothes and threw them on top of the overflowing hamper.

"Hoo-wee," Carl said. "This story just took on a whole new dimension if one of the people who died at the Plaza was friends with the president."

"Dante Costas isn't dead yet." With a silent prayer, Juni ran to the utility closet and searched through the towels in the dryer, whispering, "*Yes!*" as she came up with a pair of clean underwear. "They haven't found him yet." On the way back to the bathroom, she grabbed her robe. She shouldn't talk to Carl naked.

"Boy," he said. "Clinton couldn't have planned it better himself, could he? Ken Starr will have to back off the investigation for a while, out of consideration for the presidential grief."

Juni leaned into the mirror. "Man, you're cynical." The skin under her eyes looked bruised. She pressed a fingertip into a dark half-moon and watched the spot go from white to purple.

Carl faked a Southern drawl. "'I did not have sexual relations with that woman.'"

"Don't," she said, groaning. "I voted for him."

"The man broke my heart," Carl said. "I voted for him, too."

"When's he coming?"

"That's what Monica said."

"Jesus, Carl."

"Probably not until Friday. It'll take a few days to work out the security detail. Hey, think you can stop at the O-rena and do a piece on the morgue?"

The Ten-Cent Tour

Juni waited at the South Street checkpoint, sipping coffee. The wind was brisk this morning, unseasonably cool for April. She was glad for her coat, a charcoal gray extravagance she'd bought for a trip home to Chicago. On the walk over, she'd seen kids in shorts, spring-break volunteers bringing food and water to the rescuers.

God bless Americans.

Inside the barricade, she spotted Austin Dabney forcing his wheelchair over the debris. Juni stepped forward and handed her I.D. to the military guard.

"Welcome to hell," Austin said, waving her through. Juni resisted the urge to brush the dust off his shoulders. She clasped his grimy hand instead. He didn't let go. "How long have you been here?"

"A few minutes," she said. "You?"

"All night, I think. What day is it?" He looked at his wrist. "Son of a gun. Broke my watch." The crystal was cracked. Blood caked his knuckles.

Searching in her purse, Juni produced an antiseptic wipe. "For when you meet the governor," she said, knowing he wouldn't use it otherwise. Grudgingly, Austin mopped his hands and held them up for her inspection. She nodded, looking down the street to get her bearings. This new block of brownstones had been featured in *Southern Living*, a Floridian homage to 19th-century Brooklyn. All the windows were shattered now, curtains fluttering in the breeze. Ash covered the sills and the sidewalks like a dusting of snow.

"Let's get this over with," Juni said. Austin wheeled away and she followed, breathing through her scarf. A path led between abandoned cars and fire trucks, and she found herself trying to step in the boot prints.

There was no mistaking the crimson stains.

Juni shuddered, pulling up her collar.

At the end of the street, she knew what to expect; she'd seen the pictures on the news. Still, when they turned the corner, she had to grab Austin's chair for balance. He reached back and took her hand.

The sight of cranes and the sound of heavy machinery fooled her into thinking, for one blessed moment, that this was still a construction site, and she was here for the first time, watching the Plaza rise. Writing a blurb for the business section.

"The dogs picked up something about half an hour ago." Austin pointed to a cluster of uniformed men and construction workers in the wreckage; Juni could see yellow sparks and the blue flame of a blowtorch. "There's a steel beam in the way." Austin parked his chair at a makeshift barrier, a crumpled piece of rust-colored metal. With a start, Juni recognized it.

Once upon a time, Dante Costas had given her a tour of his masterpiece.

The grand opening had only been weeks away. Workers were scrambling to add the finishing touches. Costas had led her down the wide corridors, greeting painters and electricians by name, asking questions, listening patiently, cajoling. On the third floor, when he spotted a hairline crack in the marble—so fine she had to kneel to see—he persuaded the tiler to replace the whole section, some-how making the man think it was his idea, and a darned good one.

His personal assistant, an officious man named Pope Arnaud, had followed in his boss's wake, making notes, lugging a mobile phone the size of a lunchbox. Eventually, he excused himself to take "an emergency call from Shenzhen," and as he backed away, she heard him arguing—in a mix of English and Chinese—about a missing shipment of light bulbs.

She and Costas had wandered over to the railing, where they could look over the atrium. *Master of all he surveys*, she remembered thinking. He pointed out the hidden symbols in the Mayan sculptures, the secret patterns in the mosaic floor, visible only from this height. Across the hall, a carpenter leaned a series of abstract panels against the wall, and as he arranged them, Juni saw that their random loops and swirls were currents in a raging river.

"The piece is called 'Crossing the Rubicon'," Costas explained. "Hammered copper with bronze and pewter inlay. I met the artist in Lisbon."

So many details came back to her now.

The emerald lamps above the front desk, hand-blown, imported from Venice. The speckled Java orchids in the rooftop greenhouse. The bird's-eye maple of the lobby chairs, which Costas told her, as he made her sit and feel the wood, had been salvaged from a century-old cotton mill in Charleston.

The warmth of his hand.

Juni's throat ached, seeing the dented sheet of copper propped against a broken post in the mud.

She and Austin watched in silence as the rescuers signaled for a body bag.

"What time will the governor be here?" she asked.

"His plane lands at noon."

"Have you eaten anything?"

He shook his head.

"Carl asked me to stop at the morgue on the way back."

"I'll tell them you're coming."

Juni stared at the sky. Austin scrubbed his mouth and studied the ground. "It's a goddamn nightmare, Juni," he rasped. "My friends are down there, digging with their hands, and all I can do is sit in this fucking chair and watch."

Duty Calls

Luke Havergal, who fought fire for a living, didn't believe in love. Love of country, sure. Love of humanity, maybe. But soul mates, hearts and flowers, till death do us part? No way. He knew the statistics. Half of all marriages ended in divorce. Three in ten kids lived with single parents. Rich people signed prenuptial agreements, hired surrogate mothers and nannies. Everybody else's kids grew up in daycare.

His parents had tied the knot because the rubber broke.

And they all lived happily ever after.

It was a matter of principle that in thirty-some years, Luke had never spoken the words "I love you," though he'd been on the receiving end three times that he could remember (not counting the drunken oaths of his buddies, closing down the bar after a long shift).

His first girlfriend, whose virginity at seventeen had been an unreciprocated gift. His mom at the end, out of her mind on morphine. His dad at the firefighters' graduation ceremony.

Granted, his old man had been three sheets to the wind.

Luke caught himself searching for his father's face among the uniforms climbing over the wreckage of the Plaza. He appreciated the irony of missing a guy who'd barely spoken a civil word to him in his life. Luke envied his friends for their memories of boyhood fishing trips and man-to-man talks. Sentimental claptrap, but still, he nursed a monumental void.

At his father's funeral, he'd wanted to take a fire axe to the casket.

There would be dozens of funerals now. His brothers. What was the point of loving your fellow man if it all came down to bagpipes playing "Amazing Grace"?

How could you love a God who gave with one hand and took back with the other?

They'd pulled a hand out of the rubble, still in its thermal glove.

Luke wanted to find the bloody corpse of the fucker who'd done this and tear it limb from limb. *An eye for an eye —*

Someone heard a voice. Work stopped. The dogs came in.

Nobody breathed.

Come on. Come on. Please, God. Please.

No.

Another body bag. Another flag. Another face he knew.

It should have been him.

He wished he could fly. He was losing his mind. He wanted to be a million miles away from the smell of rust and smoke and puke, but where else could he go? This smoldering heap was home now.

Someone handed him a bottle of water, and he drank, thinking, *ashes to ashes, dust to dust.*

What he wanted was a double shot of Jameson's.

The muscles in his back seized, and he groaned, tried to stretch. He might never stand erect again. It surprised him to see daylight. Morning. Beyond the western gate was his old friend, Austin. Poor bastard, keeping watch from his chair all night.

Beside him was an angel in a gray coat.

She was staring at him—Luke—with tears in her eyes.

A peace came over him.

Love, he thought. So this is how it feels.

City's Prized Landmark in Ruins

By Juni Bruder, Herald Staff Writer/Wednesday, April 15, 1998

ORLANDO—Hailed as "a workplace for the 21st century" when it opened in 1995, the Parramore Plaza stood as one of the nation's crowning achievements in urban revitalization. Before Dante Costas arrived on the scene, investors had shunned the blighted corridor west of I-4. By the time he finished his ambitious project, dozens of companies based their headquarters in the Parramore District.

The Plaza development covered almost 20 acres, a small-town community of shops, restaurants and living spaces around a central office complex. Woven into the site were landscaped parks and gardens that attracted workers on lunch breaks and families on weekends. Scenes from several major motion pictures were filmed here, most recently "Out of Bounds," starring Harrison Ford.

The 12-story Plaza building featured so many design innovations, Virginia Polytechnic Institute used it as a study model. Its "green" roof was the first of its kind in the state. Environmental enhancements made it one of the most worker-friendly buildings in the country. According to a state health report, Plaza employees suffered fewer allergies, respiratory illnesses and mold-related ailments. Fresh-air recirculation may have prevented smoke from rising to the upper floors during the early stages of the fire on Monday. The revolutionary gas-fired cooling system is suspected in the explosion that leveled the building.

Described as "a breaking wave," the Plaza's blue-green arcs and curves became a symbol for downtown Orlando. Thousands of tourists traveled north from the theme parks to photograph the building and take guided tours. After seeing the lavish interior, Sen. Hamilton Green declared the Plaza "a national treasure."

Visitors entered the building through a soaring atrium with colorful mosaic floors, Mayan reliefs and a 200,000-gallon mangrove pool. Schoolchildren made an annual pilgrimage to visit the pool's star resident, Griffy the manatee, on permanent loan from SeaWorld. Rare tropical fish swam in aquariums throughout the main hall. The Plaza's natural wonders were matched by its decorative arts. Costas was an avid collector whose acquisitions adorned every floor. Highlights included works by Dali, Seurat, Miró, de Kooning, O'Keefe and Fra Angelico. Valued at $18 million, the collection was thought to be totally destroyed.

Also lost in the collapse was a museum chronicling the history of the Parramore District, an African-American community that thrived at the turn of the century. Exhibits included memorabilia from the South Street Casino and Dance Hall, which drew such big-name entertainers as Cab Calloway, Ella Fitzgerald, Ray Charles and B.B. King; and the Wells' Built Hotel, one of few lodgings in Orlando open to blacks during segregation.

Sculptures of local icons adorned the Plaza parks. A bust of Dr. William M. Wells, one of the area's first African-American physicians, could be seen amid the wreckage. A statue of tap-dancer Clayton "Peg Leg" Bates was recovered by firefighters, who placed an American flag in the figure's bronze hand.

Hope Dims for Plaza Survivors

By Juni Bruder, Herald Staff Writer/Wednesday, April 15, 1998

ORLANDO—Family members travel from one hospital to another, hoping to find loved ones who may be too injured or traumatized to phone home. They scour the list of survivors posted by the American Red Cross. When all hope is lost, they make the grim pilgrimage to the Orlando O-rena. There, in a place usually associated with Magic games and Britney Spears concerts, a temporary morgue has been set up to handle the bodies recovered from the Parramore Plaza.

Of 83 bodies brought to the facility so far, only 27 have been identified. Some remains are so badly burned, DNA testing will be required. Mayor Delphi Owens said that the final death toll may be "double the current number."

Hope for survivors has dimmed in the round-the-clock search. The last living victim was pulled from the wreckage Monday night. Though she was conscious when rescuers reached her, Rita Gruenberg died en route to the hospital.

On Tuesday, the mayor toured the site with Governor Lawton Chiles, who pledged the full resources of the state. "After Oklahoma City, we hoped never to see this kind of devastation again in our lifetimes," he said. Appearing visibly shaken, he crossed a security line to embrace firefighters. He described his feelings as "beyond words."

Mayor Owens praised the rescue effort, saying that the outpouring of support and donations from across the country has been overwhelming. "Yesterday, this city was brought to its knees," she told volunteers. "We will never forget that awful blow, but we will always remember you, the heroes who rushed in and offered your hands to help us stand again."

The mayor would not comment on the fate of the building, which remains intact in sections of the atrium and the outer wings. "We're focused on getting people out," she said. "This is no time to talk about tearing down."

A memorial service will be held at the Florida Citrus Bowl on Sunday at 1:00. President Bill Clinton and First Lady Hilary Clinton are expected to attend.

Trial by Fire

Between the press updates and the phone calls—the governor, the president, Oprah Winfrey—Delphi Owens didn't have time to stop and ask herself, *Who put me in charge?*

Two months earlier, she'd been a lowly city commissioner, arbiter of building permits, gazebo grants and drainage easements. Her biggest challenge had been staying awake during five-hour hearings.

Now, she had to secure a twenty-acre murder scene, feed and house the National Guard and find refrigerated storage for body parts.

Who said the Lord didn't give you more than you could handle?

She'd been proud of her work as a commissioner for the Parramore district, one of the city's most underprivileged. She liked being down in the trenches where she could do the most good.

It was Dante Costas who'd urged her to run for higher office.

The former mayor had resigned in disgrace, a casualty of the Gulf Breeze scandal. The campaign donations he'd taken were perfectly legal, but his land deals with Thomas Rhodes smelled fishy.

Fake loans, crooked investments—you name it, and Rhodes had an offshore account to hide the profits. Yet he managed to weasel out of federal charges, letting his second-in-charge go to prison for eighteen months. Rhodes went back to his job at the bank, richer and fatter than ever, while his investors got pennies on the dollar.

Delphi said a little prayer, asking the Lord for a forgiving spirit when she saw the name "Thomas Rhodes" on the Plaza victims list. She wondered if the patsy who'd taken the fall for his boss knew how lucky he was. Instead of sitting in his corner office at the Plaza, he was sitting safely in jail. If Thomas Rhodes had been an honest man, Delphi wouldn't be mayor, and someone else would be in charge of the Plaza nightmare. Or was Dante to blame? Delphi couldn't decide.

She'd become friends with him while the Plaza was still in blueprints. At first, she'd only heard that a holding company was quietly buying up Parramore rental properties, most of them vacant. As a real estate agent, Delphi assumed some nameless corporation needed the write-offs. Buildings in the neighborhood were sure to depreciate. She didn't work in commercial sales, so it didn't matter to her.

Then an eviction notice appeared on her great aunt's door, and the grand Parramore project was announced. In all the fine talk about urban revitalization, nobody had mentioned old folks losing their homes.

Nobody counted on Delphi showing up at the public hearing.

It was her first time in the new City Hall. Like most residents, she'd driven past the big bronze dome and laughed at the sculpture out front, the tower of glass dubbed the "Giant Asparagus."

They could have planted a tree, Delphi thought, and saved the taxpayers half a million dollars. In her mayoral campaign, she would promise to sell the over-priced art and add more cops to the payroll, but that day, marching up the marble steps, she was an ordinary citizen in a fancy hat. She hardly noticed the well-dressed man who held the door for her. She was busy rehearsing her speech.

The rush of pride she felt walking into the grand rotunda surprised her. *This is my town,* she thought. *This is what we built.* She couldn't help but be awed by the council chambers. Nearly two hundred people packed the seats and stood against the walls.

When it was her turn to speak, she marched to the podium and held up a picture. "This is Mabel Osborne," she told the crowd, "my grandmother's sister, who cared for other people's children all her life and never married." Delphi knew no one cared about her family tree, but she was just warming up. "Aunt Mabel worked for Reverend Hurston after his wife died," she explained. "You remember him?" She feigned shock at the sea of blank looks. Pointing north, she said, "The mayor of Eatonville? The first black community in America ever to be incorporated?"

Most white folks in the audience knew Eatonville as the place to avoid on their way to Costco.

"Zora Neale Hurston's father," Delphi added, finally getting through. *Their Eyes Were Watching God* still made the high-school reading list during Black History Month.

The old mayor—could he imagine the mouthy woman in the hat would one day take his job?—had reached for his microphone. "While we appreciate the historical significance—"

"Aunt Mabel has lived in Parramore all her life," she thundered over him. "She saw her neighborhood carved up to build your police station, and your expressway, and she doesn't even own a car. You tore down her house on South Street. You tore down her house on Hughey. The landlords made their money. Now you want to tear down her house on Ossie Street? Where's she supposed to go? She's ninety-eight years old! Her hip is bad, or she'd be here to tell you herself: All she wants is to tend her geraniums and die in the place she was raised. Is that too much to ask? Hasn't she earned that right?"

Waiting for the applause to die down, Delphi fixed the angle of her hat. (She'd loved that hat, a red felt cloche with a black ostrich feather.) Finally, she started in on the Plaza developer, "that Costas person," the greedy outsider rolling into town with his hammer and nails and eviction notices. She even called him a carpetbagger, which was probably over the top, but it won her a standing ovation.

More than a few people—Delphi included—held their breath when "that Costas person" stood and approached the podium. He was the man who'd held the door for her. Like a snake charmer, he laid out his plan for an urban utopia where working families and retired elders could live in harmony and shop at the gourmet market. He offered a sizable discount to Parramore residents. On the screen, he showed colored sketches of parks and fountains, even a museum. He vowed to preserve the district's historic integrity, whatever that meant.

After the hearing, Delphi had to scramble out of the way as people rushed the stage for brochures. She'd taken one look at a flyer and tossed it in the trash. Maybe she couldn't stop progress, but she could call a lawyer to slow it down. "Motion for preliminary injunction" had a nice ring to it.

Two days later, Dante Costas showed up at her office, hatbox in hand. In his pocket was the deed to a two-bedroom condo at Parramore Place.

Delphi stood her tallest—up to his chin—and fixed him with a glacial stare. "You think I'd take a bribe from you?"

"It's for Aunt Mabel," he said.

Until the day she died, Mabel would call Dante Costas her adopted son. Which somehow made him Delphi's uncle, but she didn't quibble. To be closer to her aunt, Delphi consented to buy a condo up the street—at full price. That's when Dante mentioned the idea of City Council. "You're a resident of the precinct now," he said. "It's time to give back to your people."

"My *people?*"

"Your neighbors, your friends," Dante said. "You're wasting your gift selling houses."

Delphi scoffed. "I'm good at it. Top listing agent again this month."

"You know," he said, "in Greece, where *my* people come from, Delphi was the center of the universe. People walked hundreds of miles to the temple to speak to the oracle, to ask her the future. 'Should we go to war?' 'Should we plant the fields?' Nobody made a move without her."

"I'm no fortune-teller," she'd said, laughing. "I can't even tell you what I'm having for dinner."

"I'm talking about power. You have it. Use it."

And so she ran for City Council, and won. Her champion quickly regretted his advice; Delphi forced so many concessions from the Plaza developer, he threatened to pick up and move. Mixed-income housing, a medical center, a school named in honor of Dr. Wells—all Delphi's doing.

Dante told her once, shaking his head, that she was the only woman who'd ever refused him. When he joked about seducing her, she invited him to church.

On his travels, he brought back hats from Paris and Milan.

With the mayor's position suddenly vacant, and a special election announced, Dante persuaded Delphi—and he couldn't resist the phrase—to throw her hat into the ring.

"Why don't you run?" she asked him.

"I'm the carpetbagger, remember?"

She hadn't thought she stood a chance. Orlando had elected a Hispanic mayor in the early nineties, but was the city ready for an African-American woman? On the other hand, Delphi didn't back down from a fight, and she loved any excuse to dress up. The fact that she'd never shaken hands with Thomas Rhodes was a political bonus; her challengers weren't so fortunate. One of them had a hard time explaining the interest-free loan on his boat.

The other, a good old boy from a downtown law firm, made a crack about women in politics—to a *Herald* reporter. The headline of Juni Bruder's article would be "Ladies, Get Back to the Kitchen." (Frankly, Delphi had been surprised the joke wasn't about race.) In the end, she won by a landslide.

Ultimately, Delphi thought, it was Juni's fault she had to field calls from FEMA, the FBI and thirteen different funeral directors.

In her first staff meeting after the election, Delphi had warned her team, "Because I'm a woman of color, we will be held to a higher standard, which I expect you to exceed. You will do nothing to dishonor this office." She'd meant the run-of-the-mill scandals: taking kick-backs, driving drunk, having sex in a bathroom stall with someone other than your wife. The former mayor's antics had shamed the city, and Delphi intended to avoid the media spotlight at all costs.

The dusty streets of Parramore were lined with trucks from every major network and cable station. Delphi's condo was part of the evacuation zone.

Yea, though I walk through the valley of the shadow of death...

The night the Plaza collapsed, she'd wanted to curl into a ball and howl, but she didn't have time to mourn, or sleep. This was a test, she knew, a higher calling. *My God is my rock, in whom I take refuge.*

Political scholars would later praise her "iron-jawed resolve in the face of chaos." The lady mayor was photographed at the disaster site consoling weary volunteers, praying with families, blocking the cameras from private moments of grief. She directed the rescue effort like a five-star general. At bedsides and gravesides, she stood regal, veiled in black.

She broke down, finally, at Officer Browning's funeral, when little Caitlin placed a rose on her father's flag-draped coffin.

Delphi's pledge at the memorial service—"We will rise again"—was now a rallying cry, a vow to build a bigger, better Plaza. Whether Delphi had meant to make a promise of faith or reconstruction didn't matter.

Dante Costas could have helped her do it. He could have answered so many questions. A dozen times, Delphi caught herself reaching for the phone.

But no. She had a crisis to manage, and Katie Couric was waiting on line two.

Valerie Rose, Mauro Abissi's sister, Wednesday, 4-15-98, 8:30 a.m.

Juni Bruder? You're the one who wrote the story?

I'm sorry—which story?

About my brother, Marko.

Oh. Yes! You caught me off guard—I just stepped out of the shower. Can you hang on a second? [background noise] Sorry. Thank you for calling. I've been trying to get in touch with his family, his wife. We didn't know about brothers or sisters. Are you here in town?

Yes. I live in Casselberry. My name's Valerie Rose. I saw the paper and figured you'd be the person to call. You're in the book.

Have you talked to anyone else?

No. No, I can't. I wouldn't know what to say. No, that's not true. I want to say to these so-called media people, "My brother could be lying trapped in that wreckage, waiting to be rescued—he could be dead, God help me—and all you can do is tear him down, destroy his name. It's wrong, what you're doing, morally wrong." But I know what'll happen. They'll just turn my words around and use them against me. That's why I wanted to talk to you, to set the record straight. I thought since you already wrote about him, you could—

Mrs. Rose, is it okay if I tape this?

Oh, hell, why not? I had to give a deposition in Marko's divorce.

I'm sorry to hear that. This is only for my notes, though. In this state, it's a felony to tape a conversation without the other person's knowledge, so I have to ask.

I hate my voice on the answering machine.

You have a lovely voice, trust me. Some people I talk to, it's like breaking glass.

Well, thank you. Marko had the voice in the family, really. You should have heard him. He wouldn't sing in front of other people, but just washing dishes or whatever, it was like having James Taylor in the kitchen. Oh, my God. *[inaudible]*

I'm so sorry, Mrs. Rose.

I just want to wake up, you know? Call me Valerie.

Sorry…Valerie. When was the last time you saw your brother, Valerie?

Sunday night. He came over for dinner. Every week.

Did he show any signs—

I want you to understand something right now. There were no *signs*, because there's no way he did this. None. I swear on all that's holy. The head of my firstborn child. Marko wouldn't hurt a fly.

What about his wife?

That little—look, I'm being polite here. That little you-know-what ruined his life. Literally.

So she deserved it?

Marko never touched her! If anything, it was the other way around. He pleaded no contest because he couldn't afford a legal fight, and his lawyer said he'd have a better shot at custody if he cooperated—

I've been told there was a call to DCF, a report of child abuse.

You ever hear of false claims being made during a nasty divorce?

You're saying his wife lied?

No, I'm saying that if you hooked her up to a polygraph, the thing would light up like a Christmas tree. Aw, hell—you can't repeat that. She'll come after me next. Part of the reason Marko didn't fight was because he didn't want to make this dirt public. He was trying to do right by his little girl.

So he was dealing with false allegations, custody issues, an ugly divorce, and then he lost his job on top of everything else. That's a lot for one man to handle.

You don't know the half of it. When Cornerstone let him go—it's so hard for men, isn't it? They define themselves by their work. I read somewhere that losing a job is as hard on a man as losing a spouse, and he lost both. Well, good riddance to the one, but then nobody would hire him because he had a criminal record. It was *so* not fair.

I meant about him getting fired from the Plaza.

Oh, that. Well, it was just the last straw, wasn't it? Fire a man the day before his custody hearing so he can't prove any visible means of support. Could they have freakin' waited until Monday?

That was part of the reason he lost custody?

One more nail in the coffin, yeah.

You said he was fired from Cornerstone—the construction company?

Yeah. He managed their job sites for almost five years. He built, like, nine subdivisions for them, those ungrateful—

Why was he fired?

You'd have to ask them. Ask Harlan, he'll tell you. Harlan Sewall. Marko wouldn't talk about it. I think the problem was missing too much work. He never took a sick day, not one, and then this court thing came up, and they wouldn't cut him an inch of slack. No severance, no benefits—

Marko's boss at the cleaning company said he had some health problems from Desert Storm.

Yeah, him and about a thousand other G.I.s. It was worse right after he came back from Kuwait, but the V.A. took good care of him. Marko liked his doctors, he said. He trusted them. The bronchitis, or whatever it was, flared up in times of stress, so of course the last few months—

Did he have any ill will toward the government?

"Ill will"? You mean, like…like Timothy McVeigh or something? My God! You see? This is what I'm talking about. Everybody's trying to paint Marko like he's this…this *terrorist,* when that's the farthest thing from the truth. He loved his country! He fought a war for this country! My God, he choked up every time they played the national anthem!

He had a right to be angry at someone.

But he wasn't! That's what I'm trying to tell you! Why won't anybody listen to me?

It must be hard to imagine someone you love—

No. Absolutely not. I'll swear to my dying breath that Marko is innocent.

He carried a package into the building a few days after being fired. He lied about his I.D. to get past security—

So he had a package! What was in it, a bomb? The police searched his apartment. They didn't find anything remotely resembling what you need to build a bomb, even if he knew how, which he didn't. And they said it was a chemical explosion from the fire, not a bomb, so what was he carrying? Gasoline? That basement was full of chemicals, ready to light if he wanted to. It doesn't make sense!

According to the investigators, the fire started a few feet from his locker.

And he called 911, didn't he? Why would he set the fire and call for help?

Maybe to be on hand when they—

Oh, please, so he could be a hero? You obviously didn't know Marko.

He said he wanted to be remembered on television.

I know. I don't understand that part—he didn't even like to have his picture taken. Ask anybody who knew him. I can give you references. Marko set up this electronic mail thingy for me, Compu-something. I can send you a list of people as soon as I figure out how it works.

I'd appreciate that. I haven't been able to get in touch with Rosanna.

Yeah, good luck with that. I'd be surprised if she hasn't hired an agent already. Talk to Mick.

Who?

Mick McGrew. He and Marko were best friends. Talk to him. Do you have a brother?

Uh, yes. An older brother.

Would he ever hurt anyone?

No. Of course not.

How do you know?

Well, for one thing, he's a priest.

My cousin was molested by a priest when he was nine, an altar boy. What's your point?

I know my brother. He couldn't hurt a soul. It isn't in him.

Well, as sure as you know your brother, I know Marko. He. Did. Not. Do. This. You have to believe me. I'm begging you.

I'm not sure it's up to me to believe.

What you write is what people will think is true. You're convicting an innocent man.

What did your brother say to you on Sunday night?

Excuse me?

What was his state of mind? What did the two of you talk about?

What else? His daughter. My niece. She was all he ever talked about. She was everything to him. He was the best father—

And he lost her.

He didn't know what to do. He kept saying, "Val, how am I supposed to live without her?" It broke my heart, seeing him cry like that, you know? This was Marko! But I told him we'd get through it. We'd hire a better lawyer. He tried to get a home equity loan, but that fell through—those shysters at Gulf Breeze, honestly. I said, "Brother, I'll take out a second mortgage. We'll do whatever it takes to get her back. As God is my witness." And he sat up and said, "Okay. Damn straight. Lawyers can't be that expensive, right?" And we both laughed. That's how it was with him. When life knocked him down, he got back up and shook it off. He didn't lie around on the mat feeling sorry for himself.

He was a fighter?

No, not like that. It's professional-wrestler talk. You know, Andre the Giant, Dusty Rhodes. We used to watch them every Saturday. No, Marko was the kid who carried spiders outside. Mom paid him a penny apiece. Bug money. He was cheaper than Terminex.

How does a boy who can't kill spiders end up in the Army?

Squishing bugs and defending your country are two different things.

Right.

You're still not getting it, are you? It's a good thing you have that tape recorder. You can run it back later. It'll make perfect sense.

No, I do understand—

You want to know Marko's state of mind on Sunday night? I baked him an extra pan of lasagna, not thinking he'd have to carry it home on the bus. I offered to freeze it for later. "No way, Val," he said. "I'm not leaving without my lasagna. That's food for a week." Those were his last words to me. Now, you tell me—does that sound like a man with death on his mind?

A Jealous God

Looking back, Marko couldn't decide exactly when the fates turned against him. Was it the night he and Rosanna met? Their wedding day? If he had taken a different road, he wouldn't have his daughter—the love of his life—so how could he regret the choices he'd made?

Watching his child come into the world, he could have died a happy man. The cosmic joke was that God let him live—long enough to watch his marriage crash and burn.

Friends had warned him that a baby changed everything, and they were right. Holding his little girl in his arms for the first time, Marko finally understood what he was meant to do. *Keep her safe.* For the first few days, he almost never put her down. That week at home—he used the last of his vacation—was the best he could remember, not counting the lack of sleep and Rosanna's mother in the house. His sister, thrilled with a niece after two rambunctious sons, bought Mozart tapes and frilly baby dresses. When Marko called her "Auntie Val," she cried.

His wife's infatuation with motherhood faded after the fourth or fifth try at breast-feeding. "Give her time," the obstetrician said.

Rosanna told Marko, "Maybe I'm not cut out for this."

They argued over her going back to work. The thought of leaving his child in a stranger's care made Marko physically ill. For someone who rarely voiced an opinion, it was a deal-breaker: his wife would stay home for at least the first year. If that made him a knuckle-dragging caveman, so be it.

He'd have taken the job himself, given the choice. Coming home one night after work, he heard his daughter wailing. The TV was up so loud, Rosanna didn't hear him slam the door. He found the baby wet in her crib, and when he crooned her name, she calmed. Marko changed her diaper and rocked her to sleep, promising never to leave her.

The neighbor lady, taking pity, offered to baby-sit during the week. She missed her grandson, who lived in Phoenix and only visited once a year. "Nana," as she liked to be called, hooked rugs and watched the baby for the next twelve months—until Rosanna decided it was time for a bigger house in a better neighborhood. She'd taken a job in an optometrist's office by then, selling designer frames on commission. His wife had a gift for making people spend more than they wanted, and the house was no different. Marko signed on the dotted line, and they moved on Easter weekend.

By Halloween, they'd bounced a check for the mortgage. The payment on the furniture was late again. Just before Thanksgiving, their daughter brought head lice home from daycare.

Sitting in traffic on Christmas Eve, Marko thought, *This isn't the way I planned it.* His boss had pulled him aside—there would be no bonus this year. That money was the only thing standing between him and a very deep hole. He'd found the checkbook, which Rosanna usually hid. It shocked him, seeing how deep the hole really was.

The Italian leather chair he'd been sleeping in most nights should have been the first clue.

To be honest, he hadn't been paying attention. Trust or stupidity, he didn't know which. Asleep at the wheel, most definitely. The month of December meant eighty-hour weeks and a glut of year-end closings, and there were times when brushing his teeth took too much energy. He consoled himself with knowing that he—husband, father, provider—was working as hard as he could to take care of his family.

Not hard enough, his wife said. Repeatedly.

Climbing out of his truck each night, Marko braced himself. He never knew which fight to expect: the one where he worked too late and never helped around the house (and when he did, he did it wrong), or the one where he needed to work even later.

The woman who'd sworn to love and cherish him until her dying breath could barely stand the sight of him.

When his daughter came running for a kiss, Marko knew why God had put him on the earth. But most nights, his reason for living would be fast asleep by the time he came home.

It was almost enough to sit by her crib in the dark, stroking her hair.

When he fell asleep in the chair, the dream was always the same: an endless fall, the icy shock of water, drowning.

Harlan Sewall, Cornerstone Homes, Wednesday, 4-15-98, 4:30 p.m.

Mr. Sewall, I'm sorry to bother you at the office, but Valerie Rose gave me your name—
Oh, Jesus, Valerie. How's she doing? How's she taking this? I wanted to call, but what the hell do you say? "Sorry about your brother?"
That's why I'm calling. My name's Juni Bruder. I work for the Herald. *Valerie thought you could tell me a little about Marko, since you two worked together.*
I still can't get over it. I mean, you think you know a guy, right? Hell, I went to his sister's house for the Super Bowl, church for the christening, all that. I knew the whole family. Well, not the wife so much. She was...I mean...I guess the point is, you just never know.
How would you describe Marko?
Great guy. Hard worker. Never missed a closing. You could count on him to get his punch list done, no excuses. You know how hard it is to keep contractors in the summer? All the subs liked him. In fact, we lost a few when he left.
Why did he leave?
I'd rather not go into that.
He was fired?
The owner could probably—
He won't return my calls.
He won't? Yeah, I'll bet the old man's busy. Son of a bitch. Sorry. Scratch that. Look, all I'm saying is that Marko was coming up on five years, which is when you're fully vested, so missing a few days of work was a handy excuse to get him off the payroll. And now a certain son-in-law is sitting in Marko's chair, screwing up left and right. Talk about your nightmare walk-throughs. The closing's at four-thirty, and they're still grouting tile, for Christ's sake—
How did Marko take being fired?
How anybody takes it, I guess. What can you do?
Was he angry?
More like surprised that anybody could be so low. I mean, here's a guy who'd give you the shirt off his back, and they stabbed him in his.
I understand he had trouble finding another job.
That's what I heard. I felt bad for the guy, you know? I mean, the divorce, well, best thing that ever happened to him, but he paid through the nose for it. I figured a few months, maybe a year, tops, he'd be back on his feet, but then—
I haven't been able to find much on his wife. I take it you didn't care for her?
No comment.
Speaking of which, do you mind if I tape our call?
This is serious, isn't it? I mean, like a criminal investigation.
No one will see these notes but me. I would like to quote you, though.
Better watch my mouth. The stuff I said about the old man, can you go easy on that? I still have to work here.
I understand. Did you stay in touch with Marko after he left?

I kept meaning to give him a call. I owed him—I mean, he helped me through a rough patch. But you know how it is, you're busy with work and budgets and stuff, you lose touch. My son plays soccer, so that's every weekend. Then this shit hits the fan, and Marko's picture is all over the news, and he's the friggin' janitor? I'm like, "What the fuck?" I couldn't believe it.

You didn't know he was working at the Plaza?

Jesus, if I did, I would have pulled a few strings. I mean, we can always use help hanging drywall or painting, whatever. You know, cash on the side. But cleaning toilets? Man, that'd make me want to kill somebody, too.

You think that's what happened? Marko snapped?

It's like I said to Russell, geez, maybe we should have seen this coming.

Who's Russell?

Russell Kincaid. Golf buddy of mine. He's the one who recommended Marko for the job, way back when. They went to high school together. I saw the news, I called Russ, and we're both like, Jesus fucking Christ, can you believe this? To be honest, I didn't recognize Marko's picture at first. He even looked like the bad guy.

It's an awful thing to be remembered for your driver's license picture.

That's not him, you know? I guess it's the quiet ones you have to watch out for. You can only push them so far. Oh, hey, sorry, I have to take another call.

Thank you for your time, Mr. Sewall.

And one more thing. This crap about Marko being Arab or Muslim or whatever— Abissi is a good Sicilian name, for Christ's sake. His baby was baptized in the Catholic Church, holy water and all. I was there. Make sure you print that.

Russell Kincaid, friend of Marko Abissi, Wednesday, 4-15-98, 5:45 p.m.

May I speak to Mr. Kincaid? This is Juni Bruner from the Herald.

He's not home yet. What's this about?

I understand Mr. Kincaid went to school with Marko Abissi. I was hoping he could give me some background —

No.

Harlan Sewall gave me his name.

Russell won't talk to you.

I'm sorry, you are...?

His wife. Look—

Mrs. Kincaid, may I leave my number? If your husband thinks of anything, he can call.

He won't.

You're sure about that?

Look, we want no part of this. I have no desire to see my husband's name splashed across the headlines in the same breath with that—that *murderer*. It makes me sick to my stomach to think he was in my *wedding*. I can't look at the pictures now! He was one of our groomsmen! You think we want people to know?

It might help people to know what kind of man Mr. Abissi was.

What kind of man? He's the kind of man who could walk into a building and set it on fire, not caring how many innocent people he killed. What else do you need to know?

But if we could find out what made him do this —

What difference would it make? Those people will still be dead. I'm so sick of giving criminals an excuse, blaming their childhoods and all that garbage. None of us had it easy growing up, but you don't see us going around killing people, do you? I don't care what made him do it. Did he give a thought to the poor people in that building? No! He can burn in hell, for all I care.

Mrs. Kincaid, do you think—

Don't call here again.

But your husband—

I'm serious. We'll report you for harassment. Do you understand?

Absolutely.

And if you mention Russell's name, we'll sue.

Janitor's Sister: My Brother is Innocent

Valerie Rose criticized news coverage of Plaza tragedy

By Juni Bruder, Herald Staff Writer/Thursday, April 16, 1998

ORLANDO—In an interview on Wednesday, the sister of Mauro Abissi, the janitor suspected of setting the blaze that destroyed the Parramore Plaza, maintained his innocence. "There's no way he did this," said Valerie Rose, who challenged the media's coverage of the tragedy. "My brother could be lying in that wreckage, waiting to be rescued, and all you can do is destroy his name. It's wrong, what you're doing, morally wrong."

Ninety-four people are confirmed dead in the attack; some fifty victims are still unaccounted for. Arson investigators have narrowed their focus to the second level of the basement, where the blaze is believed to have originated. Abissi, fired from his job at the Plaza five days earlier, was seen carrying a package into the building on Monday morning. According to Abissi's sister, police searched his apartment for bomb-making materials.

Abissi, 29, applied for the janitorial position after being terminated from his previous job as a construction manager for Cornerstone Homes. Harlan Sewall, Head of Purchasing, said that Abissi was a hard worker who suffered a string of setbacks in recent months. "I felt bad for the guy," Sewall said. "Cleaning toilets would make me want to kill somebody, too."

Abissi's sister noted that he had difficulty finding work after he left Cornerstone. "Nobody would hire him because he had a criminal record," Rose said. She added that Abissi was turned down for a home equity loan by Gulf Breeze Savings & Loan, which was headquartered at the Plaza. Chairman Thomas Rhodes and manager John Burleson were among those killed.

Abissi's employer at the Plaza added that the janitor suffered a chronic cough, which his sister says was a result of his service in the Gulf War. "It was worse right after he came back from Kuwait," Rose said. "The bronchitis flared up in times of stress, so the last few months were bad." She insisted that her brother felt no ill will toward the U.S. Army or government.

"He wouldn't hurt a fly," she said. Abissi pleaded no contest to domestic battery in January after his wife, Rosanna, obtained an emergency restraining order against him. Court papers in the custody case involving the Abissis' two-year-old daughter included a report of abuse made to the Florida Department of Children and Families. Abissi denied the charge.

According to Rose, her brother's termination from the Plaza had a devastating impact on the custody case. "It was the last straw," she said. "Fire a man the day before his hearing so he can't prove any visible means of support." Rosanna Abissi was awarded full custody.

At his sister's house the night before the fire, Abissi broke down while discussing the loss of his daughter. "He didn't know what to do," Rose said. "He kept saying, 'Val, how am I supposed to live without her?'"

Plaza Survival: A Matter of Chance

Last-minute decisions meant life or death

By Juni Bruder, Herald Staff Writer/Thursday, April 16, 1998

ORLANDO—According to official estimates, at least 350 people were inside the Parramore Plaza when the fire alarm sounded on Monday morning. In the crucial minutes after the first explosion, many headed for the emergency exits. Others stayed at their desks, sending e-mails, making phone calls. Some left by the stairs, others the elevators. A few went downstairs to the parking garage to retrieve their cars.

For a group of survivors attending a candlelight vigil on Wednesday, each of these decisions proved to be the right one.

Others who heard the same warnings, and made similar choices, died.

North or south

Sandy Miner, who worked for Fidelius Financial Group on the eleventh floor, had scheduled an early meeting with colleague Chuck Bliss. The two were returning from the ground-floor coffee shop when they heard the fire alarm. "After the drill last week, we didn't bother," she said. The explosion knocked her coffee into her lap. "My first thought was, 'It's a brand new suit!' and then someone opened the door, and we could smell smoke."

Chuck headed for the southeast stairwell a few yards from his office, but Sandy dashed across the floor to the exit on the northwest side. "It's embarrassing," she said, "but I figured the door came out on Central, closest to the dry cleaner's. Mrs. Kessler would know what to do about the coffee stain."

The northwest stairwell wasn't crowded, but Sandy made slow progress in heels. "Blahniks," she explained. "No way was I taking them off." The second explosion threw her down the steps, and she lost a shoe. "I kicked the other off and ran like hell." Outside, she located several co-workers, but not Chuck Bliss.

"The last time I saw Chuck," Sandy said, "he was holding the door for everyone else." His body was recovered from the debris of the southeast stairwell.

The right elevator

Teacher's aide Serepta Mason couldn't wait to see the Parramore Plaza with teacher Emily Sparks and a group of first-graders from Henry Elementary School. The four children—Ashley Lynn Childers, Jonathan Sayre, Trân Châu Nguyen and Willie Pennington—had won the field trip in a reading contest. "I was looking forward to the gardens," Serepta said. "The kids were all about Griffy the manatee."

The group gathered by the mangrove pool to meet marine biologist Arlo Will, who cared for the Plaza's aquatic exhibits. "He helped the kids feed Griffy his breakfast," Serepta said. Afterward, she and Emily had trouble luring the children away from the pool for the ride to the roof gardens. The group became separated at the elevators. Teacher Emily and students Jonathan, Ashley and

Trân Châu entered the left car with tour guide Marie Bateson. Serepta and the fourth student, Willie, waited for the right.

"It was a race," Serepta said. "Their car stopped on a few floors, and we caught up. The kids stuck out their tongues at each other through the glass, giggling." When the explosion shook the building, both elevators jammed below the seventh floor, high above the atrium. "We didn't know what happened at first," Serepta said. "You could look down and see people running, and then smoke, and a big, black hole."

Eight passengers were trapped in the right car, seven on the left. "Willie thought it was a ride, like 'Earthquake' at Universal, until this lady started screaming." Maintenance workers quickly arrived to pry open the doors. "It felt like forever," Serepta said, "but finally we were out, and the fireman grabbed us." She and Willie ran with him to the northwest stairwell.

"I kept looking back, thinking Mrs. Sparks and the kids would be behind us." The second explosion severed the cables to the left elevator, killing everyone aboard. An electrician who climbed atop the car to open the emergency hatch also died.

Last-minute business trip

The decision that saved Thomas Hood's life came a week before the tragedy. One of his partners from the law firm of Hood, Pantier and Beatty scheduled a deposition in Cleveland on Monday, but due to a court conflict, Thomas made the trip instead.

"It promised to be a long, boring day," Thomas remembered. "Ben [Pantier] said he'd make it up to me, and I was like, 'Buddy, you owe me big time.' In Cleveland, I almost fell asleep in the meeting, so we took a break, and I walked downstairs for coffee. Everybody was staring at the television."

Thomas's offices at the Plaza were on the eleventh floor near the damaged central stairwell, directly above the epicenter of the second explosion. Of thirteen associates in the building—two partners and eleven support staff—none reached safety. Thomas is the firm's sole survivor.

"It's hard to describe that moment, standing in a Starbuck's in Cleveland, surrounded by strangers, not knowing if my friends were alive or dead," Thomas said. "I kept calling, calling on my cell phone. Nobody answered."

'Do you want to live?'

Abella Melveny loved cars, none more than her new Mazda Miata in fire-engine red. She also loved her indoor parking space in the Plaza's underground garage. "The waiting list was two years long," she explained. "My last car faded so bad in the sun, I had to trade it in." When her number finally came up in March, she and her friends at Fidelius Financial Group held a small party at space 203B on the concrete deck.

Like many other Plaza employees, Abella was late for work on Monday due to the traffic accident on I-4. She had just stepped off the elevator when the fire alarm sounded. "It woke me up," she said, "but I wasn't about to hike down a million steps." As she and her co-workers waited for the "all clear" announcement, the first explosion knocked them into a wall. "My friends, they ran for the stairs like good little girls. Me, I hit the button."

Abella's elevator stopped on several other floors to pick up passengers and was full by the time it reached ground level. "Someone told us there was a bomb," she said. "When the door opened, the guard yelled for us to run toward the commons." She ignored him and continued down to Level B.

"It was pitch black," Abella said. "You could hear people yelling. I dropped my keys. All of a sudden, this man grabs me and starts pushing me up the ramp. I was screaming about my car. He said, 'Do you want to live? Run. Now.' So, okay, I ran."

As she reached daylight, the second explosion roared behind her, trapping other victims in their cars.

Abella later identified her rescuer as Dante Costas.

For Immediate Release:

Costas Family Announces Victims' Fund

ORLANDO, FL (April 16, 1998) — The family of the man who designed and built the Parramore Plaza has announced the establishment of the Plaza Memorial Fund for victims of Monday's tragedy. Georgia Costas, whose husband Dante is among the missing, visited the site on Wednesday to thank rescuers for their round-the-clock efforts to find survivors.

The fund will assist families of victims and survivors with short- and long-term needs, from medical bills and funeral costs to rent and childcare. "Dante would want us to do everything in our power to help," said Georgia, who served with her husband on the boards of various civic and philanthropic organizations. The family recently made news with the formation of the Wells Elementary College Fund, guaranteeing a college education to each student who earns a high-school diploma. The Wells School opened in the Parramore district two years ago. This January, its students earned some of the highest FCAT scores in the state.

"Dante couldn't wait for the first class of freshmen," said Mayor Delphi Owens, who officiated at the announcement in February. "He came to school for lunch every Tuesday. He was a friend to these kids. They're devastated."

Georgia Costas pledged that the college program will continue, along with the memorial endowment. Donations to both funds, and applications for aid, may be made through the mayor's office.

For more information, contact Henry Layton, public information officer.

Widow's Walk

She smiled, she breathed, she moved from room to room. The house was full of people eating Dante's food, drinking Dante's wine.

Georgia Costas hated all of them.

They patted her hand and pretended her husband was coming home.

She felt the lie in her bones.

If Dante were alive, she would have sensed his presence at the site. He would have kept the Plaza standing by will alone. It was a blessing he hadn't survived, she thought. Seeing his lifelong dream in ruins would have killed him.

He's gone.

The words echoed in her head as she strayed between couches, picking up napkins, straightening pillows. Someone always tried to make her stop. "I need to stay busy," she told them, when what she meant was, "The next so-called *friend* who patronizes me will be dead like my husband."

But no. She kept up the farce, kept glasses filled, the famed Costas hospitality. Dante would have expected her to entertain their guests, no matter how much it cost her. Everyone wanted to hear a story about him, or tell one, as if talking helped.

Dante had been the one who put people at ease, told tales, remembered names. She simply endured, with his hand at the small of her back. He was happy to do all the work, which was how she viewed most social occasions. She could debate post-Keynesian economics for days, but she couldn't make small talk. Her idea of a party was a few close friends around the kitchen table, watching Dante cook.

For him, the more the merrier. He would have been thrilled at this turnout, Georgia thought. He would have raided the cellar for a special bottle.

Could they hold a service with an empty casket?

Don't forget to tell Ruth to iron my black silk dress.

Her parents had taken Marissa and Tucker out for dinner, a kindness, the pretense of normalcy. The fear and hope in her children's eyes nearly destroyed her. For their sake, every time the phone rang, Georgia had to remember to hurry, to act as if the news might be good. She hated lying, but they would hate her for giving up.

As if blind faith could bring their father back.

She knew there must be something wrong with her, if a healthy son and daughter meant no comfort now. Isn't that what everyone said? "At least you have your children."

My God, did people listen to themselves?

The love of her life was dead, and she was forty-two. One minute *wife, lover, friend* and suddenly, irrevocably, *widow.* The antique word made her think of a wrinkled face, gray hair, black shawl, the portrait of the old signora in Dante's study. He'd taken the photograph in Sienna on their honeymoon, charming the elderly woman by singing, there on the cobbled street, a line from Verdi.

Il balen del suo sorriso di una stella vince il raggio!

"The flashing of her smile shines more than a star!"

He'd whispered the words to Georgia the day they met, a private joke between them. He knew her weaknesses. Even after sixteen years, he could seduce her with a grocery list: *latte, uova, pane, formaggio...*

With this ring, I thee wed. With my body, I thee worship.

Dante was dead, and there were people laughing in the kitchen.

Lupe Alvarado, LYNX bus driver, Thursday, 4-16-98, 11:30 a.m.

Mrs. Alvarado, this is Juni Bruder of the Herald. *I'm sorry to call at home, but your supervisor told me you'd be getting off your shift. Do you have a few minutes to talk?*

What did I do?

Oh, nothing. You drove the bus that Mauro Abissi took to work every day, so I was wondering —

Abissi, who is this?

The man who set fire to the Plaza.

That monster? I don't know his name. You say he ride my bus?

We think so, yes.

Santa Maria! I should have back up and run over him.

Do you remember him? Six feet tall, dark hair, brown eyes.

So far, that's every man in my family.

[laughter] He may have ridden with his daughter sometimes. She was two. Her name was Stephania. His apartment was on Clay Street, the number-five stop, if I have the map right. He probably went all the way to the downtown station. He might have worn a shirt that said "The Clean Team."

Wait—you mean Marko?

Right. That was his nickname.

Oh, no! You can't—oh, no, please, don't. I have to sit down.

Are you all right, Mrs. Alvarado?

No, no, no!

So you did know him?

Yes, I know him! Oh, please don't tell me this—

Mrs. Alvarado, can you —

This morning he don't get on the bus, I try not to think about it. I know he work in that building, but I am hoping—*Jesu Christo,* let him be safe. He won't have a job no more, the glass is broken. He can sleep late. That's why he's not waiting at the stop. Oh, my poor—

You liked him?

More than like! He was such a nice boy. Quiet. Polite. Not one of these *cholos* who gets on the bus like he owns it. Mr. Clean, I call him, before I know his name.

So you and Marko talked? You got to know him?

You can hear me. I do most of the talking. He was shy, I think, but he listen, he pay attention. He notice things, like my hair when I get it done.

Did you see him on Monday morning?

Yes. Sunday night, too. I work a double shift. *Ay, dios mio,* you mean that day—

He was on his way to the Plaza.

On my bus. My bus.

Do you remember, was he carrying something? A package?

Yes. A present, he say. I tell him it's not my birthday, but how nice of him, and we laugh. I thank him for last night's dinner—I mean, it was nothing.

Dinner?

He told me a good restaurant to try.

That's not what you meant.

Yes, it is.

Don't worry, Mrs. Alvarado. I'm not about to tell anyone. I'm only trying to piece together what Marko did the last few days, where he went, who he saw. Sunday night, he might have been carrying a pan of lasagna.

How you know about that?

His sister mentioned it.

You're not allowed to bring food on the bus. Food or drink, that's the rule. I'm not supposed to let him past the door, but this is Marko, and it's dark. What can I do? He's not *eating* on the bus.

I'm sure you're allowed to relax the rules in certain situations.

But this part, it maybe get me in trouble.

It's okay, Mrs. Alvarado. I won't tell a soul. I promise.

Here's what happen. He give me a piece of lasagna to take home, like a bribe, a joke. He peel back the foil and let me smell, and, *ay, deliciosa!* I was starving, and we only get fifteen minutes for break—

Do you remember what time you dropped him off on Sunday night?

I don't know. Eight-ten, eight-twelve? I have to be to Central by eight-twenty, so close to that. I was late by the time we figure out how to wrap the food. I have the plastic from my newspaper, so that work okay, and then we—wait, don't tell my boss I was late! I make up the time on Minnesota Avenue. There's no *policía* that time of night, so I step on the gas—I mean—*ayúdame.*

Did you pick up Marko at the regular time on Monday morning?

Yes. I stop at Clay Street, same as usual.

What was his attitude?

His attitude? I don't know attitude.

How did he act?

Oh. The same. A little more quiet, maybe. Most people are quiet on Monday.

And he said the box was a present.

Yes.

For whom?

I don't know. Not me.

What did it look like?

Shiny paper, silver, a bow.

How big?

I don't know. Like a shirt?

Did it look heavy?

Lady, I'm driving a ten-ton bus. You think I have time to shake the box?

Did you know anything about Marko's legal problems?

Legal, like a lawyer? No.

But you saw his daughter?

Ah, yes, beautiful—a little doll, with her father's eyes. Why he call her a boy's name, I don't know. *Pobrecita.* What will happen to her now?

Did Marko say anything to you on Monday, anything like goodbye?

Like what you say when you step off a bus? Unless you're some rude people, and then you don't say nothing. But Marko, he say, "See you tomorrow, Lupe," like he always did. And then he didn't.

Didn't what?

See me. I was down there, you know, at the Plaza after it happen. I drive the bus all day and half the night. No fares, free, every route in the city, anyone who need a ride. Burned people, bloody, things you never want to see.

You drove to the hospital?

Me? No. Most people just wanted to go home. I take them to Central, turn around, go back.

You must have helped a lot of people.

I needed to do something. It was a nightmare, you know? The bus packed full, nobody saying a word, like ghosts. Except this one man, the very first trip. He's standing next to me, his face all dirty from the smoke. The rule is no standing in front of the yellow line, but who follows rules that day? And this man, he ask me about connections, where the buses go, do we take cash, things like that. You think he never rode a bus before. So strange.

He was probably in shock.

It was like I tell Marko, the bus can take you anywhere! Sunday night, just me and him, I say, "Why go the same old way? Let's hit the road! Who would miss us? Where should we go? New York? Las Vegas?" And he say, "Sure, Lupe. Let's do it."

Just take a city bus and go?

[laughter] I know. It was silly. A dream. But I think God, he was speaking to me. Turn around, Lupe, he say. Get on the turnpike. Keep going. If I listen to him, we could be halfway to Nevada by now, and all these people safe in their beds.

You can't think like that, Mrs. Alvarado. You helped a lot of people that day.

People I don't know! Strangers! Marko I know, and I don't help him. Maybe he try to tell me, and I'm too busy driving. I should know to look at him, but I keep my eyes on the road. Maybe he was sick? He must have been sick to do this, and I act like a regular day. Sometimes people go crazy, just for a second, you know? You make a mistake, like my uncle who drop his cigarette at the gas station, and boom, it's all over.

I'm afraid this is a little worse than dropping a cigarette, Mrs. Alvarado.

You don't think it was an accident?

A hundred and fifty people dead, a building destroyed? No. Something like that takes a plan. We just don't know the reasons behind it, which is why I'm talking to people like you. That's where we'll find the answers.

Lady, if I had the answers, you think I'd be driving a bus?

Bad Press

"Lay off the janitor for a while."

Juni had managed to avoid the newsroom for three days, spending her time at the site, filing stories from home. It was cowardly, she knew, the same urge for self-preservation that kept her away from weddings and baby showers. Weaving through the *Herald's* maze of desks, she felt raw, exposed, missing a layer of skin.

She waited outside Carl's office, wishing she'd ignored the summons on her voicemail. Behind the glass wall, she could see him talking to Bob Davidson and Margaret Fuller. Bob was the paper's strongest investigative reporter, the one who'd broken the Gulf Breeze scandal (and never let anyone forget it). He usually worked alone, but on that story, he had teamed with Margaret. Everyone knew they were sleeping together at the time.

Like most office affairs, theirs ended badly, and now the two could barely stand to be in the same room. Staff meetings were fun, watching them rush for chairs at opposite ends of the conference table. In Carl's office, they were forced to sit together, but they angled their bodies apart, arms folded, legs tightly crossed, a parody of the Kama Sutra positions they'd probably tried in the past. Juni grinned; it was a wonder one of them didn't pull a muscle.

Suddenly Carl pointed at her. Bob and Margaret looked over their shoulders, almost bumping noses. Had they heard her laughing? Juni froze, but after a beat they turned away, and Carl kept talking. He didn't look angry, but sometimes with Carl, it was hard to tell. And then she remembered the voicemail.

"Lay off the janitor for a while."

Carl was giving the story to Bob and Margaret. It was too big for her.

Juni considered running out of the office, if only to avoid Bob's smug expression, but too late—he and Margaret stood to leave. They filed past without a word, which wasn't unusual; neither of them bothered with social graces unless they needed something. Still, she could sense no triumph in them, no excitement. More like irritation, and it had something to do with her. What was going on?

Her boss waved her in. Juni could barely breathe against the stench of Bob's cologne. He slapped it on so thickly, it haunted a room for hours. "I'm putting you on another assignment," Carl said.

She let out a gasp—he hadn't even tried to soften the blow. He must be sorely disappointed in her. "Carl, I'm sorry," she said, sick with shame and after-shave.

He looked at her quizzically. "What for?"

"I'm working as fast as I can." She tried not to babble. "I talked to a bus driver this morning. She knew the janitor. She saw the package. I'm trying to track down his best friend—"

"Whoa." Carl's vinyl chair squeaked as he held up his hands. "It's nothing to do with your work, honey. We're getting calls. Nobody wants to feel sympathy for this guy."

Juni stared at him. He hadn't shaved this morning, and gray whiskers stubbled his chin. "What do you mean, sympathy?"

"His sister, his friends, the human-interest stuff."

"We ran thirty-six pages on the rescue effort. I wrote five paragraphs about this guy. People want to know—"

"Now, there, you're wrong." Carl rifled through his papers and held up a yellow slip. "To quote one of many messages this morning, 'It is an appalling waste of ink to publish the murderer's life story while the victims go uneulogized.'"

"Is 'uneulogized' a word?"

"You get the drift."

Carl kept a little statue of blindfolded Justice on his desk. In the old days, he'd flicked ashes onto her scales. Juni made a show of dusting her off. "Since when do you let public opinion dictate news policy?"

"Since a big building fell down and killed a bunch of people, Pollyanna. We're not dealing with a regular news cycle here."

"But—"

He pulled the statue out of reach. "Besides, you're the Barbara Walters of interviews. We need to go with your strengths."

"And now you're buttering me up? What a load of crap! The biggest story of our lives, and you're—"

Carl rose to shut the door. Coming back to his desk, he leaned on the corner and folded his arms, a cover photo for *Forbes*. "Listen," he said. "It wasn't my idea. Whedon was in my office, bright and early. He had a brainstorm."

"There's an oxymoron."

"Being disrespectful of the executive editor is hardly the way to get a raise."

"He froze our wages two years ago."

"Oh, right," Carl said. "Which reminds me, circulation has tripled this week. Tragedy is good for business. We haven't sold this many copies since the *Challenger*."

"Whedon must be doing cartwheels."

"He's as giddy as a schoolgirl. And remember how much grief we gave him for his plan to charge for obituaries? Who's laughing now?"

"Excuse me while I go throw up."

"You might get a raise after all."

"I don't want a raise," Juni said. She pressed a thumb to her forehead. Her hand, touching the arm of the chair after Bob, reeked of Old Spice. "I want to do my job. I want to talk to this friend of the janitor. Maybe he can tell us—"

"—that the janitor was a great guy, called his mother every Sunday? Who gives a shit? Not our readers, apparently, and not the man upstairs. Whedon wants to bump up the coverage on the victims. Their lives, their stories. He has this idea about selling commemorative editions."

"Of course he does. We see death, he sees dollar signs."

"And one day, we can dance a jig on his grave." Carl pushed his glasses down his nose to rub his eyes. "Look," he said. "I'm tired. You're tired. I need a smoke. We'll hold a funeral for journalistic integrity later. In the meantime, we're a little busy."

She watched him go around his desk and drop into his chair again. "Here's what I'm thinking," he said. "We run profiles on the victims, one a day, starting with Costas. He's the biggest fish."

"Jesus, Carl. They haven't even found him yet."

Carl eyed her over his bifocals. "Sweetheart, the last breather came out on Monday night. This is Thursday." He checked his watch. "Four p.m. You think they're pulling Mr. Costas out of the pile, just a little dehydrated?"

"It could happen."

"And Arnold Schwarzenegger could be the governor of California. Meanwhile, we're operating in the real world here," he said. "So the fate of Dante Costas is unknown. Take that tack, the brave architect going down with his building."

"Like Captain Smith and the *Titanic?*"

Carl spread his arms wide. "I'm king of the world!"

"Please don't sing."

"The doctor says my heart won't go on much longer." He yanked open his top drawer and rummaged through it. "Anyway, I'm thinking you talk to family, people who worked with Costas, that thing you do."

"Carl, there's been no funeral. I can't call Mrs. Costas and ask her to talk about her husband like he's already dead." She watched him pull out a calculator, a penlight, a plastic spoon, an empty bottle of Listerine.

"Do the best you can," he said. "You met the guy. There's plenty of press on him. We just need general background. He came, he saw, he conquered, and by the way, folks, he's probably dead."

"Come on, man. Show *some* restraint."

He waved the spoon at her. "You want me to be all sensitive and touchy-feely? A hundred and some-odd people kicked the bucket. Firefighters, policemen, normal people punching the clock. That's reality, babe. That's the story. You can sit there wringing your hands, call me cold-blooded, but I have a job to do. If you don't like it, you can go fuck yourself." He picked up the penlight and flashed it in her eyes, daring her to respond. When she didn't, he dropped to his knees and crawled under his desk.

"Did you ever take Civil Treatment for Managers?" Juni asked after him. "Because I'm fairly certain that last little speech would have earned you a lawsuit."

"I didn't ask you to fuck *me*, did I?"

Crowing in triumph, Carl came up with a dusty, bent cigarette. He closed his eyes and rolled it under his nose, savoring the smell of stale tobacco.

"You're not planning to light that indoors, are you?"

As he climbed into his chair, he growled, "Land of the free, my ass."

"What about the others?"

"The other what?"

"The other victims. The other profiles. What do you want, alphabetical order? Social status? Salary level? What?"

"You can lay off the attitude." The unlit cigarette bobbled on his lip.

"I'm just following orders," she said. "Like you."

"Oh." He leaned back and blew out an imaginary puff. "I get it." Pointing the cigarette at her between two fingers, he said, "You expected me to take a stand with Whedon, right? Tell him to take this job and shove it, right? My kids don't need to finish college. My wife doesn't need the radiation treatments. Who needs health insurance when you can live on principle, right?"

He clamped the cigarette between his teeth and waited for her to answer. "Right?"

Juni dropped her eyes and sank in her chair, like a deflated balloon, until he laughed. "What do you need me to do?" she asked, contrite.

"I'm waiting for an updated list of victims. The three of you will split them up, you, Bob and Margaret. They're not happy about it, but they'll come around. I'm putting you in charge."

"But they—"

"—will get over it. We start with Costas, run him on Saturday. Oh," Carl said, tapping his temple. "That reminds me. We need a Sunday piece on the religious angle to run with Margaret's coverage of the memorial service. How people turn to faith in times of tragedy, yadda, yadda, yadda. You know, a quote from Column A, Column B, a rabbi, a priest and a minister walk into a bar."

"How is your wife, by the way?"

"She's fine," he said, not meeting her eyes. "Thanks for asking. Now, on Monday, we'll run with the old lady Montemayor. People know the department store, they know her name. And I want to use candid shots, not the ones from the obits. I'd like to see *her* picture—Mrs. Haversham. I swear she had birds nesting in her hair. Hey, you okay?"

Juni straightened in her chair. "I'm fine," she said, repeating the lie back to him.

It hit her all at once. Fifteen years, and she was back where she'd started. Back among the dead.

Her first job as a college intern had been the obituary page, by tradition relegated to the newest hire. Perversely, she'd enjoyed the assignment at first. There was an art to it, summing up a life in a few paragraphs, getting it right. And then two children, five-year-old twins, had died in a hit-and-run accident, and she'd been sent to the home to collect photographs. The mother collapsed at the door.

That was the summer the headaches started.

"I'd better get going," Juni said, standing up too quickly. The room tilted for a second. "Lots of work to do."

The cigarette dropped into Carl's lap. "Don't be a stranger," he said.

Cold Comfort

Juni had never been much of a drinker—a glass of wine with dinner now and then—but the prospect of getting blind drunk tonight held more appeal than food. She hadn't eaten in days. Her stomach roiled at the thought.

She leaned on the refrigerator door, weighing her options. On the bottom shelf, behind the Diet Cokes and a bag of old grapes (or raisins?) was a six-pack of beer she'd bought for a date who never showed. He'd left a lame message about mushu pork and food poisoning. According to the "born-on" stamp, the beers were ten months old. Was that bad or good?

In the door with the mustards and seven kinds of salad dressing was a bottle of Riesling, but she couldn't justify the special occasion to open it. Buried under the frozen peas, she unearthed a year-old pint of Stolichnaya—the Ghost of Christmas Past, when she and Patrick, the stockbroker, had traded the "L" word, and broken up by New Year's Eve.

She'd erased his name from her memory, the vodka-swilling bastard. "Salut," she said, and took an icy swig. After the first shudder, the stuff wasn't bad.

She poured a double shot into a mug that read, "Reporters do it daily." In her case, "annually" was closer to the truth. Sleeping alone had never bothered her, but lately (since Monday night, to be exact) she ached to turn out the lights and crawl into someone's arms.

It wasn't sex she wanted, but body heat.

Juni lit a candle instead, a heavy scented pillar she'd found buried on the top shelf of the linen closet. She remembered being in an optimistic mood one day at Pier One, envisioning a bubble bath, a glass of pinot noir and the tranquil scent of bergamot.

Yeah, right. In another life, the one where she painted her toenails and kept a gratitude journal.

What did the taste of vodka remind her of? Nyquil. That was it.

With the frosted bottle tucked beneath her arm, Juni carried her mug and candle to the couch. The wax was dusty. So was the coffee table. Downstairs, a dog yipped. Her icemaker rattled. She wished the ringing in her ears, from the jackhammers at the site, would stop.

Juni needed something to drown out the noise in her head. Searching through her CDs for music to suit the mood, she found "Adagio for Strings." Maudlin, she knew, this little ritual was. Pathetic. Self-indulgent. She had laundry to do, and stories to finish. Crying would make her eyes puffy tomorrow.

What would Peter think of her—little sister, big-shot reporter—sitting alone in the dark, getting looped on cold medicine, wiping snot on her sleeve? Maybe he'd offer a dispensation. *Hail, Mary, full of grace.* Juni picked up her cordless phone, hit speed-dial and waited for his number to ring.

She squinted at the clock. Was it really two a.m.?

"Rectory," Peter answered.

Juni knew he received calls at all hours of the night. Emergencies. Last rites. Even roused from a deep sleep, he managed to sound lucid, reassuring. "I didn't mean to wake you."

"Jun, where the hell have you been? I left like nine messages! I've been going crazy here!"

"Didn't you get my e-mail?"

"Two lines, three days ago!"

"Sorry." She concentrated on enunciation. "It's been a little hectic here. You swore."

"Damn right. I was ready to hop on a plane."

"I'm fine. Too busy to get in any trouble. We're working around the clock."

"AP picked up your story," Peter said. "The 'landmark in ruins' one." Juni heard him stretch, groan. His mattress creaked. "The chairman of the history department posted it on her bulletin board. Nice touch about Peg-Leg Bates and the flag."

"Have you seen the picture?" Her stomach growled. "Artie took this amazing shot—"

"The cop with his arms around the statue, yeah. It ran with the article."

"Didn't it just break your heart?" She was suddenly, ravenously hungry. Propping the phone on her shoulder, she weaved back into the kitchen. It'd been weeks since her last trip to the grocery store, but she couldn't help hoping food had magically appeared in the pantry.

"Where were you when it happened?" Peter asked.

"At the dentist. I spent the day stuck in traffic. Useless."

"You made up for lost time."

"Hardly," she said. Was it too late to order pizza?

"Half my students called to make sure you were okay," he said. "They know who you are. It's real for them."

"It doesn't feel real to *me*."

"You've been down there, to the site?"

"Every day," she said. Standing upright made her head hurt. She uncapped the little green bottle at the sink and downed two pills with vodka.

"God, Jun. Are you sure you should be there—"

"It's where I need to be. It helps."

"But what you're seeing—it's like a war zone! How can it help? I see the news and it's too much. The firemen carrying out their friends, the search dogs with the bloody paws. The poor families by the fence. I finally had to turn off the TV. How can you see so much pain and not—"

"What am I supposed to do, close my eyes?"

"You know what I'm saying. If you stare at the sun too long, you'll go blind."

"And then I can finally get a dog." In the cupboard, she found peanut butter. Crunchy. Saltines. Stale.

"What's that noise?"

"Dinner."

"Are you eating?"

"I just told you."

"No," Peter said. "I mean, are you taking care of yourself? Are you sleeping? No, of course not. That's why you're calling me at dark-thirty. Jun, I can't help but worry. The last time—"

"—was years ago." Juni drained her mug. In answer to the question, vodka *did* go with peanut butter. "I'm fine. Trust me."

"Sure, trust you. You're fine. The apocalypse came to town, and you had a ringside seat."

"Wow, that's good. Can I use it? Where's my pen? *The apocalypse...came...*"

"Excuse me for caring."

"You're my brother. That's what you do. And I love you for it."

"And you're drunk."

"I talked to his sister yesterday," she said.

"Who?"

"The guy who set the fire."

"Allegedly."

Abandoning the butter knife, Juni dipped a cracker into the jar. "In the words of Mr. Chaudhary, tell that to the FBI."

"The sister's name is Mr. Chaudhary?"

"No, *Valerie*. I felt so sorry for her. Can you imagine your own flesh and blood wreaking such havoc? Of course, she had nothing to do with it, but people will blame her, just the same. Guilt by association. All she did was love the guy."

Peter sighed. "He must have been a troubled soul. I'll pray for him. And his family."

"Wow, do they teach you these pious quips at seminary?"

"Do they teach you these manners at reform school?"

"Judge not, lest ye be judged," she said, smacking peanut butter.

"Imagine. I was sound asleep when you called."

"I'm sorry, Peter." Her throat closed; she couldn't swallow. "Go back to bed. It was stupid—"

"It's okay, Jun. Talk to me."

"No. It's late. I just wanted to hear your voice."

"Jun, listen to me," Peter said. "As someone who counsels people for a living."

"Hell of a living. They don't pay you anything."

"Listen to me, damn it. You can't let this day take over your life. The people you're talking to, they're in a dark place. Soul-sick. It's easy to bring their hurt home with you, like it's *your* pain, *your* loss, but it isn't. You understand me?"

"Come on, Peter. I talk to victims every day. It's my job. No difference now."

"Your reporting skills aren't the issue."

She slid down the cabinet to the floor. "And it *is* my loss."

"We all lost something Monday," he said. "The whole country. A little bit of our innocence, our trust—"

"I had friends in that building. People I knew."

"Jun, I'm sorry. You said your friends were safe in your e-mail, so I just assumed—"

"Jesus, Peter, you act like watching the nightly news gives you as much *insight* into the disaster as being here! Do you have a big, gaping hole in the middle of Chicago?"

"I didn't mean to trivialize—"

"We're standing on the edge of the grave. You're standing in Hallmark, buying sympathy cards."

"You need to get some sleep, little sister."

"Don't treat me like a child."

"You're angry, Jun. I get that. You have every right to be, but not at me."

Curling up on her side, she muttered, "I hate it when you're so patient and condescending." The tile was cool against her cheek. "And right."

"Hold on a minute." Peter tapped the receiver against something hard. "This connection must be bad. Did you just say I was right?"

"Ha, ha."

"Honestly, Jun. Go to bed. Get some rest. Call me in the morning."

"I could sleep right here," she said, staring at the ceiling. Dead bugs peppered the bowl of the fan light.

"You'll feel better tomorrow."

"Now there, you're wrong, brother dear. It's worse in the daylight."

"Here's a thought," he said. "I don't have classes on Monday. I could ask for a long weekend, catch a flight—"

"Not now, Peter. Thanks, but I'm too busy. Besides," she said, lapsing into a brogue, "ye can't afford a ticket. Ye're as poor as a bloody church mouse, Father Malloy."

He chuckled, a sound that went straight to her heart. "You're going to hell. You know that, right?"

"Already there."

"Might have something to do with whatever fifth you drank tonight. How's the head?"

"Still attached. Peter?"

"What, Bug?"

Forcing herself to a seated position, she waited for the kitchen to right itself. "Nothing," she finally said. "I'd better go to bed. You, too."

"Jun, promise me something."

"What?"

"You get in a bad way, you call me, right?"

"Like now?"

"You know what I'm talking about. This is good, tonight. You're not acting like everything's under control. It's when you tell me not to worry that I do."

"Nag, nag, nag," she said. "Don't the students get tired of your lectures?"

"They hang on every word."

"Sure they do. The cute priest. Forbidden fruit."

"I'll pray for you," he said, laughing. "Somebody needs to."

Pope Arnaud, Dante Costas's personal assistant, Friday, 4-17-98, 10:45 a.m.

Mr. Arnaud? This is Juni Bruder. We met a few years ago, just before the Plaza opened. Do you remember? Mr. Costas gave me a tour. [coughing] Excuse me. My throat's a little dry.

The reporter. Yes. Dark coat and paisley scarf. It was silk, that scarf, with a lovely muted pattern, grays and blues to match your eyes. I remember coveting it for a pocket square.

That's right! I'd forgotten that scarf. Someone stole it off my chair at Planet Hollywood.

Wasn't me, but it serves you right for setting foot in that celebration of celebrity crassdom.

Under duress. I was assigned to cover the grand opening.

You're forgiven, then, but what a dreadful way to earn a living. I assume you're calling about Dante? A story about him for your paper?

Yes. His achievements, the impact he had on the community. A tribute, so to speak.

In the past tense?

No, of course not. With every hope he'll be found alive. That would be the best ending.

But we don't believe in happy endings anymore, do we?

I'm not sure I ever did.

Ah, then. You didn't have quite so far to fall.

This must be a terrible time for you, Mr. Arnaud.

We're enduring as best we can.

Were you there on Monday?

Oddly, no, I wasn't. Dante asked me to call him on Sunday night. He was very specific about the time, but I should have remembered he'd be at the opera, even if he forgot. No matter. He asked me to drive to Tampa in the morning and pick up a box of cigars for President Clinton, congratulations for the Belfast Peace Agreement. Mr. Clinton has a particular fondness for the hand-rolled Simpaticos from Ybor City. So, on Monday, I was in my car, out of harm's way.

Cigars saved your life.

A claim not many can make. The box is sitting on my dresser. I don't know what to do with it.

Would you mind if I ask a few questions about Mr. Costas? You probably knew him better than almost anyone else, working so closely with him as you did.

I'll answer what I can. You understand, the better part of my job was discretion.

Of course. I only need a few details to fill in the gaps, and it didn't seem proper to intrude on the family.

But an employee is fair game.

No. I'm sorry. Maybe this was a bad idea. I shouldn't have bothered you.

It's quite all right, Miss Bruder. How uncivil of me. Shall we begin again?

Please.

What do you wish to know?

First, when did the Costases move to Orlando? One article says 'eighty-three, the other 'eighty-four.

May of 'eighty-four. I remember because Georgia and I looked for houses over Memorial Day weekend.

That's how you met? You worked in real estate?

Among other ventures. My true talent is in knowing people. If you need an interior designer, I can recommend the best. A driver, a personal chef, a yoga instructor, let me make the call. For someone new to town, my help could be indispensable, as the Costases found it to be.

Did you grow up here?

Oh, dear, no. No one does. Let us say that I followed my heart to these fair shores, only to find myself alone and my love in the arms of another.

Funny, that's how I ended up here.

Why else would anyone come to Orlando?

[laughter] Were you the closing agent on Casa Marquesa?

Sadly, no. The house was a hair's breadth away from demolition, after all. I merely drove the happy couple past the wreck on my way to a darling Tudor Revival on Palmer Avenue. We never made it.

You should have asked for a finder's fee.

Considering the benefits I've reaped over the years, my greed would have been shortsighted, don't you agree? Besides, I made a healthy commission on the condo they rented during the renovation.

How long did it take?

Almost two years. Georgia was pregnant for the house-warming.

With Tucker.

Yes, and Marissa, our little princess, came along two years after.

You're close to the children?

I've never missed a concert or a basketball game, unless I'm away on business, which is more than their father can say.

Mr. Costas didn't attend school functions?

Forgive me. I spoke out of turn. It's a stressful time, you understand. Of course, he attended when he could. His schedule didn't always facilitate extracurricular activities. I was available. I went by proxy.

You were part of the family.

The children call me Uncle Pope.

How did you end up working for Mr. Costas?

Oh, ancient history. I stopped by the condo one day to deliver a batch of holiday cookies, a gift I made for my clients every year. The twelve days of Christmas, a partridge in a pear tree, the lords a-leaping and so forth—handmade with fondant icing, really quite lovely. Dante mentioned having trouble with a builder, a missing stucco crew. Twenty minutes later, I had eight burly lads on the job.

And you became his personal assistant.

Et voilà! Although I consider myself more of a life manager.

Sounds like a big responsibility.

You have no idea. I'm on call twenty-four hours a day. Don't misunderstand me—the perks far outweighed the disadvantages. Dante was a very generous employer. I traveled the world with him.

What was he like as a boss?

Demanding, of course. He expected the best, of himself and everyone around him. I'll admit, he could be short-tempered at times, but then, I've never known a man of power and influence who wasn't. They live in a different world, don't they? They make their own rules. They breathe a higher quality of air. But that was his appeal, as you well know. People were drawn to him. If anyone ever denied him, I can't remember it.

If they did, they lived to regret it.

Speaking from personal experience?

Oh, no. I mean, I've heard stories, that's all. The neighbors' tree, for example.

Good heavens—that tree was on his property line. Dante was perfectly within his rights to remove it.

In the middle of a birthday party?

He wasn't privy to his neighbor's calendar.

A party to which his daughter wasn't invited?

Oh, dear. I'd forgotten the media's penchant for hearsay.

[laughter] Don't get me wrong, Mr. Arnaud. Anyone who's ever been left off a guest list loved that story. Especially those of us who grew up without a dad to chop down the mean girl's tree.

And Dante did apologize later. I hope you're not planning to include this ridiculous story in your article.

Of course not. There's no reason to bring up a simple misunderstanding.

Exactly right. And all the work Dante did with children, surely that counts for something?

I wanted to ask about that. Apparently, hundreds of children owe their education to him, the kids at Wells Elementary and now the children of April 13. It seemed to be a theme in his life.

He always said, "Knowledge is power." He read extensively—books, papers, magazines, any print he could find. He was always learning, always asking questions. He could tell you what the doorman had for lunch.

And he never forgot a name.

Of course not. He had me. *[background noise]* Let's see. Ah, yes. Miss Juni Bruder. *Herald* reporter, tour of the Plaza, January 9, 1995. Auburn hair, blue eyes. Five-foot-six, one hundred and twenty pounds.

One fifteen, if you don't mind.

My mistake. Corrected. Originally from Illinois. Moved to the City Beautiful in 1989.

How on earth do you know that?

As I recall, it was cold the morning of the tour. You said it reminded you of home. Dante asked where home was, and you said Chicago, although the name of the suburb escapes me. You mentioned "the big freeze" the first Christmas you lived here, the one that killed the orange groves. That was 1989. You also explained the concept of "snow days" for the edification of us Southerners, unacquainted with frozen precipitation as we might be.

How embarrassing.

Once, you said, your school was closed for an entire week, and you slept with your mother and brother beside the fireplace.

Sometimes I talk too much when I'm nervous.

Most people do.

I thought you were taking business notes.

I was.

You must be a veritable font of information.

If you saw my journal, I'd have to kill you. My condolences on the divorce, by the way.

We were still—I hadn't even filed then.

Marriage licenses and divorce decrees are published in your very own periodical, Miss Bruder. I read it cover to cover. Did you enjoy the flowers?

The flowers?

Ah. Perhaps I misspoke.

Oh. No. They—the irises were beautiful. Thank you.

Roses wouldn't have suited you.

I imagine Dante must have kept you busy with floral orders.

Now, we're paddling in confidential waters, Miss Bruder.

Do you know what happened between him and the janitor?

I'm sorry?

The owner of the cleaning company said that Mr. Costas called to have the man fired, which I thought was odd.

Attention to details, Miss Bruder. Dante was famous for it.

He took time out of his busy day to fire an hourly employee? Something major must have happened, something worse than water spots on the glass.

I really couldn't say.

Nothing in your notes?

I vaguely recall an issue having to do with Micaela, but I don't—

Micaela?

Micaela Singer. Our art conservator in residence. She worked on Level B, not far from the lockers. I think perhaps the janitor was bothering her.

In what way?

It's an unpleasant and irrelevant detail, given the circumstances. Suffice it to say that Dante took great pains to ensure a safe working environment for the Plaza staff. His care and concern were well documented.

I remember the art vault from the tour. I didn't realize the collection was a job in itself.

It was, but mine. No, Micaela signed on to restore an icon that Dante bought on his last trip to Athens. Hundreds of hours of painstaking work. She allowed me to watch on occasion. Gold leaf as thin as air. Tiny brushes. I was bored out of my mind. It was like watching paint dry. Literally. From what I understand, she was inches away from finishing.

I assume the piece was destroyed in the fire?

Yes. As you can imagine, she's quite distraught.

Was she there on Monday?

Fortunately, no. Micaela isn't what you call an early riser. You know those creative types, always burning the midnight oil.

Would you mind giving me her phone number?

For what purpose?

She worked at the Plaza. She knew Dante. Apparently, she knew the janitor —

Micaela is a lovely girl with a bright future. I see no reason to drag her name through the mud. What's done is done. And I couldn't give you her number, even if I wanted to. She's gone.

Wait — what mud? I'm sorry, where did she go?

She left town yesterday. Quite distraught, as I said. As are we all.

Do you have a forwarding address?

The last time I checked, privacy was still a constitutional right in this country.

Of course. I mean…it's just…you said her name was Singer?

Why don't I fax you a copy of her Curriculum Vitae? It should tell you all you need to know, and you won't have to disturb Micaela in this difficult hour.

I'd appreciate that. Thank you, Mr. Arnaud, for your time. You've been a big help.

My pleasure.

What will you do with your journal, by the way?

Keep it safe, of course. For Dante's return.

Death of the Hired Man

In her childhood room, Micaela huddled in the dark. She couldn't tell the time. The velvet curtains—new, a deep forest green—blocked out the light.

Essence of winter sleep is on the night.

Strangely, she missed the old eyelet lace, which she'd once described to an art-school friend as "shabby without the chic." Her mother had redecorated not long after she left for Baltimore—when, four years ago? The Walters Museum felt like another lifetime.

I dwell with a strangely aching heart.

Micaela could remember fabric swatches in the mail, anxious messages on her answering machine. Silk or chenille for the duvet cover? Faux paint or wallpaper? The question she never answered: When are you coming home?

Some say the world will end in fire.

Her parents had cried at baggage claim.

We love the things we love for what they are.

The Singers had taken their only daughter home and tucked her into bed like a feverish child, clearly frightened for her. Micaela had walked off the plane like the living dead. No shower, no makeup—she'd simply packed a bag and run.

Home, the place where, when you have to go there, they have to take you in.

She'd never attended church as a child; her parents had trusted her to find her own way. Late in life, her mother became a disciple of Martha Stewart. Her father, professor emeritus of English, worshipped at the altar of Robert Frost.

Because of the fears of fire and loss.

Micaela had recited poems at her father's faculty dinners without knowing what they meant. Her world was pictures, colors—every shade of red in the crayon box. The wintry stanzas about birches and walls and graveyards had been as remote to her as the man at the head of the table, and later, as quaint as a greeting card.

This saying good-bye on the edge of the dark.

Now, they seemed to be the only words she understood.

"Breakfast!" Her mother burst through the door with a tray, and Micaela shaded her eyes against the sudden light. "Fresh fruit, cranberry juice, banana nut muffins. I made them myself."

Her working mother, who'd sent store-bought cookies to PTA bake sales.

I cannot rub the strangeness from my sight.

"Let me move this vase. Every guest should have fresh flowers, Martha says. You're not a guest, you're family, of course. She clips them from her own garden. I would, too, if we had a yard. It's too early, though. Too cold."

Give the buried flower a dream.

"Were you warm enough last night? Your father wouldn't let me raise the thermostat. I should have brought an extra blanket."

How the cold creeps as the fire dies at length.

"Micaela? Honey?"

Micaela knew that if she didn't pull herself together, her mother would call a doctor. "What time is it?" she finally asked, pushing the hair out of her face.

Begin the hours of this day slow.

"Almost noon. I was going to bridge club, but now you're here—but then, I thought you might want to rest today, after…well, after the time you've had."

I'd like to get away from earth awhile.

Micaela watched her mother fuss with the flowers; their smell reminded her of a funeral home. Sitting up, she broke off a piece of muffin and went through the motions of chewing. "Go, Mom," she said, tasting sawdust. "I'll be fine."

"Are you sure? I hate to leave you alone."

One is alone, and he dies more alone.

"It'll give me a chance to unpack." Micaela smiled. Her mother smiled back. She'd said the right thing. Her mother could leave her now, safe with a task.

"All right, then. Maybe you'll take a nap this afternoon? You look—"

"I slept for ten hours." A lie, but what else was there?

Truth? A pebble of quartz? For once, then, something.

She couldn't very well say, "Mom, I'm suddenly afraid of the dark."

Visions of half the world burned black.

To her horror, she'd dozed on the plane, lulled by the passing clouds and the drone of the engines.

It was just as the light was beginning to fail.

He watched her with that dark half-smile, the old-soul eyes. Nut brown, mahogany, chocolate—she'd never been able to decide on a shade. He stood at the window, watching her work, and she pretended not to know. Soon she would turn and open the door, but not yet. Not yet.

We keep the wall between us as we go.

His silent self-possession had drawn her from the start: an inner stillness, a standing apart. He'd been content to wait. He didn't fill the space with empty words.

You have only to ask, and I can tell.

In the dream, he never spoke.

I am greatly to blame.

Not even as fire licked at his clothes.

Two roads diverged in a yellow wood.

And she sketched the brilliant colors of the flame.

Plaza Architect Shaped Orlando Skyline
Dante Costas is among the missing
By Juni Bruder, Herald Staff Writer/Saturday, April 18, 1998

Dante Costas had a knack for being in the right place at the right time. As a college student in Houston, he bought and renovated a string of dilapidated bungalows in a neighborhood destined to become one of the hottest housing markets of the 1970s. The modest investment of sweat equity netted Costas a million dollars before his twenty-first birthday.

He parlayed his profits into real estate holdings across Houston during the oil boom, turning forgotten landmarks into chic lofts and offices. In 1983, he surprised his associates by putting his properties up for sale. By the time oil prices—and Houston's economy—plummeted, Costas was out of the market with a handsome profit.

Seeking new investments and a chance to live closer to his parents, both in failing health, Costas moved to Orlando in 1984. On his first house-hunting expedition, he drove past the abandoned Casa Marquesa, a vine-covered ruin once owned by the Ringling family. The 1934 Mediterranean Revival-style mansion, designed by architect James Gamble Rogers II, was slated for demolition the next week.

Costas climbed the fence and started making phone calls.

After he saved the architectural treasure from the wrecking ball, Costas launched a two-year restoration project to turn the 18-room villa into a Winter Park showcase. *Gourmet Magazine* featured the home's brick-lined wine cellar, holding 1,600 bottles, in its annual oenophile edition. The mahogany-paneled humidor appeared in *Cigar Aficionado*.

While Costas finished his house, he was also working on a business plan to transform the Parramore District from a no-man's-land into one of the city's most sought-after addresses. By the time he completed his 20-acre Plaza complex, the American Institute of Architects would name him "an urban visionary."

Perhaps the most remarkable aspect of his achievement was that, while Costas served as the architect of record on hundreds of renovations, the Parramore Plaza was his first full-scale development.

He was last seen assisting victims from the burning building.

The Sponge Diver's Son

Dante Andrea Costas was born in Tarpon Springs in 1949. His grandparents had immigrated to Florida from the Greek island of Patmos. Costas liked to say that his father was a sponge diver, which was technically true—Nicholas Costas had spent a summer as a sponger before shipping off to South Korea with the U.S. Army. After two tours of duty, Nick earned a degree in electrical engineering on the G.I. bill. Costas Electric became one of the largest commercial contractors on the Gulf Coast.

The Costas family stressed the value of hard work and education. Nick's son planned to become an engineer like his father, but a trip to Frank Lloyd Wright's Fallingwater changed his mind. Dante Costas earned a Master of Architecture in Urban Design from Rice University in 1977.

Costas met his future wife, Georgia Reece, while both were students. Georgia received her M.A. in International Economics from the University of Houston. After completing her graduate degree, she served as an analyst at the Centre for Studies and Research in International Development at the Université d'Auvergne in France. A year later, she returned to Houston as an adjunct professor.

The couple married in 1982 and honeymooned in Italy, where Dante fostered a love of Italian opera and cooking. His *ravioli con aragosta* was legendary; he once cooked the dish for a surprised group of senior citizens on the Parade of Homes tour.

Though the Costases limited their attendance at society functions, both served on the boards of various civic and philanthropic organizations. They joined the St. Sophia Greek Orthodox Church soon after their arrival in Orlando.

Georgia Costas is currently an Associate Professor of Economics at Rollins College, where she lectures on global economics and the history of economic thought. While serving as a trustee for the Orlando Science Center, she was credited with reversing the museum's ailing finances.

The Costases' first child, Tucker, was born in 1986. Their daughter, Marissa, followed two years later. Both are students at Lake Highland Preparatory School, where Tucker plays forward for the freshman Highlanders and Marissa plays the clarinet.

Dante Costas played basketball in the "over-forty" league at the Lakemont YMCA.

"The man was an inspiration," said Mayor Delphi Owens, his long-time friend. "He was a hero to so many people in this community, and he showed his true colors on April 13."

Never Again

For his beautiful home, his perfect family, the ease with which he made and spent money, Dante Costas might have been resented, even despised, by the average *Herald* reader. Yet, nearly everyone who met him was charmed. Dante counted on it. He didn't question the power—charisma, magnetism, whatever—that opened doors for him. He used it to get what he wanted. His admirers called him a self-made man. His opponents called him a ruthless bastard.

For the record, he wasn't a womanizer. Anyone who knew him knew he loved women: their sharp minds and soft curves, cool smiles, secret heat. To him, a woman was a luscious puzzle. A Zen koan. The grassy knoll.

Dress her up in a designer suit—so he could imagine stripping off a pair of killer heels and thigh-high stockings—and he was hooked.

In his defense, he followed a strict set of rules. He limited his indiscretions to business trips. He'd never become emotionally involved. He never took off his ring. He simply laid his cards on the table—lust was trump—and countless women took him for an honest dealer. His longest relationship had lasted twelve days, the Ritz Carlton in London. The shortest, ten minutes in the Delta Crown Room at O'Hare.

If nothing else, Dante loved a challenge. A woman who said no? Now, there was something to get his juices flowing. He was in the business of changing minds. When he promised a woman she wouldn't regret a night in his bed, he wasn't lying.

The regret would be his. On the plane home, on his third glass of Scotch, Dante would contemplate his recklessness. He would weigh the long-term risks against the short-term benefits and come to his senses.

Never again. He loved his wife. She was everything to him.

He could live without heat.

For weeks, even months, he might be happy, living the life he imagined faithful husbands led. The restlessness, when it came upon on him, would be manageable. He channeled his energy into blueprints, site designs, feasibility studies.

His mission statement: Never again. Until the next time. He was only a man, after all. He needed something—someone—to take the edge off. And didn't he deserve it, for as hard as he worked? If no one found out, who got hurt?

As a student of the ancient Greek philosophers, Dante knew an argument in moral relativism when he heard one.

As an American male of the twentieth century, he'd learned to live with himself.

Bishop Gordon Liman, St. Barnabas Church, Saturday, 4-18-98, 9:30 a.m.

Good morning, Bishop Liman. Thank you for returning my call. Did your secretary explain the theme of the article?

Yes, she did, and I think it's a fine idea. Faith in times of tragedy. I'm not sure your paper does enough on the spiritual front, but that's a discussion for another day.

I'll admit, this is my first religious assignment.

Are you a churchgoer, Ms. Bruder?

Uh, no. I was raised Catholic, but it's been umpteen years since my last confession. My brother is a Jesuit, though. He teaches at Loyola.

A Jesuit, eh? Now, there's a strict order. Is he allowed to play golf, do you know?

I think so. He doesn't, but—

A celibate life is one thing, but a life without golf? That's more than God should ask of any man.

We were just talking about his vow of poverty the other night. Greens fees might be an issue.

Which is why I'm Episcopalian. Do you golf, Ms. Bruder?

No. Call me Juni. I'm with Mark Twain.

Come again?

He said, "Golf is a good walk spoiled."

Ha! Let me write that down. My favorite is, "Golf is good for the soul. You get so mad at yourself, you forget to hate your enemies." Will Rogers. Don't get me wrong—I wasn't playing golf while the Plaza burned. I haven't been out on the course all week. We're expecting standing-room-only tomorrow at church. But just between us, times like now, golf is the only thing that makes sense to me in this world.

I should tell you my phone recorder is on, for my notes, but golf won't come up in the article.

Go ahead and mention my book, if you like.

Your book? What's it called?

Ready? *Let God Be Your Caddy: A Contemporary Christian's Guide to Golf.* It's coming out in time for the Masters.

There seems to be a big market for sports books these days.

That's what my agent says. And of course, with the religious crossover, we're tapping into two demographics.

Will you sign a copy for me?

I'll give you the friends-and-family discount.

Can we go back to the quote about hating your enemies? It seems relevant to the article. I saw two men in a shoving match down at the site yesterday, a fight over a prayer. "Forgive those who trespass against us." One man had just lost his son, and he didn't want to hear anyone preaching about forgiveness. He was too angry. He wants revenge. What do you say to someone like him?

"Vengeance is mine, sayeth the Lord." I would tell that father not to worry—God will find and punish the evildoers, even if the authorities can't.

You think there was more than one?

Of course! How could one man—a janitor, no less—possess the brainpower and resources to bring down a steel structure like the Plaza? That building fell like a house of cards. It defies logic. Everyone says so. When you think about unknown accomplices still at large, why, it chills the blood. No wonder we can't sleep at night! These cowards need to be hunted down and brought to justice, for our peace of mind.

Old Testament justice?

Absolutely. Here's the God's honest truth. One of the first-graders who died, Ashley Lynn Childers? I baptized her. I sat with her mama two nights ago. That poor woman wants to die herself. Her baby was such a miracle. She nearly died, there in the incubator. Stopped breathing three times. She was a fighter, Ashley was. To think how she might have grown up? Well, it's mighty hard to love your enemies when you know what they did to that precious little girl.

I imagine you've counseled a lot of grieving families this week.

You wouldn't believe the calls. Funeral services, hospital visits, prayer vigils—I finally had to tell my secretary to limit requests to members of our church. There's only so much of me to go around. *[laughter]* Although, I will say, there's more of me lately than there should be.

Golf doesn't keep you in shape?

Not with that snack cart following me around. Satan tempts me with hot dogs.

He's a tricky devil. Going back to the Plaza, what would you say to family members who've lost a loved one in such a senseless way? How would you help them cope?

Well, first of all, I'd remind them their loved ones are in a better place. That's a given. That's a reason for rejoicing.

"Rejoice" might be a little hard to hear, so soon after—

And you used the word "senseless." Now, who are we to judge whether God's plan makes sense? To our tiny minds? "Can you fathom the mysteries of God? Can you probe the limits of the Almighty?" The Book of Job. That's a good verse for your article.

Thanks. I'll—

Take the Holocaust, for instance. You have to believe that God had a purpose, a *reason* for killing so many people, even if you can't see the sense of it. "Faith is the assurance of things hoped for, the conviction of things not seen." What good is faith if it's never tested?

So the Plaza was a test? Gee, I must have failed.

But then, you said you weren't a churchgoer.

Well, that's true. Let's just say I have a few issues with organized religion.

You're honest, I'll give you that. You went to parochial school, I'm betting?

Through sixth grade.

If I had a nickel for every Catholic who made it to legal age and cut bait, we could buy a new pipe organ.

I met a woman the other night, the wife of a policeman, one of the missing. Her name was Faith, of all things. She was holding a rosary, and it caught on my ring as we shook hands, so we were laughing, trying to get untangled. I had to apologize, because it didn't seem right to laugh. She saw my face and said, "Oh, please, don't worry. My prayers will be answered." She meant that her husband was coming home. She truly believed it.

Why wouldn't she? You don't believe in miracles?

In this case? No. Her husband's body was recovered the next morning.

The answer to our prayers isn't always the one we asked for.

You'll forgive me if I find that a cruel kind of comfort.

You might find more comfort in worship. I'll save a seat for you tomorrow.

Thank you, but my Sunday morning ritual is to go Barnes & Noble, order a café latte and lose myself in a good book.

"Some of us worship in churches, some in synagogues, some on golf courses." Adlai Stevenson.

Amen.

Rabbi Esther Judson-Stoddard, Saturday, 4-18-98, 10:30 a.m.

Hey, Esther. Is it cheating if my expert religious opinion comes from a friend?

I hardly know you. Who's on the other side?

Bishop Liman.

Arnold Palmer's disciple.

It's a cult, isn't it?

Strange clothes, weird rituals, pressure to join the club? Yep.

If I ever buy a plaid skort, kill me.

For you, I'll break the sixth commandment. So, good old Gordie. How was he?

Sanctimonious as ever. Tossing out scripture verses left and right, like he's on the holy debate team. I think he called me a heathen.

Don't take it personally. He's only trying to save your soul.

Black as it is.

He told me once, very nicely, that he would miss me in heaven.

Frankly, I'll prefer the company in hell. Especially if you're there. You're speaking at the service on Sunday?

Yep. Delphi wants a Hebrew blessing to go along with the Christian prayer and the Buddhist chant.

And the Islamic song and the Seminole drum circle.

Really?

It says so, right here in the press release. They missed your hyphen, by the way.

I'll have to raise holy hell with Delphi.

How'd she sound?

Like a rock. Amazing. I doubt she's slept six hours this week, but she's clear-headed and focused on what's best for the community. She comforted *me*.

Did you lose anyone from your congregation?

No, *Baruch Hashem*, but I led Shiva services for five who weren't affiliated with the temple. In Jewish law, the dead have to be buried within twenty-four hours, but some of these families don't have a body. Where's the law on that? They're asking me! The Torah doesn't have a chapter on high-rise collapses.

Is it hard, sometimes, being expected to know all the answers?

Every day, I'm waiting to be stoned as a fraud. *[laughter]* Seriously though, in my experience, people are grateful to hear "I don't know" if it's true. They're so used to lies and double-speak and made-up reasons.

I was hoping you could explain the whole mess to me.

Ha! A man came into my office yesterday, Josiah Tompkins. He was a Lockheed engineer before he retired. Very troubled. He had an appointment to sign papers at Fidelius on Monday morning, but something woke him up on Friday and said, "Go. Today." Which he did. Now his broker is dead, and he doesn't know whether to feel guilty or blessed.

What did you tell him?

That the Almighty planned to save him and kill his broker? How could I? So many survivors say—after a car accident, or a fire, or a tornado—that "God must have saved me for a reason." What do you tell the woman whose husband fell through the atrium floor? God wanted the father of your children to burn alive? You can't have it both ways.

So you're saying, "God had nothing to do with it"? I can quote you?

[laughter] Yeah, that'll go over well. No, I'm saying that if your God can pick and choose which people to save from a burning building, your God is the same one who stood by and let innocent children die. Little kids on a field trip to see Griffy the manatee. If you believe in that God, you're a better man than I am, Gunga Din.

I used to believe in a God who controlled the traffic lights. You know, green all the way down the street.

What happened when you hit a red?

I was being punished, or I'd been spared from an accident farther down the road.

When did you stop believing?

After my mother died.

Ah.

Let's go back to the Plaza. Bishop Liman brought up the Holocaust. I almost swallowed my tongue. He said—let me see here—that "you have to believe God had a reason for killing so many people." Won't that make a great headline?

It was Hitler's reason, not God's. Those camps, those ovens, they were built by human hands.

So what do I say about God in this case? He had an alibi? He was nowhere near the scene on the day in question?

He was there. Mourning with the rest of us.

Okay, I need to fix you up with my brother.

Why do you say that? Isn't he a priest?

It's a certain way of speaking—you both have it, you of the spiritual calling.

[laughter] Maybe Bishop Liman was right.

Help me with this damned article. Please. I have one lame quote about the Holocaust, and an admonition to rejoice in death. Our community is heartbroken, and I'm supposed to say, "Don't worry, be happy"?

Of course not. People are in pain. They're hurt. They're angry. They won't be happy until they can strike back.

At whom? The janitor? He's dead.

It doesn't matter. We'll find another target. Someone bigger. After this week, we'll launch into a long line of inquests and lawsuits and finger-pointing. You've already heard the talk about faulty sprinklers. It isn't enough that the perpetrator is dead. We want retribution. We'll embrace the rage and keep our pain at bay. Will we find peace? Will our souls be healed? No.

Wait, let me guess—this was your Shabbat sermon last night?

Oops. Guilty. Too strident?

No, I'm just not sure I can use any of it.

You need a generic quote to accept the Lord's mysteries and live in faith.

I already have one. So, okay, we're not allowed to question God's motives. What about Marko Abissi's? That's what I keep wondering. What was he thinking? What was in his mind? By all accounts, he lived a decent life until a few months ago. What happened? What drove a good man over the edge?

Showing compassion for the murderer, Juni? That's un-American.

You know what bothers me the most? His sister. She isn't allowed to grieve with the rest of us. Someone threw a rock through her window last night. She's getting death threats.

And they call themselves Christians. Poor woman. What's her number? I'll give her a call.

You see? You're the good one. Always thinking of others.

And here you are, seeking mercy for this man and his family.

I'm writing a story.

How did we meet? Same circumstances, as I recall. Wendell Bloyd's clemency hearing five years ago.

Was it that long? I remember thinking you were so young to speak with such conviction.

My knees were shaking.

And now you'll stand in front of thirty-five thousand people on Sunday.

How many?

Not counting the TV cameras.

Good Lord. I'm about to be sick.

And the President of the United States.

Stop it! Will you be there?

I don't think so.

Juni, it would be good for you—

I know. I just don't think so. Promise me something, Esther.

What?

You won't give the president a piece of your mind.

[laughter] "There is a time for everything, and a season for every purpose under heaven." It doesn't mean I won't thank him for being the reason I had to explain the term "oral sex" to my fifth-graders at Hebrew Day School.

Plaza Survivor to Sing at Memorial Service

By Juni Bruder, Herald Staff Writer/Saturday, April 18, 1998

ORLANDO—On the morning of April 13, Zenas Witt had to pinch himself as he strolled through the doors of the Parramore Plaza. He and friends Jason "Flossie" Cabanis and Joey Dixon were about to sign a recording contract with music mogul Stan Diamond, famous for guiding a string of "boy bands" to international stardom.

"It was a dream come true," said Zenas, 16, who joined the singing group B4Me in his sophomore year after an original member came down with mononucleosis. Stan Diamond heard the trio perform at his ten-year-old niece's birthday party in Windermere. "He told us we were going places," Zenas said.

After the young men arrived at the Plaza with their manager, Rami Green, they learned that Diamond was running late for their appointment. "The lady put us in a conference room with all this food," Zenas said. "There was nothing to do but eat."

He soon felt sick to his stomach. "Cream cheese and nerves," he explained. Too embarrassed to ask for directions to a restroom, Zenas left the corporate suite. As he wandered the eleventh floor, the fire alarm sounded. He followed a Plaza employee to the exit, thinking he would rejoin Flossie and Joey outside.

"I never saw them again," he said.

Zenas will sing the national anthem at tomorrow's memorial service for Plaza victims. Some 35,000 people are expected to attend, and the event will be televised. The service begins at 1:00 at the Florida Citrus Bowl.

Leap of Faith

Juni stared at the cursor. It sat there, blinking, in the middle of a blank page. She'd already erased three drafts, and each new try was worse. Those jokes about religion? Someone up there had heard, and she was being punished.

God, strike me dead, she thought. *No, seriously. Please.* No such luck. No lightning bolt from above. But then, God wasn't known for his mercy, was He? Hadn't Bishop Limon said it? "Vengeance is mine, sayeth the Lord."

Apparently, the Lord held a grudge.

Juni paced the apartment, taking deep breaths. Walking helped sometimes when she was stuck on a thought. Staring at the screen too long was like spinning her wheels to get out of a rut; it only dug the hole deeper.

She was in so deep, she'd need a ladder to climb out.

In the kitchen, she took two Excedrins; the caffeine in the pills would help her think. For good measure, she scooped coffee into the filter and set the pot to brew. What was Carl thinking? Giving her a piece on faith was like asking a vegetarian to write about steak. She could fake her way through unfamiliar territory—a basic job requirement—but this task was beyond her considerable powers of bullshit.

She would miss a deadline for the first time in her life. She would be fired. She would spend her life savings and lose her apartment, her car, her benefits. She'd be one of those women at Publix who paid for groceries with food stamps and spent her last dollar on a lottery ticket.

The odds of winning the lottery were thirteen-million-to-one.

Nevertheless, convenience stores had reported a record-breaking week for bets of 4-1-3-9-8 in the Fantasy Five. Numerologists were in a tizzy over the fact that adding the Plaza's month, date and year (4 + 13 + 98) produced the number of dead (115). That is, until fireman Cass Hueffer succumbed to his injuries, inconveniently raising the total by one.

The problem was easily fixed by removing the janitor's name from the list, dead though he might have been. Nothing like fudging the numbers to prove a point.

Juni was getting cynical in her old age. She had no business writing about faith, or religion, or golf. On her laptop, she scanned Bishop Liman's transcript, looking for something—anything—she could use. As Carl had said, all she needed was a quote from "Column A, Column B, a rabbi, a priest and a minister walk into a bar."

She could sure use a drink right now.

Esther wasn't much help, except for that line to "accept the Lord's mysteries and live in faith," which she hadn't meant. Juni sorted through her clippings from other disasters, starting with the Oklahoma City bombing three years back. One witness had said, "This is America. We don't have terrorism." *Whistle past the graveyard, my friends.*

Timothy McVeigh said, "I have come to peace with myself, my God and my cause." *His* God. Whose God? The one who kept every nut-job on the payroll?

Juni pulled out President Clinton's eulogy, a beautiful piece of writing— even his critics had agreed. Nothing like a good disaster to muzzle the howling mob. (Who'd have guessed the healthcare debate would get so ugly?) By all accounts, the president's response to the Murrah Building explosion had saved his first term. Would the Plaza save his second? The impeachment threats had died down suddenly—maybe he'd get lucky. (She could hear Carl laughing now: "That's what Monica said.")

Amazing, the vagaries of fate. Amazing, the time she could waste.

Juni went back to the president's speech. He'd quoted a letter from a widow of the Pan Am 103 bombing in Lockerbie, Scotland. Juni couldn't recall, a decade past—who'd claimed responsibility, exactly? Libya? The Palestinians? Islamic something-or-others. Weren't they the same ones who'd tried to blow up the World Trade Center in '93? And weren't they arrested for using their real names to rent a truck, the same as McVeigh?

One thing terrorists seemed to have in common: a lack of imagination. And they killed in the name of God. Ultimately, wasn't God—or Allah, or Jehovah, or whatever he called himself—the mastermind?

She should ask Valerie Rose: Had her brother gone to church?

The speech. The story. Focus, Juni, for God's sake.

The Pan Am widow had told the families of Oklahoma City, "The anger you feel is valid, but you must not allow yourselves to be consumed by it. The hurt you feel must not be allowed to turn into hate but instead into the search for justice. The loss you feel must not paralyze your own lives. Instead, you must try to pay tribute to your loved ones by continuing to do all the things they left undone, thus ensuring they did not die in vain."

Juni had a brainstorm—she'd print the quote verbatim and be done with it.

Her coffee was ready; at least she'd finished something. The smell alone was enough to clear her head. She ran to the kitchen and made a quick switch— glass pot for mug—to fill her cup as it brewed. Had she taken Excedrin already? She couldn't remember. Shaking two pills from the bottle, she cupped her hand beneath the faucet and drank. Coffee stains made a pattern of Olympic rings in the sink.

Put Comet on the grocery list. Go grocery-shopping.

With a hot, full mug and a new sense of purpose, Juni went back to her laptop.

Question: Why did people turn to God in times of tragedy?

Answer: Because they'd run out of alternatives? Because they were scared out of their wits? She remembered Pat Robertson's dire warning—the one that had made the newsroom howl with glee—when the city commissioners voted to approve rainbow street flags for Gay Days.

"I'd warn Orlando that you're right in the way of some serious hurricanes, and I wouldn't be waving those flags in God's face if I were you. This is not a message of hate. This is a message of redemption. A condition like this will bring about the destruction of your nation. It'll bring about terrorist bombs. It'll bring earthquakes, tornadoes and possibly a meteor."

Happy New Year!

Maybe Pat was onto something. He'd been right about the tornadoes, after all. Arson, not a bomb, was listed as the official cause of the Plaza collapse, but still—prophesy didn't have to be a hundred percent accurate to scare the bejeezus out of the faithful. Never mind that Gay Days became one of the city's biggest events. Lesbian, gay or straight, a dollar was a dollar.

Juni had moved on to President Roosevelt's speech after Pearl Harbor— April 13th, another date that would live in infamy—when the phone rang. "Bad news," Carl said.

He was firing her even before she missed the deadline?

"We're pulling the story," he said. "No room. We picked up Billy Graham's piece from AP, his thoughts after touring the site. Now, don't jump down my…"

"It's okay, Carl. I'll live."

"You sure?"

"Two days wasted, but whatever."

"I'm really sorry, kiddo. How can I make it up to you?"

"Well," Juni said, stretching. "You can let me talk to the guy I mentioned."

"What guy?"

"The janitor's friend."

She pictured Carl pressing the receiver to his forehead, counting to ten. "Sure. Fine. You win."

Hanging up the phone, she couldn't help laughing. There was a God after all.

Mick McGrew, friend of Marko Abissi, Sunday, 4-19-98, 10:05 a.m.

Here, take the couch. Move that junk out of the way. Kick the dog, he'll move. *He's fine.*

He's a worthless excuse for a mutt! Did you hear any barking when you knocked?

No.

See what I mean? He'll eat your tape recorder. Swallowed my good watch. Not like I need it anymore.

You'll have to check him for ticks.

Well, he wears a flea collar—

Sorry. Dumb joke. Why don't you sit down? It must be hard getting around—

You can say it. Must be hard getting around this sardine can on crutches.

No, it's a lot of room for a trailer. I mean, mobile home. Manufactured home. Whatever they're called these days.

Tornado magnets.

[laughter] I'll admit, after seeing the damage in February, I'd have a few second thoughts about living in one.

Them tornadoes ripped through a couple of apartments and a subdivision, too, don't forget. Not everybody that died was sitting on wheels.

A lady at work lost her house. Cinder block, solid as a rock, came apart like matchsticks. Was she in it?

No, thank god. How's this for timing? She spent the night with her boyfriend. She'd been meaning to break up with him, but he gave her a diamond bracelet for Valentine's Day, so she decided to wait a few weeks.

She keep the bracelet?

Kept the bracelet, dumped the guy. Eventually.

What do a hurricane, a tornado and a redneck divorce have in common?

Somebody's fixin' to lose a trailer.

Heard that one, huh?

The thing about office e-mail is, you get all the jokes.

One more reason not to have a computer, I guess. I just got the phone turned back on, right before you called.

You've had a hard time since the accident.

Goes with the territory, I guess. Crazy enough to hang off a building, you get what you pay for.

Did you like your job, washing windows?

Hell, yeah. Well, except for the summers, sun coming off the glass hot enough to melt your testicles. Uh, sorry, ladies present. But you know what I mean, up there by myself, breeze blowing, nobody hassling me, looking down on the world—yeah, I liked it.

How did you get hurt?

Stupid. I was showing off, is all. Hey, this is just between you and me, right? I don't want them Workers' Comp people coming back, asking for their money.

No. Strictly off the record.

Well, swinging on that rope, you can kick out and fly way far, and then you reach over and stick your landing with the suction cup—*ffftttt*—and some little girl at her desk freaks out, like, "Where'd he come from?"

Like Spiderman.

Right. So I'm fooling around up there, feeling pretty good, only I'm not paying attention to the weather. One of them afternoon storms is blowing in over my shoulder. I push off, swing over, and the wind picks me up like a leaf, sends me flying. I don't even have time to grab for the glass, and I'm spinning—*whoa!*—and bang! You know how the building curves up to that sharp point?

Like the edge of a wave.

A goddamned tsunami. I came down on that edge like an egg on a skillet, leg broke in three places.

Ouch.

No kidding. All that shit about your life flashing in front of your eyes? All true. They ought to make a movie.

"It's a Wonderful Life"?

"Easy Rider."

Nice bike out front, by the way.

Rusted solid for all I can do with this bum leg.

What do the doctors say?

More surgery to fix the plate. I have a few screws loose, you could say. Want something to drink?

No, thanks. Can I get you anything?

I wouldn't mind a beer if you're up. Second shelf. [*background noise*] Ah, that's better. Skoal. Yeah, you know, I've been thinking, if I hadn't been messing around, those people at the Plaza might still be alive.

You can't say that.

Sure, I can. I think about it all the time. Or go back even farther. If I was a better driver, Jennie'd still be alive, and Marko and me, we never would've met.

Who's Jennie?

My first wife. Died eight years ago this fall. We were taking the back way home from Daytona, Biketoberfest, and this RV pulled out in front of me. I ditched the bike—man, it was sweet, a Harley Ironhead. Smashed all to hell. I walked away, just a bad case of road rash, but Jennie, she weren't wearing a helmet. Didn't want to mess up her hair.

I'm so sorry. It was an accident, though. Not your fault. What could you have done?

I could have taken I-95.

You can drive yourself crazy, thinking "what if."

Which is why I stayed drunk for three months after her funeral. Lost a bet and joined the Army, just in time to ship off to Dhahran. Fucking a-hundred-and-forty-degrees in the Saudi shade, which there wasn't any. Sober a man up right quick.

You don't strike me as the military type.

What was your first clue, the tats or the ponytail?

Every Marine I know has a tattoo.

Fucking jarheads. See this scar here?

The one that makes you look like a pirate?

Arrrr. Courtesy of the USMC.

Don't tell me you picked a bar fight with the Marine Corps on R&R.

[*laughter*] Yeah, but that's not how I cut my eye. No, this was stateside. Walgreen's. I'm waiting in line at the pharmacy, and this old fart's up there bitching and moaning, waving his military discount card, how he's a retired Marine and they're ripping him off for prescription drugs, on and on, the whole nine yards. So I say, kinda loud, if he's a Marine, he must be needing his Viagra, so could they hurry it along? And the geezer takes a swing at me! I ducked, of course, but you know them metal racks for reading glasses? Caught me square in the eye. Eight stitches.

What was the bet?

What bet?

How you joined the Army.

Oh. Guy bet me twenty bucks I wouldn't enlist.

So you won.

Technically.

And that's how you met Marko.

Yeah, on the way home from Kuwait. How freaky is that? Both of us infantry out of Fort Campbell. I was Eagle Strike, he was 327th, Bastogne. Two guys from Florida going all the way to the Persian Gulf, and we end up sitting next to each other on the plane back to Bumfuck, Kentucky.

It's a small world after all.

Shit. That song gets stuck in my head sometimes, and I can't get rid of it. Yep, there it goes. God damn it. Thanks a lot. Change the subject, quick.

So you and Marko became friends.

Yeah. He liked bikes. I liked his sister.

Valerie? You went out with her?

Went out with her? Hell, I married her.

Oh, my gosh, I feel so stupid. I didn't make the connection. Her last name is—

Rose. Yeah. She went back to her maiden name after the divorce. So Val told you to call me, but she didn't mention being the old ball and chain?

It must have slipped her mind.

Well, she's ticked off at me. Child support's late. Again.

And what with everything else going on.

Yeah, that too.

Is disability taking care of you?

Sort of. Pays two-thirds of my check, so I'm not exactly living high on the hog. That job was good money, you know, because of the risk and all. Best money I ever made, which is the only reason I told Marko to take it. He needed the bread.

It sounds like he didn't have too many other options.

Guy like him should have been able to work anywhere.

What kind of guy was he?

Marko? Salt of the earth. Do anything for you. Help you move, paint your house, whatever you needed. Not like some friends, you ask a favor, they're out of town that weekend. And he was there for my kids, even when I couldn't be. That meant a lot to me. You knew he'd walk through fire for them or Stevie.

I met your boys. Did I get their names wrong? Jacob and Kyle?

Right.

Who's Stevie?

Marko's girl. My goddaughter.

Oh, you mean Stephania?

Yeah, but nobody calls her that. It's too big a name for such a little girl. No, Stevie Rose, after Marko's brother and Val's family. Get it?

No, actually, I'm feeling a little dense. I didn't know Marko had a brother.

A twin, Stephan. He died when they were eleven, along with Marko's folks. Val didn't tell you?

It was two days after the fire. I'm sure her mind was on other things.

You know the Sunshine Skyway?

The bridge? Sure.

Remember that freighter hit it, and a piece of the highway fell into the water? Had to be twenty years back.

Wasn't there a bus or something?

Yeah, and a bunch of cars, including a Buick station wagon with Marko's family in it.

My god.

Two people survived, and that boy was one of them.

What about Valerie?

Oh, no, she weren't there. They were the neighbors, the Roses. Marko didn't have nowhere else to go, so they took him in. Val's mom adopted him a year or so later, I guess, to make it legal.

I had no idea.

It didn't make no difference to Val, blood or not. She and Marko grew up together. They're kin. The rest is paperwork.

To lose your family like that—I can't imagine.

Makes you wonder, don't it? This kid gets pulled out of the Gulf of Mexico when thirty other people died. He comes back from the Persian Gulf in one piece. Somebody's keeping an eye out for him, right? All so he can end up buried under a ton of concrete?

You don't think he caused it?

Well, I'd like to say no, but I can't. Used to be, I thought you could tell what a guy was capable of, just by looking at him. But I saw some shit in Iraq, you know? Mortars landing, the whistles—"*Incoming!*"—and the dude next to you freaks out, starts shooting at anything that moves, you included. And this is the same dude that ate breakfast with you. Now, do I think Marko had anything to do with that fire, aside from being in the wrong place at the wrong time? Hell, no. Do I know for sure? No, I do not. Nobody does, except Marko and the man upstairs.

When's the last time you saw him?

God? Probably an A.A. meeting.

[laughter] No, Marko.

Oh. Hell, a couple weeks ago? He came over to look at my bike. He was headed to the store, wanted to buy something to take off the rust, shine it up.

How was his mood?

His mood? What do I look like, a shrink?

I mean, with the divorce, and the custody issues—

Come to think of it, he was okay. Yeah. We talked about the job, you know, tricks of the trade. He knew his way around the equipment by then, so he was thinking of taking up rock-climbing, but that was the joke. There's nothing higher around here than a fire-ant hill.

Marko didn't mind working at the Plaza?

Mind? I don't know. He was making the best of it. I got the feeling there was a girl.

What do you mean?

Well, we were talking about, what's the best thing you've seen through the glass so far? People forget you're out there, you see 'em humping on the desk or picking their noses or whatever. He said the scenery in the basement, that was the best thing. All I could figure, it was somebody he worked with, one of the lady cleaners.

Did he mention the name Micaela?

Nah, but it's not like we compared love notes or nothing. Hey, on your way out, can you grab me another beer?

Claire Montemayor Abuirre, Muriel's daughter, Sunday, 4-19-98, 11:20 a.m.

Mrs. Abuirre, it's Juni Bruder again. Is this a better time?

Yes. I'm sorry about earlier. They call it morning sickness, but with me, it's all day long. My mother said that's the sign of a girl.

Her first grandchild?

The world's first, to hear her carry on. I knew she'd lose her mind, so I only told her a few weeks ago. My God, the phone messages, the e-mails, ten times a day. Take your vitamins, Claire. Stay away from cemeteries. Don't look at a rabbit. The most ridiculous superstitions.

Rabbits?

Don't ask.

When are you due?

October. We're hoping for a rotation stateside as soon as the baby is born.

I understand your husband works at the U.S. Embassy.

Yes. He's a DSS agent with the State Department.

Which means…?

Security.

Ah. Living in Madrid must be exciting.

You'd think so, but ever since Miguel Blanco's kidnapping last year, Vincent won't let me out of the house. I've been to the Prado once. All these radical groups—my friend in Ecuador is scared to death that the FARC will snatch her son off the street, and the ETA is murdering people here. ETA, PLO, IRA, use whatever letters you like, they're still terrorists. Call a spade a spade. I'm not the diplomat in the family. I told Vincent, we are *not* raising this baby in a foreign country. We're going home to New York, where it's safe.

It must be difficult, losing your mother and being so far away.

For the record, it wasn't my choice not to attend the funeral. My doctor wouldn't allow it. He's worried enough about the strain. Vincent was afraid to tell me. I already knew, of course. There were only two e-mails from my mother. First, her opera recap. Three hours of beautiful music, and all she talked about was Dante Costas answering his phone. Second, her daily itinerary. Not that I ever read it, not that it mattered which doctor she saw which day. But there it was in black and white: "CFAC, Plaza, nine o'clock." And the pictures of the building on the news—with the elevators gone, there was no way she made it out. Pardon my bluntness, but pity the poor firemen who had to carry her down the stairs.

When did you get word?

I guess it was Wednesday afternoon when they found her, Thursday morning when they called. They waited until after breakfast, of course, something my mother never would have done. She was always calling in the middle of the night, which is why we let the answering machine pick up.

Do I have the time zones right? It's five-thirty there?

Correct. Vincent left a few minutes ago for the Plaza de Toros.

The bullring?
You speak Spanish?
Un poco.
I guess it's required in Florida, isn't it? My mother insisted I take French, "the language of love." A lot of good it does me with the maid. It's bullfight season here. Every Sunday night at six, just like American football.
Except the bull dies.
Don't tell me you're one of those animal-rights people.
No, it's just…can we get back to your mother?
If you insist.
I'm sorry. This must be very difficult for you.
Let's be honest. One of the best things about living here was that Madrid was three thousand miles away from my mother.
You weren't on good terms?
We hadn't spoken in months. On the phone, I mean. If the check didn't come, I called Peta.
Your mother's nurse?
She wasn't really a nurse. She came from a foster home. The poor thing. I guess she'll be out of a job now?
I'm afraid she died in the collapse.
Oh. You mean—yes, of course. Peta would have stayed with my mother, wouldn't she? Well, what a shame. She had a hard life.
How long did Peta live with your mother?
Oh, two years, give or take. It wasn't long after my wedding. We always had a housekeeper, you know, but then my mother needed daily care. Well, what actually happened was, I had to come home early from my honeymoon because Mother devoured a bag of Oreos and slipped into a diabetic coma.
Oh, no!
The housekeeper said she thought Missy Montemayor was taking a nap.
Not good.
So while we should have been snorkeling in Tortola, we waited at the hospital. As soon as Mother woke up, she said, "Does this mean you'll stay?" As if she'd planned it to keep me from leaving home. And that was it. I said, "Mother, you can do whatever you want with your life. I won't sit here and watch." And we packed for Spain.
You mean you—
—abandoned my poor mother in the hospital to fend for herself? Yes, I did. Call me heartless, I don't care. In all her e-mails, she never once apologized.
For…?
Ruining my honeymoon? Trying to control my life when she had no control over her own? Diabetes is manageable, you know, if you monitor your diet, but no, she was close to three hundred pounds! Put down the fork, for heaven's sake. And to have her telling *me* what to eat—it was unbearable.

So you kept in touch by e-mail.

Strictly a one-sided conversation. She typed and typed and typed. There must be hundreds of e-mails by now. Vincent keeps them, for some odd reason.

What did she write about?

Oh, you name it. The state of the world. Politics. Gossip. She *loved* gossip, and scandal, and rumor. She had money, so people were happy to whisper in her ear in exchange for donations. She had no life outside mine, so she entertained herself with the misery of others, which is all gossip is. I couldn't stomach it. And the baby business. What a *joy* it was to have a daughter, how *much* she loved me. Now I'd finally understand, blah, blah, blah. Mortifying. Vincent enjoyed some of her longer screeds, so he wrote back occasionally, her pen pal. Maybe her only pal.

She must have had other friends.

None that I'm aware of. Social acquaintances, mostly, people she knew through the arts council. Her pharmacist, her quack psychic, people she paid. Pathetic, really.

What about the department store? Wasn't she involved in —

Oh, no. Not even when my grandfather was alive. He didn't think women belonged in management, Mother especially, and he sold the company before he died. No, our connection to the store was in name only.

What about your father? What was he like?

I don't remember, really. He died when I was young. People say I take after him. You can draw your own conclusions.

What did he do?

He married money.

Ah.

It wasn't a love match, from what I understand.

I'm sorry.

No need to be. Most of my friends' parents are divorced. What's the difference?

So the last time you saw your mother was in the hospital?

No. She visited here in December. She had this fantasy about spending the holidays in Europe, the perfect family Christmas. What a nightmare. Aside from having to buy two plane tickets because she was too fat to fit in one seat, she could barely walk. She hated the food. Our house had too many stairs, and too many bottles of wine in the refrigerator. Two days was enough.

So your last visit wasn't a happy one.

I know where you're going with this, but I said goodbye to my mother a long time ago. She's been killing herself by slow degrees all these years. She stuffed her mouth and prayed to God for relief. Maybe he finally delivered.

Faithful See Holy Image in Plaza Ruins

By Juni Bruder, Herald Staff Writer/Monday, April 20, 1998

ORLANDO—While some 50,000 mourners attended a memorial service Sunday at the Citrus Bowl, dozens of people waited at the Plaza barricades, hoping to see a miracle. Here, on a towering section of blue-green glass, many believe an image of the Virgin Mary has appeared. The iridescent reflection covers 50 feet of the Plaza's atrium entrance, the only section of windows to remain intact.

"When you consider that two explosions couldn't shatter this glass, you have to believe it's a sign from God," said Leroy Goldman, who traveled from Lakeland to see the image and pay his respects.

"It's a wondrous blessing," Nicholas Bindle said with tears streaming down his face. "The Queen of Heaven is praying for us. You can see her head, her hands, plain as day."

Glass experts attribute the image to chemical residue and heat from the fire.

Janice Milton-Miles of College Park skipped church on Sunday to bring her two children to the disaster site. "It's a warning they need to see," she said. "The TV shows they watch, the video games they play, their rap music—it's all sex and guns and bad language. The Virgin Mary, she's had it up to here. She's saying, 'Kids, it's time to straighten up, clean your rooms and listen to your mother.'"

An engineering report notes that the wall poses a potential risk to recovery workers. "They say it's unstable," said Father Lemuel Wiley of the Blessed Trinity Church of Conway. "We know it's solid as a rock. The Lord won't let it fall." The pastor, who dubbed the image "Our Lady of Parramore," is soliciting donations to establish a shrine.

Muriel Hutchins Montemayor: The Family Name

The Dead Remembered/Profiles compiled by Herald Staff

Muriel Montemayor couldn't wait to be a grandmother. Weeks before the Plaza tragedy, the heiress to the Hutchins Department Store fortune learned that her daughter was expecting a baby.

"You'd have thought it was the world's first baby," said Claire Montemayor Abuirre from her home in Madrid, where her husband works as a foreign service specialist at the U.S. Embassy. In dozens of e-mails, Muriel shared her advice for the coming child. "She described the joy of having a daughter," Claire said. "How much love she felt for me."

Because of her pregnancy, Claire was unable to make the transatlantic journey home to attend her mother's funeral.

Muriel Montemayor, married at 27 and widowed five years later, devoted her life to her only daughter. Soon after Claire's departure for Spain, Muriel opened her home to an 18-year-old foster child, Peta Wilder. The pair became inseparable. "Wherever Muriel went, there was Peta," said a family friend.

Muriel never missed a performance of the Orlando Philharmonic Orchestra. Concertgoers recognized the woman in her customary front-row seat, her red hair swept up in an elaborate style. In later years, her walker was decorated to match her flowing gowns.

Hutchins Department Store, founded in 1949 by Muriel's father, Lambert, became an Orlando fixture. The store was the first in the Southeast to have an escalator and air-conditioning. Thousands of children took their first ride on "moving stairs" and bought their first Sunday suits at Hutchins, which grew to 23 branches by the time Allied Retail Federation acquired the company in 1982.

The Hutchins name graces a theater, a park and a wing of Orlando's Museum of Art. Poor health prevented Muriel from participating in many of the causes she supported, but she continued to serve as a director for the Central Florida Arts Council. A meeting brought her to the Plaza on April 13.

"The first item on the agenda was a new concert hall," said E.C. Culbertson, acting president. "Muriel agreed to fund a substantial portion of it. We will miss her immensely." Board members evacuated the Plaza after the first fire alarm, but due to her limited mobility, Muriel stayed behind. "We were told rescuers would be along shortly," Culbertson explained. "She had Peta with her." Both women died in the collapse.

"Peta would have stayed with my mother," said Claire, who last saw Muriel in December. It was the fulfillment of a fantasy, Claire explained, for mother and daughter to spend the holidays together in Europe. "The perfect family Christmas," she said.

Jaysukh Chaudhary, The Clean Team, Monday, 4-20-98, 2:30 p.m.

Mr. Chaudhary, it's Juni Bruder again. Do you have time for a quick question?
For you, all the time in the world. I am in your debt.
Why do you say that?
Remember my predictions of doom and gloom?
Bankruptcy, yes.
Thanks to you, I have a new account. The Sun Bank building.
That's thirty-six floors!
Indeed. My staff will quadruple. I hardly have time to sleep.
When did this happen?
Two days after you printed my name, a man from Sun Bank called me. He was unhappy with his cleaning crew and looking for a replacement. He knew my people would be out of work. He took pity upon us. And, as fate would have it, we're distant cousins. Our families come from Madurai.
How about that.
So what can I do for you? Name your favor.
I know you can't tell me why Marko was fired, but is it possible he made advances to one of the Plaza employees, a woman named Micaela?
Marko? I can't imagine. He was a gentleman. He kept to himself. Who told you this?
It doesn't matter. Could he have been involved with one of your employees?
Involved?
Dating? A romantic relationship?
What my people do off the clock is none of my concern. Besides, how would I know?
Can you think of any possibilities? I talked to Mick McGrew the other day, and he seemed to think Marko was interested in someone.
Mick? Was he sober?
Relatively.
What time did you talk to him?
Ten, ten-thirty in the morning.
Ah. The golden window of opportunity. With so much paperwork to fill out—workers' comp, unemployment, what a pain—I've learned to call before noon.
Good to know. Can you think of anyone on your staff who might have been—
How do I put this politely? The women who work for me, the Plaza ladies are...well, there's Adalia, married with five children. Keeps her head down. Noemi, old enough to be Marko's mother. Grandmother, possibly. Racine, poor thing, has a few synapses missing, along with most of her teeth. Armida, hard worker. No time for socializing, and she doesn't speak English. Her daughter, Lilia, does most of the talking. She's a big girl, Lilia. *Big* girl. Sumo-wrestler size. Not Marko's type, I think. No, he was a handsome boy. But who knows? Maybe it was love.
Hmm. Well, it was worth a shot.

What do you care if Marko had a girlfriend?'

That's a good question. I'm trying to figure out what happened to him. Why he did what he did. It's like putting together the pieces of a puzzle.

When we were young, we used to drive my father crazy, hiding pieces of the Grand Canyon or the Mona Lisa or the sleeping kittens, rainy Sundays on the porch with the card table. A thousand pieces, down to the last one—and it's missing! He would tear the house apart, with us children giggling behind his back, pretending to help. He couldn't rest! Then one of us would say, "Look, Papi, it was here all along! You should have your eyes examined."

Poor man.

Indeed. I have paid that karmic debt tenfold with my own children.

But your business is thriving.

Who knows? Maybe I was a saint in another life.

The Art Lover

The night he met Micaela Singer, Dante had sworn to be on his best behavior. Houston, the opening of the Byzantine Fresco Chapel, a museum funded by the Menil Collection. Dominique de Menil, founder of Rice University's Institute of Art, had taken Dante under her wing some twenty-five years earlier. The *grande dame* of the Houston art scene had shaped his love of Mediterranean icons and surrealism. She helped him assemble his art collection. His debt to her as mentor and sponsor was immeasurable.

Dominique de Menil had introduced him to his wife.

To show his gratitude, Dante donated to any cause his patron championed, and he opened his wallet for the construction of the Byzantine Chapel. Dominique had worked for decades—even staring down the barrel of a smuggler's gun— to recover the scattered fragments of two frescoes stolen from a 13th-century church in Cyprus. After two years of painstaking restoration, the frescos of Christ Pantokrator and the Virgin and Archangels were being shown privately to major donors.

With regret, Georgia had declined the invitation to the opening; she was hosting an auction of the Central Florida Women's League. Alone, Dante stood in the apse, admiring the golden dome. When Micaela walked through the door in a wine-red suit, he scrapped all thoughts of being a saint.

Micaela had spent a summer at the Istituto per l'Arte e il Restauro; Dante had honeymooned in Florence. She specialized in Byzantine iconography; he'd recently purchased a 14th-century triptych and was looking for an artist to restore it. She read French and German—required at the Master's level in art conservation—and romance novels. She preferred Puccini over Wagner.

With the Menil project completed, she was out of a job.

"It must be fate," he said.

Her eyebrows arched. "I don't believe in fate."

"Let me change your mind," he said.

She wasn't fooled by Dante Costas, but she couldn't help appreciating a fine work of art. If nothing else, she'd have nice scenery to look at over dinner.

Peta Wilder: Great Expectations

The Dead Remembered/Profiles compiled by Herald Staff

Abandoned on the steps of a fire station as a baby, raised in foster care, Peta Wilder had a childhood out of Dickens. She lived in thirteen different homes. She was hospitalized twice: once for malnutrition, later for injuries received at the hands of a caretaker. He is serving five years for child abuse and fraud.

Those who knew Peta said she believed in fate.

Teachers at Evans High School remembered her as a quiet student who wore the same clothes every day and often fell asleep in study hall, but who managed to earn a 3.8 grade average. "You had the feeling Peta was trying to blend into the walls," said Abby Marie Pilar, her Language Arts teacher. "She wouldn't raise her hand in class, but her assignments were a joy to read."

In a poem about family, Peta wrote:

> *Daddy was a fireman*
> *Mama the wind*
> *Sirens sing a lullaby*
> *Echoes of my kin.*
> *Home is where the heart is*
> *Walls of flesh and skin*
> *My crib was a bucket*
> *To carry me in.*

Abby hoped her talented senior might win a college scholarship, but Peta's immediate concerns were more pressing. In the foster system, children are "emancipated" at the age of 18, leaving them on their own with no money, housing, insurance or job prospects.

"I have four kids, or I would have taken her in," said Abby, who began making inquiries on Peta's behalf. At a school luncheon, she met Mayor Delphi Owens, who'd recently attended the wedding of Claire Montemayor, daughter of one of Orlando's most prominent philanthropists, Muriel Hutchins Montemayor. "Mrs. Montemayor was rambling around in that big old house," Abby said. "It seemed like the answer to a prayer."

Peta became Muriel Montemayor's companion, accompanying her to social functions, meetings, plays and concerts. "A whole new world opened up for her," Abby said. "It wasn't always easy, a young girl living in a strange place. She was lonely sometimes, but that house was a vast improvement over the other ones."

The last time Abby saw Peta, they spoke of the future. "For once, I think she was letting herself dream," Abby said. "She wanted a place of her own, maybe a dog. She wanted to go to law school and become an advocate for foster kids. She believed she'd had such a horrible childhood for a reason, so she could help others."

Thomas Hood, attorney, Hood, Pantier & Beatty, Tuesday, 4-21-98, 10:30 a.m.

Thomas, it's Juni Bruder. I wanted to see how you're holding up.

I'm more coherent than the first night we talked, but not much.

Of all the people I met at the site, you struck me as the most composed, considering what you'd been through.

A polite way of saying I'm a cold son of a bitch. My ex-wife used to say the same thing, less politely.

I'm sorry, I didn't mean to bring up—

It's okay. The other thing she hated was my habit of making bad jokes at bad times. Like when she was packing to leave and said, "You'll never find another woman like me," and I said, "God, I hope not."

You didn't.

Yeah, I did. Funny—she called me the night I came home from Cleveland, said she was worried sick about me.

Of course she would be.

Why?

Tragedy has a way of waking people up to what's important. Who.

So she left me and ripped my heart to shreds on a *good* day, but the Plaza blows up, and suddenly she remembers how much she loves me? That's bullshit.

Well, when you put it that way. [laughter] My ex called, too. We hadn't spoken in two years, not since the day we signed the papers.

What did he say?

Oh, that he and his wife closed on a house in Sarasota, and they're expecting a baby in August. I deleted the rest. There's only so much good news you can take.

Yeah. "Hey, you might be feeling down right now, what with the Plaza and all, so let me tell you about *my* life!"

[laughter] Come to think of it, empathy was never his strong suit.

Jesus, I have people coming up to me, telling me what a hard time they had when their dad died, like that gives them a window into knowing what it's like to lose thirteen of your best friends in a single day. Oh, yeah, and your job, which would have distracted you from all the funerals.

I'm not sure there's such a thing as heartbreak by degrees. When my mom died, it felt like the end of the world, so I can't imagine the kind of pain you're in.

Aw, hell, you know—right now, it feels like there's nothing left of my heart but a sucking chest wound. I keep seeing Ben and Beatty and Olive, Amelia, the rest of the girls, poor Tig—

Tig?

Ben's dog. He brought her to work every day. The sweetest dog—a racer. The greyhound people saved her. I think dogs know, right? They're grateful. She'd come by my desk, just to say hello. I kept a box of Milk Bones— *[inaudible].*

I'm so sorry, Thomas.

They can't all be gone. It's not possible. I have this dream where they're all together in a room somewhere, a safe room down at the bottom of the pile, and they're waiting for us to find them. Ben says, "Firstly, you must find another shrubbery!"

Come again?

It's from "Monty Python and the Holy Grail." Ben knew every line. I swear he quoted the movie like some people quote the Bible. You'd come back from court after getting totally creamed, ready to slit your wrists, and he'd say, "It's only a flesh wound," in this goofy British accent, and how could you not crack up?

I don't get it.

It's okay. Most women don't. It's a guy thing. Like the time Ben walked up to the witness stand—the expert witness—and said, "What is the air-speed velocity of an unladen swallow?" Every guy in the room lost it, jurors, guards, everybody. The lady judge, on the other hand, threatened to cite Ben for contempt.

Did he win the case?

Nah, but that's beside the point.

How long did you two know each other?

Since law school. We always talked about opening a practice together, but when it came down to brass tacks, it's dreams versus reality, so we both went the way of the big firm, big cars, big houses, big wives.

Your wife was a large woman?

[laughter] Miss Hawaiian Tropic, 1987.

Ah.

Ben's wife is the former Sophia Marriott.

Of the—

Yeah. You can stay at their house and order room service. Not that he was ever home much. Nineteen rooms, and he slept on the couch in his office with Tig to keep him warm. Oh, hey, I shouldn't be—

It's okay. It doesn't matter. Do you know their son very well?

Reuben? Used to. He's at one of those boarding schools up north, the kind they send you when you've been kicked out of every place else. The poor kid can't seem to get his act together, and no wonder, the way his parents went at it. And now his dad's gone. God, I remember when we opened the first office, and Reuben came to visit, maybe five or six, sitting on his dad's shoulders. Ben said, "Just think, little man. One day, this will all be yours." And I could see it, you know? Ben and me, the old gray partners, handing down the firm to the next generation.

You can still do that.

Nah. No kids in the cards for me. No Ben. No point. He's the one who made it happen. I'd still be working for somebody else, if not for him.

You guys went after a dream. Most people never take that chance.

Yeah, and I'll always be grateful to Ben for that. Not that it was all cigars and roses in the beginning. I mean, we rented this little closet over on Pine Street, two phones, one secretary. God, the things Olive had to deal with. The rats—

Your clients?

[laughter] No, the kind with tails, but yeah, our clients were vermin, too.
And then you took the Barrett case.
I keep forgetting you're a reporter. You dug that up, huh?
No, actually, I remember. I met Pauline Barrett not long before she died. I admired you for what you did.
People say we're the reason malpractice premiums are sky high, but when it's your wife dying of cancer, suddenly a lawyer's not such a bad idea.
It's not frivolous when the claims adjuster is letting people die to make a profit.
Dying is cheaper.
That settlement broke a record, as I recall.
That settlement bought us office space at the Plaza, so maybe we lost after all.
Thomas, I—
You know, people are already calling about benefits. Olive's husband, and some lady from New York who claims to be Amelia's sister, who I thought was an only child. Beatty's wife went into premature labor, and now we're fighting the HMO. All the files are gone. Ben and Olive handled that stuff. I don't even know what kind of life insurance we had. It didn't matter to me. We—
You'll sort it out.
People think we were sitting on a pile of cash, like we didn't have rent and taxes and hundreds of hours on cases that never panned out. Being a partner just means you get to split the bills. Everybody's lined up with their hands out.
Unfortunately, there will always be people waiting to cash in on disaster.
And lawyers lined up to represent them.
I know this will be hard for you, Thomas, but for the other profiles, your friends, do you mind if I call from time to time to talk about them?
No. That's fine. I don't know. There's no telling how I'll feel from one day to the next. These news people, they shove their mikes in my face, asking, "How does it feel to be the only survivor of your firm?" Well, how the fuck do you think it feels? I'd rather be in the hole with the rest of them.

Conspiracy Theories Abound in Plaza Collapse

Psychologists say speculation is human nature

By Juni Bruder, Herald Staff Writer/Tuesday, April 21, 1998

ORLANDO—While arson investigators and police officials comb the wreckage of the Parramore Plaza for clues to the cause of the tragedy, local radio shows are fielding hundreds of calls from listeners with theories of their own.

"We can't keep up with the volume," said WTKO talk-show host Bram Stroker. "People out there have a real need to talk about what happened. They're processing their anger and disbelief and sadness, and we provide the forum for that. I consider it a public service."

Stroker isn't surprised by the abundance of conspiracy theorists. "You see it with any sudden disaster, any 'man-made' catastrophe," he said. "It happened with the *Challenger*, Oklahoma City, TWA flight 800. I mean, we still have people who think the moon landings were faked."

Only one suspect, Mauro Abissi, has been identified in the Plaza case thus far, but Stroker said, "There's a real fear out there that the government is somehow involved."

Imanuel Ehrenhardt was one of dozens who called Friday to talk about the tragedy. "The collapse of a steel building from fire is unheard of," said Ehrenhardt, who took an engineering class at Valencia Community College. "It never happens. You watch the video, and it looks like a controlled implosion. You have to believe this building was brought down by professionals."

"That Abissi guy worked in construction," one listener pointed out. "He was in the Persian Gulf. He knew exactly what to do with explosives."

Other callers believe Abissi couldn't have acted alone. "There's no way a janitor pulled this off," one said. He pointed to the recent acquittal of Thomas Rhodes, CEO of Gulf Breeze Savings & Loan, as a possible motive. "The Feds couldn't get a conviction, so they went for the death penalty instead."

Columbus Cheney speculated that the Planned Parenthood office on the fifth floor was the target. "These pro-life activists, they've killed doctors and nurses. They've bombed abortion clinics. Why not take it a step further and bring down the organization that raises all the money?"

Psychologist Marcia Fieldstone explains that conspiracy theories are a common reaction to tragedy. "It's hard for us to accept death as an accident," she said. "It's too random for our peace of mind. Instinctively, we look for someone to blame." She adds that rumors serve a purpose, filling a void in the absence of hard facts. "Humans don't do well with the unknown."

Within hours of the Plaza tragedy, rumors about victims and survivors began to spread. The man found dead in his Porsche in the parking garage? True. Five others rescued alive from a Hummer? False. The lucky angelfish? True. Minutes after the collapse, a dust-covered man staggered into the Itso Sushi restaurant on South Street. Hostess Lia Schroeder offered him a glass of water. "He took one sip, looked down and patted his shirt," Lia said. "He reached into his pocket and pulled out a fish. He looked at me. I looked at him. He dropped the fish into the glass and left."

The blue and orange fish now resides in an aquarium at the restaurant.

One of the most damaging rumors suggested that the body of an OFD fire-fighter was found clutching a gold necklace from the Plaza gift shop. "This kind of story is despicable," said Fire Chief William Herndon. "To suggest that one of our men stopped in the middle of a raging fire to help himself to property is ludicrous and reprehensible." Chief Herndon points out that several firefighters were trapped in the levels below the store, and the collapse sent merchandise cascading onto the lower floors.

Rozelle Simmons, who managed the gift shop and lost her husband on April 13, notes that gold jewelry was not part of her inventory.

Walter Simmons: Clockwork Orange and Blue

The Dead Remembered/Profiles compiled by Herald Staff

Though Walter Simmons repaired timepieces for nearly thirty years, he is remembered by his children and grandchildren for the toys he created out of soda cans and watch parts: a mechanical dog, a kaleidoscope, a miniature train called the Fresca Express.

"Give him a pair of tin snippers, and he was happier than a bird with a french fry," said his son, Barry Simmons of Winter Springs. "The dentist couldn't understand why my sister and I had so many cavities. We were emptying cans for Dad."

In 1995, Barry's mother, Rozelle, opened the Plaza Gift Shop, which displayed the work of local artisans. She encouraged her husband to contribute a sample. "Preferably something without the word 'Coke' on it," she said. Walter's first piece, a silver pin made out of watch cogs, sold within hours.

"It was a godsend," Rozelle said. "He was puttering around an empty house, and none of our friends wanted another aluminum wreath."

Walter's jewelry became so popular, he set up a studio in the shop. The once shy man began to demonstrate his craft for visitors; he also traveled to art shows in the area. Last year, he won a juried award at the Mount Dora Arts Festival.

"This was the same month the Gators beat the Seminoles for the national championship," said Barry. "It was like the best year of Dad's life."

Both of the Simmons children attended the University of Florida, and Walter was a diehard football fan who "bled orange and blue," according to his family.

"The store was perfect for him," Rozelle explained. "He could fill his jewelry orders during the week and devote Saturday and Sunday to sports." On the morning of April 13, she left her husband at the store to make a bank deposit. "I was only gone twenty minutes," she said. "That's all it took."

Rescuers have already recovered several of Walter's pieces from the wreckage. "His designs were so distinctive," Rozelle said. "Everyone recognized them." Her favorite was a watch-face pin with wings called *Tempus Fugit*. "I assumed it was gone forever," she said. "Yesterday, a fireman delivered it to the house. He said he wanted to bring it personally, because 'it was the only thing of beauty he'd seen in a week in hell.' Walter would be so proud of that."

Plaza Losses Not Measured Only in Human Cost

By Juni Bruder, Herald Staff Writer/Wednesday, April 22, 1998

ORLANDO—In the shade of a fire truck, Jon Houghton rests with his dog Sadie. The Labrador retriever's paws are muddy, and Jon rinses them with bottled water to check for cuts. "She won't keep her booties on," Jon explains. He and Sadie are part of a K-9 response team from Kentucky, mobilized to Orlando within hours of the Plaza disaster. They have been combing the wreckage for eight days.

While other members of their team specialize in finding survivors, Sadie is a cadaver dog, bred and trained to detect human remains. This task of search and rescue (SAR) is considered one of the most stressful for K-9 handlers and their canine partners.

It is Jon's second trip to Orlando in three months; he and Sadie worked here in February after tornadoes struck Kissimmee and Winter Garden, killing 42 people.

The death toll for the Plaza tragedy has been set at 115. There is no count of the non-human victims.

A German shepherd in an orange vest was a common sight at the Plaza. Hondo, a mobility assistance dog, came to work daily with his owner, Francisco Turner, a proofreader for Walden Publishing. Turner was confined to a wheelchair due to a congenital heart condition. Fellow employees carried Turner down the steps to the commons, but in the confusion, Hondo was left behind. The service dog could open doors with lever handles, but not the heavy fire doors of the stairwell.

Hearing that Hondo was missing, mounted patrol officer William "Doc" Metcalf rushed into the building, leaving his horse, Billy Lee, tethered on the commons. The retired thoroughbred had been rehabilitated after a racing accident; Metcalf was said to be the only person who could ride him. Officer Metcalf failed to emerge from the Plaza after the collapse. Francisco Turner and his co-workers, editor William Jones and authors Perry Zoll and Alfonso Churchill, died as they waited in the triage area. Late Tuesday, Billy Lee's body was removed from the wreckage with the full ceremony accorded to fallen members of the police force.

The glittering aquariums of the Plaza attracted tourists from around the world. Most local schoolchildren visited the mangrove pool at least once a year to see Griffy the manatee. Griffy, orphaned after his mother's death from a boat collision, was rescued from the St. Johns River and raised at SeaWorld. The 6-year-old sea cow ate fifty heads of lettuce a day, hand-fed to him by marine biologist Arlo Will, who cared for the Plaza's aquatic exhibits. Many aquariums were shattered in the first explosion, and evacuees reported slipping on fish. Will was last seen with a bucket, trying to save rare specimens.

Patrons who picked up their clothes at Andrea Kessler's dry-cleaning shop on Central Avenue took an extra minute to pet the homeless cat, nicknamed Spot, that had wandered in and given birth to a litter of kittens in a laundry basket. Flaming debris ignited the business, destroying it. Mrs. Kessler suffered a heart attack while rescuing clothes from the fire; she died at the scene.

On the night of April 13, three dogs waited for their owners at Bark Avenue, the canine daycare center next door to Kessler's. No one came to retrieve them. Though the business was damaged and remains closed, Manager Barbara Woodhouse says she will keep the dogs—Booger, Lord Kibble and Molly—until family members can be located.

Attorney Ben Pantier never went to work without his dog, Tig, a retired racing greyhound. Saved from euthanasia by a local rescue group, Tig slept under Pantier's desk and was often seen loping through the Plaza halls. Both owner and dog died in the collapse.

According to searcher Dillard Sissman, SAR dogs assigned to the Plaza began showing signs of depression as the rescue effort turned to recovery of victims. "They know," said Sissman, who is here with K-9 partner Rex. To raise the dogs' spirits, volunteers hide in the wreckage at the end of each shift, providing the opportunity for a successful rescue. "We make a big deal out of it, cheering and thumping everybody on the back," Dillard says. "The dogs need that reward. I guess the humans do, too."

When asked what he and his dog Sadie will do when the recovery effort ends, Jon Houghton answered, "We're going to Disney World." All theme parks in the area, including the Disney resorts, Universal Studios and Wet 'n Wild, have offered free admission to two- and four-legged rescuers.

Andrea Ghiaurov Kessler: Attention to Details

The Dead Remembered/Profiles compiled by Herald Staff

Andrea Kessler never forgot a name. Patrons of her dry-cleaning business didn't need a ticket; Mrs. Kessler had their clothes ready and waiting.

"It meant something," said James Garber, who lived in a condominium above the shop. "These days you're just a number, so to walk into a place and be greeted by name made you feel special."

Kessler's Dry Cleaning, opened by Andrea's husband, Bert, in 1995, catered to Plaza employees and residents. "Bert saw it as a golden opportunity," James said. "Mrs. Kessler didn't want any part of it at first."

The couple moved to Orlando from Buffalo, New York, after Bert retired from the military. "They came to Florida to sit in the sun," James said, "and Bert sank his savings into a dry-cleaning store." The former Army supply sergeant ran the counter while his wife worked in back. "I never saw her," James said. "Bert did all the talking."

In 1996, Bert died on a hunting trip to the Ocala National Forest.

"A week later," James said, "there was Mrs. Kessler at the register. She handed me my shirts and asked, 'How is your mother, James?' She'd been listening the whole time. She took notes and coached Bert on what to say. Her file was this thick." In her file were birthdays, anniversaries, starch preferences and details of every conversation, no matter how small.

"I used to tease her about selling it, her little book of secrets," James said. "She had some powerful clients. Judges, bankers, lawyers. A little lipstick on the collar would have gone a long way."

Fire destroyed the file, along with the business. Ignoring evacuation orders, Mrs. Kessler ran into her shop several times to retrieve her clients' laundry. She later suffered a fatal heart attack.

"She saved my Bolgheri pinstripe," said James, who also lost his home. "A fireman found the bag on the sidewalk with my name on it. It's the only suit I have left. I wore it to her funeral."

The Usual

In the first ten days after the explosion, Delphi Owens went to her apartment only to sleep, shower and change. She lived at the command post on Central Avenue. Residents on the outer edges of the evacuation zone had finally been allowed to return home, but this street was still closed, a plywood-shuttered ghost town. City crews were struggling to fix a broken water main.

The mayor operated out of an accountant's office two doors down from the blackened ruins of Kessler's Dry Cleaning. Delphi's staff made do with bottled water and a portable toilet, which she refused to use. (She tried not to drink too much.) She kept a bottle of ibuprofen in her purse for the constant ache in her lower back, and a set of hatboxes in her car. Any funeral clothes left hanging in the office absorbed the smells of smoke and mildewed carpet.

Rescuers who needed medical attention went next door to Bark Avenue, where doctors and massage therapists worked beside a team of veterinarians. When the search for victims ended, the vets would go home, along with the cadaver dogs.

Delphi would miss the sweet-eyed shepherds and Labs in their DayGlo vests.

Down the street, the police and fire departments shared a space at Gap Kids. On her first visit, Delphi had laughed out loud, seeing the burly men in turnout gear surrounded by miniature outfits in lemon, lime and pink. By the time she returned, the walls were bare. Chief Herndon explained that the store manager had donated her entire neon inventory to the children of Plaza victims.

"How hard did you twist her arm?" Delphi asked.

The fire chief scratched his neck. "I might have mentioned she'd never reopen without running water."

"And you offered to help her how?"

He shrugged. "By leaning on my guys at Public Works. Who, by the way, think they'll have the street open tomorrow."

"Which had nothing to do with your leaning?"

"Nah, but the manager lady doesn't have to know."

Delphi peered over the barrier of empty racks that divided the store like the Berlin Wall. Her assistant, Lydia, sat at a table on the law-enforcement side. "Be sure to send the manager a letter of thanks," Delphi said.

Lydia flipped through her bulging calendar and made a note. "You're due at Spoon River in five minutes."

The little deli around the corner, famous for its homemade soups, was the only business operating in the restricted zone. Delphi had done some leaning of her own with the health department. Before the explosion, Spoon River was the place she'd gone for coffee, take-out dinner, Saturday lunch. The owner, Eddie, had even named a special after her (pulled pork on a roll with coleslaw and spicy mustard). The rescuers deserved better food than a cold ham and cheese sandwich from the Red Cross.

Strangely, Eddie credited Delphi with saving his life. When the Plaza fell, he'd been cleaning up breakfast dishes at City Hall. "I would have been standing here," he said, showing her the shattered glass. Plywood covered the window now, and volunteers scrawled their thanks with Magic Markers.

Delphi told Eddie to keep a tab on all the food he'd served to rescuers, but she doubted he would send a bill. Knowing Eddie, he'd already donated the proceeds of his tip jar to the memorial fund.

The frigid blast as she opened the restaurant door made her shiver. These past few weeks, she'd gotten used to life without air-conditioning. Standing in the open sun at yet another grave, Delphi thanked God for the shade of a hat and the cool breezes of April, not yet summer. Another month, and heat stroke would have doubled the death toll.

The deli was quiet this afternoon. Without any sunlight, it felt like a cave. She counted three tables of firemen, a few locals, a FEMA agent dripping mayonnaise on his paperwork. The crowd dwindled a little more each day. Eddie's place had become the official hangout for Plaza workers — rescuers, journalists, volunteers from across the country. Good, decent people, even the media. Tom Brokaw had ordered a meatball sub and posed for pictures with a welding crew from South Dakota, his home state.

Delphi had heard a rumor that the cashier didn't recognize Kathy Lee Gifford (or was it Regis?), but Eddie wouldn't confirm or deny the story. No matter. The cameras were gone now. Ten days, and the Plaza was old news.

In the restroom, Delphi bowed her head. *Thank you, Jesus, for warm water and a flushing toilet.* Sooner or later, she would have to go back to City Hall. Her staff couldn't live much longer without Internet access. Central Avenue would reopen in the next few days, business owners returning to sweep up the ashes, start over.

She was the one who'd said, "We must rebuild."

On the way to her table, Delphi tiptoed up behind the lone *Herald* reporter, camped out at her usual spot. Typing away, Juni didn't notice anyone reading over her shoulder. "Girl, I hope they pay you by the word," Delphi said, wrapping an arm around her neck, making her jump.

"Jesus, Delphi, cough or something." Juni tried to return the hug and shut her laptop at the same time.

"What are you writing?"

"Nothing."

"It looked like something. Look at you blushing!"

"I am *not* blushing." Juni covered her face. "It's just—oh, hell. Ever since the Plaza, I've been writing these...stories."

"Yes. I know. I read them every day."

"No, not for the paper. For me. So I can remember."

"Oh. Like a book?"

"No. More like a diary." Juni nodded to the mayor's table, where the group was ordering lunch. "Aren't they waiting for you?"

"Believe me, they can't think without food in their mouths." Leaning closer, Delphi whispered, "Did you get to the part where Mayor Owens collapses from exhaustion and checks into rehab?"

Grinning, Juni pretended to make a note. "Chapter twelve."

"You *should* write a book. It's important, what happened here."

"I know, but somebody else—"

"No, you."

Shaking her head, Juni said, "Trust me. I'm Sylvia Plath with all of the angst and none of the talent."

"Who?"

"Bell jar? Oven? Never mind." As Eddie approached the table, Juni slipped her computer into its case. "Let me stick to the news. It's what I do best."

"Yes, well," Delphi said, closing one of the Velcro flaps for her. "I used to sell real estate. I was the best. You think I'd trade all that money to be sitting where I am today?" She spread her arms wide, letting her voice rise. "Here, in this fine place, with these brave men and women, these people I love?"

Eddie took his pencil from behind his ear. "I thought you only loved me, Delphi."

She stood and planted a kiss on his cheek. "You and only you, baby."

"The usual?"

"Yeah. Oh, and Juni, honey, when you write about me? Make me pretty."

Kevin Potter: Hot Pie and Coffee

The Dead Remembered/Profiles compiled by Herald Staff

Firefighters at Station 2 claim that Lt. Kevin "Cooney" Potter slept with a lighted cigar in his mouth, and they have photos to prove it. Hanging in the firehouse kitchen is a framed picture of a sleeping—and smoking—Kevin.

"It's sad when a fireman sets fire to his own bed," said his wife, Katie, a physical therapist who for years begged her husband to quit smoking. "I said the cigars would kill him if the sugar didn't. I guess he had the last laugh."

Like his father and uncle before him, Kevin became a firefighter in Boston and married his high-school sweetheart. "It's a family tradition," said Katie. "Put out fires and marry the first girl who'll have you."

In 1990, Kevin followed tradition by moving to Florida. "His dad bought a house down here when he retired," Katie said. "He left it to Kev when he died, so here we are." She adds that her husband spent most of his free time working outdoors and took great pride in his yard. "It gave him no greater pleasure than to call the Charlestown firehouse in January and say, 'Hey, guys, guess what? I'm in my shorts! The windows are open! It's freaking gorgeous here!'"

Nicknamed for a 1920s Red Sox shortstop, Kevin carried on another family tradition with his sons: cheering for Boston's home team. "You can't exactly call it cheering," said Katie. "More like groaning and swearing." Nine-year-old twins Justin and Dustin took a trip with their dad to Fenway Park last May for two games, both losers. "The boys came home and painted their bedroom wall the same color as the Green Monster."

Anyone short of cash at the Parramore firehouse knew Kevin was an easy mark for a wager. "He bet on anything, the next ball, the next commercial," said his friend, Luke Havergal. "Every season, he bet the Sox to win the Series. That's the one thing he wanted to see before he died. I felt bad taking his money, year after year."

At an accident last fall involving a septic truck on fire, the OFD crew found a lake of waste surrounding the fire hydrant. Kevin made a bet that he could connect the fire hose before the truck's tires melted. He took the money, along with a lengthy course of antibiotics, after he stepped in a hole and cut his ankle.

"Any fireman will run into a burning building," Luke said. "Walking through raw sewage, now, that takes real courage."

"Kevin never talked about work," his wife said. "We had a code. He'd call, and I'd ask what he wanted for dinner. If it was a good day, he'd say, 'Whatever you guys had.' If it was bad, he'd say, 'Hot pie and coffee.' Then you knew. Monday, I had Dutch apple pie and ice cream waiting for him. Of course, he never called."

Two Kittens Survived Plaza Fire

Mother cat died trying to save her litter

By Juni Bruder, Herald Staff Writer/Friday, April 24, 1998

ORLANDO—Two kittens that lost their mother to the Plaza fire have found a new home with *Herald* Photographer Art Penniwitt. He rescued the orphans outside the charred ruins of Kessler's Dry Cleaning on the night of April 13.

"I was shooting pictures all day," Art said, "and running on fumes. I sat down on the curb to rest for a minute, and reality started to hit." Above the noise of sirens and fire equipment, he heard faint mewing from the storm drain at his feet. Using his flash bulb, he lit the interior and saw two pairs of eyes staring back at him.

"The drain was full of water from the fire hoses," Art said. "These little guys were high and dry, up in a cubby hole at the top." He scooped out the kittens, tucked them into his camera vest and returned to work. Only when he climbed into his truck around ten o'clock did he remember the contents of his pockets.

"Not a peep out of them," he said. "I guess they felt warm and safe in there." Art took the orphans home, shredded newspaper for a litter box and opened a can of tuna fish. "I've never had animals before," Art said. "Cats seem like low maintenance."

Patrons of Kessler's Dry Cleaning remembered the litter of five kittens born in a laundry basket about six weeks ago. Their mother, a stray nicknamed Spot, had wandered into the shop and taken up residence. The business was gutted by fire on April 13. Owner Andrea Kessler died of a heart attack at the scene. Art knew nothing about the kittens' origins until he asked a fellow *Herald* employee for advice on his new pets. "I've been too busy to read the paper," Art explained.

"The mother cat, she must have saved these two and gone back for more," he said. Art, who collects Gunsmoke memorabilia, has named the kittens Chester and Miss Kitty.

Rita Gruenberg: Beating the Odds

The Dead Remembered/Profiles compiled by Herald Staff

Rita Gruenberg had finally given up cigarettes. "She said it was the hardest thing she'd ever done," explained daughter Eileen Maye of Sanford. "And if she was going to be miserable, she made sure the rest of us were, too."

A family intervention had played a part in the decision. All four of Rita's children and eleven grandchildren live in the Orlando area. "None of us let Mom smoke in the house, not around the kids," Eileen said. "Grandma spent most of her time on the porch, which seemed ridiculous. One day, we finally sat her down and told her it was time to quit."

A smoker for forty years, Rita rebelled at first, despite repeated warnings from her cardiologist. "I think she would have rather cut off her left arm," Eileen said. "The fact that she was ruining her heart didn't register. She told us, 'Odds are, I'll get hit by a bus instead.' We gave her the choice of seeing her grandkids or not. To be honest, she had to give it some thought."

Rita was an avid gambler who enjoyed a weekly ritual: Friday night bingo at St. Mary's Cathedral and the Saturday night cruise on the Sterling Casino Ship out of Cape Canaveral. The weekend before the Plaza fire, she skipped both events to stay home with her family and celebrate her first smoke-free month. "We had a big cookout," her daughter said. "I can still see Mom at the picnic table, chewing her carrot sticks, looking absolutely miserable."

A native of Milwaukee, Rita worked as an accountant for Fidelius Financial Group, where a new company policy had dealt the final blow to her habit: smoking employees at the Plaza had to quit or face losing their jobs. "They blamed it on healthcare costs," Eileen said, "but I think it had more to do with people taking long breaks to walk across the street, my mom included."

Although Rita was only a year away from retirement, she considered leaving her position. "She was ready to lose her livelihood, out of sheer stubbornness," Eileen said. "I asked her, 'Mom, where will you live when you're unemployed? Not with me.' And boy, was she mad."

Rita's husband, Roy, died of emphysema in 1988. Rita was the last survivor to be pulled alive from the Plaza wreckage. Protected under a crumpled steel door in the southeast stairwell, she survived for 12 hours after the collapse. Though she was conscious and talking to rescuers, she died en route to the hospital.

"I asked the paramedic what her last words were," Eileen said. "He told me she asked for a cigarette."

Common Ground

Rita always kept the lighter in her hand as she crossed the street, but she never lit the cigarette until she reached her favorite bench. There were days when a stranger might be sitting there, and then the day was ruined. Today, all four seats around the concrete circle were empty, a lucky break.

She'd buy a lottery ticket after work.

The weather was beautiful this afternoon, not too cool, not too hot. Another few weeks and she'd be sweltering out here. It was an embarrassment, going back to her cubicle drenched in sweat, but what could she do? Smokers were banished to Outer Mongolia. At least she got some exercise, walking out to the commons a few times a day.

The honeyed scent of confederate jasmine drifted on the breeze; the vines hiding the electrical boxes were laden with blossoms. Rita found her pack, tapped out a cigarette and put it to her lips, loving the woodsy taste of the filter, the menthol cool on her tongue. She struck the lighter—that cheerful hiss, the calming smell of butane—and watched as the flame danced around the clean white tip, charring it black. Closing her eyes, she sank into peace as smoke warmed her throat, her chest, her lungs.

Life, for a moment, was perfect.

"You started without me?"

Rita looked up, happy to see Olive coming down the walk, but her friend had brought the dog this time. Rita hated the click-click-click of its claws on the pavement. She'd never liked dogs, the way they expected a pat on the head when they'd done nothing to deserve it. This one was especially pushy, shoving its wet nose under her palm. She elbowed the greyhound aside and wiped her hand on her skirt.

"Sorry," Olive said, collapsing onto the bench beside her. "It was my turn."

"Does the boss pay extra for dog-walking? He's a big-shot lawyer. He can afford it."

"I don't mind." Olive looped the leash around the armrest. "It gives me a chance to come outside." The dog sat and edged its front paws down to the ground. Olive stroked its pointy snout. Rita rolled her eyes, but Olive was too busy fondling—what was its name?—to notice. "Big case on Monday," Olive said. "The office is going nuts. I couldn't stand it anymore. I left so fast I forgot my purse."

Without a word, Rita offered her lighter and pack.

"You're a lifesaver," Olive said, exhaling as she settled back.

"That Frankie in your office, she ought to be walking the dog." Overhead, a jet trailed a long, white plume, a skywriter without a message. "A little exercise would do her good."

Olive swatted her. "Don't be mean. Frankie can't help it. She's...big-boned."

"Big bones, big thighs, big butt."

"Life is hard," Olive said. "Everyone needs a comfort. Hers is food. Ours is..." They both held up their cigarettes and laughed.

"I'll bet you've always been thin." Olive squeezed Rita's bicep, or lack thereof. "You don't know what it's like, having your—having people make fun of your weight."

Rita let out an extravagant puff. "The last time I quit, I gained thirty pounds. I'll never do that again."

"I thought you were quitting now. Or soon."

"What do you mean? I quit a month ago."

Olive eyed her cigarette. "But you're—"

"In fact, my kids are throwing a party this weekend. Thirty smoke-free days. Whoop-de-frigging-do."

"Lying to them? Rita Gruenberg!"

Rita smirked. "What they don't know won't hurt 'em."

"But what about your job?"

"I'm thinking about suing," Rita said. "You know any good lawyers, Ollie?"

Olive laughed, breathing smoke through her nose. "Ben and Thomas would love to take on a fat-cat company like Fidelius. Want me to talk to them, seriously?"

"We'll see. Maybe I'll drop dead of a heart attack and save everyone the trouble."

"Rita! Don't even say such a thing!"

"What do I have to live for?"

"Your children, your grandchildren—"

"My children?" Rita pointed across the commons to one of the other benches, where the homeless man, the guy who camped out in the parking garage, was sleeping. Or maybe he was dead. "My kids don't care if I live on the street."

"How can you say that?"

"They told me, point blank! They won't lift a finger to help if I lose my job." Rita pictured herself pushing a shopping cart, digging in dumpsters like she'd seen the old man doing. "Everything I did for my kids, all those years, and this is the thanks I get," she said. "My sons, I don't expect much from, but my daughters, they're supposed to take care of me. Isn't that how it works?"

"Yes, of course! Honor thy father and mother."

"I tell you what," Rita said, "the way my life is going? Smoking is the only pleasure I have left." She leaned down, stubbed out her cigarette and lit another. "That and bingo. Oh, wait. My kids say people smoke at bingo, so I can't go. Shoot me now."

Olive laughed and smacked her on the shoulder. They watched the traffic on the streets around the park. People dropped off their dry cleaning at Kessler's. People dropped off their pampered pooches at daycare. What was the world coming to, when people paid other people to babysit their dogs? What was wrong with a long chain in the back yard?

Rita glanced over; Olive was playing with the greyhound's ears, standing them up, letting them flop. The dog used to be a race hound, Rita remembered that much. Roy had taken her to the track once, but she'd been bored to tears. Too much time between starts, and she never picked a winner.

Horses, on the other hand, she didn't mind so much—except for that black beast, Billy Lee. He had tried to bite her once. Doc Metcalf, the Plaza policeman, was posted on his mount by the entrance this afternoon. Rita noticed when Doc sat a little straighter in his saddle, and she saw the art girl, the one who worked in the basement, walking up the sidewalk from the parking lot.

Here she comes, Miss America. The girl waved to Doc—all she needed were long, white gloves—and he touched the brim of his cap. Billy Lee pawed the air with his hoof. They were too far away for Rita to hear, but she saw the girl laugh and press a kiss to the horse's nose.

The greyhound climbed to its feet, whining in the horse's direction. *I'd pay to see them race*, Rita thought.

"Hush, now," Olive said. Rita had to give the dog credit; it minded. Olive smoothed a hand along its ribs, its skinny tail. "What I wouldn't give to be this thin."

"That thing you said before." Rita picked a bit of tobacco off her tongue. "Fletch, he makes cracks about your weight?" She'd never met Olive's husband, but from the few things her friend let slip, Rita gathered he was a creep.

"No—" Olive was suddenly busy persuading the dog to sit. "Sometimes," she finally admitted, "but I don't blame him. This isn't what he signed up for. If you saw my wedding pictures, you wouldn't recognize me." She fluffed her salt-and-pepper hair, cocked her shoulder and posed with her cigarette. "Folks used to call me a looker, back in the day. Now, look at me. Who wouldn't feel cheated?"

Rita glimpsed at her friend, seeing the same dark circles under her eyes, the same saggy skin, the same yellow teeth that smiled grimly back at her in the mirror every morning. Time hadn't been kind to either of them.

"Your husband, he looks the same now as the day you married him?"

Olive let out a little grunt. "Hardly. He's bald as a cue ball, with a gut out to here." She drew a mound in front of her and, looking at her chest, noticed the buttons gaping on her blouse. Rita waited while she tried to fix them.

"Maybe you're entitled to a refund."

Shrugging, Olive said, "Till death do us part."

Though she tried not to dwell, Rita couldn't help thinking back to the months in the hospital with Roy, watching him shrivel away to nothing, gasping for air, drowning in his own bed. Ten years gone, and she still heard that sickening rattle in her sleep. *Till death do us part.* She'd said the words so lightly to the minister in the church, thinking only about the marble cake at the reception. She'd starved for weeks to fit into her mother's wedding dress. Roy had looked so handsome in his good suit and tie.

At the funeral home, they'd clipped his suit with clothespins to make it fit, he had lost so much weight. When she saw him again in heaven, would he be wearing that baggy jacket with pins down his back, or would he be his old self again, the strapping boy she remembered? Would she be young and perfect, too, all the disappointments of this life fading like a bad dream?

Rita smiled to herself and took another drag on her cigarette, praying, *Lord, make it soon.*

Claire Montemayor Abuirre, Friday, 4-24-98, 11:20 a.m.

Claire? I can barely hear you.

You didn't print it, did you, what I said?

No—what's wrong? The baby, you're—

My baby will never know her grandmother! I realized today. Vincent's mother is dead. His father remarried. We never see him. The stepmother is horrid. My child won't have a grandmother when she's born. It's so awful! I—

Claire, calm down. What happened? What brought this on?

I said such terrible things about her. You must think I'm a monster.

No, I don't. Grief makes people say things they don't mean. I know you loved your mother.

Did I?

Of course.

How do you know? She didn't know. I never told her.

Mothers know.

I was so mean to her! All the letters she wrote, and I never wrote back, or if I did, a few lines about the weather. I did it on purpose. I knew it would drive her crazy.

It's complicated, mothers and daughters—

She wouldn't leave me alone, you know? She wouldn't let me breathe! Now, it's so quiet. The phone doesn't ring. My inbox is empty. I don't know what to do!

Your mother's been a constant force in your life.

Now, I see what it's like, being ignored, how lonely she must have felt. It's wretched. I—

Your mother isn't ignoring you. You know that, right?

I just want to tell her—

You didn't have a chance. You're on the other side of the world. It must not seem real.

When I told you I said goodbye, I was lying. I never really thought about it. Sometimes I *wished* she were dead. What kind of daughter—

Claire, you can't do this. You have to stay calm for the baby.

Something terrible will happen to this baby. I just know it.

Why?

Punishment. For what I did. Don't you see?

No! It doesn't work that way, Claire. Getting upset is more likely to hurt your baby. You have to stop. Is your husband home?

He's at a NATO conference, the Western European Union, I think—

It doesn't matter. Have you seen a doctor?

This morning, the sonogram—

Oh, so that's what—

The nurse told me I needed to gain weight, and she sounded like my mother, and I snapped. I said, "Mind your own business," and then I thought—who's going to tell me what to do now?

Claire, you still have your mother's letters, yes?

Her e-mails?

Your mother can talk to you whenever you like. You only have to read her words. She must have shared advice about babies. You said—

Of course she did! I never thought about it! There must be dozens I haven't read yet.

There you go.

And I was thinking about that psychic, the man my mother liked? He said the baby would be fine.

I'm not sure—

I was thinking I wanted to talk to him. It's Jonathan something. Do you know who I mean?

No. Claire, really, you don't need to—

But I do! He talks to the dead, doesn't he? Wouldn't my mother go to him if she wanted to reach me from the other side?

I don't know. This is—

Can you find him for me? You're there in town. Will you tell him to call me? Please? It would mean the world to me.

Okay. Fine. I'll see what I can do.

Will you promise?

Claire, I think it's a bad idea—

But it would make me feel better.

Not necessarily.

How do you know?

Call it a hunch.

Esperanza

Muriel Montemayor had dreamed of Spain, where she and her beloved daughter would wander, arm in arm, through the sun-warmed Parque del Retiro. Together they would touch the burnished heel of Christ in the Cathedral de San Isidro and ask his blessing. They would sit on the Plaza Mayor, sipping *café cortado.*

Even the coffee tasted bitter.

First, there had been the problem at the airport. After eight hours on the plane, Muriel's legs were aching, stiff. Walking was hard for her, even on a good day. If Peta had been there, they might have managed, but Muriel couldn't justify the extra expense when holiday fares were so high. To accomplish the task of disembarking had required a team of flight attendants and a Barajas policeman.

Claire had been mortified.

To appease her, Muriel offered to take her daughter shopping on the Calle de Serrano, where three pairs of suede calfskin boots (same style, three different pastel shades) had cost more than a plane ticket. Muriel paid the price, and gladly, to see Claire's beautiful smile.

Alas, the happy mood hadn't lasted through dinner.

Perhaps she *had* drunk too much wine, Muriel thought, but her son-in-law was proud of the local vintage. Spain, after all, was the third largest wine-producing country in the world. Vincent, bless his heart, had been a genial host, but even he, a diplomatic envoy, had failed to keep the peace through dessert.

Claire left the room in a huff.

Muriel never knew quite what she said to upset her. The event happened with such regularity, it seemed inevitable. They'd been discussing the meal, hen in saffron sauce, and Muriel mentioned, strictly a suggestion, that the cook might use a lighter hand with the cream, perhaps yogurt in place of—

Claire's chair fell over in her haste to leave the table.

On the second day, Muriel bought her daughter a new gold chain from Ansorena, smoothing the waters. She and Claire toured the Palacio Real, or rather, they paid for a tour, but Muriel couldn't climb the grand staircase, and there was no elevator. She never saw the famous 17th-century tapestries as touted in the guidebook, and a security guard had hustled her out, fearing she might sit on an antique damask chair.

It was at the Monasterio de la Encarnación, with its reliquaries of ancient saints, that Muriel fell to her knees before the tiny vial containing a drop of

Saint Pantaleon's blood—his actual blood!—and more than a miracle was needed to get her to her feet again.

The nuns had been most helpful.

Later, she mentioned to Claire the kindness of a group of schoolgirls who had retrieved her walker, young olive-skinned beauties with blue-black hair and shining eyes.

"They were laughing at you, Mother."

In the dark of early morning, Muriel took a cab to the airport without saying goodbye.

Benjamin Pantier: The Holy Grail

The Dead Remembered/Profiles compiled by Herald Staff

According to friends, attorney Ben Pantier quoted "Monty Python and the Holy Grail" as often as other people quoted the Bible. His favorite film provided sayings for every occasion, from his wedding day to a day in court.

Ben, a partner with the firm of Hood, Pantier and Beatty, once ended his closing argument with the words, "We have been charged by God with a sacred quest." He asked the jury to award in favor of his client, Albert Barrett, whose wife, Pauline, committed suicide after being denied life-saving treatment for breast cancer. Ben and his firm won the case, a landmark judgment that forced widespread reforms in Florida's insurance industry.

King Arthur spoke the line in the Trojan Rabbit scene.

Ben's law partner, Thomas Hood, noted that his friend's Pythonisms always helped after a bad day. "That goofy British accent," Thomas said. "How could you not crack up?" The pair met during law school at Stetson University and worked together at Somers, Keene, Whitney and Standard, one of Orlando's largest law firms, before opening a private practice in 1992.

The firm soon earned a reputation for eccentric—and successful—legal strategies. The letterhead read "Hood, Pantier, Beatty and Tig."

Tig was Ben's dog. Ben once tried to put his greyhound on the stand, claiming that she was as smart as the opponent's expert witness.

Tig was Ben's constant companion. She went to work with him every day and waited patiently on the steps of the Orange County Courthouse during trials. A client, who volunteered with the local greyhound rescue program, had given the former racer to Ben in lieu of payment.

According to a Plaza security guard, Tig had "something of a crush" on a mobility assistance dog that worked in the building. Tig and Hondo, a German shepherd, were often seen frolicking on the commons during afternoon breaks.

Both Tig and Hondo died in the collapse.

"Ben never went anywhere without that dog," said his wife, Sophia Marriott Pantier, who noted that Ben's penchant for Monty Python didn't endear him to her family. During his wedding reception at the Marriott Marquis Hotel in New York City, Ben toasted his bride by saying, "Your mother was a hamster and your father smelt of elderberries."

"No one thought it was funny," Sophia said. "Least of all my parents."

Once, Ben's sense of humor nearly landed him in jail for contempt of court. He brought proceedings to a laughing standstill by asking a witness, "What is the air-speed velocity of an unladen swallow?"

"The jurors, the guards, everybody lost it," Thomas remembered.

In the movie, knights must answer the question before they cross the Bridge of Death.

Message from Beyond

Over the years, Juni had met her fair share of scam artists—palm readers, faith healers, gypsy roofers, used-car dealers. She knew the tricks; they came in handy in her own line of work. To gain a subject's confidence, one must appear sympathetic, willing to listen, never judgmental. She mirrored body language and speech patterns to build rapport. She figured out what people wanted to hear, in order to get them to say what she needed.

A simple equation, really.

She armed herself to the teeth for her appointment with Jonathan Swift Somers.

His tasteful home in Winter Park, looking like any other on the leafy street, surprised her. She'd expected a neon hand in the window. Over the phone, Juni had told the psychic who she was, her job, her connection to Claire and Muriel Montemayor. To make him guess would have been unsportsmanlike. She had to admire the balls it took in his line of work, pretending to see the future but having to ask for the expiration date on the credit card.

Juni didn't need a sixth sense to know that Jonathan Swift Somers was doing well for himself; she only had to look at his antique collection. Her keen powers of perception told her that coffee (mountain-grown, possibly Folger's) was brewing in the kitchen. Mrs. Somers, whose arthritic fingers were weighted down with rings, showed Juni into a formal sitting room. She explained her husband was running late with a client. "The poor thing lost her daughter on the thirteenth," she whispered. "Cream or sugar?"

"Black, thanks." Juni kicking herself for not realizing—of course, the Plaza would be a boon to a man who saw dead people. She stepped around a tufted ottoman and took a seat on the white silk couch. "Your husband's been busy?"

"Oh, the phone won't stop ringing. I'm surprised he agreed to see you." Mrs. Somers watched as Juni put a fresh battery in her tape recorder. "I'm sorry, dear, but we don't allow those in the house." She fluttered her hands in the air. "The magnetic field or what-not."

"Of course." As Juni returned the machine to her bag, she considered pushing the button. *Bad, Juni. Bad.*

Alone, she turned to study the enormous oil painting above the couch. Mrs. Somers, perhaps a decade younger, sat in a chair before a marble fireplace—the one in this room—draped in satin and pearls. Beside her stood a snowy-haired gentleman in an ivory suit. Mr. Somers, Juni had to assume, or Colonel Sanders. Brushing a piece of lint off her pants, she wished she'd worn something other than black. In here, she looked like the bad guy in a Western.

A door opened at the back of the house, and heels clicked on the parquet floor. Juni tried not to stare as a portly man with a shock of white hair ushered his client down the hall. With an arm around the woman's shoulders, he blocked Juni's view, but she caught a quick glimpse—black dress, red eyes, a teary smile—before the front door closed.

Elizabeth Childers, mother of seven-year-old Ashley, dead in an elevator. Juni had gone to the house two days earlier. At the time, she'd feared for the woman's peace of mind. Now, she feared for her bank account as well.

Juni took a deep breath; she would have to be careful. Faking a smile always made her face hurt. Mr. Somers remained at the door, one hand on the latch, his forehead almost touching the paneled wood. *And the Oscar goes to...*

"Miss Bruder!" As if she'd caught him by surprise, he shook himself, smoothed his lapels and came into the room toward her. "What a pleasure to see you!"

A psychic, surprised? He'd written her name in his appointment book, even asked how to spell it. "Thank you for taking the time," she said, rising to shake his hand.

"Claire's worried about her pregnancy."

"Oh. Yes." She couldn't remember—had she mentioned the baby on the phone?

"By the way, Muriel wants the child to be named Lambert, after her father," he said. "Please, sit."

"It's a boy?"

"I certainly hope so. Lambert would be a terrible name for a girl." Unbuttoning his jacket, he took the side chair. Mrs. Somers, on tiptoe, delivered a silver coffee tray and poured two silent cups. Juni waited to see if she would bow and shuffle backwards out of the room like a geisha. "Thank you, my dear," her husband murmured as she tottered away. Turning to Juni, he said, "So," and slapped his knees. "You think I'm a fraud."

"What? No!" So much for her poker face. "Honestly, I don't know what to think."

"You wouldn't be here if not for Claire."

"True. I'd have no other reason."

"No one you wish to contact? No one you miss?"

Juni took a quick sip of coffee, burning her tongue. The china was delicate, almost translucent, too fine for everyday use. "I'm here for Claire," she said.

Idly, Mr. Somers rubbed his lip and looked at her. His eyes were a startling blue, and his cheeks were baby-smooth, though he had to be twice her age. She wondered what moisturizer he used. "You like being a reporter because it deflects questions away from yourself," he said.

Apparently, he had a gift for stating the obvious. "Claire asked me to contact you," Juni said. "She's worried about her baby, which is natural. Any woman who's about to give birth starts to understand what her mother went through, but it's too late. Muriel is gone. Claire can't say, 'I love you, Mom,' or 'Thank you.' All she has is guilt, which she's turned into fear for her baby. I suppose she wants some kind of absolution from you."

"Do I possess that power?"

"She thinks you do. Isn't that what counts?"

Mr. Somers inched his chair closer to the couch. "You want me to peer into my crystal ball and tell Claire all will be well?"

Juni fought the urge to scoot away. "I don't want anything," she said. "Claire asked me to put you in touch, so here I am. Do you really use a crystal ball?"

"Muriel gave me her daughter's phone number." Her brows shot up before she could stop them—*a message from the Great Beyond?*—and he added, "When I first met her. Each of my clients provides an emergency contact number. I will call Claire tomorrow. There. Your obligation is fulfilled. You could have done so over the phone, yet here you are. Why?"

"Curiosity? As you said, I'm a reporter."

"What story are you writing?"

The grandfather clock by the fireplace thumped, and a deep chime sounded a moment later. Juni counted: one, two, three. Throughout the house, smaller bells rang and cuckoos whistled. "Edna is a collector," Mr. Somers explained. He pulled up his sleeve—Juni couldn't remember the name of the fabric, the stripes that rich men wore in the summer—to show his bare wrist. "I don't own a watch."

A trio of Waterford clocks ticked on the side table. "I guess you don't have to."

"My wife comes from a wealthy family. She likes beautiful things. Who am I to deny her?"

Oh, so all this...?

He smiled, as if he'd overheard. "I charge a nominal fee for my services."

"What are your services, exactly?"

"What we're doing now," he said. "Sitting and talking. Asking and answering questions. No different from your job, I imagine."

Juni set her empty cup on the table. "No one's ever asked me to contact their dead mother." It came to her then: *Seersucker. Ha!* She wasn't going senile yet.

Catching her off guard, Mr. Somers grasped her hand and turned it over. "You must have been born in August," he said, tracing a line on her palm. "Toward the end of the month, I should think."

His touch, like a feather across her skin, made her shiver. "September. The eleventh," she said.

"Still a Virgo."

"Lucky guess."

Beaming, he ticked off points on her fingertips. "Modest. A perfectionist. A discriminating mind. Good communicator. Always trying to get to the heart of the matter. There, you see? No guesswork involved."

Gingerly, she withdrew her hand and reached for her cup, even though there was nothing in it. "About your work," she said. "When people come to you, they talk about their loved ones, and you listen, right? All they really want is for someone to listen and not interrupt, not tell them it's time to move on. It's grief counseling, what you do. Psychic therapy, in a way."

"Yes," he said. "For people who don't believe in psychiatry."

She had to laugh. "They wouldn't come to you unless they had unfinished business, guilt or regret—"

"Or a need to say goodbye. You had that chance with your mother. Many don't."

"My—" The hair on the back of her neck prickled. "What do you know about my mother?"

Settling back in his chair, he said, "Only that you mention Claire's name with a certain disdain, along with a greater sadness." She refused to blink under his blue gaze. "You don't approve of the way she treated her mother, although you never met Muriel. One can sense that the words, 'I love you, Mom,' have a deep and painful resonance for you. A finality. When you speak of the chance Claire will never have, you speak from experience."

"Wow." Juni felt herself sinking on the silk cushions. "You *are* good."

"It's hardly a parlor trick. She's well, by the way."

"Don't. Please."

"She fears for you, though." He tipped his head, as if he was listening to a conversation in another room. Juni noticed that he wore a hearing aid; she imagined it was a tiny receiver, with a team of researchers sitting behind a two-way mirror. "You're surrounded by death," he said. "She can't protect you this time."

Juni sat up, gripping the cup and saucer. "My job, the Plaza story, is nothing *but* death. You don't need psychic powers to deduce that."

"And you've come so close to death before."

This time she was the one who flashed her wrist. "You mean this? I'm disappointed, Mr. Somers. Somehow I thought you'd be more subtle."

"Yet you were secretly hoping I'd surprise you." He sighed and shook his head. "It never fails. The most jaded cynic comes to me, professing to believe in nothing, all the while praying for a miracle. You *want* to be proven wrong."

"I don't want anything. And it goes back to what I said before. You're a good listener. You figured out I miss my dead mother. Good for you. It's hardly a secret. The only voice you heard was mine."

Leaning forward, he murmured, "Indeed, French porcelain will break if thrown at my head." He eased the cup and saucer out of her fingers. "Limoges, by the way. A matched set. Edna would be distraught to lose it."

"I'm sorry—"

"No. My fault. I shouldn't have trespassed."

"I see why people come to you." Juni put a hand to her temple. "For a minute there—"

"You wanted to believe. Yes, I know. Your head troubles you?"

She nodded.

"You have no defenses. No barriers. Other people's pain, their feelings— you're wide open. It's a gift, you know, but you must learn to shield yourself, as I do."

"My doctor says it's low serotonin." She felt tired, suddenly, hollowed out, wanting nothing more than to lay her cheek on the cool silk tapestry and sleep.

"Close your eyes," Mr. Somers said. He touched her forehead, pressing her back against the couch. "Tell me something. How long ago did your mother die?"

"Three years."

"And yet you still hear her voice, don't you? She talks to you every day."

Juni had to think. "Yes. No. It's only my memory, my mind, imagining her. I know she's gone."

"You and I, we're talking here. When you leave this house, I'll remember your face, your voice, your lovely spirit, though we may never meet again. When you walk through that door, will you cease to exist, simply because you're gone from my sight?"

His voice was low, measured—she felt more than heard the words—and the blinding pressure at her temples eased, even as she tried to resist.

"I sense many souls around you who have passed through the door and yet linger, there on the other side. They're listening, waiting to see how you'll record their lives."

"The dead read the *Herald?*"

"You make light of me, and yet I think you feel it, this great responsibility. One presence in particular—it's very strong. A male energy, I think. A troubled soul in life, and now, I sense terrible confusion, anguish. He cannot rest until he knows his child is safe."

Gee, Kreskin, what a coincidence. How many stories have I written about Marko Abissi?

Juni lifted her head and opened her eyes. Mr. Somers' face was lost in the haze of the white room. "I should go," she said.

"You're feeling better?"

"No, but that's never stopped me before."

Mr. Somers offered a hand to help her up, but she stood on her own. Linking his fingers behind his back, he bowed slightly and gestured for her to precede him to the door.

Rude to an old man? Juniper Bruder, didn't I teach you better manners? Her mother's voice was so clear, Juni turned and looked over her shoulder.

"I hope you brought an umbrella with you," Mr. Somers said. Through the sidelight, Juni could see nothing but clear sky. He rubbed his shoulder in explanation. "These old bones ache like the dickens before the rain. The curse of the elderly—weather prediction." Smiling, he added, "There was something else you wanted to ask."

What the hell, she thought. "Have you heard from Dante Costas?"

Mr. Somers cocked his head and thought for a moment. "No," he said, as if the answer puzzled him. "But then, he was a man of great deeds, great courage. He had no need to linger on this earthly plane. His work here was done."

In the distance, Juni could have sworn she heard thunder.

Ashley Lynn Childers: Pennies from Heaven

The Dead Remembered/Profiles compiled by Herald Staff

Seven-year-old Ashley Childers collected pennies. "Everywhere we went, her eyes were trained on the ground," said her mother, Elizabeth. "She could spot a nickel at fifty paces." Ashley donated her coins to the Save the Manatee Club, a nonprofit organization founded by singer Jimmy Buffett and U.S. Senator Bob Graham, former governor of Florida. The group's mission is to protect endangered manatees and their habitat.

"Ashley was obsessed with manatees," her mother said. The first-grader from Henry Elementary School was thrilled about her field trip to the Parramore Plaza, where she would meet Griffy the manatee. "She couldn't sleep," Elizabeth said. "We'd been to Blue Springs, but all we saw were gray humps in the water. Griffy would be 'this close.' Ashley put lettuce in her backpack to feed him."

Ashley and three other students won the Plaza trip as a reward for reading the most books in their class. Ashley's choices ran to nautical themes: *Humphrey the Lost Whale*, *Baby Beluga* and her favorite, *Until the Sea Cows Come Home*. As Elizabeth learned from teacher's aide Serepta Mason, Ashley not only met Griffy, she touched him. The children helped marine biologist Arlo Will feed the manatee and give him his daily bath. "Griffy rolled over and let Ashley scrub his belly with the brush," Elizabeth said.

Elizabeth and her husband, Ted, struggled for years to conceive a child, enduring a series of painful and expensive fertility treatments. Ashley, born prematurely, spent three months in Neonatal Intensive Care. "I lie awake at night, wondering why we went through so much, only to lose her," Elizabeth said. "Why the left elevator and not the right? But then you realize what you're wishing—that someone else's child had died."

On the day of Ashley's funeral, a child appeared at the Childers' front door. "Ted answered the bell," Elizabeth said. "There was a little girl, holding a goldfish bowl." As Serepta later explained, Ashley cared for the class pets, a pair of fish named George and Martha Washington. The bowl went missing after the Plaza explosion. "The girl said, 'Ashley wants you to have them,' and she turned and ran down the steps."

Elizabeth reports that the goldfish are thriving in a new tank. Ted has trained them to eat brine shrimp from his hand. "George lets Martha eat first," Elizabeth said. "He's a real gentleman."

Several of Ashley's classmates visit the fish weekly and swim in the Childers' pool. "It's a blessing to hear children's voices in the house," said Elizabeth, who enjoys playing Ashley's favorite game—diving for pennies—with her daughter's friends. "I find pennies in the oddest places," Elizabeth said. "On the sidewalk. In my pocket. It's Ashley, I know it is, telling me she's still here with me."

Phone call, Monday, 4-27-98, 10:15 p.m. [unidentified]

You're that reporter?

I'm sorry—who is this?

You wrote the story about that girl, Peta.

Peta Wilder. Right. What's this about?

The baby that got left at the firehouse, do you know when that was?

Uh....well, it's probably in my notes. Hang on a second. [inaudible] Okay. It looks like—no, that's the first placement. Here. March 11, 1980.

Oh, Lord.

You know something about this?

No. No! I was just wondering, is all.

Idle curiosity?

She lived with that rich woman, right? She had a good life.

As I understand it, she shuffled through a dozen foster homes before she went to live with Mrs. Montemayor.

But she ended up in a nice place.

One of her so-called foster parents raped her and broke her arm. The man went to jail for molesting five children, along with defrauding the government. One of the nicer places she stayed, after her mother dumped her.

Who's to say her mother didn't have a good reason?

Enlighten me.

I'm just talking, like, hypocritical, here. Say there's money in that survivors' fund for families, for their pain and suffering and what-not? Peta, she didn't have nobody else. Say her mama's been trying to find her all these years, it just took her a little while to get back on her feet—

As I understand, in order to claim survivors' benefits, you have to prove a blood relation, which will require DNA testing, which can be quite expensive. Especially considering that Peta is already buried, so there's the cost of disinterment, labor, heavy equipment and so on. Of course, as a relative, you'd be responsible for her funeral costs. Peta's service was top-of-the-line—it was beautiful, I was there, believe me—so if you come forward now, you'll have to pay those bills, too. We could be talking thousands of dollars—

Thousands! What? That don't seem right!

Well, that's what families do, isn't it? They take care of their responsibilities.

Now, you don't need to take that tone with me—

You left your baby in a mop bucket, ma'am.

Listen, you b—

[call terminated]

Recovery Effort Ends at Plaza

Plans to raze the building anger victims' families

By Juni Bruder, Herald Staff Writer/Tuesday, April 28, 1998

ORLANDO—Two weeks after the Plaza tragedy, officials have called off the search for victims, citing the instability of the remaining structure and a danger to rescuers. The recovery effort halted at 9:05 on Monday morning, the exact time of the first explosion.

A total of 115 people died in the collapse. Three bodies remain buried in the rubble. "I announce this decision with a heavy heart," said Fire Chief William Herndon. "The lives of police, firefighters and volunteers are at risk. We made a herculean effort to find every last victim and bring closure to the families. Unfortunately, we failed." Tons of debris have been removed from the site to the Central Florida Fairgrounds, where workers continue to sort by hand to find remains.

Still missing are architect Dante Costas, repairman Rocco Purkapile and a homeless man who served as unofficial watchman in the Plaza parking garage. The man, as yet unidentified, was known only as Whit.

In a written statement, Georgia Costas said, "It's fitting that Dante will be buried with the building he loved. We pray that a proper memorial can be erected on the site, which has become hallowed ground, the resting place for so many innocent souls."

Victims' families accused City Hall of moving too quickly to raze the building. "They're destroying evidence," said Rue Burleson, who lost her husband, John, in the collapse.

After a short prayer service with rescuers, Mayor Delphi Owens said, "Our sole motive is to protect those of you who have so valiantly given of your blood, sweat and tears on this site. The ground is not safe. I refuse to risk another life after losing so many." The mayor denied reports that demolition would begin immediately. "We're only clearing personnel from the area. Our structural engineers will make that determination."

Father Lem Wiley, who is leading a drive to preserve the glass wall upon which an image of the Virgin Mary is said to have appeared, vowed to block the wrecking ball. "If it takes a court order or an act of God, we will preserve this shrine to the Virgin of Parramore," he said.

A Day's Work

"Make it quick," Delphi said, taking the chair that Hank pulled out for her. "No time for lunch today."

"But it's our last—"

She shot him a look, and he slumped into the plastic seat beside her. Austin rolled back to make room for Lydia and her calendar. The little table wasn't big enough for the four of them, but they'd been congregating around it every day for the past two weeks.

After this, the conference room at City Hall would feel like the Taj Mahal.

Our last meal. Delphi opened her folder, avoiding the thought. When Eddie came toward her, she shook her head and said simply, "Coffee." He nodded and turned away. She wasn't sure if she remembered how to have a normal conversation. "Let's talk about the wall," she said.

"It's a goddamned safety hazard." Hank loosened his tie, getting comfortable. "I say we go in and knock it down overnight, tell the TV stations the wind blew it over—" Delphi cut him off, glancing past him to the lone construction worker who was gathering up his half-eaten sandwich and hardhat from a nearby table. She caught the man's eye and smiled, a silent *thank you.*

When he was gone, she turned to Hank with a look that said, *You're lucky I let you live.* "Talk to the engineers," she told him. "Figure out how we can move the wall—safely. It could be a potential centerpiece for the memorial. Find out if we can store it at the fairgrounds."

"But Delphi, think of the cost! Transportation, security, liability, it's—"

Austin cleared his throat. Hank had the good sense to stop. "Check with the Morse Museum," Delphi said. "They know how to handle fragile glass. They've moved the Tiffany panels a hundred times."

"You know his royal holiness will make a stink," Hank said, unfazed. "Father Frigging Riley is all over the airwaves with this crusade of his, 'the Virgin of Parramore.' What a joke! Our Lady of the Blessed Bullshit. Am I right?"

Delphi glanced around to see if she wasn't the only one who'd grown tired of Hank's "smartest kid in the room" routine. Her thirty-something press secretary never stopped to question his own opinion; he was too busy talking. In the past, she'd chalked it up to youthful arrogance. Now, she knew that if the Plaza hadn't humbled him, nothing would. "Why don't we ask Father Wiley to serve on the Memorial Task Force?" she asked.

Hank scoffed. "Because he's a major pain in the ass?"

"You'll call him as soon as this meeting is over. I've asked Georgia Costas to lead the advisory committee. She'll handle Father Wiley." To Lydia, she said,

"Get out the call for volunteers. Victims' families, survivors, community leaders, anyone who wants to participate. Oh, and talk to the salvage crew at the fairgrounds. Their job is to find personal belongings, but I asked them to set aside artifacts, too. Someone told me they found a mangled bicycle. That's the kind of thing we want for the memorial."

Lydia nodded, making a note, and Delphi felt a rush of affection for her. She'd forgotten how good it felt to ask for a job to be done and know that it would be, no questions asked.

As Eddie poured coffee around the table, Austin said, "Over by the western gate, they're using a big metal panel as a fence. It's probably something we should save."

"I'm worried about the statues, too," Delphi said. "Oh, and Austin, talk to the TV stations. I picture video screens with broadcast footage, you know? See if you can get the news directors on board."

"I'll talk to Juni about the profiles, too," Austin said. "Those interviews ought to be part of the archives."

Delphi saw Eddie's head come up at the mention of the *Herald* reporter. She knew the poor man was half in love with Juni—any fool could tell by the way he waited on her hand and foot—but Delphi knew he would never act on it. With the Plaza gone, Delphi wanted to shake him and say, "What are you waiting for? Life's too short!"

But she had a city to run, and no time for a grown man's cowardice.

"Lydia," she said, "I wonder if, as belongings are returned to families, we could ask for loans to the memorial. That is, if the items aren't too personal, or too valuable."

"Or we could take photos, collect stories, that sort of thing," Lydia said.

"Perfect. And since the fairgrounds are on county turf, copy the commissioners. Keep them in the loop. How many funerals tomorrow?"

Lydia flipped to a page and began to read. "Firefighters Cass Hueffer and Kevin Potter, morning and afternoon. Oak Hill Cemetery, full honors. You're going to both?" Delphi nodded. "Also Sammy Chiroy at ten o'clock. The church is Iglesia de Dios. Gardener, no local family. His body's being shipped home to Guatemala."

Looking at Hank, Delphi asked, "Who'll take Mr. Chiroy?"

Hank tipped his chair back from the table. "I don't speak Spanish."

"Good," she said. "Less chance you'll offend anyone."

"Come on, Delphi," he whined. "A gardener?"

She grabbed the arm of his chair, and Hank came down with a thud. Close to his ear, she whispered, "My father was a gardener." He winced and turned to Austin, who pretended not to know him. "Listen carefully," Delphi said. "This man deserves our respect. You will stand solemnly—*quietly*—in that church. You will say one thing: *La alcaldesa da su más sentido pésame.* 'The mayor offers her sincere condolences.' Write it down. Memorize it. Got it?"

"*Si, señor.*"

"It's *señora,* you *cabrón.*" She waited for him to write something, but he only stirred another packet of sugar into his coffee. Meanwhile, Lydia's pen skittered across the page, slashing backwards on the accent marks.

"And if I hear you tell another joke in public—"

"*One* joke! To a policeman!"

"At a grave site! Laughing like hyenas!" Delphi looked toward the ceiling, praying for strength. "You're lucky there are decent people at the *Herald* who know how much pain and embarrassment that photo would have caused in print. Whedon would have run it in a heartbeat."

Catching her eye over Hank's head, Austin asked, "What was the joke, man?"

Hank snickered. "It's a good one," he said. "How did Bill try to get Monica out of the White House?"

Austin quietly rolled his chair out of range.

"He offered to let Ted Kennedy drive her home."

Delphi blew out a pained sigh. She might be laughing on the inside, sure, but Hank would never know. Her staff—smart people, college graduates— followed her lead, and no one said a word. Silence, a punishment worse than death. As she watched the flush rise above Hank's collar, Delphi thought, *poor little redheaded boy.* Taking pity on him, she turned and asked Lydia, "What about the arrangements for Dante?"

Lydia flipped to another section in her calendar. "The service is too big for St. Sophia," she reported. "It's been moved to First Baptist."

Laughing, Delphi said, "Dante must be rolling over in his grave." And then she remembered—he was buried in the wreckage of the Plaza, and she felt a wash of shame.

"The sanctuary seats five thousand," Lydia continued. "They've always been good about offering space."

"True," Delphi said. "Remember when Jefferson Howard was killed?"

Lydia's eyes went wide, and Delphi flinched. "I'm sorry, Austin. My mind is in a million places today." She laid a hand on his arm. "I didn't think—"

"It's okay," he said. "They told me about it in the hospital."

"I'd never seen so many uniforms in one place," she said. "From all over the country. My God, what a beautiful sight. I wish you'd been there, Austin. They did right by your partner. They surely did."

Austin nodded. "Back in the day when *one* dead cop was a state event."

The bell above the door jingled, and everyone turned. "Juni!" Delphi waved her over. "We were just talking about you. Sit! Sit! We need your advice." Eddie was there with a chair, a cup, a napkin and spoon, as solicitous as a butler, while the others peppered the reporter with questions about the memorial.

Delphi sat back, watching Eddie, knowing he was happy having Juni near. He rested a hand on the back of her chair as he filled her cup, and it struck Delphi as an intimate gesture.

Juni glanced over her shoulder, murmured, "Thanks, Eddie," and reached down to pull a notebook from her bag, forcing him to step away.

It was neatly done, and Delphi would have missed it if she'd blinked. *Oh, Eddie.* She was tired of feeling sad for people, tired of grief, tired of shaking hands above a grave. Eddie circled the table, filling other cups, and Delphi patted his back, as much to comfort him as herself.

Plaza Memorials Tax Local Funeral Industry

Mortuaries and florists are working overtime

By Juni Bruder, Herald Staff Writer/Wednesday, April 29, 1998

ORLANDO—Funeral director Jed Hawley of the Hawley-Charlemont Mortuary normally handles three funerals a week. "We're a small business," he said. "We try to space out the services to guarantee personal attention to our families." Since April 13, Hawley and his staff have worked double shifts, conducting 21 funerals in 14 days. "Not all of them were Plaza victims," Jed added. "Sadly, people die every day."

The sudden deaths of 115 people at the Plaza put an unexpected demand on mortuaries, crematoriums, cemeteries, headstone suppliers, florists and even airlines. More than 15 percent of people who die in Florida are shipped out of state to be buried, the highest rate in the country. Richard Bone from Everlast Memorials reports that grave markers are on back order.

Connie Siever, a designer for Apple Tree Florist, notes that her supplier sold out of lilies and white roses. "I never thought we'd have a hard time finding white carnations," she said. In a strange twist of fate, Connie went to the Plaza on the morning of April 13 to deliver an anniversary bouquet. "It was supposed to be delivered in the afternoon," she said. "Our driver had called in sick, and I was all mixed up."

Witnesses who reported a suspicious green van speeding away from the Plaza minutes after the first explosion actually saw Connie rushing back to her shop. "I never heard a thing," she said. "I only knew we were short a person, and the day was bound to be crazy. I had no idea."

Justine Dorcas: Smelling the Roses

The Dead Remembered/Profiles compiled by Herald Staff

Twenty-three roses were waiting at the front desk for Justine Dorcas when she arrived for work at the Plaza on Monday morning. It was her twenty-third wedding anniversary. "I didn't think she got them," said her husband, Greg, who forgot about the flowers in the wake of the tragedy. "They were supposed to be delivered in the afternoon." He learned about the mix-up later, adding, "It makes me happy, thinking of her smelling those roses."

As a senior investment analyst at Fidelius Financial Group, Justine worked long hours and was a self-confessed workaholic. "She didn't take the word as an insult," said Greg, who noted that his wife's laptop was a fixture on family vacations. The couple married in Charlotte, NC, in 1975. They had three children: Chelsea, a junior at UNC; Jordan, a senior at Trinity Prep School; and Ashley, a Trinity freshman. The family moved to Orlando three years ago when Justine accepted a promotion with Fidelius.

Justine began her financial career as a bank teller, which is how she and Greg met. "Here was this beautiful blonde behind the counter, and I'd find excuses all the time to go in and cash a check, and then have to write another one to cover it. Finally, she said, 'Why don't you ask me out and save us both the trouble?'"

A year later, Greg proposed to Justine on a deposit slip.

By the time their first child was born, Justine had moved up to management. Greg opted to stay home with the baby. "It was strange at first, being Mister Mom, but we made a choice between my teacher's salary and Justine's. She was on her way to the top." Justine became the youngest bank vice president in company history.

"I think that even though she didn't see much of the kids, she showed them by example what a woman can do in the world," Greg said. "Chelsea started cooking when she was six. Jordan does the laundry. Ashley clips coupons and makes the grocery list. Our kids know the value of a dollar."

On his first anniversary, when Greg started the tradition of giving his wife one rose for each year of marriage, it was a matter of economics. "Roses weren't cheap," he said. "I figured it'd be a long time before I had to spring for a dozen." He added, "Eventually the florists called to remind me every year. They loved that order."

"People always teased us about why we got married on the thirteenth," Greg added. "We never thought about it being lucky or unlucky. It was just the day the church was free."

Securities

Justine hurried across the commons, checking her Day-Timer. Whatever tasks she'd scheduled for the morning would have to wait. The news on the wire was grim. The Asian markets had barely stabilized from last year's meltdown, and now the ruble was collapsing. Who was next? She'd hoped for a quiet Monday, but now she'd spend hours on the phone, assessing the damage. In time, she supposed, the IMF would swoop in and bail out the Russians, same as with Thailand and Indonesia and the rest. Let failing economies fail, she thought. Let capitalism work! But did the World Bankers listen to her? No!

Feeling the beat of the pulse in her neck, Justine stopped. The doctor had warned her about her blood pressure. He'd used the word "stroke." She was taking her pills, but now she lived in fear of collapsing in public, falling ass over teakettle in front of a bunch of strangers. "Take a deep breath," her husband said, which only made things worse.

Justine crossed the street and hopped onto the curb, feeling a twinge in her knee. She was getting too old for heels, but she couldn't stand the look of flats. Nothing said "giving up" like a pair of Naturalizers. Besides, she liked being taller when she shook someone's hand. It gave her the advantage.

Stepping through the dry cleaner's door, Justine prepared herself for an arm-wrestling match. She'd picked up her favorite blouse on Friday, not seeing that a button was missing until she hooked the bag on her office door. Normally she would have marched straight back, but she'd had meetings all afternoon, and then dinner with the Matlocks.

That had been a mistake, dinner with the Matlocks. They were more Greg's friends than hers, parents of Amanda's classmate from school. Davis Matlock, an agronomist at the University of Florida, studied mite infestations in honeybee colonies, of all things. Yes, pollinating the orange groves was a problem, but the man droned on and on! And Justine couldn't think of a thing to say to his wife, Lucy, who didn't have a job, unless you counted taking care of her kids and volunteering.

Because of the Matlocks, Justine had to run an extra errand this morning.

The button, fabric-covered to match the blue silk, could not be replaced. Over the weekend, she'd spent hours digging through last year's tax files to find the Nordstrom's receipt. Now, she wanted full compensation for her blouse, plus the cost of her time and inconvenience.

She expected that Mrs. Kessler would try to lie and say the button was missing from the start, but Justine came armed with proof: a photo taken just last week for the Fidelius annual report. She wasn't happy with the picture and had demanded a reshoot—the lighting was harsh, unflattering—but her button showed clearly, third loop from the top.

Unfortunately, two other customers waited in line. She had to stop herself from barging to the front. Justine took a deep breath, which only tightened her chest. At the counter, a man with a beard unfolded some kind of coat. It was gray, trimmed in gold brocade. It looked antique. He looked like Robert E. Lee. She'd seen him in the Plaza, sitting at a desk in the Gulf Breeze S&L, where he'd probably been busy, stealing his customers' money.

Between the man's slow drawl and Mrs. Kessler's heavy Slavic accent, this conversation might take all week. Listening, Justine suddenly realized—he was one of those Civil War buffs who dressed up in costume and re-fought battles. What a way to spend the weekend, she thought.

Come and try my job for a day.

The hot, steamy smell of starch was making her ill. She checked her watch: five minutes gone. Unacceptable. Mrs. Kessler made a point of learning everyone's name, asking nosy questions, writing the answers down. Not only was the habit time-consuming; Justine thought it fostered a level of familiarity that was inappropriate in a place of business. Customers felt comfortable sharing their personal problems, making others wait. One day, she'd stood here, tapping her foot, while a woman carried on and on about her *miscarriage.*

Checking her schedule again, Justine saw that her son had a swim-meet tonight. Would Jordan mind if she skipped it? Again? Teenage boys didn't want their mothers hanging around the pool, did they? Watching kids swim back and forth was almost as boring as it was pointless, and she had tons of work to do. Greg was going, so at least one parent would be in the stands.

April 13. Something about that date besides the crash of the Russian stock market. Good Lord—our anniversary! How had she missed it? Justine did the math: twenty-three years, not one of the biggies. No party or specific gift expected. Two more years, and she'd have to buy something silver. Probably a watch. Maybe a Rolex to match hers? (Stainless steel counted as silver, surely?) Greg would send flowers, as he always did. On anniversaries, it was the husband's job to show his devotion, wasn't that right? He'd be lucky to get a card.

Something irked her about Greg buying flowers *for* her with the money *she* earned (and the price of roses was outrageous these days) but she put that thought on the shelf. Her blood pressure was high enough. They'd both decided that Greg should stay home with the kids, and all these years later, she had no right to complain.

There were days, though, when she wished she'd married a man with a little more ambition. The gentleman in front of her, for example, held an armload of pinstriped suits, and she spied a Bolgheri label. He must be doing well for himself. She hadn't seen Greg in a suit since...when, her sister's wedding, two years ago? Jeans, shorts or sweats—those were his uniform.

Robert E. Lee was still discussing his uniform with Mrs. Kessler. Justine looked back at the door, counting four new customers in line. She expected to see disgruntled faces, but everyone seemed content to wait. *Don't you people have anything better to do?* One lady hadn't even bothered to save a place; she knelt by the basket in the corner, playing with the kittens.

Bad enough when Mrs. Kessler adopted one stray cat, but an entire litter? The last thing Justine wanted on her clean clothes was cat hair. Really, someone should call the health department. If this place weren't so convenient, she would take her business elsewhere.

At long last, General Lee was making his retreat. The line moved one step forward. "Good morning, James!" Mrs. Kessler greeted the man in front of Justine by his *first* name. She'd been coming here for three years and didn't remember being called anything but "Mrs. Dorcas." Feeling a burn in her chest, Justine reached for her Tums, but there weren't any left in her purse. Mentally, she made a shopping list, in alphabetical order, so she wouldn't forget when she stopped at the drug store after work. "Anniversary card" was first.

"Duh." James, the man at the counter, slapped his forehead. "I left them on the bed," he said, and pointed to the ceiling. Mrs. Kessler told him not to worry; she would mend his pants tomorrow. Justine guessed that he lived in one of the upstairs condos, which meant he and Mrs. Kessler were neighbors. That was different. She could relax.

This close, she noticed the film of sweat on Mrs. Kessler's lip. The woman leaned on the counter, as if she had to sneak a rest. She was short and squat, often out of breath, probably destined for a heart attack, Justine thought. She'd never been here when Mrs. Kessler wasn't working. There was no Mr. Kessler, who'd apparently died and left his widow to mind the store.

Could we hurry it up? Some of us have to get to work!

Mrs. Kessler slowly finished sorting James's suits and gave him a ticket. Justine readied her blouse, her photo—

"How is your mother?"

That did it. Closing her eyes, Justine counted as the man described his mother's cruise to the Galapagos Islands, how she'd had an infection after her hip replacement, yadda, yadda, yadda.

Good Lord, was he crying?

Mrs. Kessler actually came around the counter and *gave him a hug.* Justine stumbled out of the way, bumping into the woman behind her. She had half a mind to leave, forget the whole thing, but she'd invested—she checked her watch again—*eleven minutes* in this fool's errand, and she would see it through to the end.

James looked over his shoulder and apologized to the line. Everyone shushed him, saying, "It's okay!" After blowing his nose and wiping his eyes, he finally relinquished his place at the register.

With another deep breath, Justine straightened to her fullest height. Mrs. Kessler, barely taller than the register, looked up and cried, "Missus Dorcas! I am waiting for you!" Smiling broadly, the woman reached into her pocket and held out a navy blue button.

Justine felt dizzy for a second. Was this the stroke? She gripped the counter. Mrs. Kessler snatched the blouse away, saying, "One minute. I will sew." Before Justine could argue, the woman disappeared behind the revolving rack of clothes, and a girl came out to help the next customer.

Stepping aside, Justine adjusted her purse on her shoulder. She refused to acknowledge the basket of cats at her feet. On the wall, a poster read "Make Your Wedding Gown a Lasting Memory." Speaking of wedding gowns, where was hers? Her mother's basement? She'd never thought to ask. It wasn't as if the puffy sleeves and granny lace of the Seventies would ever be wearable again. Her children's baby shoes, their teddy bears, their finger paintings—she assumed Greg had kept them. He was good that way, sentimental. Greg had told her once that he regretted not saving his marriage proposal, the line he'd written on a deposit slip. He would have framed it, he said, as a reminder of the smartest question he'd ever asked.

Justine remembered—the customers in the bank applauding, her manager popping a bottle of champagne—that she'd wadded up the slip and thrown it into the wastebasket under the teller's cage. Why hadn't she kept it? Why had she said yes?

Behind her, the cash register rang, and Justine watched another customer leave with his clothes. She pressed two fingers to her neck; her pulse kept time with the tumbling dryer. She'd lost count by the time Mrs. Kessler appeared with her blouse in a fresh plastic bag. "As good as new!" the woman said. "So sorry for the trouble!"

"No trouble at all," Justine replied, a phrase she'd rarely heard herself use.

Mrs. Kessler smiled and patted her hand. "You and your hubby are doing something special for your anniversary?"

Justine blinked. With a sense of horror, she felt tears welling in her eyes, and she dashed them away. "It's muggy in here!" she said with a laugh. She wasn't sure she wanted Mrs. Kessler coming around the counter to hug her, too.

Thank you for remembering, Mrs. Kessler. I forgot. Can you imagine? Anyway, my son has a swim-meet tonight, so nothing special. By the way, did I tell you what the doctor said about my blood pressure? Way too high. That's why I've been so tired. He wants me to take some time off, but how can I afford to? Not with three kids to put through college. You know how it is. No rest for the weary, right?

She wanted to talk to Mrs. Kessler, because she had a feeling Mrs. Kessler would understand, but there were other people waiting in line, so Justine simply smiled, took her blouse and left the shop.

Ultimately, she was only three minutes late for work.

Samuel de Jesús Arévalo Chiroy: Field of Dreams

The Dead Remembered/Profiles compiled by Herald Staff

Sammy Chiroy believed in the American Dream.

The 34-year-old father of six left his home in Huehuetenango, a village high in the mountains of Guatemala, to work in Florida's orange groves in 1991. He hoped to earn enough money to bring his family to the United States.

For the first five winters, he lived in a trailer with his uncle and five strangers, picking oranges and planting strawberries. In the summer and fall, the workers migrated north to harvest tobacco in Kentucky, tomatoes and cucumbers in Ohio, apples in New York and blueberries in Maine. They earned about five dollars an hour.

Sammy sent his wife a check every month, though he would never see her again. As an undocumented immigrant, he couldn't risk the trip. He had paid a truck driver $3,000 to smuggle him across the Mexican border.

In 1995, Sammy collapsed while cutting ferns in Apopka, an allergic reaction to pesticides. He lost his job. A local mission paid Sammy's hospital bills and found work for him as a landscaper. He moved in with a family from Iglesia de Dios, a local church. At night, he met with a volunteer from the Adult Literacy League to improve his reading skills. English was his third language; he grew up speaking Q'anjob'al, a Mayan dialect, and learned Spanish as a teenager.

"He worked so hard," said Ida Poulet, his tutor. "I came from my air-conditioned office. He came from ten hours in the sun, riding his bike. He never asked for a break. He'd say, 'Keep going, Missy Ida.' He started at the first-grade level, and by the end, he was reading *The Grapes of Wrath*."

Sammy's work ethic impressed his many landscaping customers, including Dante Costas, who offered him a job as groundskeeper at the Parramore Plaza. When Costas learned of Sammy's illegal status, he put a team of lawyers to work. Thanks to a short-lived amnesty loophole, Sammy was able to become a naturalized citizen, with his employer's sponsorship, last November. Sammy began saving money for a house. He intended to use his health insurance to fix two teeth he'd broken, falling off a ladder in the orange groves.

He planned a trip home to Guatemala in June.

"Imagine not seeing your wife and children for seven years," said Rev. Jorge Piño of Iglesia de Dios. "His youngest daughter was a baby when he left home. Sammy was living for the day when he could be together with his family again."

After his death, his church took up a collection for the Chiroy family to add to Sammy's life insurance policy from the Plaza. The congregation of Iglesia de Dios also covered Sammy's funeral expenses. Hundreds of people attended the service, including a representative from the mayor's office. Sammy's body was shipped home to Guatemala for burial. His crumpled and twisted bicycle, found in the Plaza wreckage, will become part of the permanent memorial.

Not Waving but Drowning

Juni pinned the photo of the grinning, gap-toothed man to her bulletin board. She kept copies of all the snapshots, reminders of the Plaza victims she profiled. In life, they'd been strangers to her. Now, they felt like family, watching over her as she worked.

There was Sammy Chiroy, smiling in the Adult Literacy League newsletter. Muriel Montemayor in a beaded gown at a ballet gala, her bouffant hairdo listing to one side. Kevin Potter in his dress uniform, slicked down and somber. Walter Simmons cheering at a Gators game. Ben Pantier on the couch in his office, hugging his dog.

There was Justine Dorcas, posing for a portrait in the Fidelius annual report. The *Orlando Business Journal* had featured Mrs. Kessler in a story about eco-friendly chemicals. Dante Costas stood with Delphi at the announcement of the Wells Elementary scholarships.

Poor Peta. The only picture Juni had been able to find came from the foster-care records, a black-and-white shot, creased, undated. Second grade, maybe, though the little girl's eyes were already ancient.

At the corner of the bulletin board, away from the others, was Marko Abissi. He held his daughter in his lap, lifting up her tiny hand to wave at the camera.

Stevie's first birthday, the caption read. Valerie had sent the photo, though it never ran in print. The only images the public saw were Marko's driver's license and the mug shot from his battery arrest. There was no reconciling the face in this picture—handsome, laughing, carefree—with the man who'd set fire to the Plaza.

Stevie had her father's eyes.

Stephania Rose, named for her father's twin brother, killed in a famous crash on a bridge.

"Don't let TV forget me," Marko had said. In his final moments, why did he care if strangers remembered his name? Had the thought brought him comfort? Juni wanted to believe, from his last words, that Marko regretted what he'd done, if only for an instant. *Remember me for who I used to be*, she thought he meant. Juni could understand—she'd lain at the bottom of that same black hole, looking up, straining to see light through the haze—but her last conscious thought had been, *I'm so sorry, Mom.*

Sorry for the blood and the mess and the selfishness.

Ask anyone who'd ever loaded a gun, knotted a rope, closed the garage door, opened the medicine cabinet, and they would tell you they had a good reason. *I only wanted the pain to stop.* But here was the catch: The survivors, the ones left behind, would have a lifetime to suffer.

Had Marko given a thought to his daughter?

Juni rubbed her forehead. If she weren't careful, this job would finally kill her. She stared at the photograph, drawing her finger over the faces of father and child. "Marko Abissi," she whispered. "What were you thinking?"

In the empty apartment, the dead man whispered back.

Don't let Stevie forget me.

Plaza Suspect's Wife Signs Deal with Madonna

From the AP Wire/Friday, May 1, 1998

ORLANDO (AP)—The wife of suspected Plaza arsonist Mauro Abissi has sold the rights to her story to a production company owned by Madonna, according to *Variety* magazine. Maverick Entertainment was founded as part of a $60 million deal with Time Warner in 1992. Madonna's representatives have made no comment.

Rosanna Abissi's attorney, John M. Church, issued a statement from his client, who remains in seclusion. "This has been a horrible ordeal for me and my daughter," Rosanna said. "The public needs to know the truth about the man I lived with. We've received dozens of offers from tabloids and TV shows. This is the only way to make sure the real story will be told."

Rosanna has not spoken publicly since April 13, when her estranged husband allegedly set the fire that destroyed the Parramore Plaza, killing himself and 115 others. Rosanna's lawyer said that she is receiving counseling "to deal with the terrible trauma and loss." She filed for divorce in January after her husband pleaded guilty to domestic battery. The couple was married for six years. In a court hearing on April 10, Mauro Abissi lost custody of his 2-year-old daughter.

Abissi, a Desert Storm veteran, suffered medical problems related to his service in the Persian Gulf in 1991. He lost his job at Cornerstone Homes soon after his first court appearance and began working as a janitor at the Plaza in February.

Rosanna's lawyer added that she will travel to New York for an interview with Diane Sawyer of ABC's "20/20." The segment will air in May during the network's sweeps period.

Church said that an autobiography tentatively titled *The Janitor's Wife* will be released in October, and Madonna will star in the movie adaptation. The actress's high-profile marriage to Sean Penn ended in charges of domestic assault in 1989.

Like a Virgin

Micaela traced the graceful lines of the Madonna's face, the deep blue folds of her robe. She'd spent hundreds of hours trying to match the shade of the mantle, ordering lapis lazuli from Badakhshan, grinding raw stone into powder, extracting the pigment with an ancient recipe of resin, lye and oil. Micaela liked to sit in the dark and shine a lamp on the icon to make it shimmer.

Fire had ravaged the triptych first, then flood. Centuries in a cave in Stavronikita hadn't helped the brittle wood. For months, Micaela had labored to fix the damage, a job her mentors deemed a lost cause. Another week, and she would be done.

Her throat ached at the thought. She woke every morning thinking about the icon, dreamed at night of tints and brushes and golden light. Micaela understood why Dante had gone to such great lengths to acquire the relic and have it restored. She didn't consider herself religious, but she loved the Virgin Odigitria with all her heart.

Everything about the piece enthralled her—Mary's dark, exotic beauty, the piercing sadness in her eyes. The way she held her infant son, his cheek to hers, his tiny fingers to her lips. Byzantine icons were usually idealized, remote, but this one had an earthy sensuality that Micaela had never seen in other works. Knowing what she did about the church, she wondered if the artist had risked his patronage, or even his life, to paint this flesh-and-blood version of the Virgin Mother.

He'd committed an even bigger sacrilege with the figures on the side panels. The archangels, Michael and Gabriel, were supposed to be androgynous, the pretty boys of heaven. Here, they were rugged specimens of manhood, wings and all. Over the months, Micaela had nursed a crush on Gabriel, the flaxen-haired Viking on the left, he of the lush mouth and brooding eyes. He belonged on the cover of a romance novel, not a 14th-century altarpiece.

Below him was white-bearded Saint Nicholas, worker of miracles, patron saint of sailors and thieves. He reminded Micaela of her grandfather; he looked like he might wink and pull a drachma out of the Christ Child's ear. On the opposite side, the face of the young doctor, Saint Panteleimon, broke Micaela's heart. In legend, he'd been tortured to death for healing the sick. She couldn't fathom how the artist had captured such sorrow in a few strokes of paint.

The size of the icon itself was extraordinary—four feet high, and with its hinges open, six feet wide. It was too big to fit in the storage vault, so it stayed on the center table. Hidden sensors kept it safe; any would-be thief who lifted the piece away from the metal surface would trigger a lock-down. Micaela had worked in some major galleries in her day and had never seen a more sophisticated security system. Part of the reason she'd taken this job was to learn all she could about housing and guarding a multi-million-dollar collection. The knowledge would serve her well when she became curator of a top museum.

Seeing the icon now, she could hardly remember the crumbling fragments of wood that Dante had shown her on her first trip to Orlando. The figures had been barely visible, obscured by layers of ash and grime. Saint Nicholas was missing an arm. Saint Panteleimon's medicine box had broken off in thirteen pieces.

Micaela had known that the icon's owner wasn't hiring her for her artistic skills. He'd made his intentions clear. She didn't care—the Virgin Odigitria would be the making of her career. It was obvious from the moment she met Dante Costas, the reception at the Byzantine Chapel in Houston, that he was used to getting his way. At dinner, she had watched him charm the driver, the maitre d', the coat-check girl, the waiter. After the sommelier emerged from the cellar with a gift from the house, a thirty-year-old bottle of Château Margaux, Dante had smiled and raised a glass to her as if to say, *What will you give me?*

The only way to handle a man like him was not to give him what he wanted.

When the limo rolled to a stop in front of her house, Micaela had tried not to laugh at the look on Dante's face as she offered her hand to shake. This had been a business meeting, after all. He recovered quickly, pressing a kiss to her fingertips, wishing her sweet dreams. Safe behind her door, she'd been surprised to feel a twinge of disappointment. He hadn't even tried to bargain for a nightcap.

Just one, and then I'll go.

If Micaela had invited him inside, and he'd spent the night, the story would have ended there. In the morning, Dante would have flown home to his wife, forgetting anything he'd offered Miss Singer, the art conservator in Houston. As it happened, he called from the airport, and Micaela was shopping for apartments in Orlando within the week. Now, she was sitting beside her greatest accomplishment, and a man from *ARTnews* was coming to take her picture. The Walters Museum had called—they wanted her back, this time as Associate Curator of Medieval Art.

She couldn't help but practice a smile as she waited for the photographer.

John H. Burleson: War and Peace

The Dead Remembered/Profiles compiled by Herald Staff

In a scene in the movie "Gettysburg," an officer in gray sits atop his horse at the edge of a woods, awaiting Pickett's Charge. Cannon fire explodes in the trees behind them, but man and beast remain perfectly still. The camera pulls back, and they disappear in a cloud of smoke.

"It was his finest moment," said Rue Burleson of her husband, John, who spent a week filming the movie in 1992. A native of Lookout Mountain in Tennessee, John had grown up near Chattanooga National Battlefield, playing there as a boy. As a teenager, he became a Civil War re-enactor and took on the role of a Confederate officer in the Tennessee Seventh Cavalry. In college, he published *The Gray Ghost*, a volume of essays about his military idol, Gen. John S. Mosby. After graduation from the University of Memphis with a degree in banking, John took a job in Chicago, where he met his future wife. "When I saw John decked out in his uniform, with the hat and the sword and the sash, he was hard to resist," Rue said.

While the couple lived "up North" and started a family, John remained active with his Tennessee cavalry unit. His writings appeared in Civil War journals across the country. He and his horse, a chestnut gelding named Stonewall, took part in hundreds of living-history demonstrations. In 1995, Stonewall retired from active duty at the age of 18. The following year, John's bank closed as part of a national merger. Offered a position with Gulf Breeze Savings & Loan in Orlando, John and his wife faced a decision.

"There wasn't much keeping us at home," Rue said. "Our daughter was married and living across the country. The winters were miserable. We thought the job at the Plaza would be less stressful. Little did we know."

Months after John started his new job as manager of the Gulf Breeze branch on the Plaza's first floor, CEO Thomas Rhodes was indicted for fraud. The bank became embroiled in scandal, and John faced a daily barrage of reporters and federal investigators. His wife says he stopped sleeping and lost twenty pounds. "If it hadn't been for the friends he made at the Battle of Townsend's Plantation, I don't know what he would have done," said Rue, referring to the annual reenactment in nearby Mount Dora. "The war became his refuge," she said. "He could go back to a time when honor meant everything."

"John embodied the true spirit of a Civil War re-enactor," said Matthew Arnold, a member of the 8th Florida Infantry, Company G. "He was an officer and a gentleman."

He will be buried in Tennessee, not far from the Chattanooga battlefield.

Louise Smith, Dept. of Corrections, Monday, 5-4-98, 7:30 p.m.

Yes. What's this about?

You were Marko Abissi's probation officer, correct?

I'm not at liberty to discuss the case.

I understand. We already have your case notes, the monthly reports, satisfaction of his requirement to attend counseling and all that. I just wanted to ask your professional opinion about something.

Yes?

What was your impression of Mr. Abissi?

My impression?

Did he strike you as a violent man?

No pun intended.

Ooh. Sorry about that.

Happens all the time. Look, to be honest—and I've wracked my brain on this—I was carrying a caseload of forty-five offenders in January. It's a big blur. Whatever I wrote on the intake interview, that's the extent of my memory.

You didn't write much.

What can I say? Like ninety-nine percent of my cases, he was a nice, polite guy who claimed it was all a big misunderstanding. Gosh, where have I heard that before? These men, they're like Jekyll and Hyde behind closed doors.

All of them?

Well, this one, apparently. The violence didn't stop with his wife, did it?

So he fit the profile of a batterer? Passive-aggressive tendencies, low self-esteem, alcohol or drug abuse, a traumatic childhood, denial of the issue?

You did your homework, huh? Want to know the number-one trait? The ability to fool people. I mean, look at O.J. Simpson. Here's a charming guy who got away with murder. Even after the Polaroids went public of his wife covered in bruises, he still insisted he never touched her, said *she* hit *him*. Right. I know these guys.

Sounds like you don't have much faith in the system.

I wish the system would mandate counseling for the victims, to teach them not to go back to their abusers. You can't be a repeat offender if you're locked out of the house.

I thought a restraining order only aggravated the problem.

Who needs a restraining order when your girlfriend hands you the keys to the front door? I can't tell you the times my offenders have moved back home—*before* the classes started, *while* the R.O. is still in effect. What am I supposed to do? And it's pure evil when a man puts a hand on your *child* and you take him back. God, I wish we could get to these girls in junior high to keep them from hooking up with these losers in the first place.

Speaking from personal experience?

Let's just say I learned the hard way.

I understand the burnout rate for probation officers is pretty high.

Me? You ought to talk to somebody in Parole. They have it bad. No, I like my job. I let these guys know—here's one broad you can't push around. You can tell it pisses them off, but they have to smile and take it like a man.

Is that what Mr. Abissi did?

I don't remember him smiling. Like I said, I don't remember much about him. He called every month to check in, gave me his new address, told me about his change in jobs. No hassle.

It says here the last time you talked to Marko was in March.

Technically, he should have notified me immediately after he was fired from the Plaza, so I guess he was in violation. Oh, well. Can't touch him now. But guess what? He's one less pair of fists walking the streets. That's a win-win situation in my book.

Self-Defense

Juni tightened her fingers around the keys in her pocket. Even the police avoided Westmoreland Drive after dark. She felt relatively safe on this block of empty row houses where the demolition crews parked, but the Plaza blast had blown out most of the streetlamps. In the dusk, she squinted to see address numbers above abandoned doors.

Walk confidently, with purpose.

Like other female employees at the *Herald*, Juni had taken a mandatory class in self-defense. *Make strong eye contact.* Evidently, the instructor's goal was to scare the women into buying pepper spray, which he sold at a discount after the show. *Head up, shoulders back.* She suspected he moonlighted as a beauty-pageant coach. *Even if you don't feel brave, act the part.*

One thing Juni had learned: It was possible to hurt a man in a padded suit if you kicked him hard enough.

Six months after the class, when she'd been mugged in a mall parking garage, she didn't even have time to grab the pepper spray. Her posture had been impeccable, but it hadn't saved her purse or her brother's Christmas present, the perfect Oxford shirt she'd found on sale.

"Mugged" was such an odd, shapeless word for that shattering instant—her wallet and car keys gone, the security guard in his golf cart reeking of onions. She realized Peter was the only person she could call, and he lived a thousand miles north.

After the divorce, Juni had resolved to be more social, the kind of girl who made lunch plans with friends instead of eating crackers at her desk. She saw women leaning across the table in restaurants, laughing, sharing secrets, comparing nail polish, and she wondered, *How hard can it be?*

Harder than it looked. Juni had never managed to assemble a dinner party's worth of shiny friends, and when the gang at work invited her out for drinks, she made excuses. Occasionally, she went to a movie with Audrey, the copy editor, or maybe a concert. (Both liked classical, hated jazz.) Audrey could always make her laugh. One night, leaving a singles mixer at the Chamber of Commerce, Audrey had called it "a waste of makeup."

Inevitably, Audrey fell in love, married and moved to Seattle. (Orlando was always a stopping point, never the final destination.) She was busy with a baby now, a Kewpie doll named Ruth. Juni had pinned the baptism pictures to her bulletin board.

She hated going-away parties almost as much as baby showers.

The year Audrey left, Juni realized that at thirty-five, she'd lost her friend, her husband, and her desire to start again with someone new. She couldn't bring herself to make the investment—the hope, the money spent on clothes and prophylactics, the time spent on dates and happy hours, the interminable give-and-take of "Do you have kids?" and "How'd you get those scars on your wrist?"

Instead, Juni bought a condo and painted the walls a soothing blue. She had her work, and her brother, and a view of Lake Lucerne, and that was enough.

When Audrey called, Juni quickly changed the subject from the Plaza to happier subjects—Ruthie's first steps, for instance—and her friend was happy to oblige.

Life, it seemed, moved on.

At the end of the block, Juni found the address on a mailbox by a chain-link gate. Inside the fence, a cottage sat away from the street, hidden by a bramble of live oaks and scrub palms. She'd have thought the place was abandoned, too, except that the plywood over its windows was new, not faded and warped.

The Plaza explosion had shattered glass for half a mile.

As she opened the gate, a dog began to bark inside the house, and the front door opened. The gray-haired man who stepped onto the porch looked frail—older than she'd expected.

"Mr. Schmidt?" she asked. "I'm Juni Bruder."

"Lucy!" the man yelled over his shoulder. "The liar's here."

Felix Schmidt, father of Neely Schmidt, Tuesday, 5-5-98, 6:30 p.m.

I'm sorry, Mr. Schmidt. Have we met?

No, but I know who you are.

Did I—

You wrote those stories, didn't you? Mastah Costas, savior of the world. The great white hope. How much did he pay you?

Nothing!

Give you one of his condos, did he, like his friend, the mayor?

I bought my own condo, thank you very much, and not in a Costas building. I hardly knew him. Mr. Schmidt, I know this is a difficult time for you, but I only wanted to ask a few questions about your daughter. If your wife—

Lucille can't come out right now. She's resting.

I understand.

No, I don't think you do. Otherwise, you wouldn't be here, would you? It's bad enough we have to bury our last child without you here in the parlor, asking questions.

I'm sorry, Mr. Schmidt. Truly. If there was anything I could do—

Bring Neely back? Can you do that?

No.

Can you tell me why God took my sons from me, and then my daughter— pieces of my heart he ripped out, one by one—and I'm still breathing? Why'd I work so hard to send my little girl to cooking school, to get her *out* of here, safe, away from the freaks and the bangers, all so she can be dead, and those baggy-ass punks are still warming the corner? Can you tell me that?

I understand your daughter was one of the best students the culinary institute ever saw.

Damn straight, she was! I have the medals to prove it. Look here! National Pastry Team, gold. World Pastry Cup, silver. Culinary Olympics, bronze.

Impressive.

She could've worked anywhere in the world.

But she stayed here.

To be close to her mother, yes, she did, but it's not what we wanted.

Your wife's heart—

Lucy'll be laid out herself before too long, if you need the truth, and I only have the one suit.

I hope you're wrong.

Want to see my closet?

No, I mean about your wife. I hope she's with you for a good long time.

Don't bet the farm on it.

I remember reading on the menu that Neely's mother didn't like to cook.

Lord, no. She'd burn a pot of water. If it weren't for Neely, we'd have starved.

What happened to your boys?

They got in the way of some bad people, both of them, and they paid for it. It wasn't supposed to be the same with Neely. She was supposed to leave.

You've always lived in Parramore?

Yes, ma'am, this grand mansion here.

And a fine place it is, but I notice you don't have any neighbors left.

No. Your boss, Costas, he took care of that. He owns this block now. What the world needs now is another condominium! Yes, sir! We'll see how many goons it takes to throw me out.

You've been pressured to move?

Pressured? Try threatening a sixty-year-old woman with a bad heart! When they came after Lucy, I liked to shoot somebody.

Threatened her? How?

Let me think. Foreclosure for missing a house payment ten years back? A lien or some nonsense for fixing a leak in the roof after a storm? Back taxes? You name it. They make it up as they go along.

But they can't—

Turns out they can. You ever hear of this "eminent dough-main"?

Yes, but for public use. Roads. Hospitals. A developer can't take private property—

[laughter] Girl, where'd you come from?

You're saying the city is forcing you to sell your house?

No, the city is telling me what they'll pay to steal my house.

They have to offer a fair price—

Well, now, the word "offer" sounds like they ask, I say no, and that's the end of the transaction. It's highway robbery, what's going on here. All about the tax rolls. City wants the money, Costas says he'll pay, poor man's out in the cold.

But Mr. Costas is dead.

Won't make a lick of difference. Wheels in motion. The world goes on.

What will you do?

Go live with my wife's brother in Atlanta? I don't know. Neely was always trying to get us to move somewhere safe, closer to her.

Where did she live?

She had a nice apartment over by the lake, what's it called, Lucerne?

Lake Lucerne? That's where I live.

You knew my girl?

No, I'm afraid not. To be honest, I don't know many of my neighbors.

Well, Neely weren't never home much. Early morning hours in the kitchen, here to fix us lunch, back to work in the afternoon, six days a week. She said it made no sense, that place of hers sitting empty, us living here—pastry chefs make good money, you know—but I couldn't see us leaving the neighborhood.

What about the Plaza condos? You're guaranteed a unit.

My, my, my, they've got you reciting the party line.

I don't—

They had one old black lady living up in that tower, but the rest is white kids with their cappuccinos. Walk through the parking garage, you'll see—Lexus, BMW, even a Jag or two. Hell, every person of color I know that filled out an application, their credit's no good.

But the project was built in part with taxpayer dollars. By law, they have to provide housing to low-income—

By law. Whose law? What law? The same law that's taking my house?

I'm sorry, Mr. Schmidt. I don't know what to say.

What will you say about my girl?

That she was a great talent, a pleasure to work with. And every night, she sent dinner to an old man who slept in the parking garage.

She did what?

A homeless man named Whit. He ate like a king, from what I understand.

Ah, that's my girl. That's my girl. *[inaudible]* You know, whenever I complained about my troubles, the house and all, she'd say, "Daddy, eat. The world looks better on a full stomach."

I think she was right.

And now she's gone, I hate the world, and I can't eat a bite.

Neely Marie Schmidt: The Sweet Life

The Dead Remembered/Profiles compiled by Herald Staff

This February, when President Clinton came to Orlando to survey the tornado damage, he made an unscheduled stop at the Parramore Plaza. French leader Jacques Chirac had told the president not to miss the desserts at Douze, home of pastry chef Neely Schmidt.

Neely was a member of the 1997 World Pastry Cup U.S. Team, winning a silver medal in the finals in Lyon, France. There, Chirac tasted Neely's signature dessert, a dark chocolate cake filled with Creole custard, drizzled with raspberry coulis, garnished with fresh berries and spun-sugar lattice. The recipe was passed down to Neely by her grandmother in Metairie, Louisiana, where Neely spent her summers.

Neely grew up in Parramore, five blocks away from the future site of the Plaza. After her graduation from Jones High School, she attended the Florida Culinary Institute in West Palm Beach, where she completed the program in international baking and pastry. Neely apprenticed at the Walt Disney World Swan and Dolphin Hotel.

"She could have worked anywhere in the world," said her father, Felix. Due to her mother's failing health, Neely chose to stay in Orlando. In 1995, she accepted a position with Douze, the gourmet restaurant on the Plaza's twelfth floor.

"Neely was an artist," said executive manager Wallace Ferguson. "I often wondered if our patrons didn't endure the first four courses of dinner just to sample her work. We were afraid she'd turn into the temperamental chef patisserie after the World Cup, but she never let it go to her head."

According to Wallace, Neely would have been one of the first to arrive for work on April 13. Three employees died in the collapse. "She was probably making her pecan rolls," Wallace said. "She baked them every morning for the staff."

During the afternoon lull every day, Neely walked to her parents' house to fix lunch. Felix said, "She always told me, 'Daddy, eat. The world looks better on a full stomach.'"

A Plaza security guard added that Neely prepared nightly meals for a homeless man who slept in the parking garage. "She usually sent an extra piece of cake for me," the guard said.

Customers normally had to call ahead to reserve a piece of *Grandmère's Gâteau*, as Neely called her signature dessert. President Clinton called it "a slice of heaven." The family recipe, which Neely never wrote down, died with her.

Rosetta Stone

Marko held the door of the service elevator, letting the produce guy roll out with his cases of lettuce. It was a tight squeeze. The dolly jammed in the gap, and Marko gave it a push with his foot. "Thanks, dude," the kid said, looking left and right. He was obviously new. Marko pointed down the hall toward Douze. There were no signs for the restaurant. During business hours, guests received a personal escort from the lobby.

"Be nice to Neely," Marko called, finding his keys as he walked the other way. He stopped at the etched steel door at the end of the corridor, the one disguised as a piece of artwork. Mr. Costas didn't like the help mixing with tourists, which meant that Marko had to take the service elevator to the twelfth floor and hoof it up the last flight to the roof.

Eying the stairwell, Marco took a deep breath and crossed himself. On a good day, he could make it in one push. This morning, he doubled over on the first landing, gasping for air.

The door creaked above him, and Sammy yelled down, "Okay, Marko?"

"Fine." Marko dug in his pocket, shook his inhaler and took a puff, waiting for the pressure in his chest to ease. He hated the bitter taste in his throat, hated the dizziness, hated being so goddamned weak—but here he was. Gripping the rail, he hauled himself up the steps. His boots echoed on the corrugated metal.

"Sammy, how do you say 'wind' at home?"

"*Kaq'e,*" the gardener translated. Home was Guatemala. In the beginning, Marko had asked him for words to pass the time, but now, he really wanted to learn. His daughter, at two, was already smarter than he was.

Marko coughed to clear his lungs. At the top, Sammy stood silhouetted in the doorway, light filtering through the weave of his straw hat. Marko made a gesture of shading his eyes against the sun. "*K'u,*" he said. "Right?"

The gardener beamed, showing his broken front teeth. "*Bueno.*"

"Hot *k'u* today." Marko squinted as he followed Sammy onto the roof. Before the door could slam, he stopped it with a rusty trowel; the gardeners left it there to keep the lock from sticking. The stairwell entrance was on the back wall of the maintenance shed, wrapped in a curve of the building's blue-green glass. Marko caught sight of himself in the window and tucked in his shirt. As they'd told him on his first day of work, *You are a reflection of the Plaza.*

Looked like the Plaza hadn't slept much last night.

The flat part of the roof was as wide as a football field, with a path looping out from the elevator pavilion, into the greenhouse and out to the ornamental gardens. Visitors rode up from the lobby to see the orchids and bromeliads and flowering cabbage. When Sammy's crew had to move plants and dirt, they did it at night—a huge inconvenience, but what did Mr. Costas care? The man walked on water as far as Sammy was concerned.

Marko unlocked the storage closet and hauled out his gear: ropes, bucket, squeegee, boatswain's chair. Sammy brought the hose and started mixing the soap. As Marko strapped into his harness, he studied the gardener's profile, reminded again of the carvings of Mayan kings in the atrium. Sammy arced a fountain of water into the air and asked, "What's this?"

"*Ej,*" Marko said, pleased with himself for remembering, but Sammy wasn't impressed. He tapped the crown of his hat.

Hat. Bonnet. "*Wonit,*" Marko answered. A nod. "*Soy muy inteligente,*" he added, and that earned a laugh. Sammy hefted the square bucket and waited for directions. Marko looped the ropes over his shoulder and gestured toward the northern wall beyond the citrus trees, where he'd stopped the day before. As they walked along the path through the Japanese garden, Sammy tapped one of the smooth stones with his foot.

Stone. Rock. Rock hits chin. "*Ch'en,*" Marko said. They passed the bonsai trees, where Dow Kritt was watering the big Chinese elm. Sammy had told Marko the gnarled tree was at least a hundred years old. The gardener yelled at Dow, "You're soaking the roots!"

Dow growled back, "I know what I'm doing!"

Marko couldn't help laughing. Same argument, different day. Across the roof, Neely stepped out of the greenhouse with her basket. Seeing Marko, she waved and tilted her face to the sun, showing her pleasure at being outdoors. He watched as she knelt beside a bed and began to cut herbs for the day's menu. (One morning, she'd pointed out the different plants to him, insisting that he smell each one—mint, dill, rosemary, basil—and now, whenever he passed, he couldn't resist burying his nose in the leaves like a dog.) Turning to Sammy, he tipped his chin at Neely and waited for a word.

The gardener thought for a moment and said, "*Yim.*"

"Woman? Cook? Saint? What?"

Grinning, Sammy mimed the ample curve of her breasts.

"Sammy, don't." Marko shook his head sharply, making sure Neely hadn't seen. "*Malo.*" She was one of the truly decent people he knew. "*Entiende?*"

"*Lo siento,* Marko." The gardener ducked his head. Marko knew he was sensitive about saying the wrong thing in any language.

"It's okay, Sammy. Just—she's somebody's daughter, you know?" He'd had this revelation not long after the baby was born. The guys from Cornerstone had taken him out to celebrate, and as they leered at the Hooters waitress, a girl barely out of high school, Marko had thought, "That could be Stevie one day."

It had been a bucket of cold water over his head.

Sammy looked across the roof at Neely and nodded. "*Entiendo,*" he said. "*Perdóneme.*" He'd shown Marko pictures of his own girls at home. One was seventeen and already married. The middle daughter, fifteen, worked as a guide with her brothers at the Zaculeu ruins, where Sammy had promised to take Marko one day. The littlest one (seven or eight?) was learning to weave with her mother. "*Hijas hermosas*," Marko had said, wondering how he'd survive seven days away from Stevie, let alone seven years.

His gut twisted—the custody hearing was two days away.

Hearing a clank, Marko looked toward the greenhouse, where Butch Weldy was setting up his ladder. *Well, well.* The electrician had finally decided to fix the broken light after days of complaints. Butch made a big production out of steadying the legs, and Gustav Richter came out of the greenhouse with one of his orchids. The man doted on his flowers, giving them names like "Shakespeare" and "Homer." He was always showing them off. Neely bent toward the bloom to admire it, and Butch, true to form, leaned sideways to ogle her cleavage.

Marko dropped his ropes by the wall at the roof's edge. "What do we call him?" he growled to Sammy.

"*On-on.*"

"Give me a hint."

Sammy repeated the word, grunting like a pig this time. "Name like the sound."

"Ah," Marko said. "*Perfecto.*" Waving across the roof, he yelled, "Hey, *on-on!*" Butch raised his hands quizzically. Marko gave him the thumbs-up sign. Turning back to Sammy, he lowered his voice and said, "Soo-ey."

The gardener grinned, and Marko could see him adding a new word to his vocabulary. Sammy lowered the bucket on the wall, sloshing suds. Marko leaned over the edge, checking the ground below. Cal Campbell was trimming the hedge along the reflecting pool, but there were no civilians in the drop zone.

Once, Mick claimed to have "accidentally" spilled a bucket of water on a visiting busload of cheerleaders (the "world's freaking best wet T-shirt contest," he called it), but Marko doubted the story. From what he knew of Mr. Costas, Mick would have been fired, or possibly killed, on the spot. As it was, Marko lived in fear of dropping a sponge and losing his job.

He stepped into the sling of the boatswain's chair and fitted it against his hips. Sammy clamped the rope into the roof anchor. Tightening the buckles around his chest, Marko leaned his weight against the line, testing the lock on the descender, watching the rope tighten in the bolt. The concrete moorings ran every fifteen feet along the roof, marking out his day in five-yard increments.

Letting out the line, Marko backed toward the wall and rested his wooden seat on the edge. He looked over his shoulder at the work ahead. April had been a strange month, hotter and drier than usual. Bad for the gardeners, good for him. The breeze was blowing from the east today, so soap wouldn't blow on the windows he'd already washed. This section of the building was relatively flat, which meant a day of straight rappelling. It also meant no curves of glass to break his fall. He'd done the math: twelve stories, 130 feet down to the sidewalk, give or take. Mick had banged himself up but good without even falling—but Marko didn't finish the thought. Reaching for the medal at his throat, he remembered St. Christopher in his locker in the basement. He'd worn the chain to Iraq and back, but he wasn't allowed to wear it on duty at the Plaza.

One more reason to love Mr. Costas.

Sammy sat beside him on the wall and took off his hat, scratching his head. His hair stood up in sweaty spikes. Marko guessed that they made a funny picture: same dark hair and eyes, same green work shirt and pants, one man half the size of the other.

The breeze carried a sweet citrus scent, and Marko pointed to a little tree in a clay pot. Neely had promised him a piece of Key Lime pie when the fruit ripened. "*Te*," Sammy said. With a flourish, he dropped his hat on his head and tapped it down, a gesture that meant *back to work*. As far as Marko knew, the only breaks the gardener took were to help him get started in the morning.

"*Yuj wal tyoxh*," Marko said. "As always."

"You're welcome."

Marko stood on the wall, leaned back and walked down the glass, feeding out the line. When he was far enough to hang, he thwacked his suction grip on the window and waited for Sammy to lower the bucket. After he adjusted the harness strap digging into his groin, Marko looked down and pretended to be afraid of heights. It wasn't completely an act.

"Why do we do this, Sammy, my friend?"

"*Ch'en tumin.*"

"What's that mean?"

The gardener laughed, as if it were obvious. "For the money, my brother."

Letter rec'd Wednesday, 5-6-98

Dear Miss Bruder,

Please forgive the formality of this letter, but it's easier to gather my thoughts on paper. Your message asked me to share memories of my daughter, Frances. The minister asked the same thing for her funeral, and I drew a blank. What does it say about me as a mother that my child was a stranger to me?

Frances was a quiet baby, born on a Wednesday. She was always shy, painfully so. She nearly stopped speaking after her father died. I sent her to dance classes, tennis lessons, anything to keep her active, but Frances was always the girl standing off to one side. Her weight was an issue. There weren't many little friends coming home after school. For her ninth birthday, my daughter said, "Please don't throw a party, Mom." I think she was afraid no one would come. Children can be so cruel at that age. Her red hair and freckles didn't help. When Frances was twelve, I sent her to fat camp, thinking she might develop a better self-image, but she only gained back the weight and more. Her stepfather and I spent our time outdoors, golfing or playing tennis. She was happy in her room with her books.

We hoped things might improve once Frances went away to college, but she roomed alone and didn't join a sorority. I dreamed my daughter would pledge Chi Omega like myself. We sent her to Duke for the pre-med program, or barring that, to marry a doctor, but she majored in European history. I asked her, "What can you do with a history degree but teach, and you're afraid to speak in public?" She had a notion of working on "Jeopardy." My husband found her a job with a lawyer he knew. I understand she did odd jobs and filing.

Lately, we'd become concerned about the time Frances was spending on her computer. We thought the Internet might offer her better career options. She only used it to talk to strangers. I don't understand the concept of "chat rooms," only that my daughter typed away late into the night. How she stayed awake at work, I can't imagine. She claimed to make more friends in three months than she knew in her entire life. I pointed out that she didn't actually <u>know</u> these people, never having met them face to face. "I know their souls, Mom," she said.

I would like to add that none of these so-called friends attended her funeral.

In the days since Frances's death, I have had ample time to contemplate my role as a mother, now that my job is done. There will be no grandchildren to comfort me in my old age, no one to inherit the family silver. Am I being punished? I wonder if the man who set fire to the Plaza was doing the Lord's will, meting out his divine judgment.

These are the thoughts that keep me awake at night. Please, when you write about Frances, say that she was a good girl, smart, well read, and never talked back to her mother. I buried her with my Chi Omega pin.

Sincerely,
Althea Drummer

Missing Plaza Victim Found in Jacksonville

Compiled by the Herald Staff/Thursday, May 7, 1998

ORLANDO—The body of Rocco Purkapile, thought to be buried in the Plaza rubble, was identified at the Jacksonville morgue late Wednesday. His remains had been stored at the facility since April 13. According to flight records, Purkapile was airlifted to St. Anthony's Hospital in Jacksonville on the morning of the tragedy and was removed from life support upon arrival. With no identification, hospital personnel forwarded the body to the medical examiner's office, where it lay unclaimed.

"Mr. Purkapile arrived at our facility with two vehicular fatalities," said Dr. Robert Quincy. "We mistakenly believed all three people died in the same crash." The medical examiner registered the body with the Florida Unidentified Decedents Database, which is available to law enforcement officials across the country. "Sadly, Mr. Purkapile wasn't a missing person," Quincy said. "His loved ones thought they knew where he was."

A routine audit of airlift records led to the discovery. The Purkapile family received a call from the medical examiner's office yesterday. "I thought it was a joke," said Purkapile's widow, Marlene. "We've been going to the site every day for three weeks, leaving flowers, and he wasn't there. He was in a freezer somewhere, alone."

In the wake of the discovery, the Purkapiles have hired an attorney. "This family not only suffered the loss of a husband and father, but also the pain of not being able to lay their loved one to rest," said lawyer Kinsey Keene. "They already held a memorial. Now, they have to go through the whole process again. The neglect and incompetence shown by these so-called 'medical professionals' is unconscionable."

A hospital spokesperson declined comment.

Time Flies

Walter Simmons watched through the window as three kids raced into the atrium. Two girls and a boy. First-graders, maybe? The towhead in front wore a backpack almost as big as he was. He looked like Dennis the Menace. The girl behind him had thick, toffee-colored hair that bounced as she ran. The other girl was Asian. Her hair was black, arrow-straight, tied back with a purple ribbon. Cute little thing, like a china doll. Adopted, most likely. Walter shook his head. People went halfway around the world to get a baby instead of accepting the fact that the good Lord didn't want them to have one.

Adjusting his light, he snipped the silver wire and crimped the ends with his needle-nose pliers.

Two women—teachers, he assumed—jogged past the store with a fourth kid in tow, a scrawny boy with glasses. It looked like the teachers had already lost control, and they only had four kids? Walter was used to seeing busloads in the atrium. The groups from parochial schools were the best behaved; he supposed it had to do with what the nuns carried in their pockets. Spare the ruler, spoil the child, the Bible said.

One of the teachers was young, dark-skinned, with beads in her hair. The older lady wore glasses on a chain around her neck; they kept popping her in the chin as she ran. When she yelled, "Johnnie Sayre, stop running this instant!" the kid ignored her. Walter watched him dash past the elevators, out of sight. The others looked back and slowed to a stiff-legged gallop, that walk-running thing kids seemed to know from birth. Walter had smacked his son for trying it once in church. Rozelle was mortified, and Barry bawled like a baby in the pew, but Walter didn't care. When his kids tested him in public, he laid down the law. Today, you couldn't do that, or you'd wind up in court.

Back at his work, Walter brushed flux on the watch face and positioned a tiny gear with his tweezers. He unspooled a length of copper wire, touched the tip to his soldering iron and melted a drop on the surface. Perfect. He liked the look of this new design, a little bird made out of watch dials. He'd found the perfect beak, a second hand with a filigree point, and a coiled mainspring for the tail. After he'd finished the last piece with wings, a pin he called "Time Flies," Rozelle insisted on naming it in Latin. Who spoke Latin? Walter didn't understand, but she said it would sell. He hoped she liked this one too.

And he wished she'd get back soon. He wanted his coffee. They'd stopped buying the fancy stuff from the cafe across the hall. Three bucks for a cup of Joe, for Pete's sake! Rozelle counted the money she saved by going to Seven-Eleven on her way back from the bank. By now, she could probably buy a new car.

Also, the pink-haired girl in the cafe had a ring through her lip, which was disgusting.

Walter knew he was out of touch, but why did kids these days insist on making themselves ugly? One day, they'd be sitting in a nursing home with piercings lost in their wrinkles, surgery scars running through their tattoos, and the kids taking care of *them* would laugh themselves silly.

Walter sighed. Forget the aching joints, the lousy vision, the getting up five times a night to pee—the hardest thing about getting old was becoming a joke to the young. His son laughed at him for using coffee filters twice. His grandkids laughed at him for not being able to program the VCR. Waitresses laughed at him for mispronouncing names on menus, or paying for dinner with early-bird coupons. Strangers laughed at him for driving too slow. He saw them shaking their heads (or their fingers) as they swerved around him on the road.

Since when was it a crime to follow the speed limit? Walter had worked hard all his life, and he deserved respect, but all he got was rolling eyes and honking horns. Either that, or people looked right through him.

He'd been a decent-looking man in his prime. No movie star, maybe, but he never had trouble getting a girl's attention. In school, all it took was a football jersey and a car, but he'd figured out that a wink and a smile never hurt. Now, if he winked at a cashier in the grocery line, she treated him like a dirty old man. When had it happened? And why hadn't somebody told him? He hated the idea of making a fool of himself. These days, the only time a pretty girl paid attention to a middle-aged man was if the man had boatloads of cash, like Donald Trump.

I could dump Rozelle, cash in the annuity and rake the hair over my forehead.

No, they were in it for the long haul, he and Rozelle. She joked about dying first and haunting him if he took a second wife. He threatened to marry the pink-haired girl, take her as his date to the funeral. Rozelle always laughed, but secretly, Walter knew his wife would outlive him. She walked every day, watched her weight, took her vitamins. His father had died at sixty-two, his grandfather at fifty-seven. Walter had no illusions. He was living on borrowed time. His doctor had said as much at his last physical, so he'd stopped going. What was the point? He didn't believe in medication. Every one of his friends who'd died of a heart attack took Zocor or Lipitor or a dozen other pills, lined up in little plastic boxes. What good had any of them done?

Sometimes Walter lay awake at night, listening to the beat of his heart, which he likened to an antique pocket watch with a rusted mainspring. One day it would run down, and no amount of oil or winding would start it again. In his old shop, he'd kept a drawer of broken watches that he called the graveyard. (A graver was a clockmaker's tool, but nobody got the joke.) At his retirement party, the boss had made a show of giving him the lot—not one gold watch, but forty-three, and none of them running. Walter hadn't appreciated the gift at the time, but it turned out to be a godsend. He'd turned the parts into jewelry, and people called him an *artiste*.

Outside the store, the fat girl from the law firm waddled by on her way to the cafe. Her skirt was too tight; it made her look like a sausage. She checked her hair in the window, and even though she was looking straight at Walter, she only saw her own reflection. It was the same in the old shop, where he'd worked behind a little glass partition. Customers never noticed him unless they needed something: a resized ring, a watchband, a battery. He'd heard it all—lovebirds arguing over the price of engagement rings, a man picking out a diamond bracelet for his wife and another for his girlfriend. Walter had always felt sorry for the ladies who came in alone. The salesgirls rushed the door, knowing a husband was about to be punished, and a platinum credit card charged to the limit.

Across the hall, the slime-ball repairman was back in the coffee shop. Walter wondered how big *his* bill was going to be. He'd been working on the cooler for days. And the way he flirted with the pink-haired girl—she was young enough to be his granddaughter!

Across the atrium, Walter spotted the janitor, the one named Marko, at the guard desk. He was holding a silver package with a bow. Nice wrapping job, he thought, grinning. The paper looked like cooking foil. Too bad Rozelle wasn't here to see it.

He checked his watch again: eight forty-seven. What was taking her so long? He'd have this piece done and a new one started. Walter fastened a flat brass wedge, a part called a balance cock, for the wing. Come to think of it, this little birdie was starting to look like a chicken—all it needed was a comb on its head. He dug through his tackle box and found a tiny escape wheel with teeth on its edge. The name came to him, and he laughed out loud.

"Chicken Little." Bingo.

There were times in his life when he felt happy, plain and simple. When the Gators made a touchdown. When Rozelle made mashed potatoes and gravy. Moments like now, when he made something out of nothing, something fine.

With a grin, he hopped the bird across the table, chirping, "The sky is falling! The sky is falling!" Rozelle would have to figure it out in Latin.

Frances Drummer: Trivial Pursuit

The Dead Remembered/Profiles compiled by Herald Staff

When the law partners at Hood, Pantier and Beatty needed to settle a debate or answer a trivia question, they turned to Frances Drummer. "If Frankie didn't know the answer, she knew where to find it," said attorney Thomas Hood. "We had a contest once with a stopwatch. The question was, how many Beatles appeared in Monty Python skits? She came back with the answer in ten seconds. Two, George and Ringo."

Frankie served as the office's records manager and legal librarian. "Our files were a mess when she started," Thomas said. "In two months, she organized the litigation records, streamlined our advanced client costs and cleared the books."

A student of European history, Frances graduated from Duke University last year and dreamed of becoming a researcher for the TV show "Jeopardy." Thomas noted, "We told her she should become a contestant, but she wouldn't fill out an application."

Frankie was shy, according to her mother, but also smart and well read. "She was happy in her room with her books," said Althea Drummer. This year, her daughter set a goal to memorize *The Encyclopedia of World History*. Frankie's boss sometimes quizzed her at lunch, though he rarely understood the answers.

"Who ever heard of Eochaid Mugmedon?" Thomas asked, laughing. "He was a high king of Ireland. Frankie could remember everything she read, names, dates—I asked her once to proof a legal brief, and she quoted the case back to me a month later."

Her mother added that Frankie loved technology almost as much as history. In recent months, Frankie found a new way to meet friends through online chat rooms. With the advent of the Worldwide Web, these virtual communities are connecting people from every corner of the globe. "She made more friends in three months than she had in her entire life," Althea said.

Based on where Frankie's body was found in relation to her co-workers—all of whom died at the Plaza—it's believed she stayed behind at her desk when the first alarm sounded. "Was she typing a letter? Finishing a report?" Thomas asks. "It's one question Frankie will never be able to answer for us."

Deborah Bliss, wife of Chuck Bliss, Friday, 5-8-98, 9:45 a.m.

Mrs. Bliss, thank you for putting me in touch with your husband's boss. Mr. Piersol was a big help. I shouldn't have to ask too many questions, unless there's something you'd like to add. It must be painful to talk about Chuck so soon after —

Did you know?

Did I know what?

About Chuck and Sandy? Did Bill say anything?

I'm sorry, about what?

I didn't put two and two together until I read your story, the one about people surviving. Sandy said they had a "meeting."

Right. A business meeting.

Not. Chuck told me he had an appointment with Josiah Tompkins, one of his clients. Mr. and Mrs. Tompkins are friends of my parents, people I know. Chuck specifically said that Josiah was coming in at nine to sign some papers. After the explosion, while we were waiting for word, I called Mrs. Tompkins to see if she'd heard anything, and her husband answered the phone. He was so upset about changing the appointment, and I wondered why Chuck hadn't told me, but with everything else going on, it didn't register. Then I saw your article.

Rabbi Judson is a friend of mine. She mentioned that Mr. Tompkins had a premonition about the thirteenth.

He told me at the funeral. The poor man—he thinks if he'd said something, Chuck would have stayed home that day. And of course, I know the real reason my husband was in such a hurry to get to the office, but what could I say?

Are you sure? Couldn't there be an innocent explanation?

The thing is—I can't believe I'm saying this to a perfect stranger.

Mrs. Bliss, whatever you say, it's private, I assure you.

Call me Deb. The thing is, this wasn't the first time. We went through a...bad spell...five years ago. We went to counseling at church. Father Wiley convinced us not to divorce for the sake of the kids, and I thought we were past it, but obviously—

I'm so sorry.

And now Chuck's dead, and I can't even be mad at him.

You should talk to someone about this, Deb. A professional. You can't carry this burden alone.

Guess I won't go back to Father Wiley, will I? *[laughter]* Oh, God, I'm such a mess. Are you married?

No.

Have you ever been?

Divorced.

Was it bad?

The divorce? I guess so. Are there good ones? [laughter] As it happens, my husband was seeing someone else.

So you know—

A little about what you're going through, yes. But my ex is still alive, so I can hate him. Do you?

No. Not really. I'm down to "bemused disappointment" by now. My mom used to say that holding on to resentment was like drinking poison and waiting for the other one to die.

Smart woman, your mother. How did you find out? About the affair, I mean.

I found a hotel receipt in his briefcase. How's that for a cliché? He left it open on the kitchen table, where his wife, the reporter, was bound to find it.

Sounds like he wanted to get caught. I hadn't thought about checking receipts. Chuck keeps his papers in the den—

Don't. You already know. Take it from me. You only torture yourself with the details.

I keep thinking it was my fault. The same old boring housewife in her sweats. Who wants to come home to that, you know? But they're comfortable. My jeans don't fit anymore, and I refuse to buy new ones, not until I lose a few pounds. No wonder he went for the bony career woman with her boobs out to here. Mine are headed south, halfway to Argentina by now. And all I talked about was the kids. Chuck probably thought—

Deb, it wasn't your fault. Sometimes, men don't think. My husband said he was lonely. He said he needed someone to talk to, as if that's all they did. My mom had just died, and I was working too much—but then, he said it didn't mean anything.

That's what Chuck said, the last time, and I wanted to strangle him! It meant everything to me! And I keep thinking about her. Did she for one minute stop to think about what she was doing to me and my family?

My guess is no.

Women like that, don't they realize we're on the same side? If a man cheats *with* you, he'll cheat *on* you. But no, it's like they're competing with us for the same prize. And let me tell you, Chuck was no great prize. He had the charm down pat, but—

You loved him.

I can still remember, our first date, when he came around the car to open my door. I thought, "This is the man for me." But now I see it was the same act, getting me to trust him, like he did with his clients. He used to laugh about it, "reeling in a fish."

I'm sure it was different with you, Deb.

People call him a hero for holding that door so others could escape. I can't help thinking he stood there at that stairwell, waiting for *her.*

Which doesn't discount the fact that he saved lives.

You know she came up to me at calling hours? She actually hugged me! And I'd figured it out by then. Her eyes were red, but everybody from Fidelius was crying, and it occurred to me—good Lord, does everybody know? Are they waiting to see if I'll scratch out her eyes?

I would have knocked her into the coffin.

The service was closed-casket.

Oh, my God—I am so sorry. That was incredibly thoughtless of me.

No. It's exactly what I thought. But you know what? I looked at my kids and realized, how could I damage their father's memory? The kids idolized him. He was their hero. They can never know. I have to go on pretending that Chuck was the perfect father, the perfect husband.

Which he was, in many ways.

Not any of the ways that counted.

Deb, you—

It's okay. I know. I'm making myself crazy. What was your husband's sign?

His what?

His sign. When was he born?

Oh. Let me think. June 6?

No wonder. Gemini. They change their minds like they change their underwear.

Now you tell me.

Chuck was a Leo. Faithful and true. Ha!

To tell you the truth, I've never put much stock in astrology. Six billion people on earth and only twelve types of personalities? It doesn't compute.

I know, but I still read the horoscopes every day. In fact, I saved Chuck's from that day because it was so eerie, after the fact. I keep it on the refrigerator. Want to hear it?

Sure.

Hang on. *[background noise]* Here it is. "Romance will heat up with a colleague at the water cooler. In matters of the heart, now is the time to take better care of yourself. Eat right, drink plenty of water, and take the stairs." Isn't that funny? Well, not funny, but, I mean, it's just so…it's all so…oh, Lord, I can't… *[inaudible]*

Deb, you don't have to—

I keep seeing him in that stairwell, where they found him. Did he die right away, or did he suffer? Was it quick? Was he in pain? I can't sleep at night for thinking about it, whether he knew what was happening, whether he was afraid. I can't imagine—

Don't imagine, Deb. Don't do it to yourself. You're focusing on the last few minutes of his life, as if they mattered more than all the other minutes and hours and days he lived, all the years he had on this earth. Thirty-seven years—that's a long time. A lifetime of memories. In the grand scheme of things, that stairwell was the blink of an eye.

You're right. Oh, you're right. That helps. A little. I might be able to sleep tonight.

That makes one of us.

[laughter] I always pictured us growing old together, you know? Chuck and me, shuffling off to bed in our pajamas, waking up in the morning, drinking our orange juice, eating our bran cereal.

True love.

It is, you know? Taking care of each other.

Holding hands as you walk down the street.

Yes. And opening doors.

Rocco Purkapile: Lost and Found

The Dead Remembered/Profiles compiled by Herald Staff

It wasn't the first time Rocco Purkapile had gone missing.

The Plaza victim, whose body lay undiscovered in a Jacksonville morgue for three weeks after the collapse, had disappeared once before. According to his widow, Marlene, Rocco left for work one morning in 1973 and didn't return for almost a year. The couple had been married for less than six months, and "going through the usual adjustments," Marlene said, when her new husband walked away and disappeared.

"You'd think I would have panicked," she said, "but deep down, I knew he'd be back. I loved him too much to give up." Calls to his family in Michigan provided no clues, and police found none either. "I don't think anybody suspected foul play," Marlene said, "They just assumed he'd left. My friends told me to move on, file for divorce, but I said no. We took a vow 'till death do us part,' and I meant every word."

Eleven months later, Rocco appeared on her doorstep, holding a potted hydrangea. It was Valentine's Day. He'd stolen the plant from a neighbor's yard. "How could I not take him back?" Marlene said, laughing. Over the years, Rocco's whereabouts became a private joke. "He'd say he was abducted by aliens, or kidnapped by pirates," explained Marlene. "I'd call him a mean, cruel man for tormenting me, and then we'd kiss and make up."

The couple, who had three children and two grandchildren, celebrated their 25th anniversary in January. "Rocco said that technically we were a year short, but I made him spring for the silver punch bowl anyway." Self-employed as a refrigeration specialist, Rocco worked at the Parramore Plaza for several days, repairing a deli case at the Dueling Grounds coffee shop on the first floor. When he didn't come home on April 13, Marlene thought history was repeating itself.

"I figured he'd taken another walk-about. Never for a second did I think he was one of the victims," she said. "My son had to explain it to me." Rocco was injured in the first explosion and died en route to Jacksonville, where his body lay in the morgue, unidentified, until May 8. A legal suit against St. Anthony's Hospital is pending.

"Nobody wants to say it," Marlene noted, "but my husband, who fixed coolers for a living, ended up in one. Isn't that what you call ironic?"

Sandy Miner, co-worker of Chuck Bliss, Monday, 5-11-98, 10:30 a.m.

Sandy, I'm sorry to bother you. We spoke after the Plaza collapse? I wrote the article about survivors.

Oh, right. How's life?

That's more a question for you, after everything you've been through.

Well, this may sound strange, but I've never been happier.

Really?

And I have you to thank.

Me? Why?

Your article. I'm getting married, I'm getting promoted, all because of you.

Married? Wow. I...congratulations. I didn't realize you were engaged.

I wasn't. Not until my boyfriend, the love of my life, saw my name in the paper and called me. Did you know the story ran in *USA Today*? We hadn't spoken since he moved to Raleigh, almost a year ago. I was so mad at him. I mean, he had to take the transfer, of course—he's vice president of acquisitions—but I wouldn't leave my job without a ring on my finger, and he wasn't ready to propose. Now he is. Life's too short, you know? We're getting married, and I'm moving to North Carolina.

That's...gee, I don't know what to say. It's nice to hear a good story come out of the Plaza, I guess.

And the best part is my new job. With our office destroyed, the company is being extra nice about moving us to other divisions. I'm being promoted to senior project manager in Raleigh. So you see? Everything turned out for the best.

Yes, for everyone. I'll be sure to tell Deb Bliss.

Deb? Why—what do you mean?

When I spoke to her about Chuck, she mentioned you.

She did?

She knew you two were friends. She mentioned how hard the funeral must have been for you.

Oh. Yes, it was. For all of us.

Did you know Deb well?

Not really. Mostly from what Chuck said about her.

He talked to you about his marriage?

No, not like that. He talked about his family. He had the pictures on his desk, the wedding shot, the whole thing. It was part of his spiel. And he bragged about his kids at every meeting. We heard every detail about Kevin's softball tournament, Leesa's dance recitals. The sun rose and set by those kids. And Deb this, Deb that. The perfect wife, the perfect marriage.

And now you're engaged?

Oh, don't worry. I'll keep my man so busy, he won't have time to stray.

Did Chuck stray?

No, of course not. Look, I don't know what Deb told you, but there was nothing going on between Chuck and me. Is that what you're getting at?

Not at all. You worked together. You were friends.

Exactly. We were friends. Chuck was like a mentor to me. He showed me the ropes. Maybe we took a long lunch now and then, but who doesn't? Look, I'm not stupid. In this day and age, sleeping around at the office is career suicide. It's the last thing I would do.

So it wasn't the fact that Chuck was married—

I'm not the one who took a vow to be faithful.

True. Poaching doesn't count.

Where do you get off—?

Wow, I'm sorry. That was way out of line. Really. I've been talking to so many people, I'm starting to forget where the line is. Please forgive me.

Sure, whatever.

And congratulations on your engagement. I wish you all the happiness in the world.

My mother used to say it was bad manners to congratulate the bride, as if you were congratulating her for catching a man. Although in this case, I'll admit I worked damned hard to catch him. It took me five years and a near-death experience. Not to mention the boob job.

That's dedication.

I think of it as an investment.

One word: plastics.

What?

Never mind.

```
To:        jbruder@theorlandoherald.com
From:      marquis_de_sod@aol.com
Subject:   The Dead Remembered
Sent:      5-11-98
```

A colleague forwarded the profile you wrote of my dear
friend, Francesca Drummer, whom I met through AOL. Living
as we do in the fantasy of cyberspace, it came as quite a
shock for me to learn that the woman of my dreams had died
a very real death at the Parramore Plaza. I saw her face
for the first time in your paper. She resisted the idea of
sending me a photo. We were soul mates, she said, and had
no need for the physical trappings of vanity. Had we passed
on the street, I would not have known her.

We spoke to each other, or rather typed, every day for two
months. I had planned to buy a bus ticket from Edmonton to
Orlando in the next few weeks to meet her. It was simply a
matter of waiting for my tax refund. (There's little income
from my landscaping business in the winter, and many a
lonely night.) That I will never see Francesca in the flesh
breaks my heart.

I write to you because there is a need in all of us to
solve a mystery, and you mentioned one in your article. In
the final moments of her life, what was Francesca doing? In
fact, she was writing to me. I received her last e-mail at
9:05 a.m. on that fateful day. The full contents shall go
with me to my grave, but I will share with you one line:
"Percival, you have freed me from the bondage of my heart."

I take great comfort in that knowledge, no matter what her
mother might say.

A Book by its Cover

Juni liked to hide in the photo lab. The thick, insulated walls blocked out the *Herald's* noise and fluorescent glare like a cocoon. She handed a picture to Eugenia Todd and watched the photo editor attach it to the drum scanner. As the cylinder began to spin, Eugenia settled back and took a careful bite of her sandwich.

"You okay?"

"Yeah." Eugenia tapped her jaw. "Sore tooth." Juni's mouth panged in sympathy. Her new crown ached like a raw nerve. She rolled a chair over from the corner and settled in for the upload. There was no need to wait—the photo would enter the database in minutes, along with its graphic identifiers—but she and Eugenia had a routine. They watched the image appear on the monitor, line by line. Eugenia nodded. "Good-looking man."

"Looks can be deceiving."

Wiping her fingers on her polyester pants, Eugenia typed the cutline on a keyboard caked with gunk. Juni tried not to touch anything in here. Eugenia might be meticulous about her work, but her office looked like a landfill. Stacks of photos and papers and *National Geographics* went back twenty years. When the darkroom had closed, Eugenia boxed up and moved every item, down to the food wrappers.

The old girl had threatened to retire, but Juni knew she was bluffing. This job was her life. Eugenia had started at the *Herald* in the days when stringers rushed their rolls of film to the lab to be developed, and Linotype galleys were pasted up with wax. Now, the photographers were testing digital cameras. ("I'll give you digital," Eugenia liked to say, using her middle finger as punctuation.) Whedon had shelled out fifteen grand apiece for his latest toys, even though everyone knew the pixel quality would never match film.

Eugenia couldn't stop bitching about the new software program she was supposed to learn. Photoshop, it was called, and she hated it with a passion. "If I can put my head on someone else's body," she said, "how will anyone know what's true?" Squinting at the monitor now, Eugenia read, "Charles Bliss."

"Devoted husband and father," Juni murmured.

"Dig up some dirt on him, did we?"

Juni shook her head. "Don't mind me," she said. She was startled to realize it wasn't Chuck Bliss on her mind, but her father. Where had he come from? She tried not to think about dear old dad if she could help it. He'd walked away when she was seven and Peter was eight, leaving their mom without a dime. The divorce papers had come in the mail from California. As years went by,

Juni assumed her father had died—how else to explain the long silence? Friends with actual parents often asked, "What would you do if he showed up at your door?"

Nice seeing you, Dad. Here's twenty bucks. Have a nice life. (Slam.)

A reporter's job wasn't glamorous, and perks were few, but one advantage of working at the *Herald* was access to classified data. Margaret ran criminal background checks on the men she dated. Bob looked up his neighbors' property values. Audrey had found the phone number of her high-school flame, and now the two were married. Juni resisted abusing her journalistic privileges until one day, out of boredom, she typed in her father's name—and there he was. Remarried in Sacramento with three more kids, dead at the ripe old age of seventy-two. *Be careful what you wish for, Juni dearest.* She'd made peace with a sire who wandered off and died of cirrhosis, but this? Alive all those years, walking a different daughter down the aisle, celebrating anniversaries with a different wife.

He'd traded in his old life for a new one, like a car he'd gotten tired of driving.

Juni stared at the picture of Chuck Bliss on the monitor, wondering if there was something around the eyes, some telltale sign that said, *This man is not to be trusted.* She'd seen it in Dante Costas, but then, he advertised. According to the rumors, his girlfriend walked around the Plaza like she owned it. His wife must have known—how could she not?

On the other hand, Deborah Bliss claimed to have been oblivious.

At least Frankie Drummer had died in the first throes of love, before her Percival could disappoint her and break her heart. Remembering his odd letter, Juni asked Eugenia, "What's the deal with our e-mail addresses going public? Some guy from Canada can look up my name and sent me a message? It gives me the creeps."

"It's a brave new world." Eugenia hit the return key, and Chuck Bliss's picture disappeared into the system. "Headline news goes live next month." She picked up her sandwich, something Italian with lots of peppers and oil, and offered a bite.

Juni waved her off. "Last I heard, we were only showing the classifieds and the weather."

"The Plaza changed the game," Eugenia said around a mouthful of capicolla. "We're hot stuff now. Won't be long before the whole bloody paper goes online."

"But it doesn't make sense," Juni said. "Business sense, I mean. Why pay fifty cents for a paper you can read on your computer for free?"

"Because you can't take your computer to the toilet." Licking her fingers, Eugenia peeled Chuck Bliss's photograph away from the scanner and looked around for a place to put it. She lifted a pizza box and found the folder that held the other profile pictures. Juni caught a glimpse of the last few faces she'd delivered: Rocco Purkapile, Neely Schmidt, Frankie Drummer.

"I still don't get the concept of e-mail," Juni said. "Why waste time typing when you can pick up the phone?"

"Long distance is expensive. Get yourself an AOL account, and you can type all day, pay by the month—at least now. CompuServe used to charge by the minute. I had to sell a kidney."

"You know about this stuff?" Juni realized she sounded like a Luddite next to this fifty-something woman who didn't believe in hair coloring.

Eugenia wadded her sandwich paper and tossed it toward the wastebasket. Missed, shrugged, turned back in her chair. "My Gateway tower came with a free trial," she said, "All I needed was a credit card."

Evidently, Frankie Drummer had signed up for the same service, along with Glamour Shots. Juni thought it was wrong to print the photo of a dead girl in a feather boa, but her mother had insisted. Juni pictured Frankie dressed up in her room, typing to her phantom lover in the frozen North, and it made her want to cry. She tucked the photo back in its folder. "So what's the deal with these 'chat rooms'?"

Eugenia snickered. "What do you know about them?"

"One of my interviews—they ought to be simple, you know? Born, died, boom, but they keep taking left turns, places I don't want to go. This girl, no last names, her mother said she stayed up all night, talking to people on her computer. And then, out of the blue, I get this flowery e-mail from her boyfriend, some guy named Percival. The 'Marquis de Sod.' S-O-D. Like he was a sadistic landscaper or something? I don't get it."

Eugenia clutched a hand to her chest. "Oh, honey," she said, laughing. "You don't want to go there. This girl, she was playing with some dark stuff. And his real name isn't Percival. It's Bob or Dave or Erwin."

"How do you know?"

"Trust me. What else do you have on her?"

"Not much." Juni felt like she'd fallen down the rabbit hole. "History major, worked in a law office. Struggled with her weight, I guess. Lived at home, didn't get out too often."

"Online, she was a svelte vixen in leather who liked to be spanked."

"Whoa. Back up. Too much information." Juni covered her ears and scooted away in her chair. "How'd you come up with *that?*"

Eugenia grinned. "My screen name is "38D_vorced.""

"No offense, but you're an A cup."

"Ah, but the horny husbands of the world need never know. And you can bet Mr. Marquis is married like all the rest, getting his rocks off after the wife and kiddies go to bed."

"I'm completely lost."

"It's called cybersex, honey. Don't knock it 'til you've tried it."

"What? How? It's a computer, for Christ's sake. You're *typing.*"

"The joke is how you wank off with one hand and type with the other," Eugenia said, waggling her eyebrows.

"Ew!"

"And you thought *my* keyboard was filthy."

"Double ew! Eugenia, don't tell me that *you*—"

"What else am I supposed to do, all by myself in the house at night?"

"So you talk to strange men...on the computer...about sex?"

"Well, it's more like *having* sex."

"But you're typing."

"Yeah." Eugenia leered, fanning herself. "Oh, yeah."

Juni drilled her eyes shut, fearing that the image of staid, post-menopausal Eugenia—no, too late!—would be burned on her retinas forever. "I have to go."

Eugenia cackled as Juni grabbed her purse and tripped over the wastebasket. "It's safe sex. No strings attached. Anything you want to try, no questions asked. It's the new frontier."

"I'll take your word for it," Juni called back, wondering if she knew anyone at all. She made a mental note to wash her hands at home.

Charles Bliss: The Family Man

The Dead Remembered/Profiles compiled by Herald Staff

Charles Bliss predicted the future for a living. As a senior consultant at Fidelius Financial Group, he advised clients about trends in the stock market and steered them away from potential risks. On April 13, he went to work as usual. It was one of his clients who felt a premonition of disaster.

Josiah Tompkins, a family friend, had made an appointment on Monday to sign papers for a living trust. "It meant peace of mind," Josiah said. "Chuck was making sure my family would be taken care of." The previous Friday, Josiah woke with a headache and a niggling sense of unease. "Something told me to go to the office. Now, not next week." Josiah shrugged off the warning, but when his wife asked for a ride to a hair appointment, he realized he'd be blocks away from the Plaza. "It seemed like fate," he said, "and why waste gas?"

Chuck was out to lunch when Josiah arrived, so he signed the papers without seeing his favorite advisor. "The secretary told me he'd be right back, but it came to be two o'clock, and my wife was waiting." Josiah says he regrets not telling anyone about the fear that haunted him over the weekend. "I thought I was dying," he explained. "Somebody upstairs was telling me to hurry. *Me*, not Chuck. Not any of these other poor people."

Many at Fidelius credit Chuck with saving their lives in the Plaza explosion. As smoke filled the office, he led co-workers to a stairwell, calling out to others to guide them. "The last time I saw Chuck," said project manager Sandy Miner, "he was holding the door for everybody else."

The son of an Army colonel and a Georgia belle, Chuck was famous for his Southern charm and a strict sense of manners. "On our first date," said his wife, Deb, "I remember him coming around the car to open my door, and I thought, 'This is the man for me.'" The couple was married for 15 years and had two children, Leesa, 14, and Kevin, 10. "The kids idolized him," Deb said. "Chuck was the perfect father, the perfect husband."

"He bragged about his kids at every meeting," said Sandy Miner of Fidelius. "We heard every detail about Kevin's softball tournament, Leesa's dance recital. The sun rose and set by those kids."

Josiah recalled a conversation he and Chuck had upon the birth of Josiah's youngest son. "We set up a college fund, and I couldn't help thinking I might not be around to see my boy graduate. I'm sixty-four, after all. I have a bad heart. Chuck put a hand on my shoulder and said, 'You'll see him graduate, Josiah. You'll see him marry. You'll see him take over the business. I'll be right there beside you.' We shook on it."

"Chuck could talk the spots off a leopard," said his manager, Bill Piersol, "which doesn't hurt when you're selling securities. People trusted him. He had a confidence about him. When he told you something, you believed it."

Pipe Dreams

Frankie Drummer stared out the car window, remembering all of the dirty, delicious things Percy had done to her last night. Well, not actually *done*—he'd told her what he *would* do as soon as they were alone in a room together. Percy was coming to Orlando soon, and she would finally meet her soul mate.

Meanwhile, her mother droned on about Slim-Fast. "I packed two shakes for you," Althea said, with a nod to the bag on the seat. "One for breakfast, one for lunch. And then you eat a sensible dinner."

You taste like the sweetest cream...

"Frances, are you listening to me?"

"Yes, Mom." One day soon, she'd have her own car, her own apartment. Would she and Percy live in Edmonton? They hadn't talked about it yet. She'd have to research the logistics of an American living abroad. The thought made her giggle—Canada seemed more like a northern state, not a foreign country.

The Dominion of Canada was formed on July 1, 1867, an event celebrated annually as Canada Day.

"No snacks today," her mother said, turning the car into the Plaza lot. "I wish they wouldn't sell so many fattening things in the coffee shop."

"I stay away." Percy didn't care how much she weighed. He loved her for herself, not the outer wrapping. The only part her mother saw.

They passed the janitor on the sidewalk, the one whose name was Marko. He was carrying a silver box with a fancy bow. Frankie liked Marko; he was nice to her, the only cleaning person who knew her name. The rest of the crew spoke Spanish, chattering away to each other, ignoring her, as if she didn't know what *gorda* meant.

The Spanish language evolved from Vulgar Latin, the tongue of ancient Rome.

One day soon, she'd have a man who bought presents for her, wrapped in pretty ribbon.

Frankie grabbed her backpack as the car rolled up to the curb. Jumping out, she tugged down her skirt and caught her mother's flash of disapproval. Then the too-bright smile was back, and her mother chirped, "I'll pick you up at five!" As the car pulled away, Frankie heard the singsong "Love you!" and she thought, *I'll buy an éclair and a chocolate croissant—no, a jelly donut—to go with my coffee.*

On the way to the cafe, she dropped the lunch bag in the trash.

Dueling Grounds wasn't busy yet, so Frankie was able to order, pay and chat with Archie and not lose too much time. Archie must have played with her hair this weekend; the tint was more watermelon, less cotton candy. Her sketchbook lay open on the counter, and Frankie saw a drawing of the repairman who'd been working on the cooler. Call it "Gross Old Guy with Butt-Crack Showing." Some of Archie's subjects were hard to recognize, which was why Frankie had never agreed to pose. Once, at a birthday party, she'd made the mistake of sitting for a cartoon artist, and the man had drawn her as Miss Piggy.

The repairman crawled out from under the cooler with cobwebs in his hair. He looked like something out of "Tales from the Crypt." The name "Rocco" was stitched on his pocket, but Frankie thought it must be a joke—the perfect name for a guy wearing a tool belt. When she'd come downstairs for her coffee break on Friday, he and Archie were yakking about their travels as if they'd known each other for years. Frankie hadn't been able to get in a word edgewise.

Percy said that he loved to travel. Frankie could remember in vivid detail her last time on a plane, when her mother had to ask the stewardess for a seatbelt extender.

Friendly skies, my ass.

"Venti white chocolate mocha," Archie said, handing the coffee and bag of pastries across the counter. She cocked her head and studied Frankie for a moment. "Something's different about you. What? You're looking good, girl!"

Frankie felt the blush from her ears to her pinkie fingers. Mumbling something about a new shampoo, she made a beeline for the door. A chorus of witty retorts rang in her head. "I'm in love," she could have said, or "My little secret," if she'd wanted to be mysterious. "Phone sex and donuts," if she'd had the guts. Which, of course, she didn't.

Archie called after her, "Whatever it is, keep it up!"

Hurrying past the gift shop, Frankie avoided eye contact with the old man in the window. He sat there every day with that cold, squinty-eyed look—it reminded Frankie of her mother. She wanted to pick up one of the lobby chairs and throw it at him.

There were four people waiting at the elevator—three kids and a little man with a briefcase. They looked so out of place, Frankie knew immediately where they were going: her floor, Stan Diamond's music offices. The kids were still in high school, she guessed, but they were trying to act much older (and cooler). They kept stealing glances at the atrium, pretending not to be impressed. The clean-cut one with sandy hair smiled at himself in the directory glass. He had nice teeth and the cutest dimple. If he didn't make it in this act, he could be Prince Charming in the Disney parade. The redhead, number two in the trio, kept his hands in the pockets of his suede coat and didn't look at her.

All of the kids were nervous; number three in shades and dreadlocks kept a staccato beat with his Doc Martens. The chain hanging from his pocket jingled. Frankie felt sorry for him, and not just because he was wearing leather pants at eight-thirty in the morning. She'd seen dozens of would-be singers trooping in and out of this building, and none of them ever made it to MTV. Clearly, some-one was making money—Stan Diamond could afford the Plaza rent—but it wasn't these kids or their starry-eyed parents.

The elevator door opened, and the man (their agent?) stepped inside, saying, "Come on, guys." Frankie waited behind them, irked. She was all for women's lib, but wasn't it common courtesy to let a lady go first? She couldn't really fault the man, though; she knew she was invisible. If the art chick were here, things would have been different.

That chick, she was always dressed to the nines, even though she worked in the basement. Long hair, long legs, long fingernails—everything about her was perfect. You'd think all the men would have whiplash after *she* walked through the atrium. Frankie wondered which was worse: being invisible, or being stared at like a zoo exhibit? She would kill to find out. She'd make a deal with the Devil to get into the *Sports Illustrated* swimsuit issue. Every spring, Frankie taped the pictures on the fridge as inspiration not to cheat on her diet.

Which starts tomorrow, she told herself. *I mean it this time.*

"Now, I'll do the talking," the agent was saying. His hair was jet black, an obvious dye job, and he wore purple glasses to match his lavender shirt. "Whatever Stan says," he told the boys, "you keep your mouths shut. Got it?"

She glanced at the redhead, curious to see how he would take this order. His hair was the same color as hers, but his skin was clear, without any freckles. She'd told Percy her hair was red, and he called it "ginger," which sounded sexier. Frankie still hadn't screwed up the courage to send him a picture, mostly because she was afraid he'd dump her like a hot potato when he saw it. If their love was true, looks shouldn't matter, right?

She chanted that prayer to herself every night.

The redhead had the prettiest eyes. So blue, and so sad. But he was smiling at her! Just a flicker at the corner of his mouth, but she caught it. She wanted to give him a hug. Instead, she blushed like a cow and looked away. What a moron she was!

The elevator stopped on third, and everyone shifted to make room for two more passengers. She knew this pair; they worked at Fidelius on her floor. She always saw them together. The man's hair looked mussed, and the tail of the woman's blouse was hanging out in back. Both carried cups from the coffee shop. Frankie stole a peek at their hands: He wore a wedding ring, she didn't. *Tsk, tsk,* Frankie thought. *You're not fooling anyone.*

Suddenly, she felt her backpack shift. Frankie grabbed the strap, looking over her shoulder as the tough kid *lifted the flap!* He wouldn't steal her wallet in front of witnesses, would he? But he only pulled up her book to read the title. *"The Encyclopedia of World History,"* he said, looking at her, stupefied. He'd pushed his sunglasses into his ropy hair. His eyes were bloodshot, painful-looking. "You a teacher or something..." he lifted the flap higher "...Frances Drummer?"

Her mind went blank. How did he know her name? And then she remembered that her mother had written it in indelible ink on the pocket. "So you won't lose another one," she'd said.

"I—" Frankie felt her face go hot. "I read at lunch, to memorize. I'm up to the Qing Dynasty." The words came out in a rush. Did she sound like an idiot?

"Hey, Zenas, maybe she could tutor you," the cute one said. He winked at Frankie. "He keeps forgetting the words."

"And the steps," the agent added, glaring at this boy called Zenas. His name would be easy to remember if it ever came up at the Grammies.

"Fuck you, Green," the kid said. The little man's eyes bugged out, and Frankie held her breath. The Fidelius woman turned and slowly eyed the boys, the agent, her. Frankie smiled—after all, they'd ridden in the elevator plenty of times—but there wasn't a hint of recognition in those fake-green-contact eyes.

Frankie knew right away: former cheerleader. It was the look that said *I'm better and prettier and thinner than you, and my shoes cost more than you make in a week.*

Nice shoes, though, Frankie had to admit. Jimmy Choos? Manolo Blahniks? When Frankie started working for "Jeopardy," she'd be able to afford any pair of shoes she wanted.

The elevator finally reached the eleventh floor. Frankie felt as if she'd lived a lifetime in the past few minutes! She followed the Fidelius couple to the left. The boys and their agent went right. The other elevator dinged, and Frankie looked back to see Jeremy Carlisle, one of Mr. Diamond's assistants. The girls in the office drooled over him, but Frankie figured he was gay. He dressed too well.

She supposed the same could be said of Mr. Costas, but he was rich, so it didn't count. Besides, she'd seen him staring at the art chick. Definitely straight.

Today, Jeremy wore a skinny black suit and a crisp white shirt, no tie. He stopped in the entryway beside the mirrored sculpture, newly installed this month. Frankie thought he was reading the plaque (she could have told him its name was "Narcissus") but he was only checking his reflection. No need. He looked like a rock star. Next to him, the agent looked like a used-car salesman. *Take notes, boys,* Frankie thought, watching the youngsters puff up their chests— and then she caught a different look pass between Jeremy and the sandy-haired boy who'd winked at her. *Oh, so that's how it goes.* Poor kid. She hoped the future teen idol wouldn't crack under the pressure, pretending to like girls.

Seeing the polished brass sign for "Hood, Pantier and Beatty" always gave her a little thrill. Her place of business! As she opened the door, Tig loped out to greet her. Frankie reached into her drawer for a dog biscuit. "Hi, Ben!" she called. He was probably still asleep on the couch. Amelia would be helping Beatty get ready for court. Olive, the office manager, was in the kitchen, making coffee. Frankie had tried to make friends with her, but the woman was a brick wall. Judging from the way she covered the phone when she talked, Frankie got the impression Mr. Olive was a jerk. Frankie only ever saw Olive talking to one other lady, the accountant from Fidelius, the smoker. Frankie would walk a mile for a Krispy Kreme donut, but a cigarette? No way.

Thomas was out of town, which meant nobody would talk to Frankie today. The law clerks thought she was dumb. Just because she stammered when they asked their whiny legal questions didn't mean she wasn't smart, just conversationally challenged. That's why she liked talking to Percy and her friends online. Her replies were lightning-quick on the screen, and she bantered with the best of them. She always had people Rolling-On-the-Floor-Laughing.

In private, Percy did most of the typing, but *lordy*—all she did was <moan>.

She would send him an e-mail and tell him about her morning. So much had happened, and it was only nine o'clock! She'd met a boy band, sort of, and one of the boys had winked at her. Okay, so he was gay—he hadn't ignored her. It had to be Percy's doing. He made her feel beautiful, and even strangers noticed. She had a glow about her. Maybe she would skip the donuts today—

The fire alarm sounded, an ear-splitting buzz that rattled her brain.

Ben staggered into the doorway, looking rumpled and dazed.

Beatty yelled down the hall, "For fuck's sake, not today!"

The fire department had held a big drill the week before, forcing everyone to walk downstairs and out to the commons. People stood around for twenty minutes, counting heads, a total waste of time, and it was sweaty hot besides. No way was she going down eleven flights again. The stairwells smelled funky, and her knees still ached from that exercise.

Olive ran out of the kitchen and grabbed her purse, but when she saw Frankie still at her desk, she hesitated. "Shouldn't we go?" she yelled above the din.

"Just wait," Frankie shouted, sending out her never-ending love to Percy. "It'll be over in a minute."

Plaza Suspect's Wife Saw Warning Signs

From the AP Wire/Tuesday, May 12, 1998

NEW YORK (AP)—In her first interview since the Plaza tragedy, the estranged wife of suspected arsonist Mauro Abissi said she warned law enforcement officials that her husband was a danger to the public.

"Nobody would listen to me," Rosanna Abissi told Diane Sawyer on ABC's "20/20," which aired Sunday night. "He should have been locked up."

At the time of the Plaza attack, Mauro Abissi was serving one year of probation on a charge of domestic battery. Police responded to a 911 call at the Abissi residence on Dec. 26, 1997, a night Rosanna described as "sheer hell."

She noted that her husband's violent behavior had worsened during the last months of their six-year marriage. "I had to hide the bills," she said. "You never knew what would set him off. I think it had something to do with the war."

Abissi served with the U.S. Army in Operation Desert Storm and returned from the Persian Gulf in 1991 with lingering medical problems. "The doctors treated him for headaches and a lung infection," Rosanna said. "They completely ignored the mental issues."

She added that her husband's depression worsened after their separation. "I didn't trust him alone with my daughter," said Rosanna, explaining why she filed for sole custody of two-year-old Stephania Rose. The motion was granted four days before the Plaza attack.

"Marko went insane," said Rosanna, recounting the scene in which officers had to remove her husband from the courtroom. "He was screaming, 'Kill me! Kill me now!' It was awful. I felt sorry for the bailiffs."

Responding to allegations of child abuse filed with the Florida Department of Children and Families, Rosanna said, "My daughter's privacy is what's important. People forget she lost her father. She's a victim, too. We both are."

Breaking down during the 20-minute interview, Rosanna described a domineering husband who refused to let her work outside the home after the birth of their daughter. "He left me alone with the baby," she said. "He stayed out late every night. We didn't have money for groceries."

She refused to comment on a movie deal with USA Networks.

Asked whether she could have predicted her husband's fatal actions on April 13, Rosanna said, "I told police that Marko threatened to strangle me, which was why I asked for the restraining order. The police are there to protect the public, right? The judge slapped him on the wrist and sent him to a shrink. A lot of good that did."

Diane Sawyer quoted a letter from the office of Judge Selah Lively of the Ninth Judicial Circuit Court of Florida: "The defendant's plea agreement was consistent with statutory sentencing guidelines for a first-time offense."

Rosanna replied, "They can say what they want. If Marko had been in jail, none of these people would be dead."

Orlando Police Department Log, 12-27-97

212 Roxanne Drive: Domestic battery. Victim reports husband pushed her into a wall before exiting the home. Reporting party refused medical. Couple shares a common child; emergency restraining order issued. Scene secure. 10:04 p.m.

Officer Ernie Hyde, OPD Parramore HQ, Tuesday, 5-12-98, 7:30 p.m.

Thanks for getting back to me, Ernie.

I just came from the hospital. Ballard told me to bite the bullet and talk to you.

Am I that bad? I'll try to go easy on you. How's the old crank doing?

Okay, I guess. The skin graft didn't take because of the infection, so the doctors won't be able to try again for a few more weeks. He'll be wearing his ass over his eyebrows before it's all said and done.

Like Joan Rivers.

Yeah. I told him it'd be an improvement. He told me to go to hell. And they say adversity changes people.

You can only abuse him as long as he's bedridden. Once he's up and around, look out.

I sleep with a firearm. So how do we do this? What do you need on Web?

Before we get to him, can I ask you a question? I pulled the records on the domestic dispute at the Abissi house last December.

Whoa. Where'd that come from?

It's research I'm doing on the side. Do you remember—

December? You know how many domestics we get a month?

Two hundred, two-fifty, something like that.

Wow. That many?

Here's the thing. It seems like an incredible twist of fate that one of the officers responding to the 911 call on Roxanne Drive in December ended up dead at the Plaza.

What did you say?

A twist of fate?

No. The street.

Roxanne Drive.

Hang on—you mean Abissi, the same son of a bitch? Fuck me. I didn't put it together. We never saw the guy, so I didn't—Web and me? Jesus H. Christ.

So you remember the call?

Yeah, of course, I remember. The street, and Web singing. Fucking karaoke nightmare. Pardon my French.

Your partner was singing on the job?

The address came in, and he's singing "Rox-anne!" at the top of his lungs, real high, you know how Sting does? When we pulled up, I was having a hard time keeping a straight face. This is serious, you know? We're law enforcement.

"The officer on duty was heard giggling."

Exactly. So we get out of the car, up the walk, door's wide open, lights on. Gal's on the front stoop crying. The closer we get, the higher the geyser. No neighbors, nobody peeking through the curtains, so we knew something was up.

No witnesses?

No audience. We take her inside, sit her down, get her talking, and the husband's been gone for like an hour. Huh? The call only came in six minutes ago. What the hell was she doing all that time? So I ask about injuries, which I'm not seeing any. No bruises, no buttons undone, none of that black goop under her eyes. She said her shoulder hurt, but she wouldn't let us call the EMTs.

Had her husband been violent before?

She said it wasn't the first time. Told us he'd threatened to strangle her.

Why do you say it like that?

My wife threatens to strangle me every time I leave my jockeys on the floor.

That's motive for murder.

My point exactly.

You don't think she was injured?

Pissed off, more like.

Wouldn't you be mad if someone slapped you around?

Hey, don't get me wrong—I've been at the table with a lady whose boyfriend took out her eye with a fork. I know what battery looks like. If your husband ticks you off and you want his ass in a sling, call a lawyer. Don't waste my time.

Why would she lie?

You tell me. Not my job to figure out. Up to the prosecutor. We took her statement, issued the R.O., checked the windows, checked the locks. She said something about custody, wanting to keep the baby away from her husband. Web says, "What baby?" and she looks around like, fuck if I know. So Web goes upstairs and finds the kid asleep on the floor in front of the tube.

Stevie?

Yeah, that's right. Web started singing Fleetwood Mac later. I forgot. Anyway, what did the macho cop do? He changed her diaper and put her to bed.

He had three kids, right?

And another on the way. Due in January. You do the math.

Oh, wow.

Yeah. It was, what, four days before we found him? Faith, his wife, she'd just come back from the doctor.

Having to plan a funeral in that condition—I can't imagine.

I think that's what got her through. As for me, Jack Daniels was the ticket. *[inaudible]* That was my fifth funeral by then.

Too many.

Yes, ma'am. I asked the priest to play "Roxanne," but he wouldn't go for it. Hey, is this the kind of stuff you needed? We talked about work, not so much about Web.

No, this is perfect. I'm talking to Faith this afternoon.

Tell her I'll be over later. She said the water heater's on the fritz.

You protect the peace and fix appliances, too?

No, but I can make a good show of banging the tools before we call the plumber.

Wayne Elijah Browning: Good Cop, Bad Singer

The Dead Remembered/Profiles compiled by Herald Staff

Wayne Elijah Browning, known as "Web" to his friends, loved karaoke. "Worst singer in the world," said his police partner, Ernie Hyde. "When he sang the kids to sleep," his wife recalled, "they begged him to stop." Web and Faith Matheny Browning had three children: Michael, 10, Rory, 8, and Caitlin, 3. A fourth child is due in January. Faith's doctor confirmed her pregnancy on April 17, the day her husband's body was recovered from the ruins of the Plaza.

"He was doing what he loved," Faith said. Recipient of six service awards, Web joined the Orlando Police Department in 1991. He started his law enforcement career in the New York borough of Queens. The Browning family moved to Florida to be near Faith's family. Web's mother died last year.

"Web always wanted to be a cop, ever since 'Hill Street Blues,'" said his sister, Victoria. "My mom tried to talk him out of it. She hated guns. He promised he'd only write traffic tickets." In his weekly calls home, Web faithfully reported his speeding tally. "He'd say, 'Ma, you wouldn't believe these crazy Florida drivers,'" Victoria remembered. "We didn't tell her about the hostage thing. Mom had a weak heart."

In 1994, Web was one of the first officers on the scene when the suspect in the traffic-stop shootings of Lt. Austin Dabney and Cpl. Jefferson Howard barricaded himself inside a home, taking a woman and two children hostage. Web climbed a fence to rescue a third child from the back yard, cutting his arm in the process. The injury required 37 stitches. An Associated Press photograph showed a bleeding Web holding three-year-old Tyson until the suspect surrendered and the boy could be reunited with his mother, Emma Lee Gibbs.

"He was like a superhero," said Emma, whose children became friends with Web after the standoff. "When his cruiser pulled up, all the kids came running." Web's partner maintains the weekly visits. "Tyson keeps asking where Web is," Ernie said. "I don't have the heart to tell him."

Faith added that her children always used to listen for sirens. "They would yell, 'Daddy!' Now we hear that sound, and the silence in the house is deafening."

Among those entrusted with public safety—police and firefighters alike— there's an unwritten code to watch over the families of fallen comrades. Faith believes her husband would be proud of the job his friends are doing. "I look out in the yard, and there's one of the guys cutting the grass or washing the car," she said. "We had five uniforms at Michael's baseball game last week." Faith expects a fight over which officer will be in the delivery room when the baby is born, but she hopes her sister wins.

"The waiting room will be swarming with law enforcement," Faith said. "And plenty of cigars." The baby, a boy, will be named Elijah.

A Saving Fear

Faith woke in the dark, disoriented. She moved closer to Web's side of the bed, craving his warmth—and then she remembered. The sheets were cold, and Web was lying in the ground. She'd watched his casket being lowered into the hole, watched as men shoveled dirt on top of it, watched a backhoe finish the job, and still, the thought wouldn't hold.

Buried. Dead. Gone.

She burrowed deeper into the blankets, one hand over her mouth, the other clenched to her chest. The pain—it felt as if someone had driven a frozen spike into her heart, and now her ribs were knitting around it.

Time heals all wounds. That's what people kept telling her. As if, in time, she'd forget what wholeness felt like, and she would get used to being broken. *Go back to earth and forget you knew how to fly.*

How could you leave me, Web?

They had known how lucky they were, finding each other. That recognition: *There you are.* And she had no regrets, as some of the other wives did, about not telling Web she loved him. She told him every day, and kissed him goodbye. On the morning of the fire, Maggie Heston had scolded her husband, Roger, for leaving his cereal dish in the sink, and now she couldn't stop saying, "I was such a bitch to him!" No one contradicted her. She'd treated Roger like a child—a grown man, one who risked his life for a living—and he let her. It was something Faith and Web had never understood, how couples belittled each other at parties, like some kind of sport.

Truth be told, they'd felt a little smug about it, curled around each other in bed.

But Faith had thought, by being *grateful* for her husband, by getting down on her knees each night and thanking God for such a man, that she could keep him safe.

Hey, babe, while you're down there, why don't you show me just how grateful you are?

Faith moved her hand lower, trying to imagine the tiny life taking root inside her. The thought of this child was no more real to her than the death of its father. She'd gotten pregnant the night of Web's nightmare, she was sure of it. Web had been so shaken, he couldn't go back to sleep, and then neither could she. Her husband rarely remembered his dreams, so the fact that this one was so detailed, and so clear—it rattled them both. They'd cut their teeth on Irish premonitions.

In the dream, Web was climbing Mount Everest, a trip he never would have taken in waking life, for as much as he hated snow. He was alone at the top, he said, alone and freezing cold. The mountain was deathly still, without any wind. In the black sky above, a single star. Below, a veil of clouds, like smoke. The only sound he heard was his breath. "I was so scared, Faith," he told her, "and everything hurt." She hugged him tight to stop the bed from shaking. "I knew there was no way down."

"That's it. No more ice cream before bed," she'd said to make him laugh, and then she distracted him with sex, but in her head, she chanted a feverish prayer: *Holy Mary, Mother of God, protect him, please, I beg you. Holy Mary, Mother of God...*

How greedy she had been.

Faith slid out of bed and knelt on the cold, hard floor, begging God's forgiveness for her sins, but she knew she was too late.

Web had already been taken from her.

Eugene Carman, busboy, Douze restaurant, Thursday, 5-14-98, 10:30 a.m.

You didn't bring the police, did you?

No, I—you're Eugene, aren't you? I'm Juni. We spoke on the phone.

Are they coming to arrest me?

No, of course not. At least, I don't think so. Is it all right if I come in?

Oh. Yeah. Sure. Sorry. Watch that, whatever it is. Shit, every time the doorbell rings, I think it's the cops. All I do is walk the floor. I'm going fucking nuts.

Why would you be arrested?

I can't—oh, Jesus. *[inaudible]*

Be careful! Eugene, sit down. Please. You'll hurt yourself. You've been drinking, haven't you? Let me get you a glass of water. Do you have any aspirin?

Above the sink.

When's the last time you ate?

I don't remember.

How about a banana? This one doesn't look too ripe.

It's my roommate's.

I'm sure he won't mind. Here. Try this. I think potassium's good for…something. Now, tell me what's going on.

I started a fire, is fucking what!

You—I'm sorry, do you mind if I sit down?

Oh, hey, I'm a total fuckwad. Here, move those newspapers. I've been reading everything, you know? It's been a fucking month! I keep thinking somebody'll figure it out sooner or later. You people are smart, right? There's evidence and shit.

Figure out what? You set the fire at the Plaza?

Yeah, in the kitchen.

Oh, you mean the restaurant fire. That's—I haven't heard much about that one. It probably didn't—

That's why Abner didn't get out, or Neely or Lucius either. They were there, all three of them. Oh, God! I—

Abner? Oh, you mean—Eugene, start at the beginning. Tell me what happened.

I was frying an egg, that's what! We went out after work on Sunday night, and I got home around, like, four, and I was still, you know, wasted. I mean, I never went to bed, and Wallace—he's the boss—Wallace always rides my ass, and setting tables is bad enough when you're straight, and that stupid necktie was choking me to death, so I thought food would be good, right?

Right.

And Neely's pecan rolls wouldn't be done for like, seven minutes, which was way too long, so I threw an egg in the pan, and then the fire alarm went off, so I went to the door, and people were running and shit, so I figured, hey, good time to catch a smoke, which I did, and then things got *fucked up!*

Totally.

Yeah! And it wasn't until, like, four hours later, when I'm finally home, and I'm still hungry and shit, so I thought, an egg sounds good, and then it was like, oh shit! I left that pan burning on the stove!

But you don't know it caught fire.

It was either that or the oven, and the pecan rolls never caught fire before, did they? Neely would have been watching them. She told me, "You go ahead. I'll be here when you get back." That's what she said. If she would've come outside with me—and Abner had the hots for her, which is why he stayed, and they both—

Eugene, you don't know that the kitchen fire had anything to do with them.

Why didn't they get out?

A hundred and fifteen people didn't make it out, Eugene. Listen, I've talked to the investigators. No one said a word about the kitchen fire. The fire in the basement, the explosions—they were enough to level the building. Trust me.

You mean I didn't kill anybody?

Of course not. Did your kitchen have a fire extinguisher?

Yeah, like a bunch.

Neely was a trained chef. Don't you think she knew her way around a grease fire?

I guess so.

We may never know why she and Abdur didn't make it out, but I'm pretty sure you can't blame a fried egg.

Really? You mean, seriously? Oh, Jesus, it's been— *[inaudible]* I wanted to kill myself!

I know. Why don't you tell me about Abdur—I mean, Abner. That's why I came.

Oh, man, Abner, he was the best. Like, the greatest ever.

How long did you know him?

I don't know. Maybe six, seven weeks? I started just before Thanksgiving, so about that long.

Last November? That would be…five months ago.

Five months? Really? Wow. Time flies, I guess. That long? Huh. I was supposed to get a raise after ninety days.

It must have slipped Wallace's mind.

That really blows, you know? I was busting my ass—

So you and Abner became friends?

Yeah. It's not like we partied together or anything. He was into that Muslim crap, being pure and shit. He was always lecturing me about how I polluted my body and my brain and whatever. His dishwashing sermons, I called them. But we goofed around, you know? When he got behind on the dishes, I'd load the racks. He blasted me with the hose, I ran his English book through the rinse. Wallace got pissed because the paper clogged the drain, but, hey.

Abner was studying English?

Yeah. Not like the language—he spoke English, and Swahili, whatever they speak where he comes from. No, he was studying English, like the writer stuff. Baywatch, Baywolf, something like that.

You mean "Beowulf"?

Hey, I don't know. Abner said it had monsters and stuff.

Right. Grendel. I think that story scares most students away from English.

Oh, shit! I totally forgot about Grendel! I don't even know what Grendel eats!

Pigs, sheep, drunken men? I don't—

No, Abner's dog! Do you know if anybody's taking care of him? I totally forgot. Just like the fucking egg! Jesus, I am a fucking loser!

Wait—Abner has a dog named Grendel?

Right!

He must have friends or family to look after—

Not here. They're all back in India or Ethiopia or wherever.

I think it's Pakistan.

Can you check on Grendel? I can't keep a dog here. My landlord's an inch away from evicting my ass already.

I don't know—

That would be, like, fucking awesome. I don't have a car. Abner lived over by the Valencia campus so he could walk to class. They don't let you bring dogs on the bus. Hey, uh, now that I know the cops aren't hot on my trail, I've got some errands to run, if you get my drift.

Oh, right. Thank you for talking to me.

Say, you don't pay for interviews, do you? Some spare cash for...whatever?

No. Sorry.

Never hurts to ask, though, right? Hey, you can't bust me or discriminate me or shit, just talking about doing something that's not, like, legal, can you?

No. A reporter can't be compelled to testify or provide information to the state.

What's that mean in, like, English?

My lips are sealed.

Abdur-Rahman Peethala: A Hero's Quest

The Dead Remembered/Profiles compiled by Herald Staff

On his first day at Douze, the gourmet restaurant on the Plaza's twelfth floor, Abdur Peethala told his boss, "I will be the best dishwasher you ever had." Executive manager Wallace Ferguson says that Abdur lived up to his promise. "He was always here early, always ready to work hard," Wallace said. "We never had a complaint about dirty flatware."

Abdur worked full time at Douze while attending classes on the east campus of Valencia Community College. This spring, he would have received his A.A. degree in English, which guaranteed his acceptance as a junior at the University of Central Florida. "He wanted to make a name for himself as a writer," said his composition professor, Patricia Newcomer. "It was his quest."

Abdur's friend and co-worker Eugene Carman added that Abdur named his dog after a character in the epic poem "Beowulf." The dog, a three-legged fox terrier named Grendel, is being cared for by Abdur's landlord, Ralph Burchard, until a new home can be found.

Valencia teachers and administrators took up a collection to bury Abdur, who was estranged from his family in Pakistan. "As I understand, he refused an arranged marriage, and his parents disowned him," Professor Newcomer said. "The boy had a romantic streak."

Abdur remained a devout Muslim, encouraging his friends to abstain from drugs, alcohol and gambling. "His dishwashing sermons," Eugene recalled. "He was all about being pure." Wallace noted that his best dishwasher helped his worst line cook, Lucius Atherton, stay sober for the last six months of his life. "Lucius finally cleaned up and got his act together. We were ready to fire him. He would have been long gone if it weren't for Abdur."

Wallace adds that Abdur had one vice: pecan rolls. "Our pastry chef baked a fresh batch every morning," Wallace said. "Abdur was always first in line." According to his professor, sweets also figured in an epic poem he was writing. "It was about a Pakistani immigrant who falls in love with an American girl in a bakery," Professor Newcomer said. "He couldn't ask her to marry him, not until he was worthy. So he bought a pastry every morning and loved her from afar. It was wonderful, the parts he showed me."

According to Abdur's landlord, all of his papers and belongings were sold or thrown away to make room for a new tenant.

The Valencia English Department selected the last lines of "Beowulf" to be carved on Abdur's headstone:

> *The mildest of men*
> *and the gentlest,*
> *most kind to his people,*
> *most eager for fame.*

Good Boy

Despite having three legs, the fox terrier hopped and strained against his leash, pulling Juni along the sidewalk toward the firehouse.

"Slow down, boy," she said, trying to imitate the obedience training she'd seen on the Animal Channel. "We'll get there soon enough." Grendel seemed to know where he was going.

Abdur Peethala's landlord, a monster himself, had kept the little dog chained to a pipe in his garage. Why Ralph Burchard hadn't simply dumped him, another stray on the street, Juni couldn't guess. Burchard had charged her fifty dollars for "room and board," which amounted to table scraps and slimy water. She didn't have the heart to argue. Grendel had looked up at her from his circle of urine-stained cement as if she were his savior, and maybe she was. No one else had come looking for him.

"Nothing but trouble," Mr. Burchard had said, slicking his greasy hair over a bald spot. "All he does is whine and dig and bark. Pissed all over the carpet, scratched the hell out of the door. I was well within my rights to sell the contents of the apartment to cover my losses. I checked the statute."

Juni used her best reporter's voice to ask, "How long after the explosion before you checked on the dog?"

"Hell, I don't know." Burchard hadn't met her eyes so far in the conversation, and he didn't start now. "Probably a week. These kids, they skip out on the rent all the time. It's not my job to keep track of their comings and goings."

She looked up at the house, which was divided into four numbered apartments. It wouldn't have surprised her to find illegal units in the attic and the storage shed out back. Mr. Burchard lived above the garage—six feet from Abdur's window. Juni pictured Grendel waiting by the door, growing more and more frantic as the days went by. With one good paw, he would have had to balance on his hind legs to scratch the wood. It broke her heart to think about it—the poor dog's master dead and gone—while this toad of a man ignored his whimpers.

She made a mental note to talk to her friend in Code Enforcement, the one who handled housing violations. Mr. Burchard was guilty of something more than being drunk and ugly, she was sure of it. "Did you know Abdur worked at the Plaza, that he was missing?"

Burchard looked at her, finally, and spit on the ground. "Maybe you don't get it," he said, narrowing his bloodshot eyes. "I don't give a shit where these people work, where they get their money. I only care if they pay the rent on time."

"Did Abdur pay on time?"

"Mostly."

"What about his deposit?"

"Like I said, there was damages."

"Of course."

"And it's not like anybody came to pick up his stuff. I had to clean out the place myself."

"Did you keep—"

"Nothing but junk. Notebooks and paper and books, worthless shit. The kid didn't even own a TV. I made twelve bucks on the bookshelves."

"And the rest?"

"Landfill. Now I'm spending money to keep this gimp fed and watered. I'm thinking he'll make good pit-bull bait."

Juni swallowed, tried hard not to react. Bob Davidson had done a series on the underground world of dog fighting in Orange County. She'd wanted to believe he fabricated the story to win an award. The Florida Society of News Editors had already bitten the hook.

"How much do you want for the dog?" she heard herself ask, appalled. She had no use for a dog. She wasn't supposed to get involved.

Now, with Grendel freshly bathed and dipped, she walked toward Station 2, wondering how she'd hide the vet fees, not to mention the landlord's bill for pet-care, on her expense report.

Luke Havergal, a firefighter she'd met at the site, came out to greet her. The sun bronzed his face, and Juni stopped in her tracks, dazed.

"Lady," he said, grinning at her, "if you paid money for that dog, you got robbed."

It was a crime for a man to look that good.

"This is Grendel," she said, regaining her senses. As if on cue, the little dog sat and offered his paw. Luke crouched down, accepted the shake and ran a hand over Grendel's smooth head.

"Pleased to meet you, Grendel."

Juni felt something turn over in her chest.

"I thought your house could use a mascot," she said.

Sheila Gray, wife of George Gray, Friday, 5-15-98, 11:45 a.m.

No bother. I could use the break. All these papers you have to fill out to prove somebody's dead, it's driving me up the freaking wall. I put it off too long.

When my mom died, Social Security kept sending checks, even after we mailed the death certificate. My brother said, "Don't cash anything, they'll figure it out." When they did, they wanted their money back, plus interest. It took us months to straighten out.

Oh, hell, that reminds me, I need to order more death certificates. When the funeral director asked how many I needed, who knew?

Sometimes I wonder if all the paperwork isn't just to keep you distracted.

It's working.

The worst part is the junk mail. I still get letters addressed to my mother. It's always a shock to see her name on the envelope.

George just got a notice from Publishers' Clearing House.

Is he a winner?

With his luck? No way. Tell me it stops soon.

My mom just got a summons for jury duty.

Thanks for cheering me up.

Do you feel like talking about George?

Well, I've seen the articles. I know what you're going for.

What I'm "going for"?

You know—the perfect husband, the great father, the wonderful life.

I just write what people tell me.

And nobody wants to say anything bad about their dead heroes.

Nobody said—

Well, that's the problem, ain't it? Nobody says. Everybody that died on the thirteenth was an American saint. What are the odds they all worked in the same building?

Maybe this isn't a good time to talk. I'd be happy to reschedule—

No, this is a perfect time to talk. I just know you won't print a word I say.

Mrs. Gray, I'm sorry to bring up painful memories. It wasn't my intention.

And that's how the road to hell was paved. Call me Sheila. I know you don't mean any harm. Let's talk. What do you want me to say about George? If he had any balls, he wouldn't have been in the damn building in the first place? He didn't want to work for Fidelius. He let me push him into it. He would have been happy at his old job until they forced him into retirement or he keeled over at his desk. He never spoke up for himself a day in his life. My God, he kept getting the same bad haircut for years—years!—because he didn't want to hurt the poor girl's feelings. The salon had to go out of business for him to switch hairdressers.

So he didn't like change.

No shit, Sherlock. Guess what he ate for lunch every day.

I don't...

Tuna fish on rye with lettuce, dill pickle and extra mayo. Every damn day! The people at the deli saw him coming, they had his sandwich bagged and ready. The Gray Special, they called it.

Which deli?

Please, so you can go down there and get a quote about what a good customer he was?

No, actually, I was hungry.

[laughter] Oh, hell, I'm sorry. I'm being a royal bitch.

It's okay. You're entitled.

You know he called me from the lobby? He was an hour early, worried about traffic. Human Resources didn't want him there until nine-fifteen. So he's sitting there in the atrium like a big doofus, and he calls me on the pay phone. I told him to go across the street and grab a cup of coffee, buy a newspaper, something, but no, he couldn't walk into a strange Seven-Eleven. Too far out of his comfort zone. So he sat there counting fish.

Fish? The aquariums?

Yeah, and he thinks I give a flying fart that he's up to, like, a hundred and forty-three, and this is my life.

He liked fish?

More than anything in the world, including me or the kids.

You don't mean that.

You should have seen the look on his face the day we got cable, the Fishing Channel. This look of pure bliss like I never even saw during sex. Not that there was much of that—

Did he take your boys fishing?

That's about the only thing they did together, and not very often. He said the kids made too much noise. Scared the fish.

Where did they like to go?

Lake Maitland, Lake Virginia. Ramp fishing, mostly. He talked about buying a boat, but he could never make up his mind. It would have been nice taking a trip down the St. Johns River some weekend—oh, my God, what am I saying? For our honeymoon, he tried to take me ice fishing. You live in Schofield, Wisconsin, what else do you do? Like I wanted to be sitting on Lake Wausau, freezing my ass off, hooking a frozen worm on a hook? No sir. We went to Myrtle Beach. But he put more work into that stupid ice shack of his, hauling it up to the lake every year. It was nicer than our house. Better carpet, at any rate.

I've always wondered—how do the shacks get out onto the ice?

Oh, it's a huge production. You need a trailer with a winch, first, and a truck big enough to haul it. And then with the heater, the floor melts to the ice and freezes solid, so you have to chisel it up in the spring, and you need an ice pick or an ax. George used a chainsaw. That's how we ended up in Florida.

What do you mean?

He was trying to chip it loose, but he cut too deep. The ice cracked, and down she went.

The whole thing?

[laughter] Like the *Titanic.* Wish to God I'd been there. He came home crying like a baby, threatened to burn the trailer, said he never wanted to set foot on the ice again. So I mentioned, real casual-like, that you can fish in Florida all year round, just drop your pole in the water, no long-johns involved. My brother lives in Cocoa Beach. He raves about the deep-sea charters. Next thing you know, we're packing the U-Haul.

And George took the job with Mid-Florida Title?

Right. His old boss gave him a good reference. Same job he did up north.

He worked there for ten years? Chelsea thought so, but she wasn't sure.

Eleven, give or take. They passed him over for three promotions that I know of, moved him into a smaller office, took away his window. He ended up in a cubicle with two other guys, and one of them smoked. George never complained, though. Never said boo. Never asked for a raise either, and they sure as hell didn't offer.

Did he like his work?

How would I know?

He never talked about it?

Here's what happened every night. He'd come home and ask when dinner was ready. He'd take off his tie, flop down in his La-Z-Boy and read the paper. If you asked how his day went, he'd say, "Fine." We'd eat. He'd ask Culver if he did his homework. He'd tell Cory to stop fidgeting. He'd ask if for once we could eat a decent meal in peace. He'd be too tired to help with the dishes, even though I worked, too. He'd fall asleep in front of the TV, and I wouldn't bother to wake him up when I went to bed. He'd have cereal for breakfast. Cheerios with skim milk, no sugar. Then he'd blow it on a donut at ten o'clock. He folded his socks. He wore boxers, not briefs. He was a weird kind of colorblind—he couldn't tell maroon from brown, so his ties never matched. He always listened to talk radio in the car because he couldn't concentrate on driving with music. If you rode in the car with him, you had to listen to him rant and rave at the idiots on the air, which is something he'd never have the guts to say to their face. Are you getting any of this?

Every word.

Oh, right. The tape recorder. You warned me.

Would you rather I turn it off?

Nah. I'm used to it. You know I'm a court stenographer, right? That's what I do, write down what other people say. Which transcript service do you use? Not Acu-Write, I hope. They suck.

No. I run the tapes through a speech-to-text program on my computer.

Digital tapes?

Right.

Putting me out of a job, in other words.

Sorry.

My last job was the Merrill Iron plant, stamping the same damned piece for eight hours. I thought this job would be less boring. Huh. Be careful what you wish for. You know I was there that day, the custody hearing? They had to take the guy out in handcuffs.

What guy?

The janitor.

You can't be serious. You were there?

Me and my little steno machine. It didn't take long. Five, six minutes, tops. I was ten feet away. If I'd had a gun in my purse, I could have saved us all a world of hurt.

Would you have done it?

What, shoot him? Hell, yeah. Twice. Who wouldn't? That's a no-brainer.

What did he say?

In court, not much. His lawyer did most of the talking. Or should I say stutter-ing. Judge Lively, she runs her show by the book, and this poor schmuck, he filed the wrong motion. Good night, folks. Thanks for playing.

And the janitor started yelling?

He didn't yell, exactly.

His wife, in one of her interviews, said he went insane, started yelling, "Kill me, kill me now."

It was more like begging the judge to listen, but she'd already moved on to the next case, so she called the bailiffs. Maybe he said that last part, but I didn't hear it, he was crying so hard. To tell the truth, I felt sorry for him at the time. Now, it's like I'm glad he suffered. I remember wondering whether George would be that upset if we split up and he lost custody of the kids.

Of course he would be.

Did you know him?

No, but you said so yourself—he took the boys fishing, he wanted to buy a boat. He told Chelsea he was planning to build a swimming pool, now that he had the new job.

He did?

Yeah.

That's—he never said anything about it. He— *[inaudible]*

Your husband loved you very much, Sheila. You and the boys.

I know he did. It's just—oh, Jesus, this can't be what you're looking for.

[laughter] Everybody's different.

What do they say?

Who?

The other people, the ones you call.

Oh. Well, some are still in shock. They give me names of family or friends to contact. Some are angry, of course, about what happened. Some don't want to be taped. Too personal, I guess. Too raw. Others are happy to have someone to talk to. It seems like so many people don't have family down here, no support system, you know? Not like the old days, when you had relatives living next door.

Family's not all it's cracked up to be. God help me if we lived next door to George's mother. She'd be dead by now. I would have killed her.

Off the record.

You just say it's my fault George is dead, and leave it at that.

Surely you don't blame yourself?

Sure, I do. If it weren't for me, he would have been clear on the other side of town that morning, eating his donut, happy as a clam.

I think we're each responsible for our own decisions in life, don't you?

Here's what I keep thinking. The investigator told me George died right away, in the first explosion. Know how they could tell? Because of where they found him—in his chair. Or what was left of it. He never knew what hit him.

Maybe the best way to go.

Of all the dumb luck, you know? Half an hour later, and he would have signed the papers. We'd have benefits, life insurance. Not that it's about the money.

What do you mean? Isn't Fidelius taking care of you?

Well, technically, George didn't start the job, did he? The damn place blew up first.

Do you have a phone number, your contact there?

Sure. What for?

I just want to check a few things. And do you mind if I call back in a few weeks to see how you're doing?

You think a few weeks will make any difference?

[laughter] Maybe not.

Call after the article comes out. I'm sure I'll have a few choice words.

George Gray: Early for Work

The Dead Remembered/Profiles compiled by Herald Staff

It was the first day of his new job. George Gray arrived at the Plaza an hour early, not sure how long the drive from Maitland would take in rush-hour traffic. He missed the accident that snarled I-4 and kept many employees safe in their cars when the explosion occurred. "He called me from a pay phone in the lobby," said his wife, Sheila. "They didn't want him upstairs until nine-fifteen. I told him to go across the street, buy a cup of coffee, a newspaper, something. But he didn't. He counted fish."

Fishing was George's favorite hobby. He often spent Saturdays at Lake Virginia with his sons, Culver and Cory. "He talked about buying a boat," Sheila said. "It would have been nice to take a trip down the St. Johns River."

George's love of angling started in his hometown of Schofield, Wisconsin, where ice fishing is the state sport. George's father and grandfather kept ice shacks on Lake Wausau, and George carried on the tradition each year. That is, until a fateful accident brought the family to Florida.

"That ice shack was nicer than our house," Sheila said, explaining that over the course of a winter, shacks melt to the ice and require an ax to loosen in the spring. George used a chainsaw. "He cut too deep," Sheila said. "The ice cracked. The whole thing went down like the *Titanic*." George was distraught, according to his wife. "He never wanted to set foot on the ice again." Sheila's brother had recently transferred to Cocoa Beach, and she mentioned the benefits of year-round fishing in the Sunshine State. "Next thing you know, we're moving."

In Orlando, George found a job with Mid-Florida Title as a mortgage refinance specialist. He worked for the company for eleven years before accepting a position with Fidelius Financial Group at the Parramore Plaza. George's former co-workers hosted a going-away party for him at Bennigan's on April 10.

"He seemed a little nervous," said Chelsea Olson, an assistant in George's department. "We teased him about moving on to a bigger office, a bigger paycheck. He said he might be able to afford a new pool. I think it made him feel good to know he could do that for the boys."

The employees at Mid-Florida Title have raised enough money to buy the swimming pool George wouldn't live to see. Artesian Pools provided the labor and materials at cost. The pool will be finished by the time Cory and Culver began their summer vacation.

A scholarship fund for George's sons has been established by Fidelius Financial Group.

Trân Châu Nguyen: Pearl from the Gulf

The Dead Remembered/Profiles compiled by Herald Staff

Customers at the Gulf Seafood Market often saw six-year-old twins Trân Châu and her brother Trai doing their homework at a little table behind the cash register. When the children weren't studying, they stacked shrimp on ice and played games with empty oyster shells. Their parents, Huy and Kim Nguyen, ran the market seven days a week. The company supplies restaurants in the area with shellfish from Plaquemines Parish in Louisiana, where the Nguyen family has fished for twenty years. Like many other Vietnamese refugees, the Nguyens settled on the Gulf Coast after the fall of Saigon in 1975.

Fishing is a tradition Huy didn't intend to pass on to his children. "We moved to Orlando for the good schools," he said. The twins attended Henry Elementary in separate homerooms, and both were straight-A students. Trân Châu won a trip to the Plaza by reading the most books in her class. Her brother insisted on beating her total, even though his class didn't participate in the contest. Huy said his daughter planned to become a doctor when she grew up, although she sometimes changed her mind to a ballerina. His son wants to be a fighter pilot.

Huy's father worked for the U.S. Army during the Vietnam War, ferrying soldiers up the Mekong River in his fishing boat. "When the Americans left, my father knew he would go to prison," Huy said. "He put us in the boat in the middle of the night—my grandparents, aunts, uncles, cousins." After being picked up by a tanker in the South China Sea, the family spent 11 months in a United Nations refugee camp before receiving sponsorship to come to the United States. They settled in Pointe-à-la-Hache, Louisiana.

"The Mississippi Delta reminded my parents of home," Huy said. His father scraped together enough money to buy an old fishing boat, and every relative went to work. "My ninety-year-old grandfather picked shrimp," Huy explained. "My five-year-old sister cleaned buckets." In the wake of the Plaza tragedy, Huy's wife wants to return to Louisiana to be closer to relatives. "She believes we were cursed," Huy said. "Coming here." He added that his son has not spoken in the month since his sister's death. "Trai's name means 'Oyster,'" Huy said. "He is closed up in his shell right now. One day soon he will open."

His sister's name meant "Pearl."

Longing for the Sea

George hung up the pay phone and checked for quarters, but the change slot was empty. *She's always mad at me.* After Sheila had yelled at him for being early, she told him to go across the street and buy a cup of coffee. He didn't tell her he could stay right here and buy one. The Plaza had its own coffee shop, a place called Dueling Grounds, across from a gift shop where he'd spotted a glass paperweight for his mother's birthday. His new workplace had everything he needed, apparently.

The atrium was massive. George counted twelve floors going up to the roof. With all the stone carvings and columns, the place looked like the inside of a pyramid, except that a pyramid didn't have so much glass—or fish! These aquariums were amazing. And the mangrove tank! Who'd ever heard of an office building having its own manatee?

He was going to like it here, he could tell.

It hadn't been his idea to leave Mid-Florida Title. Sheila had nagged and nagged until he sent a resume. But she'd been right. He needed a push. Eleven years he'd stayed at his old job, watching others get the promotions he deserved. Now was time for a fresh start with Fidelius.

He was nervous, though. Petrified, actually. There'd be new procedures to learn, new people looking over his shoulder. He'd have to prove himself all over again. Still, Sheila couldn't help but be happy with the bigger salary, the better benefits. Hell, Fidelius even contributed to employee pensions.

His wife would finally be proud of him.

George strolled across the lobby, loving the solid echo of his shoes on the marble floor. New shoes, new suit, new man! Inside the coffee shop, he closed his eyes and inhaled the exotic aromas. He'd been going to Dunkin Donuts every morning for...what, a decade? The choices here were dizzying: Kenya Peaberry, Sumatra Mandheling, India Yelnoorkhan.

He usually drank House Blend. This morning he ordered Hawaiian Kona.

George almost told the girl behind the counter what a momentous occasion this was, but he decided to wait. Soon she would recognize him as a regular customer. She might even remember his name and his usual drink.

She had a silver ring through the middle of her lip, and her fingernails were painted black. Her hair was bright pink. She scared him a little, but she was nice when she took his money. When she said, "Have a good day," he caught the glint of a metal stud on her tongue.

He imagined his sons growing up and bringing home such a girl, what Sheila might say. She'd probably grab that little ring and drag the poor girl out by her lip. Sheila could be…difficult, but she wanted what was best for Culver and Cory. She was a good mother. George knew he didn't always spend enough time with the boys, and he was lucky his wife was there to pick up the slack.

Starting today, he would be different. He would make the effort. Maybe he'd finally buy that boat and take the boys on a fishing trip, just the three of them. He might even coach Little League. Or soccer.

Were the boys on a team this year? Which sports did they play in the spring? What if someone asked him? What would his new co-workers think of him, being so out of touch with his own kids? How embarrassing! He'd make a point of finding out—tonight. He would turn off the television, and they'd have a family chat.

Monday night. Which shows were on?

Carrying his coffee across the lobby, George stopped to admire the mangrove pool. Striped bass and spotted gar—some as long as his arm—swam in and out of the rocks. The tank was bigger than his house. The lone manatee drifted at the bottom, trailing its flippers in the sand. The sign said it was an orphan, that it ate fifty heads of lettuce a day. As George stood at the glass, the manatee did a slow roll and floated over to him. The thick glass magnified its face: the droopy eyes, the wrinkled forehead, the whiskers on its rubbery snout. It reminded George of his mother's basset hound, except that this animal moved more gracefully in the water. All that dog ever did was waddle and poop.

George couldn't imagine living alone in a tank with only fish for company, even if it meant all the lettuce you could eat. But if anybody asked him, he would use a fifty-pound line and a minnow lure to catch that spotted gar.

Most of these fish were saltwater, he knew. Why did salt make their colors so much brighter? Take the angelfish in that tank, for instance—you could see its blue and orange stripes from clear across the room. Practically a neon sign for sharks!

Sharks. They were the real reason George didn't go deep-sea fishing. His brother-in-law kept asking, but in his head, George always heard the theme from "Jaws." Any sport where you had to wear a life preserver meant you were risking your life in the first place. Why take the chance?

One of the elevators rose into the atrium, and George imagined a parachutist jumping off the top, drifting down, getting tangled in the palm trees. Maybe falling into the manatee tank and drowning. No, thank you. He would take a nice, safe chair on the ground.

He chose a seat next to the lionfish. He'd seen them on his first interview, trailing their poisonous spikes like peacock feathers. According to the sign, they'd come all the way from Palau. One minute they were floating above the Indonesian coral, minding their own business, and the next, they were in a net, bound for Orlando.

George checked his watch: eight forty-five. Only half an hour to kill. His stomach did a flip—he didn't want to think about his first day at work. It was the same nervousness he'd felt as a kid on the first day of school, meeting new teachers, trying to find his way around a strange place.

The black security guard at the front desk kept a watchful eye on visitors. The man had stopped George and made him sign the guestbook. Tomorrow, he, George, would have a badge like everyone else, and he would walk past the desk and into the coffee shop with the same "I belong here" attitude.

He watched a man in jeans come through the front door with a package. The guard waved him over. George could read the conversation by their gestures: *Where's your badge, son? Must have left it downstairs. Don't forget it next time. You got it, man.* George reminded himself to keep his badge in his briefcase where he wouldn't lose it.

There were a few other visitors this morning. While he was on the phone, he'd seen some kids feeding the manatee—wouldn't Cory and Culver love that?—and now they were over by the waterfall, hooting and hollering. One of the boys was trying to jump in. The lady tour-guide pointed up, and everyone, including George, watched the elevators climb toward the roof. He wondered why he hadn't seen more passengers waiting in the lobby, and then he remembered that employees parked downstairs, where he too had been promised a spot. One more perk for the successful corporate executive.

George noticed that the coffee shop was busier now, people rushing in and out, taking quick sips from their cups. He finished his own coffee, thinking that maybe tomorrow he'd try Jamaican Blue Mountain. This new stuff tasted bitter, but maybe that meant it was good.

He checked his watch again. A few more minutes to go. The woman from HR had said she'd come downstairs to meet him. What was her name again? He wanted to call Sheila back. His wife would remind him of the things he tended to forget: make eye contact, keep your handshake firm, don't talk about fishing unless the other person brings it up first.

His palms were clammy, so he wiped them on his pants. Something smelled burnt—was it his coffee? Did he have a breath mint? As he dug in his pocket, a buzzing echoed, far away, and then he heard a second ringing, closer. What was going on? The desk guard picked up his phone, but he didn't seem too concerned. The sound reminded George of the buzzer on an elevator with too many riders. He noticed people on the floors above him, leaning over the railings, and it dawned on him: *We're having a fire drill!*

He didn't need this excitement. His gut was jumpy enough already. But now, he'd have a good story to tell Sheila. There I was, counting the fish, minding my own business, and the next thing you know—

Local Charity Indicted on Multiple Fraud Counts

Money from angelfish pins didn't go to Plaza victims

By Juni Bruder, Herald Staff Writer/Monday, May 18, 1998

ORLANDO—The founder of a local organization selling "Rocky" angelfish pins to raise money for the families of April 13 victims was arrested Monday on multiple counts of charity fraud. Clarence Fawcett, who formed the nonprofit "Pins for the Plaza" shortly after the collapse, is charged with the theft of nearly $15,000.

The blue-and-orange angelfish known as "Rocky" became a symbol of hope in the days after the Plaza tragedy. As the story goes, a dust-covered man staggered into the Itso Sushi restaurant on South Street minutes after the collapse. The man sat down to catch his breath, and hostess Lia Schroeder brought him a glass of water. After a sip, the man looked down at his shirt, patted his pocket and produced a wriggling fish. Without saying a word, he dropped the fish in the glass and walked out. The man has never been identified.

The Coral Beauty angelfish, a dwarf specimen from the Great Barrier Reef, had come from an aquarium in the Plaza atrium. Given the name "Rakki" by the hostess who rescued him, he now resides in a saltwater tank at the restaurant and has become a local celebrity. His name means "lucky" in Japanese.

Clarence Fawcett began producing and selling "Rocky" pins within weeks of the tragedy, advertising that all profits would go to families of Plaza victims. Sales were boosted by the fact that the fish bears the orange and blue colors of the University of Florida. Actor Sylvester Stallone generated further interest by wearing a Rocky pin to the MTV Movie Awards in Los Angeles.

According to a spokesperson from the Orlando Police Department, officers seized a list of items from Fawcett's house allegedly purchased with donations, including jewelry, clothing and Beanie Babies collectibles. Fawcett called the charges "a misunderstanding." If convicted, he faces five years in prison.

The arrest comes amid growing controversy over the distribution of relief monies collected by such organizations as the American Red Cross and the United Way.

Mayor Delphi Owens noted that a task force has been formed to investigate Plaza donation abuses. "There's a special level of hell reserved for people who seek to profit from others' misfortune," she said. "And if it were up to me, I'd cut off a few hands, like the Bible says."

Mayor Owens Collapses at Plaza Razing

By Juni Bruder, Herald Staff Writer/Tuesday, May 19, 1998

ORLANDO—Moments after the first wrecking ball crashed into the ruined east wing of the Parramore Plaza, Mayor Delphi Owens collapsed while speaking to protestors. A hospital spokesperson said that the mayor was suffering from dehydration.

Demolition crews began work at 6:30 a.m. on Tuesday to bring down remaining sections of the building that collapsed on April 13. The recovery effort for victims ended after engineers deemed the wreckage unsafe. According to a city official, heavy winds have further weakened the structure.

"I was told it could come down at any time," said Police Capt. Reilly Killion. "If it goes the wrong way, we'll have an even bigger problem on our hands."

Victims' families questioned the move, calling it "hasty" and "insensitive." Some 3,000 people signed a petition to block the demolition. "We come here to grieve," said Elizabeth Childers, whose seven-year-old daughter, Ashley, died in a Plaza elevator. "They want to smooth everything over, as if nothing ever happened."

Rodney Brown, who lost his wife, Sarah, in the disaster, spoke to reporters as Mayor Owens was transported to Orlando Regional Medical Center. "There are two victims still buried in this wreckage," Brown said. "This site is a crime scene. It's almost like they're trying to hide something."

According to Capt. Killion, the unstable wreckage has hampered the police investigation. "We can't do our work," he said. "I won't risk my people. With the walls down, we can go through the rubble with a fine-toothed comb."

All but two of the Plaza's 115 victims were recovered in the days following the collapse. Still missing are architect Dante Costas and a homeless man who served as watchman in the Plaza parking garage. The man, known only as Whit, was recently identified by Salvation Army officials as Harmon Whitney.

The body of Rocco Purkapile, believed to be buried in the Plaza rubble, was found at the Jacksonville morgue.

FBI and ATF agents and local investigators continue to gather information about janitor Mauro Abissi, suspected of setting the Plaza blaze. Abissi's estranged wife revealed in a recent interview that she warned law enforcement officials her husband was "a danger to the public." Fire Chief William Herndon would not comment on the progress of his arson investigation.

Thousands of pieces of evidence have been removed from the wreckage, along with artifacts that will be displayed in the April 13 memorial. A campaign will be launched in the next few weeks to select a design.

Before she collapsed, Mayor Owens told the assembled families, "It's a sad day. A terrible day. But we must move on." According to a hospital spokesperson, Mayor Delphi Owens will remain overnight for observation at ORMC.

Harmon Whitney: Veteran of the Streets

The Dead Remembered/Profiles compiled by Herald Staff

Like nearly a fifth of homeless Americans, Harmon Whitney was a military veteran. At 19, he landed with the First Marine Division at Inchon, Korea. He later received a Purple Heart for wounds sustained in combat at the Chosin Reservoir, one of the bloodiest battles of the Korean War. After the armistice, he came home to Ellsworth, PA, married his high-school sweetheart and started a family.

At 32, he disappeared.

Salvation Army volunteers in downtown Orlando remember a grizzled man named Whit who passed through the food line several times a week and occasionally stayed in the men's shelter. Employees at the Plaza often complained about the homeless man who slept in the shade of the parking garage and recited poetry to passersby, but the building's owner, Dante Costas, refused to evict him.

A pastry chef at the Plaza restaurant, Douze, sent dinner downstairs to Whit when she could. On other nights, he ate at the Salvation Army shelter. "He kept to himself," said shelter director Cathy Booth. "With 300 people coming through on an average night, we didn't always have time to chat."

Shelter rules require residents to refrain from alcohol, and records indicate that Whit lost his dormitory privileges several times for drinking. According to the National Coalition for the Homeless, up to half of all single adults on the street suffer from drug or alcohol addiction. On the morning of April 13, witnesses saw Whit "passed out" near the garage entrance. His body was never recovered, and published reports identified him only by nickname for several weeks after the disaster.

A Salvation Army volunteer notified the *Herald* after she recognized Whit's description among the Plaza victims. "I knew we hadn't seen Whit in a while," said Cathy Booth, "but our people disappear for weeks at a time, and we didn't want to think the worst." Cathy, who set up a local outreach program for homeless veterans, described Whit as "a proud man." She noted that he refused to discuss his eligibility for veterans' benefits. "I made the mistake of patting his hand once, and he laughed at me," she said. "He didn't want anyone's pity."

Whit's ex-wife, Beverly, waited two decades before filing for divorce on the grounds of abandonment. According to her son Russell, the divorce attorney in Pittsburgh performed an obligatory search but found no trace of Harmon Whitney. "My mother never spoke about him," said Russell, who last saw his father in 1963. "I don't think she ever forgave him." Beverly Whitney died of congestive heart disease in 1996.

Cathy Booth noted, "These men in the shelter, they all have stories. They all have family somewhere. I don't know if it's shame or regret or guilt that keeps them from picking up the phone. You learn not to ask."

Fire Drill

"Come on, buddy. Wake up." Kevin Potter nudged the sleeping man's shoulder with his boot.

"Maybe he's dead," Cass Hueffer said. He took off his helmet and held it to his chest.

"Knock it off." Potter looked up; fortunately, the wall of the parking garage blocked the view from the street. Hundreds of employees milled around on the commons, waiting for the "all clear" sign to go back in the building. Fire drills made everybody cranky. The last thing he needed was for a civilian to see two firemen kicking a homeless guy. "Grab his shoulders. I'll take his feet."

Hueffer shook his head. "No way, Cooney. You can't move an unconscious victim without a spine board. It's regulation."

"Jesus, Mary and Joseph." Potter pinched the bridge of his nose. Why his shift? A few more hours and he could have been home, mowing the lawn. "He's snoring, you idiot. He's not unconscious." Even though it was eighty-plus in the shade, the rookie had his turnout gear buckled to his chin. This was a drill, for Christ's sake, not a three-decker fire. Dumber than a sack of hammers, this kid.

"The B corridor's clear." Luke Havergal came up behind them, scudding his boots on the concrete. He'd already slung his coat over his arm. "You two waiting for the Second Coming?" Potter could feel sweat trickling down his back, but Havergal's T-shirt was dry as a bone. The freakin' OFD calendar boy, as usual.

"I'm not moving him," Hueffer repeated. "You're my witness, Skywalker."

Havergal rolled his eyes and looked to Potter, who growled and tapped his wrist. "Six more minutes to clear the building," he said. "Or I owe the chief ten bucks."

"Sucker bet," Havergal said, laughing.

"It's coming out of your hide if I lose."

The firemen turned and studied their problem. The old man slept in a corner where the wall of the ramp met the floor. One hand rested on a grungy knapsack. His pillow was a garbage bag filled with clothes; threadbare flannel poked through a rip in the plastic. His hair and beard were gray, matted. His coat looked gray, except for a lighter patch where the pocket had ripped off. A faded label on the lining said "Burberry."

"Think he's warm enough?" Hueffer pointed with his toe to the old man's jeans. The knees were torn, stained with dirt and old blood. Another layer of khaki showed underneath. Below the hem, a yellowed cuff of long underwear sagged at his ankles.

"Nights get cold when you're sleeping on cement," Havergal said. Kneeling, he lifted the flap on the knapsack. The old man stirred but didn't wake; the strap was wrapped around his wrist. With two fingers, Havergal lifted out an empty bottle of Early Times. "Oh, he likes the good stuff."

"Gentlemen, is there a problem?" They turned to see Ernie Hyde and Web Browning coming down the ramp, hands on their guns. Potter laughed. "Cheese it, the cops!" The two men walked with the same measured stride; their black uniforms were nearly the same size. With their close-cropped hair and lantern jaws, they could have been brothers.

"It's a good thing you're here, officers," Havergal said, climbing to his feet. "This man is in possession of stolen property." He held out a water-stained book and pointed to the library barcode on its spine.

Hyde leafed through the swollen pages, shaking his head, making a "tsk-ing" sound. His mirrored glasses reflected the text. "Roll on, thou deep and dark blue ocean, roll," he read. "Anyone?"

The old man murmured, "Ten thousand fleets sweep over thee in vain."

Startled, Hueffer took a step back. "It's alive."

Slipping his nightstick out of his belt, Browning sang into it. "You're...so *vain*—hey, the acoustics are great in here!"

"God help us." With a sigh, Hyde went down on one knee. "Whit? Hey, there. Time to wake up." The old man groaned and hugged the knapsack to his chest. Hyde managed to return the book to its pocket.

"Ernie, you know this guy?"

"He lives here, more or less." Hyde stood and tipped his head back and forth, cracking his neck. "Management says to leave him alone."

"Could we move the old fossil, just for today?" Potter asked. "We can't close this drill until everybody's off the premises."

A metal door slammed behind them, and they turned, forgetting the problem at hand—a woman in high heels strode across the floor toward the ramp. Potter glared at Havergal. "I thought you said B was clear."

"It was! Everything okay, ma'am?"

"Yes!" she called out. "Sorry! I was in the middle of something." Her peach-colored suit was tailored and short. Her long, dark hair was tousled in that "just out of bed" look that probably took hours. She smiled, pointed toward the exit and waved as she kept going. Her heels echoed on the pavement.

"Think I've died and gone to heaven," Hueffer mumbled. Walking sideways, he tried to keep her long legs in sight as she disappeared up the ramp. He stepped over the old man, who yelped and clutched his arm.

"Try not to kill any civilians, for Christ's sake!" Potter thwacked the kid on the helmet. "Can we get this show on the—" The Level B door slammed again, and this time, a man in a dark suit hurried out.

"Son of a—" Havergal took three steps toward the straggler and stopped. "Mr. Costas!" All of the men came to attention. They knew who he was.

"Is Whit all right?" Costas loosened his tie as he came toward them.

"Yes, sir," Potter said. "We just need to move him out of the building. For the drill, sir."

"Of course." Unbuttoning his jacket, Costas bent beside the old man and said, "Whit? Let's take a walk." He slipped an arm under his shoulder and waited for one of the men to take the other side. Hyde quickly obliged. "Ready? One, two—" On three, they lifted Whit to his feet.

"Where are we going?" The old man teetered, and Hyde adjusted his hold.

"Come on, my friend," Costas said. "You need some fresh air." The men guided Whit up the ramp, one halting step at a time. Havergal grabbed the knapsack and followed. Potter motioned for Hueffer to take the plastic bag.

Hueffer shook his head. "Sorry, L.T. I haven't had my rabies shot."

Turning to Browning, Potter said, "Web, may I borrow your gun?"

The cop shrugged and handed his Glock to the fireman. Potter grabbed Hueffer's hand and slapped the pistol into it. "Shoot me now, Hueffer. Do it. Because the next time you question an order, you get us both killed. You understand?"

"Yeah."

"Yeah, what?"

"Sir. Yes, sir."

"Thank you, Web," the lieutenant said, returning the piece. He noticed his hands were shaking. What the hell? When he called Katie tonight, he'd ask for blueberry pie and coffee—his usual fix on a bad day. To Hueffer, he pointed up the ramp and growled, "I don't want to hear you. I don't want to see you." The kid picked up the plastic bag and trudged toward the top. Potter rode herd.

Browning, singing, brought up the rear. "I shot the *sheriff...*"

At the top, the glare was so bright, the men had to stop to let their eyes adjust. Hundreds of spectators watched them from the commons. Hooves clattered on the pavement, and Doc Metcalf trotted his horse up the driveway. "Well, now it's a damned parade," Havergal muttered. "If he bites me again, I'll turn the fire hose on him."

Browning laughed. "You mean Doc or Billy Lee?"

The mounted policeman cleared a path for them, guiding his sleek black horse through the crowd. As they neared the circle of benches, Potter noticed Doc zero in on a guy on a phone, blocking the path. Billy Lee lifted his hoof and brought it down—*crack!*—on the sidewalk. Potter felt the vibration from where he stood. The jerk scrambled out of the way, and everyone applauded.

Potter had to hand it to Doc; he knew how to make a point.

Mr. Costas and Hyde deposited their charge on the bench. Whit sat and squinted in the sun. Glancing around at the other seats, Potter noticed a girl sketching—it was hard to miss the bubble-gum hair. She stared intently as

Hueffer deposited the plastic bag on the ground beside Whit, and then her pencil flew across the paper. Better her than a photographer, Potter supposed. Too slow to capture anything truly damaging. Just to be safe, he sucked in his gut.

"Thank you, sir," Whit said to Hueffer.

"Uh, you're welcome?" The kid looked pole-axed, as if he'd never been called "sir" before.

The old man shook hands with Ernie, and then with Mr. Costas. "Thank you, gentlemen, for your kindness."

"Our pleasure, Whit." Turning to Potter, Costas asked, "Are we done?"

Potter checked his watch. "With a minute to spare." Speaking into the radio on his shoulder, he said, "Engine Two to dispatch. Levels A and B, all clear. Tell the chief he owes me ten bucks."

Archie Higbie: Drawing On Experience

The Dead Remembered/Profiles compiled by Herald Staff

When Archie Higbie wasn't brewing coffee, she was sketching. The pink-haired barista at Dueling Grounds, the cafe on the Plaza's first floor, often asked customers if she could draw them. "She always had a notebook," said her father, Archibald, for whom Archie was named. "From the day she could pick up a pencil, she drew."

Archie dreamed of attending art school, but "life got in the way," explained her father, who lost his wife to cancer in 1988 and soon after, his job as a NASA engineer at Cape Canaveral. With no money for tuition, Archie became a caricaturist at Epcot Center. In 1992, she was picked to work at the opening of Euro Disney in Paris. Despite the commitment to long hours and six months overseas, "she jumped at the chance," said her father. "She loved everything about Europe, the people, the culture, the art."

At the end of her term in France, Archie set off on an adventure across the continent. "I didn't see her for three years," her father said. She bartered her skills as an artist and barista, working in Berlin, Amsterdam and Rome. "She'd stay in one place until her visa expired and then move on," Archibald said. "If she hadn't run out of money, I might never have seen her again."

Back home in Orlando, Archie answered an ad for a part-time job at the Plaza cafe. In her spare time, she sketched. According to Rozelle Simmons, manager of the Plaza Gift Shop, Archie had recently placed several of her portraits in the gallery. "They had a unique style," said Rozelle, "much like the artist herself."

Archie was a vivid presence in the coffee shop, sporting bright pink hair and a lip ring. "The hair, the black polish, the lip—I think she did it to keep herself from going back to a safe job," her father said. The Disney dress code forbids piercings and requires natural color for hair and nails. "Archie told me she didn't want to waste any more time. She wanted to make it as an artist, now or never."

Her father adds that her notebook and all of her finished sketches were lost in the fire. "I have a framed drawing she did of me when she was nine," he said. "People ask me if it's Abraham Lincoln."

Ruth Weldy, mother of Butch Weldy, Wednesday, 5-20-98, 4:30 p.m.

Your house is lovely, Mrs. Weldy. How long have you collected plates?

Ever since the Bradford Exchange opened, I guess. They ought to give me stock.

Which is your favorite?

Tough question. Princess Diana, there, or "Marry Me, Scarlett," or my new ones. They're a series, see? "Holiday Memories" by Thomas Kinkade. You know him?

I don't think so.

He's famous, the "Painter of Light." They'll be worth a fortune some day. Butch gave me this one for Christmas, and then the others came in the mail every couple of months. The last one showed up the day of calling hours.

I'm so sorry.

Oh, no, it was good, like Butch went off and dropped me a gift in the mail.

How've you been holding up?

To be honest, I had a lot of practice for Butch's funeral. Here, come sit in the kitchen. Not that you're ever prepared, but I never thought he'd see eighteen.

Why do you say that?

Aside from me wanting to kill him? Butch was what you call accident-prone. Bloody noses, broken bones, every childhood disease known to man. Even a tornado. He just came off medical leave the month before.

He was hurt in February? I didn't realize.

That twister flattened his house, threw him into a cow pasture. He went to the hospital with three cracked ribs, a busted foot, head to toe in manure. Tea?

It's amazing he survived. No, thanks.

Story of his life. He jumped out a bedroom window at five. Second floor, mind you, sprained his ankle. Fell out of a car. He almost drowned once, doing bike jumps into the canal. The neighbor pulled him out, blue. We racked up frequent-flyer miles at the hospital.

This is why I never had kids.

See this hair? Gray at twenty-nine. It's a wonder they didn't lock me up for child abuse. Aidan—Butch's oldest—that acorn didn't fall far from the tree. See these spots on my nice lace tablecloth? The kids stay with me after school. Yesterday, I'm in the bathroom, Aidan drags a chair over to the microwave, puts his sister's ballet slippers on high. Hears me coming, jumps down, bangs his chin on the counter. Blood everywhere, Sylvie yelling about her shoes, and the smoke? Oh, my Lord.

That explains the burnt rubber smell.

It'll never come out of the curtains.

How do you babysit with all these...breakables?

Family room's off limits. Aidan and Sylvie understand. They're good kids.

Was their father a good kid?

Once upon a time. A sweet kid. It changed with the drinking, but when he was little, he'd crawl into my lap and say, "I love you, Mama," for no reason at all.

He had an alcohol problem?

Well, two DUIs, if you call that a problem. I can't count the cars he wrecked. Some of them weren't even his.

Did the drinking contribute to his divorce?

Diane stood by him. That girl, she's like a daughter to me. She tried. I finally told her, "Honey, you need to cut your losses and run." It wasn't safe anymore.

Butch hurt her?

Physically, no, but I think the words, they cut deeper, don't they?

Emotional scars take longer to heal, yes.

They do. I still remember the things my old man used to say.

I understand Butch and Diane remarried in March.

Thanks to the tornado. Next thing you know, he's asking her for a second chance, like he'd seen God or something. Ha! More like the thirty-ninth.

The thirty-ninth what?

Chance.

Oh. So you didn't approve.

My honest opinion? He had nothing. His house was a cement pad, everything else scattered to the four winds. Where else could he go?

Home to his mother?

No, ma'am. I wouldn't take him. I said so.

How did the second marriage work out?

How long did they have, a month? Diane was happy, I guess. The kids were thrilled to have him home. And then, bam, it all went to hell.

You have to wonder, he survived a tornado and died at the Plaza two months later?

After the twister, Butch told me, "Ma, I thought my number was up." It's funny, but I always figured he'd be electrocuted. I had nightmares.

Was he good at his job?

When he told me he wanted money for electrical school, I said, "We're talking live wires here! Why tempt fate? Why not go be a bull rider in the rodeo?" I should've had my head examined, letting him play football. That was the start. You know those electrical thingamajiggies, when a bone doesn't mend?

Sure. I interviewed an Olympic hurdler once. He wore one for a broken leg.

With Butch, it was a fractured elbow. The doctors hooked him up to this electric box, and he took it apart. I don't know how much it cost me. Then he decided to play with electricity full time. Maybe it kept him out of jail. I don't know.

Butch saved eight people in that elevator.

That's what they say.

Some men would have run screaming out of the building. He stayed. He was a hero.

I wonder, you know, if maybe he didn't think he was bulletproof. I can hear him thinking, I'll get out of this one, too. It's like the boy who cried wolf, kind of.

Not a bad way to live, if you ask me. No fear.

Maybe. He didn't have to worry about getting hurt. Just everyone around him.

Some day you'll have to stop being mad at him. For leaving you.

I know, honey. Just not yet.

Diane Weldy, wife of Butch Weldy, Wednesday, 5-20-98, 7:30 p.m.

Diane? Hi. This is Juni Bruder from the Herald. *I just came from your mother-in-law's.*
She told me you'd be calling. So you've seen the Museum of Crap.
I'm sorry?
A retirement pension blown in three easy payments of $19.95.
Oh. Right. I've watched the commercials and wondered who bought the commemorative Elvis plates.
Now you know. Don't get me wrong, I love Ruth to death, but this Franklin Mint thing, it's completely out of hand. A serious addiction.
If it makes her happy, I guess—
I know. I'm terrible. She's been nothing but good to me.
She speaks very highly of you.
Really? I figured different.
Why?
It's been weird since the funeral. Before, even. The thing is, Ruth didn't want us getting back together, Butch and me. She tried to talk me out of it. Now, when I drop off the kids, it's like, don't let the screen door hit you on the way out.
I didn't get that impression. She said your second marriage was happy, even if it was terribly short.
Huh. I figured—see, she and Butch weren't exactly on speaking terms towards the end. I talked to her and all, but not him. She wouldn't come to the wedding.
I'm sorry to hear that.
Yeah. I'm sure she regrets it. Especially the way he died. She called him selfish.
We talked about Butch being a hero.
Damn straight, he is. The kids, they're so proud of their daddy. It makes a big difference, how they're treated at school. Better now. People know. One of the ladies from the first elevator, she called the other night to thank us. She said Butch winked at her through the glass, which was so like him.
I heard that story. I also heard that he bet one of the other electricians a C-note he could open the second door in less time.
Marty—that's who you're talking about—he went downstairs with the first group. To make sure they made it out, he said. He tried to give me a hundred-dollar bill at the funeral. I told him to keep his money.
You can't blame him.
I don't. He'll need it for therapy.
Survivor's guilt?
Something like that.
How would you describe Butch?
What did Ruth say?
Mostly we talked about his childhood bumps and bruises.
The constant trauma she had to endure, right? It's all about her.
I guess it's hard for a mother to see her child hurt so many times—
Where was she after the tornado? He got tossed around like a football!

She mentioned being in the emergency room with him.

And that's the last time they were in the same room together. I don't know what happened. He finally turned his life around, and she disappeared. I don't get it.

Sounds like part of her concern was for you.

Oh, is that how she put it? He's dead, and she's hanging the dirty laundry out to dry. Did she mention his so-called drinking problem?

Briefly, yes.

A few beers, and all of a sudden, he's a raging alcoholic, and I'm an enabler, whatever the hell that means. Psychobabble bullshit. When the fire chief asked about drugs, I almost lost it. Ruth will say anything to get attention—

When did you talk to the fire chief?

That first week. It was nothing. Routine procedure, he said. He just asked, did I know if Butch used drugs, and I said, "Absolutely not." I think maybe because he wouldn't leave the building, you know? They couldn't buy that it was bravery. He had to be high, right? Nobody believes me, but that tornado changed Butch. For the better.

How so?

He wouldn't let anybody touch his foot at the hospital until he called me. My phone rang, and it was him, begging me to take him back. Out of the blue! I couldn't understand him, he was crying so hard. Crying! And he only got that way when he—I mean, you could tell he was different. And then he said, "I love you," and the doctor in the background goes, "I love you too, man." We couldn't stop laughing.

How else did he change?

For one thing, he stopped drinking. Well, maybe a touch now and then, but not in front of the kids. And the flowers, my God, once or twice a week, and not after a fight or anything. He came straight home from work. He started going to church with me. Oh, and get this—he actually washed the dishes. All kinds of chores around the house.

Like a second honeymoon.

Yeah. It was. It really was. Oh, Jesus. *[inaudible]*

At least you had the last two months together. That's something.

I know. I'm sorry. *[inaudible]* That's what I keep thinking. I always knew he'd come back. It was just a matter of time. But, I mean, what if he had died before he got the chance? Wouldn't that be tragic?

People always think they have more time.

But they don't.

I'd hate to see you and your mother-in-law make the same mistake.

Did she tell you to say that?

No, of course not.

She owes me an apology.

I'm sure that's true.

You think I should be the one to make the first move?

It's not my place to say. I think it might be good for your kids if the two most important women in their lives could talk to each other.

You won't say anything about this in the paper, will you, about us not getting along?

No, of course not. It's irrelevant.

But you'll say Butch was a hero? The people he saved?

I think I'll say he was a lucky man. Not just surviving all the catastrophes in his life, but getting his family back.

That's what he said in his wedding toast. "I'm a lucky guy. Somebody buy me a lottery ticket."

Not many people get a second chance.

When we went to see his house, or what was left of it, I couldn't believe it. "Baby," I said, "God must have saved you for a reason." And he laughed. He said, "I wish to hell somebody would tell me what it is." It just goes to show you.

What?

That everything happens for a reason. I mean, if that tornado had taken a right turn and hit a different neighborhood, Butch and me, we never would've gotten back together.

Or, like his mother said, if he hadn't broken his arm in high school, the people on that elevator would have died. It's like a ball of twine unraveling.

You know, we even met by accident. I mean, seriously, a car accident. A fender-bender.

Whose fault?

His, probably. We never reported it. He was driving an old beater. Mine burned so much oil, I had to keep extra cans in the trunk. I said, "Give me your driver's license number," and he said, "Give me your phone number." So we started dating.

One way to avoid the hassle of insurance.

Oh, he didn't have any. He didn't believe in it. He said, "If something bad happens, it happens. If it doesn't, we saved the money."

What about the tornado? He didn't have health insurance?

No. He could've, with his job at the Plaza, but he opted out. The bill would've been something like two hundred a month. Once we were married again, the family rate, forget about it. So the hospital's letting me pay a little at a time.

Wait a minute—you're still paying on his hospital stay from the tornado? You ought to be able to work something out, especially after what happened at the Plaza. Do you have a phone number?

Sure, it's right here. Butch said not to worry, we'd find the money, and now, with the Plaza settlement, I'll have enough to cover everything. Isn't that strange? Butchie's dead, and here's this money to pay the bills. Just like he said.

Randall Weldy: A Lucky Guy

The Dead Remembered/Profiles compiled by Herald Staff

After a tornado leveled his Kissimmee home and left him lying in a field with three cracked ribs and a broken ankle, Randall "Butch" Weldy told his mother, "I thought my number was up." The divorced father of two called his ex-wife from the emergency room, asking for a second chance. "I always knew he'd come back," said Diane Weldy, who agreed to remarry Butch on St. Patrick's Day. "It was like a second honeymoon."

Surviving the February 22 storm that killed 42 people was hardly Butch's first brush with disaster. "We never thought he'd live to see eighteen," said his mother, Ruth, who recounted a laundry list of childhood mishaps, including a 15-foot jump from a bedroom window, a fall from a moving car and a near-drowning in the backyard canal. "We racked up frequent-flyer miles at the hospital," Ruth said.

Butch's career choice resulted from a high-school football injury. When his broken arm wouldn't heal, doctors used a bone growth stimulator, a machine that generates electric current to mend fractures. It became Butch's favorite toy. "He took it apart," Ruth said. She admitted having mixed feelings when her son announced plans to become an electrician. "I thought, why tempt fate? But he loved it."

Butch was one of several Plaza maintenance workers who ignored evacuation orders and stayed behind to dislodge the jammed doors of two elevators. He succeeded in freeing eight passengers from the first compartment and died trying to save half a dozen others. His medical leave had ended only a few weeks earlier.

"He survived the tornado for a reason," his wife said. "He just didn't know what it was." At his wedding in March, Butch told the assembled guests, "I'm a lucky guy."

Fire Chief William Herndon, OFD, Friday, 5-22-98, 4:25 p.m.

Hey, Chief.

Don't start nagging me because it took so long to return your call.

You're busy. And I never nag.

Ha! So what is it this time? Let me guess, the sprinklers. I heard about the recall. You can look into that company's future and see a big fat Chapter Eleven, but hey, that's not my—

You asked Diane Weldy if her husband used drugs.

What?

The electrician's wife.

What's that have to do with the fire?

You tell me.

Routine question.

Is he a suspect?

Of course not. The guy died.

So did Marko Abissi.

Look, I was just covering my bases.

You were fishing, Will. Why? Was Butch Weldy involved in the fire?

Honey, you're way out in left field here.

So set me straight. It's not my story. I'm just doing some fishing myself.

All evidence to the contrary, I'm not a total idiot. What I say here better not end up in black and white tomorrow.

When's the last time you talked to Bob Davidson?

Ah, hell, had to be two months ago, the fire at Tijuana Flats. He didn't even quote me. I blamed it on the tequila.

Which should tell you something.

Yeah. He's a lousy reporter.

No. The fact that he's not hounding you about the Plaza. He'll wait for the official report, like everyone else. Case closed. Mystery solved. It doesn't matter if you tell me why you talked to Diane Weldy. Nobody cares.

And you'll keep bugging me if I don't.

I prefer to call it recreational stalking.

Off the record?

You, me and the lamp post.

Okay, fine. Here's the thing. This guy Weldy, he tested the Argonite system—

The what?

—in the maintenance wing on Thursday. Inert gas fire suppression, so you don't get water damage. The rest of the building was on wet pipe, but the art vault and the other rooms on B level, the servers and data storage and such, they were on this Argonite system, which Weldy tested on Thursday, like he did every month.

Do we know if it passed?

He signed the checklist and mailed it off to the manufacturer, who, as you can imagine, is struggling mightily to cover its corporate ass.

So there's no way to know why the system failed.

A system doesn't work if it's shut off.

What do you mean?

The monthly test involves shutting down power to the control panel. My guess is Weldy forgot to re-arm the system. It's the last step. So what might make this guy forget something he's done a dozen times? Drugs would be my first guess.

What about being tired, spacing out?

One of the security guards saw some kind of transaction take place between him and Abissi in the locker room, same day.

So we're adding drug-dealer to Marko's long list of crimes?

Look, all I'm saying is, money changed hands. Weldy's toxicology screen came back negative, which is not to say he wasn't using. It was five days to time of death. Given the right metabolism, coke and speed can flush out of your system in forty-eight hours.

Who was the security guard?

A guy named Harry Wilmans. Want his address?

Sure.

Mount Carmel Cemetery.

Very funny.

He made a comment to another employee, who repeated it to management. That's all I have.

How did he know it was drugs?

He saw Abissi take the money. He saw Weldy put something in his mouth, drink some water and swallow. Sounds like what to you?

Aspirin? Vitamins?

You pay your friends for vitamins?

No, but—

Look, I'm not putting drugs in the report. There's no proof. It's hearsay. Weldy did a brave thing, and he lost his life for it. I'm not about to tarnish a good man's reputation on speculation. All I know is, the fire suppression system in the maintenance wing failed. We'll let the courts fight it out.

Are you any closer to a lead on the fire itself?

You mean which of a hundred flammable chemicals and compounds ignited first? Hell, it could have been an oily rag, for all I know.

Like a Molotov cocktail?

Nothing so fancy. Spontaneous combustion. Happens all the time.

I didn't take you for an X-Files kind of guy.

Hey, I've seen a body melt like bacon fat without a match in sight, but that's another story. Jack London's house, Sonoma County, 1913?

A little before my time.

Smart ass. Carpenters used cotton and linseed oil to wipe down the woodwork, called it quits for the night, place went up like a torch. Remember the Meridian fire in Philadelphia?

Doesn't ring a bell.

What the hell do they teach you in journalism school? One of the worst high-rise fires in U.S. history. Workers left a pile of oily rags on the twenty-second floor, and that's all she wrote. Of course, that building didn't have sprinklers, but—

Wait a minute. You're saying the Plaza might not have been arson at all?

Hold your water. I'm saying fire's a tricky bastard, and it's my job to rule out every possibility. Turpentine, kerosene, any kind of oil, you have to be careful. The Plaza workroom had an airtight storage container for oily rags, like any good art class. I confirmed it with Miss Singer. I wish she'd been more careful with some of the other products, but—

What do you mean?

This is just me talking off the top of my head, you understand? Off, off record.

Okay.

Miss Singer mentioned using some old-fashioned methods to make paint dyes. Sodium amide for indigo, that sort of thing. One reason they stopped using sodamide in the old days is because it blows up in reaction to water or fire.

Blows up, as in explodes?

I'm not even speaking to you, you understand? Sometimes I talk to hear the sound of my own voice. You print this, some kid goes out and builds his own chemistry lab. What I'm saying is, we have an inventory list of at least a hundred chemicals that react to each other—cleaners, pesticides, fertilizers—all used in the building. Oh, and did I mention a guy repairing a cooler in the coffee shop? Refrigerants. Boom. And then my crime scene was flooded with half a million gallons of water and buried under tons of debris.

A needle in a concrete haystack.

And no matter how much you nag, you'll be waiting for the official report like everybody else.

Cathy Booth, Salvation Army, Saturday, 5-23-98, 6:30 p.m.

Thanks for calling me, Cathy. It must have been quite a shock.

Like seeing a ghost! Thanks for coming so quickly. I wasn't sure how long we could keep him here.

Is he agitated?

Not necessarily. It's more to do with being indoors, I think. That's normal for these guys—they're used to sleeping under the stars—but he keeps watching the ceiling, like it might come down on him at any minute.

So he was there.

It's a safe bet. And he's talking more than usual. Not making much sense, but—

That's him there? The one who looks like Walt Whitman?

I always thought it was the other way around, Walt Whitman looked homeless, but yeah, that's him. Here. Take this pie. A piece for you, too. It'll give you an excuse.

No, I'd feel guilty eating—

Believe it or not, we have extra food most nights. Looks like you could use it. Don't argue. Go. Keep him talking. The doctor's on his way.

Yes, ma'am. [background noise] Uh, I brought dessert for you, Mr. Whitney. Do you mind if I sit here?

How do you know my name?

Cathy—Mrs. Booth? She told me. In fact, she said to sit down and eat my pie with you, direct orders. I was afraid to argue. She scares me a little. My name's Juni, by the way.

Like the month?

Juniper, like a character in a book my mother liked.

My daughter's name was April.

That's a beautiful name. They say babies born in the spring have sunny personalities.

She was born in December.

Oh. Like a hope for spring?

I hated winter.

I hear you. Sixty degrees and I'm shivering. Where does your daughter live?

I don't know. Are you eating the rest of your pie?

No. Here, take it. I have to be honest with you, Mr. Whitney. I know a little bit about your family. In fact, I've spoken to your son.

I have no son.

His name is Russell. He lives in Ellsworth, Pennsylvania? He works at the Bethlehem mine. He's married and has two boys.

Sorry. Wrong man.

You're a decorated veteran of the Korean War. There are benefits waiting, people to help you.

How do you know me? Are you an angel?

[laughter] Hardly. I'm a writer for the paper. When the Plaza collapsed, a lot of people were worried about you, Mr. Whitney. They couldn't find you. They thought you were dead. I talked to your family. I wrote a story about you.

The Plaza—
No, it's okay, Mr. Whitney! You don't have to go anywhere. You're safe here, I promise. Please, just stay and talk to me for a minute.
Why?
I want to know what you saw that day at the Plaza, anything you remember.
Did you see Beverly?
Your wife? Let's get to her in a minute. Do you remember where you were that day? You used to sleep in the parking garage. Neely sent food to you?
Neely's chocolate cake.
That's right, her famous dessert. Do you remember eating dinner?
Yes. I saw a penguin walking in the moonlight.
Try to concentrate, Mr. Whitney. I know it was scary. You had chocolate cake for dessert the night before. The next morning, you woke up in the garage. Did you see anything? Hear anything?
Bombs, like Inchon.
Explosions. More than one?
I saw a mermaid on fire. I saw the ghost of a horse.
Is that a line from a poem, Mr. Whitney?
The bright sun was extinguished.
Yes. Very dark, very smoky. Where did you go? Do you remember?
Beverly was there. She took my hand. She was waiting for me. All these years!
Did you miss your wife, Mr. Whitney, all these years?
When I woke up, she was gone, and a great white bird was waiting to take me across the water to the rainbow. A swan with a cold, white breast.
It must have been very confusing—wait a minute, Mr. Whitney. A swan? Do you mean Lake Eola? The swan boats, the colored lights on the fountain? That's where you woke up?
One touch of her hand was all I ever wanted, but no—I could never go back. I kept her picture, though, here in my pocket. Where is it? What did you do with it? Give it back! You're as faithless as she was—
Mr. Whitney, I don't—Cathy, help!— [tape ends]

Herald Reporter Injured by Plaza Survivor

Missing man reappeared at Salvation Army shelter

By Robert Davidson, Herald Staff Writer/Sunday, May 24, 1998

ORLANDO—Harmon Whitney, a homeless man presumed dead after the Parramore Plaza collapse, walked into the Salvation Army Shelter on Saturday night, disoriented but unhurt. Recognizing him, Director Cathy Booth notified medical personnel and the *Orlando Herald* reporter who had written the man's obituary. According to witnesses, the man known as Whit became violent while talking to the reporter, Juni Bruder, and knocked her to the ground. Several other residents stepped in to restrain Whitney until police arrived.

Both Bruder and Whitney were transported to Florida Hospital. Bruder is being treated for a concussion and a fractured wrist. Whitney was admitted for observation. The Orlando Police Department is investigating possible assault charges.

Whitney, 67, disappeared from his home in Ellsworth, Pennsylvania, in 1963, leaving behind a wife and two children. Little is known about the Korean War veteran in the ensuing years, only that he came to Orlando in the early 1990s. He often ate at the Salvation Army shelter and slept in the Parramore Plaza parking garage. After the collapse, Whitney's name was added to the casualty list, and Bruder located his son and daughter in Pennsylvania. Police contacted the family late Monday night with news of Whitney's reappearance. According to a police spokesperson, Russell Whitney and April Whitney Zebrewski are en route to Orlando to meet their father.

Bruder is scheduled to undergo orthopedic surgery on Monday.

FIRST REPORT OF INJURY OR ILLNESS
Florida Department Of Financial Services
Division Of Workers' Compensation

Name: Juni Bruder

Address: 20 W. Lucerne Circle, Orlando, FL 32801

Date of Birth: 9-11-62

Occupation: Reporter

Employer: The Orlando Herald

Address: 633 N. Orange Ave., Orlando, FL 32801

Marital Status: Divorced

Spouse's employer: N/A

Date of accident: 5-23-98

Time of accident: 6:45 p.m.

Location of Accident: Salvation Army Men's Shelter, 624 Lexington Ave. Orlando, Florida 32804

Employee's description of accident: A scuffle broke out during an interview at the men's shelter. I slipped, hit my head and cracked my wrist on a table.

Injury that occurred: Concussion, distal radius fracture

Medical/surgery treatment required: Surgery for orthopedic implant/fixation with plate and screws, 8 stitches on forehead

Employee has been advised of the following regarding return to work:
1. ___ Return to work immediately with NO restrictions.
2. ___ Medication has been prescribed. Please indicate any restrictions on the employee's work activities as a result of medication _____.
3. _X_ No return to work until (date)___ 7/5/98___.

(Please complete Form DFS-F2-DWC-2 regarding current pay and wage loss.)
Claims-Handling Entity Information Next Page

Plaza Survivor Admitted to Rehab

Lone Survivor of Singing Group Suffered Overdose

From the AP Wire/May 27, 1998

LOS ANGELES (AP)—Singer Zenas Witt, a survivor of the Parramore Plaza, checked into an undisclosed rehabilitation facility on Monday after suffering a heroin overdose. According to his publicist, Witt was in Los Angeles to announce his starring role in a new series for the Disney Channel. Production was set to begin next month.

Witt, 16, was the lone survivor of the singing group B4Me. Fellow members Jason "Flossie" Cabanis and Joey Dixon were killed in the Plaza collapse, along with manager Rami Green. The group had traveled to the Plaza on April 13 to sign a recording deal with music mogul Stan Diamond, but the meeting never took place. Diamond, head of a $300-million entertainment empire in Orlando, has since fled the country and is under investigation for defrauding investors.

Questions about Witt's health surfaced after his performance at the Plaza memorial service on April 19, when he fell off the stage after missing a verse of the national anthem. "Zenas is fine and will be back to work very soon," said his publicist, who reports that Witt is in negotiations with Hollywood Records to record his first album.

Valerie Rose, Marko's sister, Tuesday, 6-2-98, 10:30 a.m.

Juni! It's so good to hear your voice! I was worried! The paper said you had surgery? Are you okay?

Yes, I'm fine. Bored out of my mind. I can only type with one hand. Technically, I'm not allowed to work until the Fourth of July, so this is a social call.

I'm glad to hear from you, whatever. What did that crazy man do to you?

Nothing! Seriously. Everything's been blown out of proportion. He got upset while I was talking to him, but he didn't mean to hurt me. The poor man didn't even know where he was.

But the paper said—

Yes, and I'm embarrassed to be a member of the media. Whedon—my boss's boss—had to make a bigger deal out of it than a man coming back from the dead, which is news enough. The good news is that Mr. Whitney was reunited with his family, and he's getting help. I persuaded the police to drop the charges.

Well, it must have been scary. Is someone taking care of you?

My brother. I told him not to bother, but he was at the hospital by the time I came out of surgery. Now he insists on cooking soup and acting like my mother. I had to wait for him to go to the pharmacy so I could call you.

Maybe we shouldn't be talking.

Valerie, I'm fine. I'm going stir crazy. Talk to me, please—but cut me off if I start rambling, okay? These drugs make me loopy. How are you?

Hanging in there, I guess. Stevie's with me, so she takes my mind off other things.

You're babysitting?

I don't know what you call it. Rosanna dropped her off, what, three weeks ago? She was leaving for New York and her big interview with Diane Sawyer. We haven't seen her since. She called the other night to tell me she was flying out to L.A. to meet with a screenwriter.

Wow, they're not wasting any time. Doesn't she have to write the book first?

Sounds like somebody's writing it for her. A ghost, she said. The entire time on the phone, she never asked about Stevie. Not once. She went on and on and on about how *nice* Diane Sawyer was, how she was even prettier in person, and whether Madonna had time to meet with her—she's promoting an album or something, like anybody cares.

We all have our priorities. How's Stevie?

She's an angel. Sent from God. Every time I look at her, I see Marko smiling back at me. She's sitting on the floor coloring at the moment. She's been helping me put papers in a box for work, haven't you, baby?

You're keeping busy?

Knock on wood. Most of my clients stayed with me. I lost a few, but good riddance. You can't trust your bookkeeping to a lady with criminal connections, can you?

Are you still...is it getting any easier? The threats, I mean?

Comes and goes, depending on which story gets printed which day.

Have you given any thought to moving?

What? No way. This is my home. Always will be. Marko and I used to talk about starting over in a new place—maybe the mountains, snow—but we were never serious. My parents are buried here. His folks, too. And his brother. Now *my* brother is buried here. Who would put flowers on Marko's grave if I moved? How would Stevie visit her daddy? *[laughter]* I'm sorry—when I said that, she looked up at the ceiling. Come here, precious. Give Auntie Val a hug.

Have there been any more problems at the house?

No, not since we put in the new alarm system. It goes off every time the wind blows. But enough about my hearing loss. How's the investigation? Any word?

I wish there was more to report. The other day, when I talked to the fire chief, he mentioned something. Do you have any idea what medications Marko was taking?

Like prescriptions? Some. He kept extras here for when he couldn't go home. I didn't throw anything away. I like seeing the bottles in the medicine cabinet, you know? Let me go look. Come on, baby, let's take a walk. *[background noise]* Okay. We have Theophylline, two hundred milligrams. He took that for the bronchitis, but it made his headaches worse. And he always had his inhaler with him.

Do you see any tablets in a foil pack?

Sure, the Imitrex. Those puppies are expensive.

I know. That's what I take.

Really? You have bangers like Marko?

Did he get migraines before the war? I read a report that said one in four vets came back from the Gulf with neurological symptoms.

Not according to the government, they didn't. But Marko was healthy as a horse when he left, never took so much as a baby aspirin. Now look at all these bottles. You tell me.

Do you know if he took anything…unprescribed?

You mean, like "drug" drugs? No. When he was younger, maybe. We all did. But not when he grew up. No. In fact, we talked about it once, what to tell the kids when they were older, whether to admit the truth or not. My story for the boys was that I never drank or smoked or swore, ever, and I stayed a virgin until I married their dad, and by God, so would they. *[laughter]* But Marko, he said he'd be honest with Stevie and tell her he made a few mistakes when he was a kid, and he hoped she'd wait until she was old enough to know better.

Smart man.

He was, Juni. He really was. Which is why I keep going back to how this whole thing is impossible.

You don't think the war could have changed him? Seeing terrible things? Being in constant pain? I know what that's like—sometimes you just want to end it.

That's you, honey. Not Marko. He had a reason to live, and she's sitting here in my lap. Hey, you're not thinking like that now, are you?

No, of course not. Don't worry about me, Valerie. I'm fine.

Okay. I trust you. So you're looking at six weeks off? My, my. What will you do with all that free time? I'm jealous.

I guess I'll have time to organize my notes for the Plaza, the transcripts and everything. They're going to the memorial archives.

Notes about my brother?

Yes, those too.

The truth about him?

I hope so.

I'm counting on it, Juni. Stevie, too. Right, baby? That's her daddy you're writing about. Remember that.

I will. Give her a kiss. Hey, it sounds like my brother's back with the sleeping pills. We'll talk again soon—

Side Effects

Butch was used to working with a hangover, but his head banged louder than usual this morning, and the Tylenol bottle in his locker didn't rattle when he shook it. Empty. Great way to start a friggin' Thursday.

"Hey, Marko?" He didn't know the janitor all that well, but they started their shifts at the same time, so they usually shot the breeze for a few minutes. Tried to, anyway. The guy was about as talkative as a rock. "Got any drugs?"

A toilet flushed around the corner, and Marko eyed the camera at the ceiling. "Sorry, man. Not my thing."

"Relax." Butch laughed and clutched his temples, regretting it. "For a head-ache." On the way home from work last night, he'd bought two six-packs and stashed them in his trunk. It'd been a game for him, coming up with reasons to go out to the garage. Emptying the trash, replacing a burned-out bulb, even patching a hole in the wall. The beers were gone by eight o'clock, so he offered to drive to the store, where he picked up a pint of ice cream for the kids, flowers for Diane, and another six-pack for himself. Life was good.

This morning, not so much. He concentrated on focusing both eyes while Marko folded his sweatshirt. A picture of a little girl was taped to his locker; Butch didn't know whose kid she was. "So, do you?" he repeated.

"Yes and no."

"It's not a trick question." Butch couldn't figure the guy out. He appeared to be relatively smart, good-looking (not that Butch was a homo or anything, just making an observation) and white. So why was he doing an immigrant's job?

Butch thanked his lucky stars for being a wireman. Without his apprentice-ship, he didn't know what would have happened to him. His mom said he would have died or gone to prison, and maybe she was right. His mom said a lot of things. She said he drank too much. She said he was no good for Diane or the kids. She said he might kill somebody one day, driving the way he did.

It made his head hurt, thinking about all the things she said. He felt like shit, knowing she wouldn't speak to him, would hang up the phone if he called. He missed his mom. How fucked up was that? She was the one who—no, he couldn't lie about it anymore. His mom was right. Diane thought he'd changed; he'd just gotten better at hiding.

But he *was* getting tired of it. He wasn't a kid anymore. His body didn't bounce back like the old days. He used to be able to drink a case of beer with-out breaking a sweat. Maybe his body was trying to tell him something. Time to cut back. Not yet, but soon. And when he did, he'd patch up things with his mom. He wasn't sure what he'd need to say, how much crow he'd have to eat, but Butch figured he had until Mother's Day to work it out.

He watched the janitor take a chain from around his neck and hang it in his locker. Plaza rules: no bling. It looked like one of those religious medals. Catholics, man, they had a saint for everything. What was the patron saint for a hangover? Butch screwed up his face, letting Marko see how miserable he felt. Butch thought of it as his "pitiful" look. It worked like a charm on Diane. Marko stopped in the middle of shrugging into his work shirt. With a sigh, he said, "I have a prescription, but it's not a good idea. You might be allergic."

"Hell, if it works, what do I care?" After the tornado, the doctors had pumped him full of drugs. He missed it, that float-away feeling where nothing mattered. "Come on," he said. "I'll pay. How much? Tylenol costs five bucks a bottle, fifty pills a pop, that's…what, a penny apiece?"

"Ten cents, actually."

"Huh. I always sucked at math." Truthfully, he sucked at most subjects. His reading teacher had called him retarded, the dried-up old bitch. Sometimes the letters in the words jumped around on him, he couldn't help it. His kids, they got straight As. They got their smarts from Diane. Except for the part where she trusted him. She was dumb about that.

Butch decided that at lunch, he'd stop for gas and buy a bottle of Pabst, just one to get him through the day. In the meantime, his head was pounding like a jackhammer. "So, Marko, how much do these pills of yours cost?" He couldn't remember exactly where they'd been in the conversation. "Twenty, thirty cents?"

"Five."

"Cents?"

"Dollars."

"Apiece? Jesus! You'd have to be dying to need a pill that bad."

"Yeah."

Butch found a half-empty bottle of water in his locker and drained it. His mouth was dry as dust. He'd forgotten the rule about drinking a glass of water for every beer. He made a note to fill a couple of plastic jugs and keep them in the garage. He'd tell Diane they were hurricane supplies. "Do these pills of yours work?"

"Not really."

"So you don't need 'em, right? Come on, dude. I'm dying here."

Marko shook his head. "They can make you dizzy."

"And that's a bad thing? Look," Butch said, "I've got a shit-load of work to do today, and unless you help me out, the art babe's gonna have my ass."

"Who?"

Butch didn't know her name, the fancy gal who worked on the paintings. She'd introduced herself to him once, but he'd been too busy staring at her tits. He nodded toward the door. "The little honey across the hall," he said. "I'm supposed to test the Argonite system, but I can't when she's in there. The room has to be empty."

"So? You've got all morning. She doesn't come in until noon."

"You know the lady's schedule, huh?"

The janitor ignored him.

"I'll say one thing," Butch said. "She is one fine piece of ass." She looked down her nose at him like he was something she'd scraped off her pointy shoes, but he didn't mind. He liked the whole vibe. Chances were, a cock-tease like that was all show, probably lousy in bed, but he'd give his left nut to find out. *Dear Penthouse, I never thought this would happen to me, but I'm an electrician…*

The janitor was suddenly standing too close. "What did you say?"

"Huh? Nothing, man. Back off."

"Take it back."

"*Take it back?* What is this, fucking third grade?" Butch stepped over the bench, putting it between himself and the janitor. He'd never realized how tall the guy was. "Give me a pill, I'll take it back. Deal? Five bucks in your pocket, everybody's happy."

"Stay away from her."

Butch grunted. "Like the ice queen looks at me twice. Chill, man. Besides, I don't poach on the boss man's territory. I *want* to stay out of her way, but I can't do the test with my brain bleeding out of my ears. *Capisce?* That's where you come in." His vision went blurry, and he realized he could use it. Pretending to stumble, he sank to the bench and dropped his head between his knees. Out of the corner of his eye, he could see the janitor wavering, so he groaned for effect. Finally, Marko reached into his locker and produced a foil square. "You start feeling weird, you don't know me."

It was so easy sometimes. "I don't know you anyway," Butch said. He counted out five bills from his wallet. "Pleasure doing business with you." Punching the tablet out of the packet, he swallowed it, took a swig of water and belched. "Better already."

Someone cleared his throat, and they turned to see Harry Wilmans, the security guard. Those geezer orthopedic shoes let him sneak around like a cat.

"Gentlemen."

"Hey, Harold," Butch said as Marko slammed his locker. "How's it hanging?"

The rent-a-cop stood in the doorway with his arms crossed, feet in a wide stance, and Butch wanted to say, *At ease, soldier.* There were two desk guards on the day shift: Harold Arnett and Harry Wilmans. Butch liked to call this one "Harold" to bug him. The real Harold was black, six-two, with biceps like tree trunks. This Harry was white, middle-aged, going soft in the middle. He kept his gray hair buzzed on top, even though he'd been out of the Army for decades. He reminded Butch of the sergeant on "Gomer Pyle."

"The D-zone cameras shorted out again," Harry said, nodding over his shoulder. "Can you take a look?"

Butch shook his head. Harry was eyeing him and Marko like they'd robbed a bank or something, and it pissed him off. "Not this morning. I've got a job list as long as my dick."

"In that case, it ought to take you all of three minutes."

"Ha. Good one."

"This afternoon?"

"Can't make any promises," Butch said, watching the guard's neck go red. "Put in a work order."

"I'm asking *you*."

"Official channels, man. You know the drill." Butch shrugged, the picture of helplessness. Last time, it'd taken him thirty seconds to climb up the ladder and jiggle the wires, but he wasn't about to tell Harry, who was trying to stare him down. Even though Butch's eyeballs felt like they'd been rolled in cobwebs and put back crooked, he didn't blink. *Let the cameras stay broke for a while, old man.*

The poor coot couldn't even slam the door—the pneumatic hinge was a long time closing. Butch listened as Harry's shoes squeaked all the way up the hall.

"God, nothing I like better than jerking his chain," Butch said, slapping his knee. "He thinks being in the Army during the Crimean War makes him better than me?"

"Harry was in the Navy," Marko said. "And it was Vietnam." Butch noticed that the janitor wasn't laughing. What was his deal? The guy probably needed to get laid. "Harry took a bullet in the gut," Marko said. "He saved two buddies from his unit. He won the Medal of Honor." Marko wasn't even looking at him. "Normally you have to die to get that ribbon."

"Huh." Butch didn't know what else to say. He'd nearly died plenty of times, but he didn't go around bragging about it. Hell, the twister that ate forty people for breakfast had chewed him up and spit him back.

He watched Marko hunt for something in his locker, and then the janitor put a silver tube to his mouth and took a breath. That sound, a hollow puff, made Butch's skin crawl. He knew right away that it was an inhaler—the neighbor's kid had asthma—but for a second there, he'd heard the wind hissing in his ears, and he thought, *Storm's finally coming for me.*

Luke Havergal, OFD Station 2, Thursday, 6-4-98, 7:30 p.m.

Hang on a second, Juni. I can't hear you. Let me get into the kitchen.

What's that noise? Are you washing the trucks?

No, we've got the doors open to listen to the rain.

Aw, you guys are a bunch of romantics.

We are not. It's cooler this way. Temperature-wise.

Right.

Wish you were here, though. What's going on? How've you been?

Fine. Good. I was calling to check on Grendel.

Oh. *[background noise]* Hey, little buddy, it's for you. Yeah! The pretty lady. He doesn't like the thunder, which is why he's hiding in the kitchen. He's great, though. The guys—everybody loves him. He's a good boy, aren't you? He has a cushy bed upstairs, a silver bowl next to the fridge with his name on it. One of the wives made him a little hat, like a chief's hat, and a little red coat—

Oh, my God.

It's a total riot. The women go nuts. Hey, he was riding on the engine in the Memorial Day parade. Didn't you see him?

I missed the parade. Sorry.

Hot date?

No, actually, I had a little…accident. Some minor surgery.

Christ—what happened? Do you need help? I'm coming right over—

Whoa. First of all, I'm fine. Second of all, you don't know where I live.

You forget what I do for a living. I can plug you into the GIS system and have an address in three seconds. Do you like Chinese?

No. I mean yes, I like Chinese, but no, you can't come over. I was calling about Grendel.

I could bring him with me. Wouldn't you like to see him? Wouldn't that make you feel better? Tell me what happened. What kind of accident?

It's nothing. Don't you read the paper?

Nothing but bad news.

Gee, thanks.

No offense. You were in the paper? This can't be good.

It was nothing. A work thing. I fell, that's all. Now there's a ton of paperwork to fill out, and I have to stay home for a month. It's driving me batty. I'm not allowed to work. My boss says that if I touch a keyboard, the Worker's Comp police show up to arrest me, so I'm doing what we call "personal research on a non-work-related basis." An article about working at the site. Do you have time for a couple of questions?

So this isn't a booty call?

[laughter] Sorry, no. Totally non-work-related work. And to check on Grendel.

No Chinese food either?

No. I'm sorry. It's just—

I'm not your type? You can't date a man who puts his life on the line every day?

[laughter] No, that's not what I meant—

So I have a shot?

Wait. No! This isn't —
Are you married?
No.
Gay?
No!
Not that there's anything wrong with that. Kinda hot, actually. But, okay. You can ask your questions, I'll be my charming self, and one thing will lead to another — *[alarm sounding]* God damn it!
Saved by the bell.
Hold that thought. I'll call you when I get back.
I was planning to take a sleeping pill and go to bed early.
I'll come over and watch you sleep.
Don't you dare!
Relax, I'm kidding. I'll wake you up, I promise.
[laughter] Just be careful out there, okay? I worry about you guys.
All of us guys collectively, or one of us guys in particular?
You know what I mean.
Yeah, I know what you mean. But hey, it's not fire you need to worry about. Judging from what's cooking on the stove, I'll be dead from food poisoning later.

Plaza Guard Dies of Burns at ORMC

Harold Arnett, 43, was last to see janitor

By the Herald Staff/Friday, June 5, 1998

ORLANDO—Parramore Plaza guard Harold Arnett succumbed to injuries he sustained during the April 13 tragedy. He died yesterday in the Burn Care Unit at Orlando Regional Medical Center. Arnett, 43, was pulled from the rubble with second- and third-degree burns covering sixty percent of his body. The Plaza death toll, revised two weeks ago with the discovery of survivor Harmon Whitney, stands again at 115.

Arnett had worked at the Plaza since it opened in 1995. He was on duty at the front desk when alleged arsonist Mauro Abissi entered the building on the morning of April 13. Arnett was placed in a medically induced coma for six weeks while undergoing multiple skin grafts and had responded well to treatment, according to his doctors. He regained consciousness late Wednesday night. Family members say he became distraught upon learning of the fire, and his condition deteriorated rapidly. He died shortly after noon on Thursday with his wife and son by his side.

Arnett will be buried at Oak Hill Cemetery. Service arrangements are pending at the New Bethel African Methodist Episcopal (A.M.E.) Church. In lieu of flowers, the family asks that donations be made to the Plaza Memorial Fund.

Note rec'd Saturday, 6-6-98

Juni,

Thank you for the lovely flowers. How did you know daisies were my favorite? They brightened a sad day. Poor Harold—he's finally at peace. I sat with his mama and daddy, but the nurses wouldn't let me stay. I felt so useless. Sleep, the doctors keep saying, as if there's anything else to do. Why did you go to a different hospital? We could've shared a room. It's quiet as a tomb all day, and then people show up at visiting hours, asking favors. Don't they know the mayor is sick and needs her rest?

Speaking of favors, Reilly Killion told me the assault case was resolved to your satisfaction. The captain was none too happy about dropping the charges, what with his "tough on crime" stance and an election to win in the fall. I may have suggested you won't be asking any more questions. (FYI, he's golfing buddies with Will Herndon.) Girl, don't go making a liar out of me. Like I told Reilly, we all want the same thing, which is closure and peace for the Plaza families.

Dante's wife came by with a sketch for the memorial. I cried so hard, the nurse brought a sedative. The design is so beautiful, just what we wanted. Georgia says if we're not ready by the anniversary, she'll eat my hat. I missed the big meeting last week, thanks to chemo, but the doctors said I might go home next week.

Thank God, they caught the cancer early! If I'd been drinking water like a normal person, instead of trying to avoid those stinky Port-o-lets, I wouldn't have passed out and landed here for urinalysis and a bunch of other tests. It might have been years before my next check-up. (You wouldn't catch me dead in a paper dress!) In other words, the Plaza saved my life. I don't know what to make of that, except that the Lord moves in mysterious ways. I only wish the public didn't have to know my bathroom habits.

Visit when you're feeling better, and fill me in on all the latest news. I want to hear more about your story. How does it end? Does Mayor Owens marry Denzel Washington and move to Aruba? I would buy a ticket to see <u>that</u> movie.

Love and kisses,

Delphi

Luke Havergal, OFD Station 2, Saturday, 6-6-98, 11:50 p.m.

Man, sixty channels and nothing on. So, where were we?

I was asking you a few questions.

Right. Well, my favorite color is blue. I like sunsets and long walks on the beach. My pet peeve is people driving slow in the left lane. You know what it's like, reaching for the horn and realizing you're in your Honda and not the rig? Major bummer.

[laughter] I meant a few questions for this article.

Oh. Normally, when a woman calls at midnight on a Saturday, I'm not thinking work-related, but whatever.

I thought you were working.

Not really. It's dead around here. I'm watching TV, and a bunch of fat guys are snoring upstairs.

But you said it was okay to call—

Relax, I'm messing with you. Yes, I'm on duty, and this is the best thing that's happened to me all day. Hey, you're best buds with the chief—you haven't heard any rumors, have you?

Rumors about what?

I don't know. Cutbacks?

Where?

At the house.

Your house? No way. You're still understaffed.

That's what I said, but the guys are all—

Want me to ask around?

No. It's nothing, I'm sure. Besides, you're off the clock. Rest and recuperation, doctor's orders. In fact, what are you doing up?

These pills, they either knock me out like a zombie, or I'm wide awake all night.

Sounds like me. I don't sleep much anymore. You know.

Are you seeing someone?

That's direct. Nope, I'm available.

[laughter] I meant a therapist.

Oh. Yeah, I talk to a lady. They make us go. That's confidential, right?

If you say so. Does it help, talking to her?

Maybe. I don't know. Sometimes I wonder. It just keeps bringing everything back, when I'd rather forget.

How are you doing, forgetting?

Not too good. Thanks for asking.

Nightmares?

Look, I don't want to waste time talking about it, the whole "post-traumatic stress" thing. Yeah, I have bad dreams, same as everybody else. We lost too many good friends. Saw things we shouldn't have. Things we can't get out of our heads. No use talking about it to anybody who wasn't there, because you wouldn't understand, not in a million years. I don't mean you. Other people.

I know.

I mean, I'm sitting here, talking to you. That makes me one of the lucky ones. I have a job to do, a place to go. I can't sit around feeling sorry for myself, guilty for *surviving*. It wouldn't be fair to the guys who didn't, you know? They'd kick my ass for it. They made the ultimate sacrifice, so I'd better be damned grateful for every breath I have left in me. All of us.

The people you saved are grateful, I know that.

Please. I didn't save anybody.

Excuse me, but you went back into that building at least four times. I've talked to people who remember you by name and/or number. Serepta and Willie described you vividly. I think Willie said you were wearing red tights and a cape.

Ouch. How's the little geek doing, anyway? Have you talked to him?

Not lately. He's busy touring the country. You know Tim McGraw recorded his song?

Get out.

The kid's a rock star, thanks to you. His hero.

Juni, don't say that. Please. I'm nobody's hero. The heroes are the guys who aren't here. I did my job, that's all. You act on instinct, do what you're trained to do. You don't even think about it at the time.

From what I hear, the hard part comes when you start thinking about it later.

Well, that's the truth. And it's not like you *want* to think about it, but once you start, you can't shut it off. It's like having somebody else's memories, somebody else's dreams. And you can't—Oh, I get it. Smart, lady. Very smart. I don't want to talk about it, so you get me to bring it up on my own.

I'm sorry. You don't have to talk about it at all. I'm going through the motions of writing this article, when it's my own selfish curiosity, something I need to under- stand—how you deal with it. I'm having a hard enough time, and I wasn't even there. What bothers you the most?

I don't know. Maybe the randomness of it. Why one person lived and another one died. How somebody like you could march into the flames and lead strangers to safety, while others trampled their friends to get out. Why it had to happen in the first place.

There's no good answer to "why?" I figured that out right quick. Some sick bastard decided he wanted to kill as many people as possible. Where's the "why" in that equation? Why does a dog bite? Hey, not you, little buddy.

Grendel's with you?

Yeah, here on the couch. He couldn't sleep either. I think, some nights, he misses…what was his name?

Abdur.

Right. Poor little guy. Maybe I'm making it up, but sometimes I find him sitting by the window upstairs, and he has this look on his face. Do dogs get sad, you think?

Sure. Why not? Or maybe they pick up on their friends' feelings.

Who's sad? Not me.

[laughter] What bothers you the most?

What bothers me? Well, not that day. After. The digging. We didn't find any survivors on my detail. We found bodies. Parts. Not what I signed up for. I mean, we did it for the families, but after a while, you just wanted to bulldoze the site. Leave 'em where they lay, you know? That's what I dream about. Digging. Up to my eyeballs in dust, fingers bleeding in my gloves. Nothing but junk. Concrete, insulation, wires. Every once in a while, a piece of a phone or copier you recognized, but mostly junk. And then I see this hand sticking up, and I think, finally! Someone alive! But when I reach out to grab it, it crumbles. Poof.

Was this real, or a dream?

Real, but it's not what you're thinking. It was one of those art things your kid makes for you in school, that white stuff, what's it called — plaster of Paris? You know, like a cast of a hand. It was sitting on somebody's bookshelf, made it through the fire, the collapse, everything, and when I touched it, gone.

That would have freaked me out. Anybody, I should think.

Well, good, because I had to go home that day. Couldn't take it anymore. Guys are losing sleep over corpses, and I'm having nightmares about a plaster hand.

Are you, still?

Not so bad now. I figured out, you don't sleep, you don't dream. Problem solved.

You catch some great infomercials at three in the morning.

I almost bought the Ronco Rotisserie.

"Set it, and forget it!"

[laughter] So we're both sitting up, watching the same bad TV. I could help you sleep, you know.

This may sound like a weird question, but when you were digging, was it always bad?

Hang on. I just got whiplash from changing the subject.

What I mean is, in really awful situations, sometimes you end up laughing because there's nothing else you can do. Like when my mom was in the hospital, after the doctors had turned off the respirator, and my brother and I were standing by her bed, holding hands, waiting for the…well, you know. Anyway, this little candy-striper bops into the room on her rounds. She kind of shoves Peter aside and sticks a thermometer in my mom's mouth. We all wait for the beep. She looks at it and says, "Ninety-eight-point-six! Perfect!" And she bops out. We looked at each other and laughed until we cried.

Was she blonde?

My mother?

No, the candy-striper.

Oh. Yes, as a matter of fact.

Little fantasy of mine, the blonde candy-striper.

Too much information.

Sorry about your mom, by the way.

Thanks. But you know what I mean. You can't tell the story to anybody else.

Yeah. Only the people who were there.

Right.

I've got one, but you have to promise not to repeat it.

You're no use to me.

You want to hear it or not?

Yes.

Swear.

Fine. I promise not to repeat it. Cross my heart and hope to die.

Excellent. Now, remember the rain, the second week?

The monsoon, you mean. I swam to work.

Yeah, but it watered down the dust, so we were glad for it. We were into the atrium level by then, and the smell—well, let's not go there, but you can imagine. Not just what the dogs were sniffing for, but melted plastic, rotten fish from the tanks, coffee grounds, this fireplace smell that wasn't bad, like wood smoke.

From the trees in the atrium?

Makes sense.

Imported Chinese palms. Fifteen hundred bucks apiece.

Wow. Expensive kindling. Anyway, there'd be this nice woodsy smell, and then you'd hit a pocket of something really rank. Everybody puked at some point, don't let 'em tell you different. I mean, the thought alone, and then this constant assault on your senses. I still get the smells in my nose sometimes. The taste.

One of the cops I interviewed said he was putting up drywall at his dad's house the other day, and the smell gave him the shakes.

That would do it. Or ceiling tiles. Changing the oil in the car. In places where the heat got really intense, that's what it smelled like, a hot engine. But we were in the atrium, and we found a body. It was under a slab we thought was floor, but it turned out to be one of those Aztec-looking pieces, the things on the wall?

The Mayan reliefs.

Right. Mayan. Just checking to see if you knew your pre-Columbian art. So we find this body. And it's awful. Doesn't look like anything human. Charred beyond recognition. And it's big. Huge. We're thinking, geezus, the poor bastard must have been too fat to get down the stairs.

How did you know it was a man?

I don't know. He was bald?

Wasn't the hair burned off?

Man, you're gruesome.

Sorry. Hazard of the job.

I thought *we* were bad. Bald, burned, whatever, we weren't thinking too clearly. Besides, we would have heard if the world's fattest *woman* was missing, right?

[laughter] Right. They'd already found Mrs. Montemayor by then.

I cannot believe you're laughing about dead Plaza victims.

God, I'm so sorry.

Honey, you're way too easy. Now, as I was saying, we're in the pile, every-body's yelling—*get the chaplain, get the flag!*—because you know how everything stopped when we brought out a body.

Yeah. It was hard to watch.

I remember you being there a few times.

How did you know it was me?

How many women did you see on site?

I can't really—

What kind of reporter are you, anyway?

Observant, obviously.

I used to watch you.

Me? Why?

Well, let's see. It was a choice between the ugly guys in bunker gear or the pretty girl in the grey coat. What do you think?

So you found this body.

I'm starting to figure you out. Don't think I'm not. So we found this body, and we're getting ready to bring it out. The men are lined up for the moment of silence, and we're draping the flag, trying to wait as long as possible, because how the hell will we lift this guy? He weighs a ton! What if we drop him? Won't *that* make a great picture on the news? And then we see the flipper.

The...what?

It's the fucking manatee!

Oh, Jesus.

That's what we said! Talk about a crispy critter—we're having a moment of silence for a fucking *fish!*

A mammal, actually.

You couldn't let it be, could you?

Poor Griffy. What did you do? I didn't hear any of this.

You weren't there. I made sure. We looked like idiots. We said the debris was shifting, sent everybody home. We draped Griffy with a tarp, waited for night-fall and hoisted him out with a crane. The SeaWorld people took him away on a flatbed.

And nobody said a word.

Some things are better left unsaid. You think the poor little school kids weren't traumatized enough already?

Good point.

But I have to tell you, say the word "manatee" in the firehouse to this day, and the guys crack up.

I'll remember that.

You can't use it. You promised. All of this, off the record.

Come on, Luke. You're tying my hands here.

Now, there's an interesting idea. If you're into that.

Gee, look at the time.

Misguided

Marie Bateson checked her watch: four minutes behind schedule. She'd spent too much time arranging the Japanese tourists in front of the window, but they were all quite short in stature and needed a good view. She was glad to see Micaela working. In the mornings, Marie had to speak about an empty room, which made her task more difficult. Once, a visitor had written on the comment card, "The basement was a [ ] waste of time." (Profanity excised.) She had to bite her tongue when young men failed to remove their baseball caps indoors.

The Japanese were a polite race, thank heaven, but Marie wasn't sure how much this group understood. The leader translated constantly, and everyone smiled and bowed, but how did one convey the more technical aspects of Level B? How did one say "gas-fired cooling system" in a foreign tongue? Several times, Marie caught herself searching for smaller words, which caused her to lose her train of thought. Upstairs, she had actually referred to a Masson sketch as an Ernst.

Gathering her composure, she gestured through the glass and said, "Here, you see one of Mr. Costas's most prized acquisitions, the 14th-century icon of the Virgin Odigitria." (She pronounced the name slowly—*oh-dee-GEE-tria*—and waited for the group to repeat it.) Marie had started the description of the Plaza art collection on the twelfth floor, using the Duchamp sculpture as a focal point. On the fifth floor, she explained the rotation process (each piece in a new location every three months) and the work of the interns. She refrained from saying that an intern's job seemed to involve lounging about the art room, cleaning a frame or two with smudge-free newsprint and gossiping with Micaela. When necessary, Marie put a bug in Pope's ear, and Mr. Costas's assistant saw to it that the least industrious among them disappeared. To be a Plaza intern was an honor, a plum on any art major's résumé, and Marie believed that one should show the proper gratitude.

Today was Thursday, though, an intern-free day. Micaela worked alone. Marie always looked forward to this part of the tour, seeing a tiny bit of progress each time: a postage stamp of paint, a gilded centimeter. She couldn't help but feel a burst of pride. Her employer, Mr. Costas, who never forgot her birthday or her favorite bloom, was responsible for saving this exquisite treasure. Was he not the best man she knew? Whatever lapses he'd made in his personal life, he deserved accolades for his service to the arts.

Marie smoothed her pearls and told the group, "You're privileged to be here today, as our artist is completing the gilding process. This is the culmination of a year's effort." She waited for the news to register, hoping to see looks of awe, but her visitors were too busy filming with their video cameras. "Gold on an icon represents heaven's light," she said. "As you can see, the gold is brightest in areas surrounding mother and child. Our expert has been working on Mary's halo for over a month."

Retrieving a bowl from the refrigerator, Micaela heated it over a double boiler. She wore a lab coat over her skirt, which made her look like a very pretty doctor. "This is bole," Marie explained, "a mixture of clay and rabbit-skin glue." She pitied the poor translator, but she found this technique fascinating and tried to do it justice. "Our conservator has already painted and sanded fifteen coats of gesso, or plaster. Over it, she will apply the bole and a sheet of 24-carat gold."

Marie hadn't always approved of this girl and, truth be told, had given her the cold shoulder at first. Like everyone else, Marie had heard rumors, and she saw with her own eyes the attention paid by her employer.

But as time went by, Marie began to realize something was off. Micaela worked too many hours to be a *femme fatale*. She started late each morning, true, but she also stayed late every night, and weekends, too. The guards confirmed it. Even when the interns begged, Micaela never joined them on their silly karaoke outings. Once, Marie had found the girl sitting alone in the art vault, eating her salad, and when Marie asked why, she pointed to the bubble-wrapped paintings and said, "I like to keep them company." Marie, widowed now for almost ten years, had felt *sorry* for her.

Monday was Micaela's birthday, and Marie had offered to take her to lunch. Unlucky to be born on the thirteenth, wasn't it? Still, the girl appeared not to have suffered unduly in life.

As Micaela prepared her brushes, Marie explained to the group that this last coat of bole would dry for at least six hours before the actual gilding started. Since the Japanese tourists would be long gone, Micaela went to the vault and brought out a book of gold leaf to show through the glass. "If we were inside this room," Marie said, "we wouldn't be allowed to breathe. The gold is so fragile, it tears at the slightest draft."

The translator blew a puff of air, and Marie was pleased. *Well done.* When he finished, the art conservator gave a final bow. The group bowed in return and zoomed their lenses. The girl waved to Marie and turned away. The show was over.

Marie offered her usual closing. "In olden times," she said, "travelers prayed to the Virgin Odigitria for safe passage." She pressed her palms together in demonstration. "You are welcome to make a request of her for the plane ride home." At the last minute, she wondered if a Greek Orthodox blessing was kosher in Shinto, but she didn't see any offended looks. Who could tell? These people had been unfailingly courteous for the past ninety minutes.

Scanning their faces, she was surprised to see a janitor lurking at the edge of the crowd. The cleaning people were under strict orders not to mix with the public, and Marie tried to catch his attention. He wouldn't look at her, though. He only had eyes for Micaela.

Marie had never spoken to him, though she knew his name. He washed the windows; she often saw him hanging outside the glass when she led her tours on the upper floors. Just this morning, she had heard a disturbing story about him from one of the guards. Harry Wilmans, a military veteran, wouldn't lie about something as serious as drugs. She must let Pope know.

Better yet, she would talk to Mr. Costas. He was coming down the hall.

Vandals Destroy 'Virgin Mary' in Plaza Glass

Atrium section moved to the county fairgrounds

By Juni Bruder, Herald Staff Writer/Monday, June 8, 1998

ORLANDO—Three weeks after the demolition of the Parramore Plaza, vandals threw a rock through the glass wall that had been painstakingly removed from the site to the Central Florida Fairgrounds. The wall was meant to become the centerpiece of the Plaza memorial.

Within hours of the tragedy on April 13, visitors began to notice an iridescent reflection covering a 50-foot stretch of glass, the only section of windows from the Plaza atrium to remain intact.

Many believed they saw the Virgin Mary, and the faithful traveled from across the country to witness the so-called miracle for themselves.

Glass experts attributed the image to chemical residue and heat from the fire.

Father Lem Wiley, who launched a campaign to preserve the glass wall, said, "This is a very sad day. How some godless hooligan could pick up a stone and destroy the blessed image of the Virgin of Parramore is beyond me. I hope they rot in hell."

A spokesperson from the Orange County Sheriff's office said there are as yet no leads in the case.

City to Lose Historic Parramore Firehouse

Chief cites lower call volume in wake of Plaza tragedy

By Robert Davidson, Herald Staff Writer/Tuesday, June 9, 1998

ORLANDO—Fire Chief William Herndon confirmed yesterday that Station 2 of the Orlando Fire Department will close at the end of the month. The chief cited fewer emergency calls since the Plaza disaster, saying, "It may take years for the neighborhood around the Parramore station to recover. We can better serve the community by reassigning manpower elsewhere."

The station has been in operation since 1926.

According to Chief Herndon, firefighters from the Parramore unit will be transferred to other stations. "Our first priority is to get Station 1 back up to full coverage," he said of the downtown unit, the city's largest. "In addition, the reduction in operating costs will help us replace equipment damaged in the Plaza collapse."

A total of 31 OFD firefighters died on April 13. Station 2, known as "The Pride of Parramore," suffered the heaviest casualties: it lost eight men, a fourth of its roster. The station at the corner of Central and Parramore avenues was a block away from the Plaza, and its three trucks responded to the scene within minutes of the first alarm.

Usually the city's busiest firehouse, Station 2 has been on a reduced schedule since April 13. "Runs are down about sixty percent," the fire chief said. "I owe it to my men to let them do the jobs they were hired to do, which is to protect the citizens of Orlando."

Mayor Delphi Owens responded from her bed at Orlando Regional Medical Center, where she is being treated for bladder cancer. "As someone who grew up down the street from Station 2, I was sad to hear the chief's plan, but I understand his reasoning." She added that the city has hired an employment firm to recruit new firefighters from across the country. "We anticipate being back to full strength by the end of the year."

After the announcement, a spokesman for the Plaza Memorial Foundation also released a statement. "Station 2 is an important part of this city's history, and an even more important part of the history of April 13," said Pope Arnaud, newly appointed to the managing board. "We plan to preserve the station as a museum in honor of the brave men and women who gave their lives at the Plaza."

Georgia Costas, widow of Plaza architect Dante Costas, is the legal owner of the property. Her husband purchased the land in 1994 and leased it back to the city for a dollar per year.

Pope Arnaud, Wednesday, 6-10-98, 2:30 p.m.

Mr. Arnaud, it's Juni Bruder. I wanted to congratulate you on your new position with the foundation.

Thank you! It's quite exciting. I'm so glad to be busy again. These past few months have been an eternity without something productive to do.

Tell me about it. I can't even twiddle my thumbs.

Your accident, yes, of course. I trust you're on the road to recovery?

The doctor says the bones are mending. Yesterday was my two-week check-up. I looked like Frankenstein with the stitches in my forehead, but they're out now, thank goodness. They itched like crazy. Now, I just stagger around the apartment bumping into things with my splint.

Oh, my. You're not alone, I hope?

My brother was here for the first week, but I sent him home. Too much hovering. All of this attention has been embarrassing, to be honest. Thank you again for the flowers. They were beautiful.

My pleasure. Who's helping you now?

Oh, don't worry about me. I have more help than I need. The doorbell never stops ringing. My boss, the guys from the fire department, all day long.

The fire department?

My friends from Station 2. They were just here for lunch, in fact. Four men and a dog. They parked the truck out front. My neighbors must have thought the building was on fire.

I had no idea the fire department delivered.

Calls have been a little slow in Parramore, as you know. I think they wanted to feel useful. They're still trying to adjust to the fact that their house will become a museum.

It must be hard for them, I know, but we couldn't ask for a better opportunity. The entire community will benefit, you realize. This new museum will be state-of-the-art—interactive exhibits, multi-media displays, a 3-D movie. Georgia has hired some of the best consultants in the industry.

You're working closely with her?

She's been involved in every detail.

I'd hoped to interview her at some point, but she's never available.

Georgia has always been a private person. It wouldn't be in her nature to discuss the trials of the past few months. Whatever pain she suffers, she keeps to herself. "Act well your part, there all the honor lies."

This may not be an honorable question, but in several interviews I've done, people suggested that the Costas marriage might not have been as solid as it appeared, that Mr. Costas was involved with someone else. Could that have been possible?

Why on earth would it matter now, even if such a thing were true?

It may have something to do with Marko Abissi's motive. He might have had feelings for the same woman.

Let me cut to the chase, Miss Bruder, and put an end to these scurrilous rumors. I worked with Dante Costas for nearly fifteen years. I knew his life and his work habits intimately. He may not have been a saint at all times, but he was committed wholeheartedly to his marriage, to his wife and children. Nothing could shake that foundation. The "someone else" to whom you refer? She is innocent in all of this, I assure you. *She* behaved honorably. I would ask the same of you. *I would never suggest—*

But you did, just now. Speculation and innuendo are every bit as damaging as cold, hard fact. Perhaps more so because they're impossible to counter. A bell cannot be un-rung. Should a man be judged for a foolish intention? A fleeting thought? No. We judge a man by his actions. God help us all if we were to be judged for every fantasy we entertained and discarded.

But you're saying there might have been some basis to the rumors, once upon a time.

I'm saying no such thing, and shame on you for suggesting it.

Have you spoken to Miss Singer recently?

How is her name relevant to this discussion?

I'm sorry, but you and the fire chief were the only people who had contact with her after the Plaza. I haven't been able to find—

And I hope it stays that way. There is no earthly reason for her to be contacted by you or anyone else. She's having a very difficult time, from what her mother says. She needs privacy in which to heal. Now, I really must be going, Miss Bruder. You called to congratulate me, as you said. Thank you very much for your kind wishes. When we speak again, I trust that our discussions will be conducted on a more professional level?

Yes, of course.

And you will be mindful that the Costas name is an honorable one, with many defenders. Legal and otherwise. Do you take my meaning?

I do, yes. My apologies.

Apologies accepted. You too have suffered in this tragedy, Miss Bruder. I understand. Your accident must have been quite traumatic. Quite…debilitating. I can hear it in your voice. You are not yourself.

You're probably right. In fact, I'm feeling a little tired now. I'd better go. Thank you again for your time, Mr. Arnaud, and best of luck in your new position.

Reservations

"Good evening, Mr. Costas! Your table is waiting. Right this way!" Wallace pitched his voice so that everyone in the kitchen could hear. Neely peeked around the pass as the manager, strutting like a rooster, led the landlord and his wife to their spot by the window. Typically, conversation in the restaurant hushed when the couple arrived. Tonight, Mrs. Costas wore a pale, sleeveless dress that flowed like cream as she walked. Her husband wore a tuxedo, something Neely rarely saw in Orlando, except at weddings. She had a feeling Mr. Costas didn't rent his suits at Formal Penguin.

"Georgia, you look ravishing this evening," Wallace gushed as he held out her chair. "A special occasion?" Of course, he was the only person on staff permitted to use her first name. Everyone else was on strict orders to bow and scrape and call her "ma'am."

"The opera," Mrs. Costas explained, gathering up her skirts. Her honey-blonde hair was coiled at the back of her neck, and an almond-sized diamond twinkled at her throat. Neely caught herself tucking a stray braid into her beanie and stopped—no skinny white woman would make her feel *less than*. She was the queen of pastry, dammit. Presidents and prime ministers knew her name.

"Behind, my love." Abdur brushed past Neely, carrying a tub of dishes. When she glanced over her shoulder, he winked. His face was so beautiful—caramel, velvety textured—that he almost made her forget her troubles.

Ever the showman, Wallace whipped a napkin off the table, tossed it high in the air and let it float into Mrs. Costas's lap like a parachute. Her husband laughed and loosened his bowtie. "Wallace, I wish you'd teach me that trick."

"Rubber bands and fishing line, sir." Beaming, the manager looked toward the kitchen, and his smile fell. Neely leaned out to see Eugene, the busboy, lounging near the door. She whispered, "Water!" and he shook himself, as if he'd been napping. Honestly, she didn't know why Wallace kept the kid around. He dropped more than he carried, spilled more than he poured. (And he was the one who'd come up with the awful nickname "Abner," another reason not to like him.) Eugene managed to fill the glasses at the Costas table without trouble.

Pity, Neely thought.

Wallace hovered like a mosquito until Eugene was gone. "Our specials," he said, clasping his hands as he turned toward Mrs. Costas, "are bronzed gulf grouper with meunière sauce." She nodded. "And porcini-crusted filet with truffle risotto." Costas tipped his chin. "Something by the glass, or a bottle?"

"The glass," Mrs. Costas said, though clearly her spouse disagreed.

"Shall I put in an order for dessert?"

Neely prayed *no, no, no.* Mrs. Costas shook her head and looked across the table. "He'll never stay awake for all three acts."

"What's on the bill this evening?"

"Rigoletto."

"Ah." Wallace hummed a tune Neely recognized. *La-la-la, LAH-la-la.*

Mr. Costas applauded. "Bravo!" Wallace clicked his heels and headed toward the bar.

Neely had never heard the word "sycophant" until Abdur whispered it to her one night, watching their manager in action. She'd looked up the word in her dictionary, a book she needed constantly, now that she knew Abdur. He was so smart, and he'd been so many places. She didn't want him to find out his *"jani"* was as stupid as Eugene. People assumed that because she'd gone to France, she knew something about culture and music and art. (Wallace, who'd trained in Switzerland, spoke five languages.) Neely could make a *mille-feuille* in her sleep, but she couldn't ask a Frenchman for directions. Lyon had been a blur of sugar and chocolate and pastillage, an endless slog of practices and timed events, bending over the showpiece until she thought her neck would break. She didn't even remember getting the medal, she'd been so tired. Training for the U.S. pastry team, she'd seen some nice hotels and airports, but that was it. Back at home, her world shrank to its former borders—the restaurant, her condo, her parents' house.

Her father wanted her to leave Orlando, see exotic places, work for big-name chefs in big-name restaurants. Not that Douze was McDonald's, but it wasn't Le Cirque. "Get the hell out of this town," her father said. "Don't even stop at a red light." But Neely knew she couldn't leave. Her mother's second heart attack had put an end to the discussion. Neely wondered, sometimes, about the strangeness of life; that she'd stayed in one place, while Abdur traveled eight thousand miles to wash dishes in her restaurant. He never spoke about going home to Pakistan, but he wanted to take her to Istanbul to see the churches, to Cairo to see the pyramids, to Dublin to see a famous painted book, which sounded crazy, but she let him talk.

"Neely," one of the waiters called. "Three *gâteaux*, table four." She wasn't going anywhere but back to her station.

Wallace burst through the door, barking orders, clapping his hands as he marched down the line. "Bread! Salad! Quick!" *As if we haven't done this a thousand times before.* The joy had gone out of her work. Her parents' home—the roof above their heads—was being stolen, and she blamed Dante Costas.

The lawyer she'd found in the phone book said they didn't have a chance of fighting the city. *Eminent. Domain.* Two more words she didn't understand. She'd looked them up, and nowhere did the definitions say "highway robbery." That was the phrase her father kept using, over and over, to anyone who'd listen. His friends had stopped coming by the house—he sounded like a broken record. "Felix, take the money and run," they told him, but he wouldn't hear of it, and he branded anyone a traitor who offered to help with the packing.

He had always been a good man, her father. Quiet, a little gruff sometimes, but quick to laugh. Neely and her mom were like two peas in a pod; only after the deaths of her brothers, one year apart, did she and her dad become close. He needed her then, it seemed, and was always the last to let go of a hug. Now, he had so many sharp edges, she was afraid to go near him.

She couldn't sleep at night. She wanted to fix things.

Neely had even gone to City Hall for help. The lady at the front desk sent her upstairs. She would never forget the name on the door of the records office. Christian T. Dallman. *Christian*, of all things. He had explained it all quite slowly and carefully to her, as if she were simple-minded: the city had every right to take the house, and her family should be grateful for the offer.

"They will reap what they sow," Abdur said, explaining the concept of karma to her. He promised that justice would be done—if not in this lifetime, then in the next. "I can't wait that long," she whined, and he laughed. "Patience, *jani*."

Patience was his middle name (after "Rahman," which she'd told him was a word for Chinese noodles). Abdur had waited so long for her to make up her mind, and she wasn't quite there yet. He talked about love as if it were safe, a shelter from the sorrows of the world. In her experience, love was the *definition* of sorrow. Her beloved grandmother, her brothers up in heaven—she missed them every day, with an ache that threatened to choke her. In the mornings when she started her baking, she could hear *Grandmère* saying, "Take it slow, baby. Take it slow."

Words she lived her life by.

"Hurry up, Neely! I don't have all day!" Shope—the Buddhist waiter, every-one called him—stood at the pass with his chin in his hands. For as much as he claimed to be about peace and light, he was one of the crabbiest people she knew, always irked about something, always trying to argue religion or politics with Abdur. Wallace had finally declared a moratorium—her dictionary was coming in handy—on kitchen debates that didn't involve food.

Neely finished saucing the dessert plates. The raspberries were so plump and gorgeous, she couldn't resist popping one in her mouth. (If her fingers didn't touch her lips, no foul.) Propping the sticky sugar lattices against the warm cakes, she carried the tray to the window. Shope huffed, rolled his eyes, and took her prized creations away without a word of thanks. "Namaste," she called after him. Back by the dishwasher, she could hear Abdur laughing.

She really did love the boy.

To make herself useful, she wiped down the pass. Across the dining room, she noticed the Costases deep in conversation, leaning over the table with their faces almost touching. *How romantic*, Neely thought. *I want to throw up.* But then she realized they weren't being lovey-dovey—they were arguing, the kind of sweet-faced fight that couples had in public. The staff at Douze was used to it (alcohol had a way of bringing out the darkness in people, which was why Neely never drank), and the servers knew to tally the check for an early exit.

Trouble in paradise? Maybe Abdur's karma really works!

"Neely?" Shope was back at the pass. "My customers want a word with you." He nodded over his shoulder to table four, where two grim-faced couples stared into space. *Uh-oh.* Three clean plates, so what was the matter? Maybe she'd been a little slow, but didn't good things come to those who waited? She straightened her beanie and pushed through the door, preparing herself for a lecture on disappointment.

When the diners saw her, they burst into applause. "The star herself," one of the men cried, pumping her hand. "We wanted to meet you, to say thanks."

"That was the best dessert I ever had," the wife added. "Better than anything we ate in Paris."

"If I wash dishes in the kitchen, will you pay me in cake?" This from the other gentleman. As Neely grinned and scuffed her clogs and played the humble baker, she couldn't help but notice the other lady who hadn't eaten. She saw Neely eying her empty place and said, contritely, "I'm on a diet."

Neely patted her juicy hips and said, "That's a foreign word to me." Laughter all around. "Thank you for joining us. Y'all have a good night, now." She never used "y'all" at home—her mother wouldn't allow it—but customers seemed to like a homey touch, even if the menu was *haute cuisine.*

Taking the long way back, Neely cruised by the Costas table, hoping to overhear a snatch of conversation, a clue to the quarrel. Mr. Costas leaned back in his chair, stone-faced. His wife hunched forward on her elbows, hands fisted tightly over her mouth. White knuckles, blood-red lips. As Neely passed, Mrs. Costas lifted her head, pointed her steepled fingers at her husband and said, very quietly, "I will not…" Glassware clinked and shattered, and Neely spun to see Eugene making a mess of table ten. "…that girl."

What girl? Who?

Out of the corner of her eye, she saw Wallace staring in the same direction. *Eugene, damn you!*

By the time Neely made it back to the kitchen, she felt guilty on multiple levels: stooping to eavesdrop on customers, cursing a busboy, thinking evil thoughts in general. Mr. Costas had done enough damage in her life—she mustn't let her heart be eaten up with bitterness. The man would pay for his sins soon enough. She had to believe it, or nothing else in this life made sense.

Forgive as the Lord forgave you. If Neely stood at the pearly gates tomorrow, would Saint Peter let her in?

Maybe if she cooked for him.

Oh, merciful Jesus, Whit's dinner! She looked at the clock. Andy, the night guard, would be on his way from the lobby. Shame on her for feeding her anger while a homeless man starved. She ran to the grill and asked Lucius, the line cook, what he'd saved. He reached across the range with his tongs and grabbed a filet.

"It's a little past rare," he said.

"My fault. I'm late."

"I think he'll forgive you."

Neely did a double-take.

"What'd I say?"

"Nothing." She smiled as he spooned risotto onto a plate. She had a soft spot for Lucius, who'd worked in kitchens all his life with little to show for it. No telling how old he was now—his earring and graying ponytail made him look like a poorer, sadder version of Willy Nelson, almost as beaten-down as Whit. Sometimes at the end of a shift, Lucius would say he'd been "ridden hard and put away wet." Neely thought it had something to do with motorcycles, but she wasn't quite sure.

She'd just finished wrapping two *gâteaux* (one for Whit, one for Andy) when the guard rolled through the door, twirling his flashlight. "Delivery!" she called out, and Lucius brought a box for the plates. Abdur added a bottle of Perrier from the walk-in, two napkins, two forks—Whit carried his own knife—and folded the lid.

"High five, man," he said, but Andy missed.

Lucius caught Abdur's palm on the downswing. "Remind me later," the cook said, lowering his voice. "I burned a pork chop for Grendel."

Through the pass, Neely saw Wallace scowling at the care package. He didn't dare meddle—she knew all about the fine French wines that went home in his briefcase. Any lip from him, and she would walk out that door. Let his precious customers go to bed without dessert.

Walk out that door.

The urge was so strong, Neely felt light-headed.

After the World Cup, she'd been courted by all the resort hotels. The Disney headhunters had her on speed-dial. Neely always gave the same answer, that she was loyal to Douze, but why?

When one door closes...

Maybe it was time for a fresh start.

Her folks couldn't hold out much longer in Parramore. In another month, Abdur would move across town to start his classes at UCF. He fretted about finding time to see her—what if they lived together, all four of them? With the money she'd saved, plus the sale of her condo, Neely could afford a nice house, one with a magnolia tree out front, and pink hibiscus bushes for her mother.

Why work so hard, if not to take care of the people she loved?

Her father would never let her live in sin, which meant one thing: She'd have to propose to Abdur. (A wedding? Neely felt dizzy again.) She'd be jumping the gun on his three-year plan, but it wasn't *her* dream to marry a famous poet. Abdur could write postcards, for all she cared. He loved her. She loved him.

Honestly, what had taken her so long?

Tomorrow, first thing, she would sit Abdur down and tell him. No, better yet, she'd wait until the pecan rolls came out of the oven. He'd take his first bite, close his eyes, groan in rapture—that low, sexy groan—and *then* she would tell him.

Oh, the look on his face. How sweet it would be!

Hurry up, Monday, and get here!

Criminal Investigation into Plaza Arson Closed

Police and fire officials say Abissi acted alone

By Robert Davidson, Herald Staff Writer/Tuesday, June 17, 1998

ORLANDO—Police Capt. Reilly Killion announced Monday that his department has concluded its criminal investigation into the Parramore Plaza tragedy, confirming that Mauro Abissi, 29, acted alone in setting the fire that caused the building's collapse on April 13.

According to Capt. Killion, investigators from the Orlando Police Department interviewed hundreds of witnesses, including at least five who saw Abissi carry a package into the building minutes before the fire started. Abissi later made a 911 call from the basement level where the fire originated, and he was the last person known to have been granted access to the secured area. The suspect, fired from the Plaza five days earlier, died in the collapse.

The specific cause of the fire remains undetermined. "We may never know," said Fire Chief William Herndon, who led the arson investigation. "Due to the catastrophic nature of the crime scene, my forensics team faced a monumental task, finding the proverbial needle in a haystack." The Plaza was razed on May 20, and tons of debris have been removed to the Young Pine Landfill on L.B. McLeod Road. "We continue to sift through the rubble," Chief Herndon said. "We're looking for the one piece of evidence that will give us the answer."

Capt. Killion added that investigators found a receipt for petroleum distillates in Mauro Abissi's apartment. The purchase was made at a local hardware store. The police captain declined to provide further details, saying, "We have probable cause to believe Mr. Abissi acted with criminal intent in setting the Plaza fire. As far as we're concerned, the case is closed."

PART TWO

Memorial to be Dedicated on Plaza Anniversary
President, governor, other dignitaries will attend

By the Herald Staff/Tuesday, April 6, 1999

ORLANDO—More than 15,000 people are expected to attend the dedication of the Parramore Plaza Memorial next week in downtown Orlando. Mayor Delphi Owens will officiate at the ceremony, which begins at 9:03, the exact time the first fire alarm sounded on April 13, 1998. A moment of silence will be observed at 10:04, the time of the building's collapse. Names of the 115 victims will be read aloud by relatives.

The youngest Plaza survivor, Willie Pennington, 7, will sing "Walk to the Light," a song he composed about his experience. Now in second grade at Henry Elementary School, Willie became a national celebrity in the months after April 13, appearing on morning news programs and "The Tonight Show." His song, recorded by country artist Tim McGraw, topped the Billboard charts. All proceeds were donated to the Plaza Memorial Fund.

Also scheduled to perform was survivor Zenas Witt, 17, but he checked into a Manhattan hospital earlier this month and will not be available. According to his publicist, Witt was suffering from exhaustion after recording the final tracks for his debut album. The release date for the album, tentatively titled "Out of the Ashes," is unknown.

Special remarks at the dedication ceremony will be made by President Bill Clinton and Florida governor Jeb Bush. The governor will be joined by his parents, former President George H. W. Bush and former First Lady Barbara Bush, and brother, Texas Governor George W. Bush, who recently announced plans to seek the Republican presidential nomination.

Georgia Costas, widow of Plaza architect Dante Costas, also will attend. As a leading force on the Plaza Memorial Task Force, she was credited with the project's speedy construction. The first phase, completed ahead of schedule, includes the central memorial and gallery; surrounding museum spaces will open later this year.

Visitors enter the memorial complex through a jumble of broken glass nearly three stories high. One arching panel, suspended above the others, bears the etched names of Plaza victims. During the day, the names appear to be written on the sky. At night, they glow against the stars.

Inside the memorial walls, a gallery stands at the far end of a reflecting pool. The building's blue-glass curves create a haunting image of the Plaza in the water. "This is sacred ground," Georgia Costas said in a press release. "We will never forget those who died here."

Cennino Cennini, Curator, Walters Art Museum, Wednesday, 4-7-99, 10:30 a.m.

Thank you for returning my call, Mr. Cennini. You must be busy, so I'll make this brief. I was trying to reach Micaela Singer. The lady at the switchboard referred me to you.

Micaela. Ah, yes. Unfortunately, she is not here.

Would you mind giving me her extension?

I mean that she does not work here.

Oh. I'm sorry. I was told she accepted a position with you in Baltimore.

Yes, that is true. She accepted but later declined. A change of heart, sadly.

Do you have a number where she can be reached?

Yes, but I prefer not to share it. Micaela will not speak to me, her old friend, so I rather doubt she will talk to someone she does not know. I gather you were not...close?

No. I'm writing an article about Plaza survivors. Do you know where she works now?

She does not.

Doesn't what?

Work.

Oh. Anywhere?

No. The recovery from her injuries has been...slow.

But she wasn't there that day. She wasn't hurt.

Physically, no. I will speak to you in confidence, how they say, off the record? Micaela's mental state is fragile, even now. Her mother says she blames herself, the poor girl. Clearly, she is not in her right mind. How could she be?

Many survivors seem to share the same guilt.

For Micaela to be sitting in her room, staring at the four walls—ah, what a waste. The loss of a talent such as hers is a tragedy.

Is she getting help?

I do not know. The family is...how shall I put this? Quiet. Reserved. The opposite of Italian. They do not wish to share their problems with strangers. What is the expression, "Time heals all wounds"? Micaela's parents believe this, I think.

Do you believe it?

Such has not been the case in my own life. *Mia cara*—my wife—has been gone for eight years, and I miss her with every breath. Perhaps "time" is relative.

I think the more time passes, the more time we have to miss the ones we love.

Yes. Exactly right.

On that cheery note. [laughter] I'm sorry to hear about Micaela. I hope she's back at work very soon.

You will not mention this conversation, her troubles?

No, of course not.

She will recover, I am sure, and return to us, stronger and wiser.

That which doesn't kill us makes us stronger.

Or weakens us for the final blow.

[laughter] I'll put that on a T-shirt.

Oprah Cancels Plaza Anniversary Episode

Host says show 'gave too much time to the janitor'

From the AP Wire/Thursday, April 8, 1999

ORLANDO (AP)—Talk show host Oprah Winfrey decided to pull an already-taped episode marking the first anniversary of the Parramore Plaza collapse, saying that it focused too much attention on the arsonist who set the fire, rather than on the victims.

"After reviewing the tape, I thought we gave too much time to the janitor," Winfrey said. "We should all say a prayer for the Orlando community next week. The thirteenth will be a hard day for them."

The show was taped at the Bob Carr Performing Arts Centre, three blocks away from the Plaza site. The audience of more than 2,500 included families of Plaza victims and survivors. Special guests included Mayor Delphi Owens; Georgia Costas, widow of the Plaza architect; *Orlando Herald* reporter Juni Bruder; and Dr. Nancy Knapp, a criminal consultant who specializes in the psychology of arson. Mauro Abissi's wife was interviewed by phone from Los Angeles, where she is pursuing an acting career.

Luke Havergal, FDNY Ladder 21, Friday, 4-9-99, 8:30 p.m.

Hey, sweetheart. How are you? How's the arm?

Okay. I can almost make a fist. How are you? How's life in the Big Apple?

It ain't Orlando, but I'm adjusting.

[laughter] You miss all the culture?

Yeah. There's nothing to do here.

Is it what you expected?

Well, I wanted a change of scenery, and it's definitely that. The house is great, though. Coming from the Plaza, there's none of the usual new-guy bullshit, you know? This crew gets all the high-rise calls, so it's like, "Leave Havergal alone, he knows what he's doing." I don't want to tell anybody the Plaza was only twelve stories high.

Shhh.

They'll figure it out eventually and bump me down a grade.

You know what's coming next week.

Yeah. I know you didn't call because you missed me.

Do you mind talking about it?

I don't know. It's part of the reason I left. No memories here. Nobody asks.

Are you sleeping better?

I have to. I'm exhausted. All we do is hump up and down stairs all day.

Is it okay if I mention you in the story, what you're doing now?

Sure. "He was the pride of Parramore. Now, he's the pride of Hell's Kitchen."

Hey, that's good. Say something else quotable.

I can't stop thinking about you.

Luke. We talked about this.

Yeah, well, the fact that you didn't want to take a chance on me doesn't have anything to do with how I felt about it.

I'm sorry. Honestly, I am.

I know, babe. I know. You caught me at a weak moment. Say the word "Plaza" and I get all girly.

[laughter] And I do miss you.

Whatever. Ask your damned questions.

What made you decide to leave Orlando, Mr. Havergal?

Aside from the part about being rejected by the only woman I ever loved?

Yes, aside from that. Hi, I'm Juni Bruder from the Herald.

I left Orlando because of the climate change. It turned cold all of a sudden.

Luke.

I needed a clean slate. Is that what you're after? I saw my dead friends riding on the back of the rig. I didn't want to lose any more, okay? Here, I don't know anybody. They don't know me. I do my job. I go home to my broom closet of an apartment. I fall into my lumpy bed, and I'm too tired to dream.

Are you happy?

No. Are you?

No.

Jesus, Juni—

Don't. I can't—

I can't talk to you like you're some stranger and we never—

Do you stay in touch with the guys?

No.

Not even Grendel?

He's not much of a correspondent.

Have you seen his new calendar?

He autographed a copy for me. Misspelled my name.

Are you coming back for the memorial dedication?

Will you see me?

I don't think—

Then no, I'm not coming back. Too many painful memories.

Luke, please don't—

There's the alarm. I have to go. If you change your mind, you know where to find me.

Year of Challenges for Plaza Survivors

By Juni Bruder, Herald Staff Writer/Sunday, April 11, 1999

ORLANDO—On Tuesday, Sheila Gray plans to be in the middle of the ocean with her sons, away from any radios or TVs. "We're going fishing," Sheila says. Her husband, George, was an avid angler who loved to spend weekends on the water with his family. The last time Sheila spoke to George, he was sitting in the Plaza lobby, admiring the aquariums. He died in the first explosion.

For the Grays, April 13 is a date they'd rather forget. "It feels worse now than it did a year ago," says Sheila. "I was numb for the first few months. Now I go from tears to rage to panic, all in five minutes. When does it get better?"

Many Orlando residents ask the same question. Though the visible scars of the Plaza are gone—a glittering memorial stands in place of the charred ruins— the mental and emotional wounds have been slower to heal. "Our hearts were shattered that day," says Deborah Bliss, who lost her husband, financier Charles Bliss, on April 13. "Meanwhile, the world goes on as if nothing happened." She adds that the anniversary will be a difficult time for her family, "but we'll get through it, one day at a time."

"There's no such thing as closure," says Rabbi Esther Judson-Stoddard of Temple Shir Hadash. "We want answers no one can give us." As a licensed therapist, the rabbi began counseling congregation members in the days after the Plaza tragedy. She expected the need to dwindle over time, but her therapy practice has tripled to include patients of other faiths. "Phone calls spiked this month," she says. "The anniversary brought everything back to the surface."

Though treatment statistics are confidential, many mental-health professionals in the community say they continue to see after-effects of the tragedy, from depression to substance abuse to post-traumatic stress. "Unfortunately, isolation is common, along with self-harming behaviors and suicidal ideation," says psychologist Dr. Marcia Fieldstone. "The sooner trauma victims start therapy, the sooner they can recover."

A program established by the Plaza Memorial Fund provides counseling to more than 200 children who lost a parent on April 13. Various support groups have sprung up to help surviving spouses, many of whom find themselves in the new role of single parents. With the help of a PMF education grant, Deborah Bliss went back to nursing school. "I never dreamt I'd be working again," she says, "but now I have a purpose, a reason to get dressed in the morning."

In the line of fire

For first responders and rescuers who spent weeks at the Plaza site, returning to work after April 13 posed unique challenges. Officer Ernie Hyde of the Orlando Police Department had to train a new partner. "I was not happy," says Hyde, who buried his best friend, Officer Wayne "Web" Browning. The two served together for seven years, "as close as brothers." Hyde opted to work alone in traffic enforcement, where he has found a small measure of peace. "Just me and my radar gun," he says.

The crew of Fire Station 2, "the pride of Parramore," had to cope with the loss of eight friends while digging through the rubble to find survivors. "We saw things we shouldn't have," says firefighter Luke Havergal. "Things we can't get out of our heads." After April 13, the exhausted men had no time to rest before a new crisis erupted—forest fires raged across the state in June. "We were pushed to the wall," says Fire Chief William Herndon. His teams battled the 300,000-acre blaze with the National Guard and volunteer firefighters from across the country. "It felt like a kick in the teeth, having to fight that monster without our best guys."

The OFD lost 31 firefighters on April 13. According to the mayor's office, the department is still trying to fill empty positions. "We didn't anticipate the number of people retiring this year," said Austin Dabney, chief of staff. He adds that medical and disability claims have put an added strain on the city's budget. Station 2 closed last summer, and its members were reassigned to other units.

Instead of taking a transfer, Luke Havergal took a job with the New York Fire Department. His new unit, Ladder 21, specializes in skyscraper fires and is known as "the pride of Hell's Kitchen." Asked why he left Orlando, Havergal explains, "I needed a clean slate." He chose not to attend the Plaza Memorial dedication, saying, "Too many painful memories."

New life from loss

When memories of her lost daughter became unbearable, Elizabeth Childers turned to a psychic for help. "He told me he saw kids running through the house," Elizabeth says. "I thought he meant Ashley's friends who come over to swim." Ashley was one of three children killed at the Plaza, classmates on a field trip from Henry Elementary School. Elizabeth and her husband, Ted, struggled for years to conceive a child, and they believed the Plaza had destroyed their only hope of a family. An article about Russian adoptions changed their minds. After traveling to an orphanage in Volkhov, they discovered that their prospective baby had two older brothers in foster care. The Childers are now the proud parents of Pavel, 7, Nikolai, 4, and Anisya, 2. "This house is never quiet," Elizabeth says, laughing. "We hardly have time to think."

A new baby also helped Faith Browning survive the death of her husband at the Plaza. The mother of three confirmed her pregnancy on the day the body of Wayne "Web" Browning, a decorated police officer, was found in the wreckage. "Web was with me in the most physical sense," Faith says. "His child was inside me, keeping me sane." A son, Elijah, was born on December 13, 1998, with dozens of cops in attendance. "They're my family now," Faith says of her husband's fellow officers. "My kids will never lack for father figures."

When her mother died at the Plaza, Claire Montemayor Abuirre was three months pregnant and half a world away. "Of all the times in my life, I needed my mother the most," says Claire, who lived in Spain at the time. For comfort, she turned to her mother's e-mails, eventually compiling a book, *Letters to My Daughter: The Legacy of Muriel Hutchins Montemayor*. The book has sold nearly 50,000 copies. Claire and her husband, a diplomat with the State Department, now live in Manhattan with their infant son, Lambert. "He's named after my grandfather," Claire notes. "But he looks just like my mother, baby fat and all."

Alicia Beatty was seven months pregnant as she watched the Plaza burn on live television. The collapse sent her into premature labor. Her husband, Tom Beatty, was one of thirteen employees who died at the law firm of Hood, Pantier and Beatty on the eleventh floor. When the lone surviving partner, Thomas Hood, visited Alicia in the hospital, the two became friends. "Our grief gave us something in common," Alicia says. "Love grew from there." Thomas was present at the birth of her daughter, Hope, and the two plan to marry in the fall.

"It's hard to explain," Alicia says, "but I feel like Tom had a hand in this. He knew his partner would take good care of us." Thomas Hood has opened a new law practice specializing in the issues of Plaza families, from insurance claims to suits against the sprinkler company.

All of the families who gather at the Plaza Memorial on April 13 will share a common bond: the struggle to rebuild their lives after everything they've lost.

Rozelle Simmons, Wednesday, 4-14-99, 10:30 a.m.

I'm sorry to bother you, Juni, but you said to call if I remembered anything.

Of course, Mrs. Simmons. How are you? I phoned a few weeks ago, but your number had been disconnected.

Oh, I moved! It was time. You know. I'm in a smaller place now. No yard, no mowing. Walter would have hated it. No tinkering allowed. But I don't have to cook! We have a nice, big dining room with a salad bar.

That's wonderful. I'm glad to hear you're doing so well. You sound good.

Better now. Getting by. Say, I read about you on the Oprah show. That must have been exciting! I wish we could've seen the finished product.

Why didn't you come to the taping? All the families were invited.

It would have felt too much like ripping off a bandage, you know? I'm only just now—well. I'm fine. Everyone's fine. How was Oprah? Amazing?

A force of nature. Delphi gave her a run for her money, though.

What do you mean?

Well, picture the mayor up on stage in this gorgeous red hat, silk bow, flowers all over. She and Oprah were talking about the city's recovery, and then it got personal—a possible run for the Senate, Delphi's health scare, all that. Oprah asked if she thought her cancer was as much a "disease of the spirit" as it was a physical illness.

What did Delphi say?

She said nobody ever suggested a broken arm was a disease of the spirit, so why tell a cancer patient her broken cells were her own fault?

Ha!

Delphi said, "Oprah, I loved God before I got sick, and I love God now that I'm well, and praise be to the students who paid attention in medical school." It brought down the house. Oprah made a joke of turning to Georgia Costas, who probably wasn't expecting to talk about her dating life so soon.

What?

Well, not right away. Oprah's trickier than that. First, she asked about the settlements, which was interesting, because the foundation has been so secretive—

They've been very nice to me, those people. I won't say a bad word against them. Mr. Arnaud, especially. He delivered the check personally, gave me his pen to sign, lent me his handkerchief. A true gentleman.

I'm glad to hear it. He runs a tight ship. Anyway, the conversation moved on to Mrs. Costas's life as a Plaza widow, and Oprah asked if she was ready to start dating again.

No.

"Opening up her heart to love" is how Oprah put it.

What did Mrs. Costas say?

She said that her love for her husband was the kind that came around once in life, and there would never be another man for her.

Ah.

Thank God, they went to commercial. Poor Faith Browning was sitting next to her.

What do you mean?

It isn't public knowledge yet, but Faith and Ernie Hyde are getting married when his divorce is final. Ernie was her husband's partner on the force.

Oh, my.

It's more common than you think. I've lost count of the Plaza divorces.

Juni, there's something I haven't been able to tell anyone else. Oh, dear.

What is it, Mrs. Simmons?

In my support group, there's a man. His name is Rodney. His wife, Sarah, worked on the sixth floor. We're only friends, but—

That's great, Mrs. Simmons.

No, it isn't. My children will think I'm a terrible person, dishonoring their father's memory this way.

There's no honor in being lonely. People need love, companionship. It's what we're built for.

You think so?

Of course I do.

He's such a nice man. And he hates sports. Do you know what that means?

[laughter] I think so. No football?

Yes. It's heaven.

I'm happy for you, Mrs. Simmons, truly I am. And I met Mr. Brown once for an interview. He's a nice man. Please invite me to the wedding.

Juni, don't say such a thing! We're only friends! He's good company, and I've been so alone. He helps me with the store.

What store?

Oh, of course, you wouldn't know! Once the settlement check came in, I decided to start over. We're leasing a space across from the memorial on Central, next to the dry cleaner's place. Remember it? We open next month.

How exciting! It's great to watch that street coming back to life. I didn't see your sign, though.

Next week. Rodney takes care of all the details. He's been such a blessing. He likes paperwork, which I hate—oh, my goodness, that's why I called!

Why?

The papers! We lost most of them in the fire, which made this year's taxes a nightmare. I hate April 15th almost as much as April 13th. Anyway, I went through the boxes in the car—our filing cabinet, the trunk—and here was a receipt in Walter's handwriting. That's what made me notice, his crooked scrawl, and then I saw the customer's name: Marko Abissi. It jumped out at me. And the date, April 7. That man, he was in our store a few days before—

Does it say what he bought?

Yes. A piece by Watty Harjo. He's a Miccosukee Indian who lives on tribal land in the Everglades. He does these traditional pieces—you've seen the palmetto dolls in patchwork clothing?

Sure, with the little kerchiefs.

Right. Well, Watty was experimenting with other forms, other cultural icons, like Uncle Sam, Marilyn Monroe, Elvis Presley.

Which one did Marko buy?

The Madonna.

Material Girl or Vogue?

No, not the singer. *The* Madonna. The Virgin Mary. She was part of Watty's religious series.

Marko was Catholic. I suppose it makes sense, with everything else going on in his life, to buy an icon of the Virgin Mary. For comfort, maybe, or strength.

But it wasn't for him. He had it gift-wrapped. It says so on the receipt, "Foil." We had a silver paper for all occasions. Walter called it aluminum foil, like you could bake with it, the silly man. He was a terrible wrapper. His corners looked like an unmade bed. Wrapping was my job, but since I was gone that day—

There it is.

What, dear?

You solved the mystery, Mrs. Simmons.

What mystery?

The mystery of what Marko Abissi carried into the building on April 13.

I thought it was a bomb.

Witnesses said they saw a silver package. Nobody knew what was inside. Until now.

You can't be sure it was the same—

It's an awfully big coincidence, don't you think?

A gift from my store?

Right. The question is, who was it for?

Walter probably knew. He would have asked. He was nosy that way.

Did Marko ever come in your store before?

I don't think so. The cleaners, they maybe looked in the windows when they mopped, but nobody ever came inside. Mr. Costas frowned upon it. Maybe Walter knew him. I don't know. That's the hardest part, not being able to ask Walter. Ten times a day, I go to ask him a question, and he's not there.

But he is.

He used to pretend not to hear me when he was alive, so I guess nothing's changed. No, that's not true. Everything's changed. The world.

Yes.

Some days I just—no, let's not talk about it. You know. Everyone knows. My watch doesn't work. Isn't that odd? I bought a new one, and it stopped, too. I can't take it to anyone to fix, because then I'd be unfaithful to my husband. As if seeing a new watch repairman would be worse than seeing Rodney!

Georgia Costas Accepts Clinton Post

From the AP Wire/Friday, April 16, 1999

WASHINGTON (AP)—Georgia Costas, widow of Parramore Plaza architect Dante Costas, accepted a position with the Clinton Administration yesterday. She will serve on the Council of Economic Advisers, an agency that advises the president on the formulation of domestic and international policy.

Effective immediately, Costas will be on leave from Rollins College in Winter Park, FL, where she is an Associate Professor of Economics. Costas received her M.A. in International Economics from the University of Houston and later served at the Centre for Studies and Research in International Development at the Université d'Auvergne, France.

Costas has been applauded for her decision to dissolve her late husband's company and liquidate assets to pay settlements to Plaza victims and cover the health costs of rescuers. She spearheaded construction of the Plaza Memorial, which opened this week on the first anniversary of April 13. Her 18-room home, Casa Marquesa, was sold to the city of Winter Park last month and will become an arts center.

"I am deeply grateful to the president for this opportunity," Costas told reporters on the White House lawn. President Clinton used the occasion to announce his plan to pay off the national debt and add $1 trillion more to the budget surplus over the next 15 years. The president said he intends to use the money to add decades of solvency to the Social Security and Medicare systems, which are expected to go broke as the Baby Boom generation retires.

"If we maintain our fiscal discipline, America will entirely pay off the national debt by 2015," Clinton told reporters.

The president declined to answer questions about his recent meetings with Premier Zhu Rongji, fueling speculation that China may soon join the World Trade Organization.

Grim Reaper

Juni locked her car and hurried toward the employee entrance, steeling herself for bad news. The last time Whedon had called a staff meeting, seven people lost their jobs: four copy editors, two designers, a photo tech. The joke was that if you didn't learn computer programming, your career was headed down the tubes. "Robots will write your obituary," Carl liked to say, but nobody laughed.

Ad sales had dropped to pre-Plaza levels.

Whedon, expert in all things profitable, claimed that the entire newspaper industry was doomed. "If the Y2K virus doesn't kill us," he wrote in one cheerful and alliterative memo, "we're destined to die a quick death in the Digital Age." He spoke as if, in the 21st century, intelligence and reverence for the printed word would go the way of the horse and buggy. His doomsday clock was set to ring in eight short months. Maybe Juni ought to be more scared, but she couldn't muster the energy. The tech editor had told her not to worry, that the Y2K thing was mostly a hoax, and she trusted his judgment. Either that, or he was lying through his teeth to avert panic.

Oh, well. Let doomsday come. Let the lights go out. She didn't want to live in a world without newspapers. What would she do every morning, drinking her coffee—especially on Sundays? Without newspapers, how would people look for jobs, or sell used furniture?

Would she be the one drawing circles in the classifieds tomorrow?

No, she couldn't go there. Peter had made her promise to be a "glass-half-full" kind of girl this year, another pointless resolution. (What had she asked in return? Oh, yes, an end to the nagging.) Her brother woke up *whistling* every morning, for pity's sake. It was all she could do not to smother him with a pillow.

Juni reached for the door and caught herself. She wasn't a right-handed person anymore. In the beginning, the orthopedic surgeon had promised "as good as new." Lately, he'd downgraded his prognosis to "functioning." She tried to will her bones to knit together, but they didn't listen. Traitors. If pain was a state of mind, as the physical therapist kept saying, she belonged in a padded room. She woke up hurting—head, hand and heart—and the drugs made her sick to her stomach. If she could only type without feeling a twinge, she'd be grateful, but—

Stop. Her mother, even in her darkest hours, had never complained about the pain. How wimpy was she to whine about a sore wrist and a migraine?

One of the sports reporters passed her in the lobby, humming "La Vida Loca." God save her from happy people—they gave her a headache on top of the old one. Hadn't this guy seen Whedon's memo? "Staggering news of import to us all." No way that sounded good. Juni ducked into the restroom to fix her hair and practice her brave face in the mirror.

The face that looked back at her was as cheerful as an inmate on death row. A toilet flushed behind her, and Margaret Fuller came out of the stall. Unlike Juni, who'd thrown on black jeans and a sweater, Margaret had dressed for the occasion: red jacket, white blouse, a gaudy printed skirt that looked like graffiti.

"Hi, Margaret. You look nice today."

"Thank you." Margaret eyed her outfit and didn't return the compliment. In the weird fluorescent light, Juni could see a stripe of concealer running down the side of Margaret's nose, but she opted not to mention it. Mags would never forgive her, any more than she'd forgiven Carl for putting Juni in charge of the Plaza profiles—God, it didn't feel like a year ago. She'd heard through the grapevine that Margaret was engaged, a pharmaceutical rep that nobody knew. Juni assumed he was the kind of guy who liked being told what to do.

Remembering her manners, she added, "Congratulations." Margaret grinned a Cheshire smile and flashed the rock on her finger. Juni couldn't help thinking she washed her hands like a raccoon in a river. "I hear you're moving to Portland."

"Yes," Margaret said. "After the wedding. I'll finally have time to write. Like you."

Carl, you're a dead man.

Juni had made the mistake of telling Carl about her Plaza stories—she'd been high on pain pills, her only excuse—and now, she couldn't set foot in the building without somebody hassling her. Whedon had cornered her in the elevator, demanding to use his publishing connections. (As if a sorry book by a *Herald* reporter might actually *boost* circulation.) Bob offered his editing skills and a blurb for the cover. ("An unremarkable work of stunning mediocrity.") Artie wanted to shoot the photo for the inside flap, something "dark and moody," as if that weren't her usual look.

Her stories weren't meant for publication. She'd never intended to show them to a soul. They were only a diary, her private thoughts. Even if she let somebody read them—and she wasn't saying anything of the sort—she'd have to change all the names. She hadn't exactly pulled any punches. Thanks to the nose jokes, Bob and Margaret would be first in line to sue, followed by a long list of Plaza families.

Juni smiled at Margaret—she could hear her mother saying, *Your face might freeze that way*—and followed her down the hall.

The crowd hadn't gathered in the newsroom yet. A few early-birds huddled by Bob's desk, watching the TVs mounted near the ceiling. For once, Juni missed her desk. She would have had a chair to sit in and something to do with her hands until Whedon arrived. Seeing Art, she walked over and stood beside him. He smiled and patted her shoulder. Good old Artie. He had sent her pictures of his kittens, now full-grown. Juni imagined him at home in his bathrobe, talking to Chester and Miss Kitty, and she felt sorry for him.

Until she remembered her life was no better. She didn't even have a cat to talk to.

The news on both channels, as it had been for days, was Columbine. Thirteen dead, scores wounded—the numbers didn't register. Whedon's editorial (a gutsy stance against automatic weapons in schools) had mentioned fifteen shootings in the past five years. Was that possible? Juni could only remember Paducah, Jonesboro, a couple of others—the Kinkle kid in Oregon. Angry young men with bags of guns had lost their power to shock. If you counted bombs and gift-wrapped packages, the casualties exceeded a few small wars.

"Dallas, Lee Harvey Oswald." Bob said, out of the blue, and Juni tried to pick up the thread of the conversation. "Nineteen sixty-three."

"Memphis." This from Art. "James Earl Ray. 'Sixty-eight."

"Tampa," one of the older proofreaders said. "Hank Earl Carr. 'Ninety-eight." A month after the Plaza, the convicted felon had shot his son, two cops and a state trooper. *Killers with three names?* Juni wondered.

"Camden," Bob said, as if everyone knew it. "Howard Unruh. 'Forty-nine." He always played the game this way. Seeing he'd stumped the panel, he added, "Thirteen dead. And he only had a pistol."

"You covered that story, Bob?" Art winked at Juni, and she tried not to laugh.

"New Orleans," the proofreader fired back. "Mark Essex. 'Seventy-two." Bob's smile slipped; he'd been outflanked by an obscure reference. "The guy killed nine on New Year's Eve. Five cops. I was there."

"Kent State." This from the intern next to Juni. Everyone turned to stare at him. "What?" he said, blushing. His hair was spiked like a pincushion. "My grandpa was a freshman there. He saw it. The students getting shot, I mean."

Bob rolled his eyes. "First, name the year."

"Uh, I don't—

"And second, name the shooter."

The poor kid. Juni wanted to help him. "The year was nineteen seventy," Bob said in his best game-show voice, "and the men with the guns were the *National Guard.* Bzzt!" He hit the buzzer on his desk. "Sorry, folks. Wrong category. We were looking for *lone gunmen* here." With a snicker, Bob rocked back in his chair. "I'll bet ol' Gramps was in the theater when Lincoln got shot, too."

Art wrapped an elbow around the kid's head and whispered, "Washington, John Wilkes Booth, eighteen sixty-five." While the intern fixed his hair, Art told the group, "Don't forget the granddaddy of them all. Austin, 'Sixty-six." No response. "Charles Whitman? Clock tower?"

A chorus of "Oh's."

On the TV, grainy surveillance footage showed a crowded school cafeteria, busy, a normal day, and suddenly, kids were scrambling, diving for cover.

"Yep," Art said. "Whitman sat up there for ninety minutes, picking people off. Sixteen dead. His wife and mother, too."

Bob snapped his fingers. "Speaking of Texas—the Luby's in Killeen. Twenty-three dead. The record, I believe."

"Name the shooter," Art said.

"God dammit."

"Loser." Artie grinned and made an "L" on his forehead. "I wanted to say the McDonald's in San Diego, but I couldn't remember that guy, either."

"And he only killed twenty-two," Bob said.

"You want fries with that?"

Margaret, who'd joined the group by now, shook her head as everyone laughed. "You men and your violence. It's disgusting."

"Don't look at me," Art said. "I can't even put a worm on a hook."

Margaret stepped closer to Juni, as if their gender made them compadres. "I don't see any *women* shooting up schools—" she flicked her painted nails in the air "—or blowing up buildings."

Bob snorted. "That's because they're too busy crushing the souls of their sons and every other male they come across."

Amid the hoots and guffaws, Juni kept her eyes trained on the news. The same black-and-white video played in an endless loop, always ending with an empty cafeteria, dozens of backpacks left behind on empty chairs.

Whedon finally made his grand entrance. Juni watched him shake a few hands near the door, pat a few backs—he looked more like a winning football coach than an executioner.

Just in case, she glanced around the newsroom, looking for a safe place to hide if someone pulled out a rifle.

Herald Captures Three Pulitzer Prizes

From the AP Wire/Friday, April 23, 1999

NEW YORK (AP)—The *Orlando Herald* won three Pulitzer Prizes on Thursday, including the public service award for its "sustained and comprehensive coverage" of the Parramore Plaza tragedy. The announcement by the Pulitzer Prize board came a week after the dedication ceremony for the April 13th memorial in Orlando.

The award for feature writing went to *Herald* reporter Juni Bruder for what the board called her "detailed and compassionate" profiles of the Plaza victims and survivors. In breaking news photography, Arthur Penniwitt won for his moving photograph of a police officer hugging the statue of "Peg Leg" Bates amid the wreckage of the Plaza.

The Pulitzer Prizes, awarded annually by Columbia University, will be presented at a luncheon on the school's New York City campus on May 24. Individual prizes in the journalism category carry a cash award of $10,000. The winner of the public service award, widely considered journalism's highest honor, receives a gold medal.

Other awards included: Breaking News Reporting, staff of the *Arkansas Democrat-Gazette,* for its coverage of the shooting deaths of five students in the Jonesboro massacre; Investigative Reporting, Julian Scott of the *Dallas Morning News,* for his series on the landmark sexual-abuse settlement reached by the Catholic Diocese of Dallas; Explanatory Reporting, English Thornton of the *Los Angeles Times,* for his profile of the new Google search engine developed by computer-science students at Stanford University; and International Reporting, Staff of *The New York Times,* detailing the Russian financial crisis and the collapse of Russia's stock market and banking industry.

Phone message, Friday, 4-23-99, 10:28 a.m.
Juni, it's Bob. I didn't get a chance to congratulate you in all the hubbub. Way to go. I knew you were a lock, what with the homeless-guy attack and all. The Pulitzer board loves that shit. Carl said any other year, and he would have nominated my dog-fighting piece, but hey, the Plaza trumps. My luck, eh? Guess I'll have to be satisfied with the FSNE award, which is no small potatoes. Anyway, I'm waiting to see a draft of your little book. When's the ETA? You're not exactly working full time, right? No excuse for not pounding the keyboard. Hey, just kidding. Carl says you're having some trouble with the wrist. Too bad you can't sue. It figures you'd get clobbered by a bum and not some rich guy with deep pockets. Poor planning, I say, but then, you'll have a great story to tell your pal Oprah and her book clubbers. If you ever finish the book, that is. What's it called, *War and Peace?* Yikes. Like I said, send a draft. I can't promise I'll get to it right away, but you know, whenever. We'll talk next time you decide to pop into the office. Must be nice. Later.

Phone message, Friday, 4-23-99, 11:47 a.m.
Hi. This is the brother of the world-famous Pulitzer winner. Unbelievable. You couldn't call to tell me? I had to read it in the *Chicago Tribune* and spit coffee all over myself. It's amazing, Jun. I'm so proud of you. God knows you've earned it. Give me a call. Where are you, anyway?

Phone message, Friday, 4-23-99, 12:32 p.m.
This is Trainor's Pharmacy, calling to let you know that your refill is ready for pick-up. We'll be open until six. Thank you.

Phone message, Friday, 4-23-99, 2:10 p.m.
Hello! This is Shirley Buchanan with the Clarion Literary Agency. You may have heard of me—I represent your friend, Delphi, who asked me to give you a call. I understand you're working on a book? That's exciting news, especially considering yesterday's bombshell. The Pulitzer! Good heavens! It's an honor just to be speaking with you. Well, we're not speaking yet, but we will be. Soon. I'll try back later. Enjoy your day!

Phone message, Friday, 4-23-99, 4:27 p.m.
Oh, my God, Juni, it's Audrey! Oh, my God! Oh, my God! I know you! Call me!

A Few Small Repairs

Juni unbuttoned her coat as Shirley, the literary agent, spoke to the hostess. The restaurant was small and painfully elegant, the tables packed so close together that Juni had to turn sideways to wriggle out of her sleeves. She nearly elbowed a man in the head. She started to apologize, but he went on talking to his lunch companion as if nothing had happened. That was the trick in New York, she realized. Ignore everything, even a punch in the face.

Shirley came at her in a cloud of Estee Lauder and, seeing the coat slung over her arm, snapped her fingers at the hostess. "I'm fine," Juni started to say, but Shirley stopped her with a curt shake of the head. As Juni watched her coat disappear—no name, no ticket—she assumed she'd never see it again. Fortunately, the weather in New York was unseasonably warm for May.

Following the hostess was like threading a needle. Juni tried to remember the advice from her self-defense class: *Walk confidently, with purpose. Make strong eye contact.* No, that didn't work here. *Don't look. Don't look.* Still, it was hard not to stare. There was Charlie Rose at a table in the corner, reading the *Times.* Dominick Dunne was by the window in his owlish glasses, dining with two well-dressed women. He was probably writing a piece for *Vanity Fair.* His lady friends looked bored, but Juni realized there was no way to know how they really felt. Their faces were pulled so tightly, they couldn't show human emotion. *Make my eyebrows look like aqueducts,* she imagined them telling their plastic surgeons.

Juni kept her expression blank as she took her seat. *Pretend you belong here.* The waiter smirked as he draped a napkin in her lap—what mistake had she made? Was it wrong to thank him? She watched Shirley arrange her plum-colored shawl and ignore him completely, along with the boy who poured the water and the one who brought a silver dish with a single fleur-de-lis of butter.

Shirley might ignore the staff, but she noticed everyone else in the room. She waved here, blew a kiss there, made the sign for "call me" with her thumb and pinkie finger. Juni let herself crack a smile. (She wanted to ask the waiter to pinch her.) Here she was, in a five-star restaurant in Manhattan, meeting a famous agent to discuss her book. Tomorrow, she was getting a Pulitzer.

On Tuesday, she'd marry George Clooney.

"What's so funny?" Shirley leaned across the table as if they were old friends. In fact, they'd spoken exactly twice on the phone. Delphi seemed to think highly of her; the mayor's memoir, *Drop of a Hat,* was climbing the best-seller list. Listening to the woman wouldn't hurt.

"Delphi told me you knew everyone who was anyone," Juni said. "I didn't realize she meant it literally."

Shirley threw back her head and laughed. The gesture was so theatrical, Juni felt compelled to laugh along. "As I told Delphi," the agent said, "any friend of hers is a friend of mine." She nodded as the sommelier poured a sample of wine. "And it helps if that friend is a Pulitzer Prize-winning writer!"

Juni stole a look at the sommelier, whose only interest was the cork.

"Speaking of which," Shirley said. "We need to strike while the iron is hot. The Pulitzer is gold, literally. I've shopped the first few chapters, the ones you sent, to my friends at Doubleday and Random House. They're very interested."

Juni watched as Shirley swirled her glass, sniffed, sipped, swished. She almost missed the point. "Really?"

"Don't look so surprised, cookie. We only need to make a few small changes." The sommelier, given consent, filled both glasses. The waiter returned with two plates and presented them with a flourish. Shirley clapped her hands. "Yummy!" On each sat a single scallop with a drizzle of pea-green sauce.

"I didn't order—"

"It's *prix fixe*, darling." Taking a bite, Shirley murmured, "Heavenly. This is the freshest seafood you'll ever eat. It tastes like the ocean."

Juni reached for her silverware and couldn't decide, for a minute, which hand to use. Clumsy left or shaky right? She managed to get the fork to her mouth without spilling. The scallop was raw. A sip of Sauvignon Blanc helped wash down the brine. "What kinds of changes?"

"The names, of course, as we discussed, to reassure the legal department." Shirley dabbed her mouth, leaving a fuchsia kiss on the napkin. "And perhaps the point of view. I was thinking, when you speak of yourself, why not use 'I'? 'I did this.' 'I felt that.' Bring us into your world instead of keeping us at arm's length."

"But that's almost why—"

"And here's a thought. The Plaza is so *personal*, isn't it? So upsetting, to so many people. What if we changed the venue?"

Juni glanced away, wondering how she'd gotten drunk on one sip of wine. At the next table, two Wall Street types pretended to fight over the check. "You want to put the Plaza somewhere else?"

With a shrug, the agent said, "It wouldn't have to be the Plaza, would it? We could call it anything. A fictional name. That way, we put some distance between your version and the actual event."

"But I thought you wanted to get closer."

"Apples and oranges. I'm just saying." Shirley patted her hand. "It's *your* story, of course. But consider this. Once you take away the constraints of facts and history, you have all the creative license in the world. You can fill in the holes and tell us what *we*, the readers, really want to know."

"Not the truth?"

"Oh, good heavens, no," Shirley said, rapping the table as she laughed. "The truth is very hard to sell." Other diners turned to look, which was impressive. "Would you think about it, at least? A quick rewrite to show the interested parties?"

"How quick?"

"A couple of weeks?"

The fork slipped in Juni's hand. "Rewrite a book in a couple of weeks?"

"Is it hard? I just thought you could do a quick find-and-replace." Shirley cooed as the next course arrived, three delicate slices of fish on a strand of kelp. The waiter solemnly narrated the selections—salmon, hamachi, bluefin tuna— in more time than they would take to eat.

Feeling something wet, Juni patted her chest and looked down to see a long, green dribble of sauce on her blouse. Shirley puckered her lips. "Oh, honey. That'll leave a spot." She snapped her fingers at the waiter and pointed at her guest. "Club soda," she ordered. Juni wanted to crawl under the table. She'd squandered a week's salary on two outfits for this trip. Now, her top for today was ruined, and she wouldn't see her hotel room again until dark.

"Don't worry," Shirley said. "You can hardly see it." The waiter returned and, with a stiff bow, presented a fresh napkin and a glass of sparkling water. He didn't even try to hide the condescension this time. *Yeah?* Juni wanted to say to him. *Which one of us is getting a Pulitzer?*

Dabbing at the silk, she knew it was pointless. The stain would dry like a scab, puckering around the edges. Whedon and Art were meeting her for a special tour of Rockefeller Center, followed by dinner with their publisher. She would look stupid wearing her coat in a restaurant even fancier than this one.

You can't call Luke now.

Like the coward she was, Juni hadn't let him know about her trip to New York. She was playing it by ear, she told herself. She'd picked out her clothes, wanting everything to be perfect. Today, at some point, she planned to pick up the phone and dial his number. If he answered, it was meant to be. If he didn't, so be it.

With the chance gone, at least for today, she felt a strange sense of relief.

Dessert arrived, a precious assortment of chocolate truffles sans seaweed, and Juni gave up trying to fix her blouse. Glancing up, she met the eyes of Charlie Rose. *Oh, God, please strike me dead.* But he smiled. This famous man, who'd interviewed celebrities and heads of state, shrugged as if to say, *It happens to the best of us.* She thought Charlie Rose was the kindest man on the planet. Juni folded her napkin, straightened her spine and smiled back at him. He nodded, shook out his paper and went back to reading.

As Shirley continued to talk, Juni sat back in her chair and took a long sip of wine. If she'd been looking for a sign, she had one.

Herald Staffers Accept Pulitzer Prizes

Journalism winners honored at luncheon in New York

Tuesday, May 25, 1999

NEW YORK—Executive Editor James Whedon accepted the Pulitzer Prize Gold Medal for public service on behalf of the *Orlando Herald* yesterday for the paper's coverage of the Parramore Plaza tragedy.

Herald staff writer Juni Bruder received the Pulitzer Prize for feature writing for her articles and profiles of Plaza victims. Staff photographer Art Penniwitt received the Pulitzer Prize for spot news photography.

The Pulitzer Prize luncheon was held in the rotunda of Low Library on the campus of Columbia University, which administers the annual awards.

"While we are deeply honored to receive these awards today, we can't help but remember those who died a year ago," Whedon said. "When the Plaza fell, it was our job to tell the world, and we rose to the challenge. For that, we can be proud."

Lazarus

On a bright spring afternoon at Columbia University, esteemed writer Juni Bruder left the Pulitzer luncheon with a smile on her face and a check in her pocket.

You like me. You really like me.

It was a beautiful day in New York City.

As she waited on the steps for Whedon and Art, she studied her campus map. The dome of Low Library, where she stood, marked the center. To the left was Kent Hall. To the right was the School of Journalism. Across the lawn, the imposing building with its grand colonnade was Butler Library, which, according to the brochure, housed two million books.

Realizing she looked like a tourist, Juni opened her folder—the fancy, gold-embossed job they'd given her to hold the certificate—and hid her map inside. The brick path running in front of the library was College Walk. The pattern of red squares at the foot of the steps was Low Plaza. Halfway up the granite rise was the statue of "Alma Mater," seated with its back to her and arms outstretched.

The man sitting at the base of the sculpture was Dante Costas.

In the still, echoing space between heartbeats, Juni tried to remember who she was.

"Juni, are you okay?" Art's hand was on her shoulder.

"All the excitement," she said, blinking to clear her sight.

No. He was still there. Waiting for her, it seemed. Hunched on the stone ledge in a worn duffle coat, he looked like any other homeless man, risen from the grave.

"A fine day, my friends." Whedon jogged from the top like a visiting dignitary, nodding and smiling at the strangers he passed.

Art rolled his eyes at Juni. "Want to grab a drink?" He yanked off his tie and stuffed it in his camera bag. "The only thing that got me through the past two hours was the thought of a vodka gimlet in the lobby bar."

"No can do, my man," Whedon said. "More shopping before we depart."

With a dramatic shudder, Art stepped aside to frame the view with his thumbs. "Buy a T-shirt at the airport, why don't you?"

"Sorry. If I don't come home with a little blue bag, I'll be in the doghouse."

Art turned to Juni for a translation. "Tiffany's," she said. She stole a glance at the statue, hoping she'd hallucinated, and her heart sank.

"Just the two of us, then? I'm buying."

"Arthur." Whedon wagged a finger. "No alcohol on your expense report."

Arthur snorted; everyone knew the boss charged pay-per-view porn to his room. "Come on, Juni. One celebration drink. Or several."

Pretending to admire the scenery, she looked again at Costas, ten yards away. He tipped his head at the empty seat beside him. "The weather's so nice," she heard herself say. "I think I'll walk."

Whedon made a show of checking his watch, the shiny new toy he'd bought in Chinatown. "Meet us back at the hotel, say, five-thirty? Plenty of time to catch our flight."

"What time is it now?" Juni didn't know why she asked—it felt as if the world had stopped.

"One-forty-six," Whedon said.

Art shook his head. "Sorry, sir, but it's twenty after two."

"What?" Whedon held the watch to his ear. "Are you sure?"

Behind his back, Art mimicked shock to Juni, hands on his cheeks. "We talked about this, sir. A Cartier for forty bucks?" He bounced on a step while Whedon fiddled with his dials. Juni closed her eyes. The sun was warm on her face, but she felt frozen inside.

Minutes—days—passed, and she heard the click of Artie's camera. She turned away before he could take another shot, and he groaned. "Juni! It's great, the pillars behind you. A little bright, but c'est la vie. One more. For posterity. Please?" With a sigh, she faced him. "No offense," he said, adjusting his lens, "but you look like a funeral." She forced a smile, a crack in the ice. Art pressed the shutter and checked his screen. "Good. Yeah. Bit of a halo, but it works."

Straightening suddenly, Whedon muttered, "I have to make a return." They watched him bound toward the bottom and onto the plaza, where he broke into a dignified run.

"Hope he saved the receipt," Art said. He tucked his camera into its padded slot and hoisted the bag on his shoulder. "Well," he said, saluting her. "Vodka's calling." With a step back, he pretended to fall off the edge. Juni held her breath. The Herald photographer whose "poet's eye for detail" had won him a Pulitzer strolled past the statue without looking up.

She wanted to call him back, but she didn't have the words. Forcing herself to move, she walked toward Costas, a step at a time. When she reached him, he climbed to his feet. He kept his hands in his pockets.

"Have you ever been to the Acropolis?" he asked.

She stared at him. His hair was longer now, gray at the temples. His eyes were as lifeless as the bronze face above him.

"No," she said.

"You stand at the foot of the Parthenon—" He cleared his throat; his voice sounded rusty "—looking up at this massive Doric temple, and you're in awe. The most glorious structure ever built." Pointing toward the library entrance, he waited for her eyes to follow, as if he were leading a tour. "You think it's perfect—all straight lines, right angles—but everything about it is an illusion. The columns bulge in the middle, and they lean toward the inside. The floor slopes away from the center. Those Greeks, they knew how to fool the eye."

"You're alive."

He shook his head. "Not really."

"I have to sit down," she said.

"There's a place around the corner. It's quiet. I go there on my days off." He watched her closely, as if she might decide to bolt at any second.

With pain blurring her vision, she'd be lucky to crawl away on her hands and knees. "You work?"

He nodded, gesturing across the campus to the southern skyline. "I clean toilets," he said, "in one of the tallest and ugliest buildings in the city. Yamasaki's eyesore, the north one." She stared at him dumbly, and his shoulders sagged. Somehow, she'd disappointed him. "The architect—" he pointed at himself and mimed the action of mopping a floor "—works as a janitor."

This much she understood: He wanted her to feel sorry for him.

"You'll tell me everything?"

"Yes," he said.

He angled his head, and she followed. Instead of taking her down the steps, he led her around the corner of the library. As students hurried past, she waited for someone to point at them and scream. "Don't worry," Costas said, taking her arm. "It's New York. No one looks at anyone here."

The Hour of Our Death

In the stillness of St. Paul's Chapel, Dante Costas made his confession. Juni sat beside him, head bowed, hands clasped. A casual observer might have thought she was praying. In truth, she knew no one would listen.

"When the fire alarm went off," Costas said, "my first thought was Micaela, where she might be. I knew she didn't work that early, but—"

"Where were you?"

"In my office." He picked at a scab on his knuckle. There was a hole in his sleeve. "The phone rang, one of the guards. As soon as Harold said 'second level,' I knew."

"Knew what?"

"That it was my fault."

Juni stared at the stained-glass windows, willing herself to concentrate. The inscription on the center panel read *Add to your faith, virtue.*

"You did it deliberately," she whispered.

"No!" He scrubbed a hand over his mouth. "Yes. I did something…stupid. That night, the night before. But not—not the fire."

"What, then?"

He let out a hollow breath. "I destroyed the icon. The Virgin Odigitria."

"The icon? Why?"

"To make her stay."

"Who? The Virgin?"

"Micaela! If the icon was damaged, Micaela would have to stay. She'd have to fix it. She couldn't start the job in Baltimore. The janitor would take the blame, and she would hate him for it."

Juni noticed a crack in the vaulted ceiling. This was a very complicated nightmare, she thought, but any minute now, she'd wake up.

"That was my plan, anyway. Two birds with one stone." Costas shook his head. "Something happened. I remember standing over the icon, thinking, *She's with him.* I picked up a can." Slowly, he brought his fist down on the wooden seat and raised it again.

"A can." Juni stopped his arm. "Linseed oil?"

"Yes!" He nodded eagerly. "Some of it got on my shoes, and I had to clean up the mess, but then I remembered, *They'll blame him anyway.*"

Yes, she thought. *Because I told them to.* "It was just like the fire chief said. The rags, the oil—"

"I locked the door and went back to the opera—"

"And a hundred and fifteen people are *dead*." Her voice echoed in the empty church.

Costas blinked, as if he were coming out of a trance. "But I didn't—"

"You destroyed a priceless piece of art out of...*spite?*" Juni put her fist to her forehead, and he flinched, as if she'd meant to hit him. "Marko Abissi had nothing to do with the fire." She focused on the pressure of her knuckles against her skull. "I was so busy trying to find out *why* he did it, but it wasn't—"

Costas grabbed her wrist to make her look at him, and she saw a light in his eyes for the first time. "It *was* his fault."

"He didn't do anything, except be in the wrong place at the wrong time—"

"He wasn't supposed to be there at all! I fired the bastard, didn't I? But no, he had to come back. He couldn't stay away from her. That night—it was his own damned fault!"

"Of all the stupid, selfish, senseless—he wasn't with her! He was eating dinner at his sister's house on Sunday night!"

"No, he was—"

"It was one of the few facts I got right!"

The roar in her ears was as loud as the sea.

Hail Mary, full of grace.

She struggled to remember the words.

The Lord is with thee.

How many years had it been?

Blessed art thou among women, and blessed is the—

Fruit of the Loom, she could hear her brother giggling.

Blessed is the fruit of thy womb, Jesus.

She was going to hell.

Holy Mary, Mother of God.

Would they take back the Pulitzer?

Pray for us sinners, now and at the hour of our death.

The truth was a slippery thing.

Amen.

"A hundred and fifteen souls," she whispered. "No, what am I saying? One less—you didn't die! You don't count!"

"It was an accident, Juni. I never meant—"

"You're sitting here—"

"If I could take it back, don't you think I would?"

"What day is this? Monday?" She looked at her watch. "Your wife and kids are laying flowers on your grave!" He had the grace to look ashamed. "Wait," she said. "Witnesses saw you. You took people out of the garage—"

"No. People saw what they wanted to see. I was one of the first people out. I didn't take anyone with me. I took the bus."

Juni closed her eyes. The seat behind her head felt solid, that much was true. No—she couldn't even cling to that illusion. Wood, bone, flesh, nothing but atoms spinning in space, the universe dissolving.

She pictured the faces of Georgia Costas and her children, all of the other grieving families who consoled themselves with knowing that the man who'd caused their pain was dead.

"I ran downstairs as soon as Harold called," Costas said. "I knew. I could smell the goddamned oil on my hands. I didn't think—it was like the nightmare where you're running as fast as you can, but you never get there. Everything in slow motion. The alarm was screaming." He covered his ears. "I'll never forget that sound."

The church's brick walls muted the outside noise—taxi horns, the subway rumble, the constant sirens—that had kept her awake at the hotel. Lying in bed, staring at the ceiling, she'd wondered how anyone lived in New York without going insane.

"I made it to the lobby and saw a man sitting in a chair," Costas said. "He looked like he didn't know where to go, so I took a step toward him—to tell him to get the hell out—when *boom*, he disappeared. Blasted straight to hell. The floor opened up and swallowed him whole."

Gazing at the marble under her feet, she wished the same would happen now. Costas stared at his hands, opening, closing, making a fist. "Juni, let me tell you something," he said. "There comes a time in every man's life when he has to make a choice." His nails were dirty, she noticed, bitten to the quick. "You think, when my time comes, I'll do the right thing. I'll be brave. I'll be the hero." He snapped his fingers. "One second. That's all it takes. And then you find out what kind of man you really are."

Juni knew the truth about herself. She wasn't brave enough.

"That man in the chair, I looked right at him." Costas tapped his temple. "I saw his face. I ran."

"His name was George Gray," she whispered. "Husband, father of two."

Costas sighed, a ragged, broken sound. "Have mercy on me, Juni."

She shook her head. "You're alive."

"Punishment enough."

"It's not for you to say."

"Why do you think you're here?"

She shook her head, terrified of the answer.

"You have to write the ending," he said.

Y2K Warning Prompts Market Sell-Off

Economist predicts 'worldwide disaster'

From the AP Wire/Saturday, May 29, 1999

NEW YORK (AP)—New warnings about the Y2K bug prompted a stock sell-off on Friday as the Dow Jones Industrial Average plunged nearly 500 points. The market rallied to close at 10,434. Analysts called the sell-off a "temporary setback" in an epic bull market, saying that fears of a worldwide collapse of banks and public utilities are overblown.

The Dow made history in March when it closed above 10,000 points for the first time. The record was quickly broken at 11,000 on May 3. The meteoric rise has been fueled in part by billions of dollars in venture capital pouring into Internet start-ups, known as "dot.coms." The advent of day-trading, or buying and selling stocks in the same day, has added a new element of volatility to the market. Thousands of novice investors have joined the so-called gold rush, thanks to changes in SEC regulations allowing stocks to be traded electronically.

Computers are at the heart of the Y2K issue, a software design flaw called the "Millennium Bug" that uses two digits to designate the year. Experts warn that on Jan. 1, 2000, many computers—from ATMs to air-traffic control systems to electric power grids—will fail. Threats of blackouts and food shortages have prompted many Americans to begin stockpiling canned goods and camping supplies. An online article posted by the Christian Coalition last month speculated that President Clinton would use the resulting chaos to seize dictatorial power.

At a hearing for the Senate Committee on the Year 2000 Technology Problem, a leading software engineer said that many companies will not finish their mission-critical systems in time for the millennium rollover. Chairman Sen. Chris Dodd concluded, "We're past the point of asking whether there will be power disruptions. We're now forced to ask how severe the disruptions will be."

In a recent *Time* magazine article on the Y2K issue, economic historian Gary North said, "In all of man's history, we have never been able to predict with such accuracy a worldwide disaster of this magnitude."

Sleight of Hand

Even though he knew it was coming, Dante jumped when his cell phone rang. The *faux pas* would have been embarrassing in any case, but to ruin the tenor's opening aria—an unpardonable sin.

Nevertheless, he'd told Pope to call at exactly eight-fifteen.

During his exit, Dante suffered the eye rolls, the exasperated huffs and checking of watches. Even the gray-haired ushers clucked their tongues. Into the phone, he said loudly, "Hang on, man. I can't hear you over the orchestra."

Any kid who'd learned magic tricks knew the power of misdirection.

They would all remember what a jerk he was.

He continued the loud discussion—*cigars,* of all things—into the lobby, past the bar and down the long, empty hall to the men's room. Inside, he quickly hung up, waited a beat and stepped out again. The exit to the courtyard was a few feet away. Home free.

Outside the theater, Dante loosened his tie and breathed the cool night air. His new shoes were stiff in the heels; he'd have blisters tomorrow. Still, it was a nice night for a walk.

He made it to the Plaza in under six minutes. Lit from within, the building glowed like a great, blue iceberg in the moonlight, rippling in the ghostly mirror of the surrounding pools. Something was wrong—a blank spot in the lights along the northern roofline, a burned-out bulb. He'd tell maintenance to fix it in the morning.

As he strolled down the ramp of the parking garage and around the automatic arm, he rehearsed his excuses—a business call, something left on his desk—but nobody stopped him. Smokers were so predictable. Andy would spend his dinner break on the roof, sucking as much nicotine into his lungs as humanly possible.

Why not put a bullet through your head and be done with it, Andy?

Because, Mr. Costas, security guards don't carry guns.

At the door to the maintenance wing, Dante scanned the I.D. card he'd tucked into his breast pocket. The tiny light turned green, and the latch clicked open. The inner corridor was deserted. Keeping his keys quiet, Dante let himself into the art room, half-hoping to find Micaela working late as she often did. No. She was home tonight, he knew, and not alone.

The thought made him want to break something.

The icon lay on the center table, oddly exposed. Dante had designed his security system to prevent all manners of theft, but now he saw the fatal flaw:

he hadn't considered random vandalism. It had never occurred to him that someone might want to hurt a thing of such beauty. And yet, here he was.

He turned the handle on a cabinet filled with bottles and jars, Micaela's secret potions. It amazed him, the magic these caustic chemicals could work on a fragile coat of egg tempera. He studied the labels—gum arabic, tellurium dioxide, nitric acid—wondering which of the restoratives would, in the wrong hands, do the most harm.

It was Professor Plum in the library with the rabbit-skin glue. The idea occurred to him as he closed one side of the cabinet and opened the other: *Wrong hands. Fingerprints.* Of course, his name was on the short list of people allowed in this room. He owned the building and every piece of artwork in it. Just to be safe, he wiped down the doors with his monogrammed handkerchief.

When police checked access records, they would see that a recently terminated janitor had entered the building on the night in question, intent on destruction. What a shame the cameras were on the blink. The authorities would have to figure out how the criminal got a key—copied or stolen? Heads would roll in HR for failing to confiscate his badge.

And oh, but wouldn't Micaela be furious. She might spend months repairing the damage. The job at the Walters Museum would have to wait. Dante wondered why she'd kept it a secret from him. Hadn't she thought he had a right to know?

She'd played him for a fool.

Dante slammed the cabinet shut, not caring how much noise he made. The door bounced back; there was too much *stuff* in the way. He shoved jars around, but the crowded shelves were like a Chinese puzzle. Nothing fit. Snarling, he pulled out the biggest can, a heavy quart of linseed oil, and looked for a place to stash it. The icon lay there, almost mocking him, and —smash—he brought the can down on the cursed Virgin's face. With a brittle crack, the panel split in half—a sound of eggshells breaking—and chips of enamel and gilding skittered in all directions.

Later, Dante would swear he only did it once.

When he stopped, he didn't recognize the splintered pieces of wood. They looked like kindling. The sensor sat on the table, undisturbed.

My God, what have I done?

The can slipped from his fingers. It hit the floor with a hollow *thunk,* and the lid popped off. He heard the cap roll into the corner. Oil poured out, spreading in a viscous pool on the polished cement. He danced away like a puppet on a string, but too late—a trail of greasy footprints led away from the scene of the crime.

Dante didn't know too many janitors who wore Prada Oxfords.

Thinking fast, he grabbed a handful of rags from the interns' pile and wiped at his soles, rubbing until he could step on the floor without leaving a mark. The other prints wouldn't come up, no matter how hard he scrubbed, so he poured a wider circle to hide them. For effect, he dribbled some oil across the table. An anointment of sorts. Last rites. Wiping the empty can, he placed it carefully beside the spill, the vandal's calling card.

All it needed now was a chalk outline.

Dante climbed to his feet, holding the oily rags away from his tux. He wrapped the mess in newsprint, careful not to use too many sheets. He couldn't look at the table. The Virgin Odigitria, he knew, was lost. No one, not even Micaela, could save her now.

He hated himself for remembering, just then, that the icon was fully insured.

Finding his keys, he opened the janitors' closet, which he'd designed so cleverly. The double-door system allowed the maintenance people to empty the trash without gaining access to the art room, or the treasures inside. *I protect the things I love.* Dante dropped the bundle in the garbage can and locked the door behind him.

The morning crew would dispose of the evidence, no one the wiser.

In his head, he practiced his statement for the police. *I can only think of one man who had a motive for this, Officer.*

Retracing his steps and taking one last look around the room, Dante opened the door, peered into the hall—all clear—and gently closed the latch. He made a quick stop in the locker room to wash his hands. The inside camera, he knew, would be aimed toward the benches, out of range.

In the mirror, he straightened his tie, smoothed his hair and practiced a smile. Remote, amused, the mask he always wore.

Micaela would leave him now.

The ache in his chest, like defeat, was something new.

Exit Interview

Marko held his breath as he walked across the atrium, wondering which of the guards would stop him. One hurdle down: Harold Arnett sat at the front desk, not Harry Wilmans. The other day in the locker room, Harry had given him and Butch the evil eye. Not that Marko blamed him—Butch had acted like an ass. Still, Marko's chances of bluffing were better with Harold.

The guard held up a hand. "Where's your badge, son?"

Marko went through the motions of patting his pockets. "Geez, I must have left it in my locker," he said, hoping Harold would forgive him for the lie. Remembering the Indians cap that the guard wore off-duty, Marko asked, "Hey, did you make it to Winter Haven for spring training?"

Harold nodded, pleased to find a fellow Cleveland fan. "Five games."

Marko rested the package on the counter. "How'd they look?"

"Well, you know, losing the Series last fall, I was ready to kill myself," Harold said. He pushed the guestbook forward. "This is our year, though. I can feel it. We're going all the way this time."

"I hear you." Marko wrote his signature, but in his head he was thinking, *Not in my lifetime, buddy.* "I'm just going down to my locker to drop this off," he said, nodding at the box.

"Whose birthday?" The phone rang, and Harold turned away without getting an answer. "Let me see your badge on the way back."

Marko nodded and moved toward the elevator, surprised he'd made it this far. When Mr. Arnaud had walked him out of the building on Thursday, he assumed the news went up by smoke signal that afternoon. Now, he saw why they'd gone through the parking garage—so no one would know. Life went on at the Plaza as if nothing bad had happened. *If a man gets fired in the woods and nobody's there to hear it…*

The B-level corridor was strangely quiet, but then Marko remembered the wreck on I-4. Everybody would be late this morning. Poor Jay must be beside himself—an entire cleaning crew behind schedule, and short-handed, too.

Don't kid yourself. He's already replaced you.

Pushing through the door at the end of the hall, Marko set the gift on the bench in front of his locker. On the way out, he'd leave the package in the janitor's closet next to the art room, where Micaela would be sure to find it. He hoped she'd understand why he couldn't give it to her in person, why he didn't say goodbye. As he counted out the numbers in his combination, he realized he could forget them now.

Inside the locker, his medallion hung on its hook, and he slipped the chain around his neck, feeling instantly better. Mr. Arnaud had said his things would be shipped to him, but he couldn't wait that long. His mother, his real one, had given him the necklace for his first communion, and he never took it off, except for work. He felt naked without it, unprotected. Micaela had said she wished she had a saint for protection, and he'd found one for her.

In a few days, she'll be gone. Marko had to sit down. From the bench, he surveyed the contents of his locker: two clean T-shirts, a bottle of deodorant, a plastic grocery bag from last week's lunch. Not much to show for three months of work.

It hurt his head to think about what he would do now.

As luck would have it, there was one more pill on the top shelf, the last of his prescription. *One for the road,* he thought, tasting the bitter grains as he cupped his hand to drink from the faucet. He'd told Butch the pills never worked, but he couldn't help hoping this time would be different.

As he peeled Stevie's picture off the door, he caught a whiff of smoke.

That asshole's bucking to get himself canned, he thought, assuming that Butch had lit a cigarette before starting his shift. But then he realized the smell was stronger, more acrid. Something worse. Marko slipped the picture in his pocket and went to the door.

It was cool to the touch—he remembered that much from safety drills—so he cracked it open and looked outside. To the right, a ghostly haze floated at the ceiling, drifting in the flow of air toward the parking garage. To the left, dark ribbons of smoke curled from beneath the door to the janitor's closet.

The door next to the art room.

Micaela.

Jesus, he prayed, *let her be home, safe, away from here.*

Coughing, Marko ran to his locker and wrapped a shirt around his face. *How had the smoke spread so fast?* His mind went blank. Where was the little red handle, the thing to pull for the fire alarm? Where was the nearest fire extinguisher? Where was the freaking phone? The package caught his eye, and he wanted to put it somewhere safe, but there was no time.

In a crouch, he slipped through the door and crawled along the wall to the art room. The metal doorknob scorched his hand, but he gripped it long enough to know it wouldn't budge. He banged, tried to yell, choked instead. The only sound inside was the tinkle of breaking glass.

Where was Micaela? Where was everybody else?

Marko doubled over, wheezing. *Please God, not now.* As he tore at his pockets, he could see his inhaler, clear as day, sitting on the nightstand at home. He couldn't see his hand in front of his face. Feeling along the wall, he touched a hard edge, passed it, went back—the fire alarm. The lever was stiff, but he jammed it down, and the siren came on, a deafening shriek. He remembered now—the emergency phone was on the outside wall beside the key-card swipe. He stumbled in the direction of the parking garage.

The red glow of the EXIT sign came at him through the smoke, and he had a second to think, *I made it*—when a roaring *whoosh* hit him like a freight train from behind. Covering his head, he went down, rolling toward the wall to escape the searing heat. His skin felt blistered, but he couldn't see. Everything was black—either the power had gone out, or the lights had shattered, or he'd gone blind.

For one dizzying second, he was back in the water, sinking in darkness, gasping for breath—

Do you want a bullet in your ass? On your belly, maggot! His drill sergeant's voice was a blast of hot air in his face. Startled, Marko dragged himself forward across the cement. Reaching up, he found the latch, pushed the door open and rolled through, slamming it shut behind him. Sprawled on his back, he gulped in the warm, clean—*heavenly*—air. Cobwebs wafted in the rafters above him. For a minute, he couldn't get up.

The phone on the wall had a dial tone—*thank Christ*—and he dialed 9-1-1. Wait—should he call Security? Or "0" for the operator? Before he could decide, the emergency dispatcher answered.

"There's a fire at the Parramore Plaza," Marko rasped. "Level B."

"What address are you calling from, sir?"

"I don't know—the Plaza! Parramore Avenue, the big blue building with all the glass!" Exhausted, he sank against the wall. "Look, I'm in trouble here. It's too far gone for fire extinguishers, and the sprinklers aren't coming on."

"Are there any injuries?"

"I don't know! You have to hurry!"

"Are you safe, sir? You need to get out of the building. Is there an emergency exit nearby?" Marko looked up the slope of the ramp to the square of daylight at the entrance. As he watched, it grew dimmer and dimmer, a curtain drawing across the sun. Through the smoke, he could see a woman running toward a little red sports car, and he realized there were other people coming from the elevators.

Didn't anyone listen in fire drills?

"Sir? Are you still there?"

"Yes," he said, pushing to his feet. He needed to tell these people—it hit him all at once that the floor he'd been sitting on was hot to the touch—to *get out.*

Into the phone, he said, "Ma'am, can you do me a favor?"

As he ran toward the cars, he prayed that Stevie would get the message.

That his daughter would know, in the end—always—her father was thinking of her.

Herald Reporter Found Dead

By Robert Davidson, Herald Staff Writer/Tuesday, June 1, 1999

ORLANDO—Juni Bruder, the *Herald* staff writer who received a Pulitzer Prize for her coverage of the Plaza tragedy, was found dead in her apartment late Monday. An autopsy is expected to confirm suicide as the cause of death.

Bruder, 37, earned the Pulitzer Prize in feature writing for her "empathetic and moving portrayals of grief" after the collapse of the Parramore Plaza in 1998. She had returned from New York last week after receiving the award at Columbia University.

A reporter at the *Herald* for nine years, Bruder was perhaps best known for her personal-interest stories. In the aftermath of April 13, she interviewed hundreds of people for her series on the Plaza victims. "She was trying to put together the pieces of a puzzle," said her friend and co-worker, Margaret Fuller. "She needed to make sense of it, as we all did."

Like many of the survivors and rescuers she interviewed, Bruder struggled with depression in the wake of the Plaza disaster, compounded by injuries she sustained in a physical assault. Six weeks after April 13, she was attacked by a homeless man at the Salvation Army shelter in downtown Orlando, suffering a concussion and a broken wrist. She underwent two surgeries and had not recovered full use of her right arm.

"Juni was one of the bravest women I knew," said Carl Hamblin, managing editor of the *Herald.* "She worked through the pain every day. She didn't let anything stop her from going after the truth."

A private graveside service will be held at Mount Carmel Cemetery.

Bruder was born in Lewistown, Illinois, in 1962. She attended the University of Chicago, where she majored in journalism.

Bruder is survived by her brother, Peter.

Being Catholic, and a priest, I'm supposed to believe that my sister, in taking her own life, committed a mortal sin. I do not. I don't believe in much of anything anymore. A kind and loving god, an ordered universe, a chosen fate—all seem like childhood dreams, as innocent and wishful as the tooth fairy. Love is the only faith I have left.

I loved my sister. I can't remember how to pray.

Not surprisingly, my superiors have advised a leave of absence.

My duties as executor of Juni's estate will keep me occupied for now. She arranged her papers on the kitchen table, as neat as a game of solitaire. God damn her. My sister, who appreciated irony, named me the beneficiary of her life insurance. In a will revised a few days before her death, Juni left the Pulitzer money and the rest of her estate to little Stevie Abissi, in a trust to be administered by the girl's aunt and guardian, Valerie Rose. I haven't spoken to the family yet. The proper words escape me.

Nor did I speak at Juni's funeral, as bad as that sounds. It wouldn't have been right. I haven't forgiven her yet.

Juni's colleagues at the *Herald* established a journalism scholarship in her name. One of her friends, Bob Davidson, is writing a biography. Juni's papers will go to the April 13 archives. I like to sit in the memorial gallery and watch the footage that plays in an endless loop on the video screen. Juni is standing at the site, talking to a fireman. She's smiling. The sun is shining. She looks so beautiful and strong, it breaks my heart.

The Plaza Memorial has become one of the city's top attractions.

Grief is our vocation now. We plant our trees. We build our monuments. We establish our foundations. The job of the living is to preserve the memory of the dead. The things we remember, the details we choose to forget—the stories we tell are loving works of fiction. Myths, parables. Our heroes meet their rightful destinies. The villains will be punished in the end.

I would give anything to believe it all again.

Acknowledgements

To the families of 9-11 and Oklahoma City, for their courage and strength in the face of unimaginable loss, and to the first responders, for their sacrifice.

To the management team at AAA Publishing, for persuading me to keep working while this book took shape, and to my dear friend and editor, Kim Nicastro, for her faith, love and encouragement.

To Erick Pace, lead singer of the godAmsterdams, for reminding me that a guitar left leaning against the wall for too long may lose its song.

To Glenn Gordon, author of the Mack Fraser series, for showing me how it's done.

To Gaelic scholar and cousin, Paula de Fougerolles, author of *The Chronicles of Iona*, for her inspiration and publishing expertise. *Is fhearr fheuchainn na bhith san duil.*

To the folks at Mansfield House Books, for their generous support, and especially to Alice Mansfield White, whose wisdom and love of literature helped bring this story to life.

And to my far-flung family—the Reinhardts, the Kaminskys, the Whites, the Purintons, the Bennetts, the Drewniaks, the Zarlinos—all the love in the world.

About the Author

Alison R. Lockwood grew up on a farm in Wooster, Ohio, and earned a degree in creative writing and journalism from Wittenberg University. She began her career as a reporter for the *Daily Record* before moving to Florida to become an editor for Harcourt Brace Publishers. Later, she joined AAA Publishing as a travel writer and photographer. In between jobs, she also worked as a waitress, a carpenter, a bookkeeper and a professional Christmas tree decorator. She and her husband, Graeme, have lived in Orlando for the past 25 years. *The Arsonist's Last Words* is her second novel.